Find You First

Linwood Barclay

W F HOWES LTD

This large print edition published in 2021 by
W F Howes Ltd
Unit 5, St George's House, Rearsby Business Park,
Gaddesby Lane, Rearsby, Leicester LE7 4YH

1 3 5 7 9 10 8 6 4 2

First published in the United Kingdom in 2021
by HQ

A CIP catalogue record for this book is available
from the British Library

ISBN 978 1 00406 088 7

Typeset by Palimpsest Book Production Limited,
Falkirk, Stirlingshire

Printed and bound by
T J Books in the UK

MIX
Paper from
responsible sources
FSC FSC® C013056
www.fsc.org

For Neetha

PROLOGUE

Outside Springfield, MA

Todd listened to the phone ring, waited for a pickup. Two rings, three. You had to give these old folks time to get to the phone. Maybe they had to use a walker, or were in a wheelchair. Even if they had a cordless next to them, half the time it was tucked down into the BarcaLounger and when it started ringing they didn't know where the hell it was.

'Hello?'

Good, okay. A woman, and she definitely sounded elderly. You had to be careful. Sometimes their grown kids would be visiting the home when Todd made his calls, and if they answered, the best thing to do was just hang up. They'd know something was up from the get-go.

Todd said, 'Grandma?'

It was always a shot in the dark. Did she even have grandkids? And if she did, were any of them boys?

The old lady said, 'Eddy?'

Bingo.

1

'Yes, yes, it's Eddy,' Todd said. 'Oh Grandma, I'm so glad I got hold of you.'

'How are you?' she said. 'Hang on, hang on, let me turn down *Jeopardy!* I haven't heard from you in so long. Your father, he was going to come by the other day and I waited and waited but—'

'Grandma, I'm in trouble.'

'What?'

'I'm in trouble and you're the only one that can help me.'

'What is it?' she asked, her voice filled with grandmotherly alarm. 'What's happened?'

'I got arrested.'

The old lady gasped. 'Oh no, Eddy, where are you?'

'At the police station,' he said. Which, of course, was not true. Todd was sitting at the kitchen table in his mobile home. In front of him, a laptop flanked by a can of Bud Light and a half-eaten slice of pizza.

'What did you do?' the old lady asked.

'It's not my fault. The other person cut me off, and I swerved. I didn't want to hit this lady, she was pushing a stroller? You know? With a baby in it?'

'Oh my, oh dear—'

'And I hit the tree, but the cops found some stuff in the car, that was definitely *not* mine, it was something one of my friends left in there, and it was only an ounce, you know? But because it was in my car . . . so they're holding me unless I put

2

up this bail thing. I don't know what I'm going to do.'

'Well, you have to call your father. He'll—'

'No, I – I just can't. He's just going to kill me. I'll need time to explain what happened, and you know what he's like. He might even leave me in here, try to teach me a lesson, which isn't fair, because, honest to God, it wasn't my fault, and in the meantime, I have to pay this bail and—'

'How much is it?' she asked.

Todd smiled to himself. The hook was set. Now all he had to do was reel her in and get her in the boat.

'It's twenty-five hundred,' he said. 'I just don't have that kind of money. I was wondering . . . I hate to ask . . .'

'If you don't pay how long will they keep you in jail?' Her voice sounded increasingly concerned.

'I don't know. A few days, I guess. They'll throw me in with the general population, you know? Some of those guys in there, I just . . . some of them are big, and really mean, and probably . . . I just hope no one tries to . . . I mean, you know what can happen to a kid in jail.'

Was he laying it on too thick? You could overdo it. Todd believed that the first few times he ran this game, he went a little too far, made it sound as though he was about to be gangbanged by the Aryan Brotherhood. Best to let the mark use her imagination some.

The good thing was, most oldsters still used

landlines. You got the address of a seniors' residence through some online trolling, used a reverse directory to get the names of everyone who lived there, and you had a long list of potential marks. If they'd all owned cells, this would be a hell of a lot harder. Todd, of course, used cells. Always used disposable burners when he was doing this. Switched to a new one every week. Didn't want these calls getting traced back because, eventually, Grandma would discreetly ask a family member if poor little Eddy or Timmy or Walter sorted out his troubles with the police, at which point someone would say, 'Oh no, how much money did you send?'

Todd always asked for $2,500. A nice round, believable number, he figured. You didn't want to go so high that the oldster was scared off, but not so low as to make it not worth your while.

He'd been thinking, maybe this would be his last one. He was making okay money at the computer store. Just part-time, but it looked like they were going to up him from three shifts a week to four. And ever since he'd met Chloe – talk about having your mind blown, connecting with a half sister you never knew you had – he'd been feeling kind of ashamed about how he'd been supplementing his income. So, yeah, maybe this was it. Last time.

Maybe.

It'd be nice to tell her when she came for her next visit, driving up from Providence in that ancient Pacer of hers, that he wasn't going to do this anymore. Of course, that would mean confessing to it in the first place. It was funny how he felt a need to unburden himself to her. She'd had that effect on him. He believed she suspected he was up to something illegal. She spent a lot of time around old people – her grandfather was in some kind of home and she visited him often – and wouldn't think much of him taking advantage of them.

'I . . . I could give you the money,' the old lady on the other end of the line said.

Todd's mouth was getting dry. He had a sip of beer.

'Grandma, if you did that, you'd like, you'd be saving my life.'

'Do I bring it to the police station? I could get one of the staff here to take me. I could ask Sylvia. She's really nice and—'

'No, no!' Todd said quickly. 'No need to do that. The police said all you have to do is call Western Union. You can do it over the phone. Soon as they have the money, they give it to the police and they'll let me out of here. Have you got a pen and paper? I can give you all the information.'

'Hang on.'

Todd heard her set down the receiver, some paper shuffling. Her voice, distant: 'I think the pen slipped down between the cushions. Oh, wait, I think . . .'

5

God, they could be so pitiful. Todd comforted himself with the thought that these people didn't have that much longer, anyway. They got swindled out of a few bucks, was it really going to make all that much difference? If they ran a bit short one month, they could always ask their own kids for—

Someone banged on the door of his trailer, so hard that it made him jump. Three times. BANG BANG BANG.

'Mr Cox! Todd Cox!'

A man, shouting. What the hell was this? Especially at this hour. It was after nine at night. Todd didn't get a lot of visitors here. His mobile home sat just off the road but was shielded by a line of trees. It was pretty quiet, except for the occasional blast of sirens from the fire station on the other side of the property line.

Todd glanced out the window, squinted. There were two people on the steps he'd fashioned from several cinder blocks, lit dimly by the outside light. A man and a woman, late thirties, early forties. What was that clipped to the belts of their jeans? Badges? Fucking badges?

'Todd Cox, are you in there?' the man shouted.

'Who is it?' he yelled back, like he didn't already know.

'Police.'

Shit shit shit shit shit.

'I've got pen and paper!' Grandma said, her voice now clear as a bell.

Todd flipped shut the burner he'd bought online for twenty bucks. Next to the laptop were printouts of old folks homes across the country, as well as an overdue Visa bill and a recent Verizon statement for his personal iPhone. He grabbed the printouts and stuffed them into the utensil drawer as he headed for the door.

How'd they find out? How'd they get on to him? He'd been so careful. New phones all the time, different Western Union accounts, always covering his tracks. Todd figured, given that they weren't in uniform, they were detectives. Not good. Not good at all.

'Mr Cox, open the door, please.' The woman cop this time. She sounded like a ballbuster. Deep voice, commanding.

Where the hell could he go? The trailer's back door was on the same side as the front door, so he couldn't sneak away. So he went to the door, took a breath, tried to look like he didn't give a fuck about anything in the world, and opened it. When he did, he was able to see a dark panel van parked next to his ten-year-old Hyundai.

They flashed their badges.

'Detective Kendra Collins,' the woman said.

The man said, 'Detective Rhys Mills.'

'So, like, what's up?' Todd said.

'We'd like to come in and talk to you,' Mills said.

'What about?'

'We can talk about that when we get inside.'

Todd nervously shifted his weight from one foot to the other.

'You got a warrant?' he asked.

Kendra Collins frowned. 'Why would we need a warrant, Mr Cox? Have you been doing something you shouldn't?'

'No, shit, no, nothing like that,' he said hurriedly, forcing a grin. 'I just thought that's what you're supposed to say when the cops want to come into your house.'

Todd backed away from the door, allowing them room to step in. They each gave the trailer a disapproving look as they crossed the threshold and found themselves standing in the kitchen area. There was a small living room, if you could call it that, to one side, and a narrow hallway leading to two bedrooms and a bathroom on the other. The sink was filled with dishes, and the counter was buried in beer cans and empty takeout containers.

Todd said, 'Look, I don't know why you're here, but I'm clean, like, if you're looking for drugs or anything, I haven't been doing anything. I don't do that stuff. Seriously.'

Rhys Mills surveyed the mess in the sink. 'You're Todd Cox? Twenty-one years old? Born in New Haven, September tenth, 2001?'

'Yeah, one day before all the shit went down.'

Kendra, standing behind him, asked, 'Your mother is Madeline Cox?'

'That's right,' he said, turning to look at her, his

8

back to Detective Mills. 'This got something to do with her?'

Kendra took out her phone, opened up the photo app, and said, 'There's something I'd like you to have a look at.'

She extended her arm, holding the phone low so Todd had to bend over to look at it.

'I can't really see—'

'Look closer,' she said.

Todd tried to focus, leaned in. That was when Rhys came up behind him and jammed the needle into his neck.

'What the—' Todd turned abruptly, slapping his neck as though he'd just been stung by a bee. But Rhys was quick, and had not only completed the injection but withdrawn the syringe before Todd could swat him.

Almost immediately, Todd became unsteady on his feet. 'Jeshush . . . wha the fu was . . .'

He looked quizzically at Rhys, who stood there, smiling grimly. 'Sorry about this, Mr Cox.'

Kendra, 'Back in a sec, Rhys.'

She exited the trailer.

'Where's your pardner go . . .' Todd said, throwing a hand up against the wall to steady himself.

'It shouldn't take long, and you shouldn't feel any pain,' Rhys said, a hint of sympathy in his voice. 'It'll all be over soon.' He'd taken some rubber gloves from his pocket and was pulling them on, snapping them when he had them up to his wrist.

9

Todd began a slow slide down the wall. When his butt touched the trailer floor he rested his head against the wall, watching the room spin.

The trailer door opened and Kendra, who had also donned gloves, came in with two large canvas bags. She dropped them to the floor, unzipped the first one, and took out something shiny and black that had been folded several times. She unzipped it and opened it wide.

A body bag.

'Best to get him stuffed in here before he shits his pants,' she said. 'I don't want to have to clean up any more than necessary.'

Rhys nodded in agreement.

Todd wasn't dead yet, but he didn't have enough life left in him to be at all cooperative when it came to getting into the bag. Rhys got his hands under Todd's arms and dragged him on top of the bag, worked the sides up and around him, and then started to zip it up, starting at the dying man's feet.

He paused before closing the bag over Todd's face and looked into the dying man's unfocused eyes, his dazed expression.

'This is always the interesting part,' he said. 'The moment of passing.'

He zipped the bag shut. From inside, one muffled word from Todd: 'Dark.'

'How much longer?' Kendra asked Rhys.

He shrugged. 'Minute, tops.'

There was some minor rustling inside the bag

for a few seconds, then nothing. Kendra watched the stillness for a moment, then opened the second bag and started taking out cans of Drano, scrubbing brushes, spray bottles of bleach, cleaning cloths, paper towels, garbage bags.

Rhys said, 'Bathroom's all yours.'

Kendra frowned. 'Come on.'

Rhys shook his head adamantly. 'You know I can't handle that. If the bathroom's only half as bad as this kitchen, it's going to be like a latrine behind enemy lines.'

God, Kendra thought, Rhys could be such a germaphobe. He could kill a guy, but ask him to clean a toilet and he looked like he was going to lose his lunch.

She said, 'What d'ya think this guy was into? He was scared shitless we were real cops.'

Mills looked at the phone sitting on the laptop. 'Burner. Drugs, maybe.' He paused. 'Doesn't matter.'

Kendra said, 'Be a lot easier if we could just torch the place like the last one.'

'If there wasn't a goddamn fire station on the other side of those trees, I'd say yeah. But they'd be here in seconds. Place'd never have a chance to burn.'

They were methodical. Kendra, giving in to her partner's squeamishness, found her way to the back of the trailer and attacked the bathroom. She cleaned out the sink and shower, then poured Drano into the drains, ensuring that anything in the traps would be dissolved. This was followed by a thorough cleaning of every surface with the spray bottles of bleach. Toilet, walls of the shower, even inside drawers and cupboards.

Into a garbage bag she tossed Todd's hairbrush, razor, toothbrush, partially used bars of soap, every toiletry item he might have used. She didn't just empty the small trash container. She bagged the container, too. Plus towels, washcloths.

'How's it going up there?' she called out.

Down the hall, from the kitchen, Rhys said, 'Gettin' there.'

Kendra, needing a break, traveled the narrow hallway to where it opened onto the kitchen. The countertops were clear and clean, the empty stainless steel sink glistened, and the front of the fridge didn't have a single, visible smudged fingerprint.

She whistled. 'This place almost looks good enough to move into, if it weren't a fucking trailer.'

It took the better part of four hours. The last thing they did was go back out to the van for a high-powered vacuum to give the place one last, good going-over. Gathered by the door were the body bag and ten stuffed garbage bags that included, among other things, all the clothing from Todd's bedroom closet and drawers, the laptop, the bills, some list of seniors' facilities found in a cutlery drawer, all the cutlery itself, trash from under the sink, the half-eaten slice of pizza.

'You look under the bed?' Rhys asked her.

'Not an idiot,' Kendra said. 'Good thing, too. Found an empty beer can. I'll do a walk-around outside, in case he tossed any.'

Rhys dangled a set of car keys from his index finger. 'I'll take the Hyundai. Let's load as much as we can into the car. Anything that won't fit, we'll throw into the van. Hit the funeral home first, then the junkyard.'

She glanced at her watch. 'Nearly two.'

'Any luck, we'll have everything done by day-break. I'm gonna sleep for a day.'

'You wish.'

They each took an end of the body bag and tossed it into the trunk of the Hyundai. They managed to get several bags in there, too, then filled the back seat. The remaining bags went into the back of the van.

They took a moment to catch their collective breath.

'I reek of bleach,' Kendra said. 'Calling us cleaners, that's supposed to be a euphemism.'

'You want to follow me or you want to head out first?'

'I'll follow you. Not sure I remember the turn.'

'Shit. The phone.'

'I bagged the phone. It was by the laptop.'

'No, that was a burner. Cheap flip phone. He must have had a personal phone. There was a Verizon bill by the laptop.'

Kendra said, 'It's probably with him, in his pocket, in the body bag.'

'We'll look for it later.'

They were both silent a moment. Rhys tipped his head back, put his right hand to his forehead as he looked up at the stars.

Then he brought down the hand, let out a long sigh, and said, 'Two down. Seven to go.'

THREE WEEKS EARLIER

CHAPTER 1

New Haven, CT

'You're dying.'

Dr Alexandra Nyman was expecting some reaction when she delivered her diagnosis, but Miles Cookson was busy looking at his phone.

'Did you hear me?' Alexandra asked. 'I know that's blunt, but you've always told me to be straight with you. There's no way to sugarcoat this.'

She'd come around her desk and was sitting in a leather chair next to Miles's, angled slightly so that her right knee was inches away from his left. She held a file folder with half an inch of paperwork stuffed into it.

Miles, still staring at the phone, both thumbs tapping away, said, 'I'm looking it up.'

'You don't have to look it up,' she said. 'I'm sitting right here. Ask me anything you want.'

He glanced at her. 'You're wrong, Alex. I can't be dying. I'm fucking forty-two years old. It's something else. Has to be. Look at me, for Christ's sake.'

17

She did. Miles presented as someone in good shape. Five-eight, trim at 160 pounds. She knew he'd run marathons into his thirties, and still jogged a few times a week. Nearly bald, but he made it work in a Patrick Stewart kind of way.

'Miles, we did the tests and they—'

'Fuck the tests,' he said, putting down the phone and looking her in the eye. 'All my so-called symptoms, you can put them all down to stress. Are you telling me you've never been short-tempered, or restless, or have things slip your mind now and then? And yeah, okay, I've been a bit clumsy. Falling over my own feet. But it can't be what you're saying.'

She said nothing, but decided to let him vent.

'Jesus,' Miles whispered. 'How could I . . . It's tension, stress, simple as that. You fucking doctors, you're always looking for trouble where there isn't any. Finding a way to justify all those years you went to school.'

Alexandra frowned, but not critically. She understood the anger.

'Sorry,' Miles said. 'Cheap shot.'

'It's okay.'

'It's . . . it's a lot to take in.'

'I know.'

'It's not stress, is it?'

'If all you had was some restlessness, a bit of forgetfulness, even the odd mood swing, I would agree with you. But stress doesn't explain the

18

involuntary body movements, the jerking, the twitching you've been—'

'Fuck,' he said. 'Fuck fuck fuck.'

'And I should clarify what I said, about you dying. There's no cure, there's nothing we can do. I can prescribe tetrabenazine, which will help with your symptoms when they become more pronounced, but it's not a cure.'

Miles laughed sardonically. 'Why couldn't it have been cancer? There's stuff they can do for cancer. Cut it out, hit it with chemo. But this?'

'There's no getting around it,' Alexandra said. 'Huntington's . . . it's like you take Alzheimer's, ALS, and Parkinson's and put them all into a blender. Your symptoms are very similar to any of those.'

'But worse.'

She said nothing.

'The other day,' he said, 'I wanted to put one foot in front of the other, something as simple as that, and my brain was like, no way, Jose. Not happening. And then, a second later, it was okay. Dorian, my assistant, had set up a meeting, told me all the details. Five minutes later, I could barely remember any of it.'

'I know.'

'I go through periods, I feel restless, like my skin's crawling, I have to do something, I can't relax.' He paused. 'How bad will it get?'

'It's a brain disease,' she said matter-of-factly.

19

'You'll lose more and more motor control. Unlike ALS, where you can remain mentally sharp while your body's ability to do things deteriorates, Huntington's will impact your cognitive abilities.'

'Dementia,' Miles said.

The doctor nodded. 'There will come a point where you will need constant care. There is no cure. They're working on it, and they've been working on it for some time. One of these days, it'll happen.'

'But not soon enough to help me,' he said.

Alexandra said nothing.

'Who's doing the research? How much money do they need? I'll cut them a check so they can get off their asses and do something. What do they need? A million? Ten million? Tell me. I'll write them a check tomorrow.'

The doctor leaned back in her chair and folded her arms. 'This isn't something you can buy your way out of, Miles. Not this time. All the money in the world won't bring about a cure overnight. There are some very dedicated people working on this.'

Miles turned his head, looked out the window as he took that in. 'How long?'

'Well, that's the thing. Whether it's Huntington's, or cancer, or your heart, whatever, predicting life expectancy is a mug's game. Look at Stephen Hawking. When he was diagnosed with ALS – you know, Lou Gehrig's disease – they gave him two years. He lived for several more decades. Last year,

I had someone in for a checkup, gave the guy a clean bill of health. Dropped dead two days later of a heart attack.'

'This isn't helpful,' Miles said.

'I know. For you, it could be four or five years, maybe less, or maybe you've got twenty years. When we did your genetic test, we were looking for a high nucleotide repeat. Below thirty-six the likelihood of Huntington's is much less, but when you get up around thirty-nine, then you're—'

'I don't know what you're talking about. Apps, I understand. DNA stuff, not so much.'

Alexandra nodded her understanding. 'Sorry. Too technical. Look, we're going to want to do regular assessments, see how you're doing. That may give us a better understanding of your long-term prognosis.'

'I could live a long time, but it could be hell,' he said.

'Yes. Here's the bottom line. You know what you've got. If there are things you want to do, things you want to accomplish – amends you want to make – now is as good a time as any. Maybe you end up doing it with plenty of time to spare. But a diagnosis like this, it sharpens your focus. Helps you set priorities.' She sighed. 'I'm sorry, Miles. I'll be with you every step of the way.' She paused. 'There's something else we should talk about.'

'God, not more bad news.'

21

'No, but let me ask you about family history again. Did either of your parents have Huntington's?'

'No,' he said. 'I mean, not that I know of. I suppose one of them could have but it never had a chance to show itself. They died in a car accident when they were in their forties. My dad was a drunk. He ran their Ford Explorer into a bridge abutment on the Merritt Parkway.'

'You have a brother, yes?'

Miles nodded. 'Gilbert.'

'The thing about Huntington's is, it's very much an inherited condition. You're right that one of your parents might have developed it had they not died prematurely. You could have inherited it from one of them. If a parent has Huntington's, there's a 50 percent chance that any of their children will have it, too.'

'Pretty high odds.'

'Right. So, there's a high probability that your brother has it, too. I think he should be tested.' She hesitated. 'Are you close?'

'He works for me,' Miles said.

'That's not what I asked.'

'We're . . . close enough. Things got a bit strained after he married Cruella de Vil.'

'I'm sorry?'

'Caroline. I'm not . . . a fan. But I'm not exactly her favorite person, either.' He thought about what the doctor had said. 'I'll talk to Gilbert. Suggest he get tested. Or maybe . . .'

'Maybe what?'

22

'Nothing,' he said.

Alexandra waited, trying to will him to be more forthcoming. When he wasn't, she forced a smile.

'There is one tiny piece of good news,' she said.

'This isn't like that joke, is it?' Miles asked. 'Where the doctor says, "I have bad news and good news. The bad news is you're dying, but the good news is I'm sleeping with Brad Pitt"?'

Alexandra said, 'No, not like that.'

'Okay. Tell me.'

'Well, you're not married. You have no children. If you did, this would be devastating news for them. It'd be terrible enough to learn you've had this diagnosis. But on top of that, they'd have to deal with the news that they might have it as well. One chance in two. That would be, for you, I think, an extra emotional burden you really don't need at this time.'

Miles stared at her, expressionless.

'Miles?' she said.

'Sorry,' he said. 'Just blanked out there for a second.'

Alexandra grew concerned. '*Do* you have children, Miles?'

And Miles thought, *Isn't that just the fucking million-dollar question?*

23

CHAPTER 2

Providence, RI

Chloe Swanson had the minitripod set up and ready to go. She wasn't using anything fancier than her iPhone for this. That was all she needed for this project. After all, didn't Steven Soderbergh shoot an entire movie with an iPhone? If he could do that, couldn't she? But she didn't want the camera to be all shaky for the interview, so she'd brought along a minitripod to attach it to. Bought it used at a Providence camera shop for a third of what a new one would have cost her.

She positioned it on a stack of books on an end table, which she had moved around in front of her grandfather's wheelchair so that it was aimed at him at eye level. She wanted to frame the shot so she wouldn't see his bed in the background. The room was so small it wasn't easy.

Chloe was initially going to film this in one of the nursing home's common rooms, but her grandfather didn't want to go down there. He'd had something going with one of the other residents,

24

a woman in her mideighties, but they'd had a recent falling-out. Chloe had tried to piece together what had happened, and astonishingly, at least to Chloe, it appeared to have something to do with sex. The old lady was interested, but Chloe's grandfather, not so much.

Anyway, Chloe hadn't wanted to do the video in the common room anyway. Too much background noise. There was one guy, had to be close to ninety, who was always making these unbelievable horking noises, like he was trying to cough up something that was all the way down in his shoes. Chloe wasn't without sympathy. Her heart went out to a lot of the residents of the Providence Valley Home, the place her mother most often referred to as the Fairfield Valley Home for the Bewildered.

Chloe didn't like it when her mother made jokes about old people. What was funny about losing your balance, falling down, having to wear diapers, forgetting your loved ones when they came to see you? Where were the laughs in that? Sure, Chloe was only twenty-two and didn't have to worry about getting old for a very long time, but that didn't mean she didn't have to care. She'd been here often enough to visit her grandfather that she'd made friends with several of the residents, and had started thinking about a more ambitious project that would involve interviewing a number of them, not just her mother's father.

Everybody had a story to tell.

And it was Chloe's hope that interviewing her grandfather would fill in some of the gaps in her own story. Not all of them, of course. There was one huge, missing chapter in her life it was unlikely she'd ever know anything about. Kind of like a five-hundred-piece jigsaw puzzle with one missing piece. Problem is, that piece takes up half the puzzle.

Chloe wanted to know who she was.

Her grandfather was thin and round shouldered, with a few wisps of hair that did little to hide his array of liver spots. Most days, Chloe might find him sitting in pajamas and a bathrobe, but today he had put on a jacket, white shirt, and tie. Chloe thought she could fit her entire hand between the collar and the old man's leathery, wrinkled neck.

'That's really a camera?' he whispered.

'It's my phone,' she said. 'You've seen my phone before. It does all kinds of things.'

He licked his dry lips. 'But where's the film?'

'It's digital. Are you ready?'

'Fire away. I'm not going to need my lawyer, am I?' He grinned, flashing his dentures.

'I don't think so,' Chloe said. 'Unless you're going to confess to something awful you did back in the day. Were you a hit man or something? Did you work for the mob?'

He shook his head. 'Just Sears.'

'I'm going to pick up from where we talked last time. Is that okay?'

He nodded.

'Don't look into the camera. Just look at me. We're just having a conversation. Okay?'

'I get it,' he said weakly.

Chloe tapped the screen on the phone, settled into her chair opposite her grandfather, and said, 'So how did you handle it, when Mom came out?'

'Came out of what?' he replied, grinning slyly.

Chloe chuckled. 'When she told you she was a lesbian.'

'Oh, that, well,' he said. 'It didn't happen all at once, you know. She kind of hinted about it. The clues were there if we were paying any attention. Your grandmother, Lisa – bless her heart – and I couldn't help but see the signs, but sometimes, even when it's right there in front of your face, you pretend not to see it. Any boyfriends she had, it never lasted long. I think I took it better than Lisa did, to tell you the truth. I think Lisa was always counting on a big wedding for whenever Gillian found Mr Right. You know?'

'Sure, I get that,' Chloe said.

'Twenty-five, thirty years ago, it wasn't all "I'm here, I'm queer, I don't care what you think." It's different now.'

'Maybe not as much as you think. Tell me more about how Gran felt.'

The man's face saddened. 'She had a hard time with it. People'd ask, hey Lisa, when's Gillian settling down? She'd always say she hadn't found the right guy yet, or she was working on her career, that kind of thing. But she was already living with Annette at that time. Lisa, she'd tell anyone who asked that they were just roomies, saving money by sharing accommodations.'

'I liked Annette,' Chloe said. 'She was a good mom.'

'That still sounds strange to me,' he said. 'When you've got two of 'em. How long's it been? I lose track of time these days.'

'I was ten,' Chloe said.

'Wow.'

'Anyway, did there come a point when Gran accepted it?'

'I guess. She had to move with the times.'

'How did she handle it when Mom told you she was pregnant?'

Her grandfather let out a little hoot. 'Boy, that was something. Turned her world upside down. But not for long. She figured your mom finally started playing for the right team. That she was sneaking out on Annette and having a real goddamn heterosexual affair. Be the first time she'd have approved of adultery, I'll tell you. She had no idea for some time that there was – gotta watch how I say this – no kind of hanky-panky going on. That the whole thing happened in a doctor's office.'

'A fertility clinic,' Chloe said.

'Yeah, right, one of them. We didn't know much about those. A child needs a father, your grand-mother kept saying. A mother *and* a father. Two mothers, that was just unnatural. When she found out it *wasn't* an affair, she was disappointed.' The old man looked down, unable to look his granddaughter in the eye. 'I won't lie to you. I kind of felt the same way, at first. It took me a while to realize that as long as you were loved, that was the only thing that mattered.'

'Did you talk to my mom around that time? About the choice she'd made? About having a child that way?'

'You could ask her that yourself.'

'She doesn't like to talk about it.'

He grinned slyly. 'So I'm telling tales out of school?'

'Maybe a little.'

'Yeah, we talked. I was asking her, who's the father? She said she didn't know. I said, how can you not know who it is? And she says, she knew things *about* the father, just not who he actually was. Like, what he looked like, what he did, what his interests were. A whaddaya-call-it.'

'A profile?'

'Yeah, a profile.'

'And what did she say about the profile?'

The old man's eyes rolled skyward. 'Honestly can't remember much.'

'Try,' Chloe said. 'Anything she might have told you.'

'She hasn't told you *anything*?'

'She says it doesn't matter. It's like he doesn't exist, like he *never* existed. Like it was some kind of immaculate conception. If I can't know him,

29

she figures, what's the point? He can be anyone you want him to be, she says. Imagine he's Bill Gates or Robert De Niro. As if either of them donated sperm.'

Her grandfather winced.

'What?'

'It's just . . . that word.'

Chloe tapped his knobby knee and smiled. 'So you don't remember anything she said about the donor?'

'Just that he was . . . what was the word? Suitable. That's it. A suitable donor. Oh, and smart.'

'Smart?'

He nodded. 'He was supposed to be very smart. That was in the profile. I guess maybe he had to give information about where he went to school, degrees, that kind of stuff.' He paused. 'What time is it?'

'Uh, almost three. You getting tired, Grandpa?'

'A little.'

'I think we're good for today.' Chloe tapped the screen. 'I was about to wrap it up anyway. My shift starts at five and I'm gonna go home and change first.'

'I want to eat there one day. Where you work.'

Chloe laughed. 'Dad, as bad as you think the food is here, it's better than where I work. If I didn't wait tables there, I'd never set foot in the place.'

Chloe removed the phone from its stand, collapsed the tripod, packed up her gear, and gave her grandfather a kiss on the head.

30

'See you this weekend,' she said.

'Okeydoke.'

'We can talk about other stuff. Like when you were in Vietnam. You must have a lot of stories from then.'

'Not many I want to talk about. But sure, we can do that.'

She slung her bag over her shoulder and went out into the hall. She was passing the nursing home reception desk when she heard her phone ping with an incoming email.

Chloe stopped, dug the phone out of her bag, pressed her thumb to the Home button, tapped on the mail app.

And stopped breathing.

It was an email from the WhatsMyStory people. The ones she'd sent her DNA to weeks ago for analysis. The ones who said if there was anyone out there she might be related to, who was willing to be contacted, they'd connect her.

The phone was trembling in her hand. She took a deep breath, steadied her thumb, and tapped the screen.

CHAPTER 3

Merritt Parkway, north of Norwalk, CT

Miles Cookson spotted the flashing lights in his rearview mirror before he heard the siren. He glanced at the dash, checked the speedometer. Ninety miles per hour. Okay, that was definitely above the speed limit, but in a Porsche Turbo, that was a notch above idling.

He had the Sirius tuned into the Beatles station, which was playing tracks from *The White Album*, and when 'Back in the U.S.S.R.' came over the speakers, Miles tapped the volume control on the steering wheel until the music drowned out the sound of the roaring engine behind him, which was no small accomplishment considering a 3.8-liter turbocharged boxer-six engine, rated at 540 horsepower, was pushing him forward.

Just as well Miles happened to see the flashing lights, because he'd have never heard the siren.

He had no doubt he could outrun the police, even if it was one of those supercharged cop cars. Didn't matter how powerful an engine you put

32

under the hood of some stock Ford or Chevy or one of those snappy new Dodge Charger models. Sure, they might have speed on the straightaway, but if Miles decided to take the next off-ramp, he'd be hitting the curve at sixty or seventy. One of those cruisers tried to take the ramp at that speed and it'd be flying through the air like a cop car in *The Blues Brothers*.

But Miles wasn't about to lead anyone on a chase. He didn't want to get anyone killed. Not an officer of the law, and not some innocent bystander pedaling along in a Prius. The smart and responsible thing to do was pull over and take his medicine.

So he took his foot off the gas, put on his blinker, and steered the car over to the shoulder, gravel kicking up noisily into the wheel wells. The police car pulled over behind him, lights flashing. The cop didn't exit his vehicle right away. He was probably entering Miles's plate into a computer, waiting to find out if it was a stolen car and whether the driver needed to be approached with more than the usual caution.

I'm harmless, Miles thought. *I'm only a danger to myself.*

He sat in the leather bucket seat, waiting patiently. Turned the ignition to off so that when the cop was approaching, he wouldn't hear the purr of the engine and think Miles was going to make a break for it.

The cop got out of his car and walked purposefully

up to the Porsche, stopping at the driver's window. Miles had already powered it down.

'Good day, Officer,' he said.

'You have any idea how fast you were going?'

'I think you picked me up when I was doing about ninety,' Miles said.

'License and registration,' the cop said.

Miles had already retrieved the registration from the small leather folder in the glove box. He'd set his wallet on the passenger seat after removing his license. He handed everything to the officer.

The cop looked at the two items and said, 'Wait here.'

He walked back to his cruiser and got in.

Miles turned the radio back on. 'While My Guitar Gently Weeps' came through the speakers. This had always been one of his favorites. He leaned his head back and closed his eyes, letting the music envelop him. The song was interrupted by a persistent *whoosh* of cars and trucks passing by on the highway.

The track was just finishing when Miles heard the police officer's boots crunching on pebbles as he approached.

'Mr Cookson,' the officer said gravely.

'Yes sir?'

'You need to slow down,' he said, handing him a ticket.

'Yes sir.'

Miles offered a respectful smile as the cop

34

headed back to his car. Miles leaned over, opened the glove box again, and tucked the ticket in there with the other three he'd received since getting the bad news from his doctor a few days earlier.

Fuck it, he thought, slamming the glove box door shut.

Before long, he figured, they'd take his license away. But by then, he'd probably have to give up driving anyway. In fact, earlier that day, coming up on a red light, when he went to put his right foot on the brake, it had done this weird wobble, like his foot had a mind of its own. There'd only been a momentary hesitation in applying pressure to the pedal, but driving safely was all about response time, instant decisions. When a little girl ran into the street after a ball, you couldn't send a message to your foot via snail mail to hit the fucking brake.

Scared him.

It was enough to convince him his driving days were limited.

Might as well get out on the road and drive like a son of a bitch while he could. Put the Porsche through its paces before he had to give it up. Hadn't even had the car a year. Dropped nearly two hundred grand on it. Added every possible option he could.

You make a few mill a year, you gotta spend it on something.

Miles's reckless, don't-give-a-flying-fuck attitude had not been limited to driving. He'd been drinking to excess every night. Not that having a few drinks was living on the edge, but Miles had pretty much given up alcohol more than a decade ago. Went through the whole 'body is a temple' bullshit. Drank eight glasses of water a day. Even followed Gwyneth Paltrow on Twitter, not that he agreed with even half of her life philosophy.

But in the last week, he'd renewed his friendship with Absolut Vodka. And he'd found that it went very well with Cheetos. Fucking *Cheetos*. He'd been through the McDonald's drive-through twice, gorging on Big Macs and fries. He couldn't believe how good this shit tasted. Took home Domino's one night. Ate the whole goddamn pizza himself. Woke up at midnight with the worst heartburn of his entire life. Briefly wondered – and at some level hoped – it was a heart attack and things could be over now.

Driving too fast and eating crap weren't the only risky things he'd been doing.

Two days earlier he'd gone skydiving. Not for the first time, but it was something he hadn't done since his twenties. When it came to the moment when he was to pull the rip cord, he thought about whether to bother. What a perfect way to go out. Okay, sure, the doc said he could have quite a few years left, but what was the quality of that life going to be? Maybe this was the way to end things. One big splat and you're done. Skip the part where someone has to help you go to the bathroom and wipe your ass. Skip the part where it takes an hour and a half to walk from the bedroom to the kitchen because your arms and legs are all fucking akimbo. Skip the part where it takes you five minutes to give the waiter your order because you can't form the words and get them the fuck out of your mouth.

But he yanked on that rip cord. The parachute deployed. Miles drifted safely back to Earth.

Miles had spent much of the week playing the 'Why Me?' movie in his mind. Why him? Why did he have to get this? What the hell had he done to offend the gods that he had to be saddled with this?

Pretty un-fucking-fair, that's what it was. Sure, other people had problems and serious diseases and millions of them were living in poverty or fleeing drug cartels south of the border or dying of starvation and dehydration in Africa, but Miles didn't give a rat's ass about any of them. He didn't care about rising oceans or climate change or how the world was eating too much beef which meant cattle were farting too much methane into the atmosphere. He didn't care about the rise of right-wing extremism or that every country in the world seemed determined to vote into power the stupidest knuckle-dragging politicians they could find.

And yet, as much as he was focused on his own situation, his own future, something was nagging at him. A sense that this was not *all* about him.

There is one tiny piece of good news . . . You have

37

no children. If you did, this would be devastating news for them.

'Are you going to tell me what this is about?'

Miles was at his desk, staring at his computer screen. Before him were the detailed proposals for several new apps his company had in development, but he wasn't seeing any of it. He couldn't focus. It wasn't vision related. He couldn't concentrate.

At first, he wasn't even aware that his personal assistant, Dorian, was standing there.

'Hello?' said Dorian, who was holding a metal Coke can. 'Is this what you wanted?'

He turned, looked at the can, and said, 'You were careful not to touch the top?'

'Yes.'

'Put it in a plastic bag and seal it,' he said.

'You're the boss, I get that, and lots of times I have to do things you want without knowing what it's about, but this crosses a line.'

Dorian, thirty-eight, had been working alongside Miles for nearly a decade, and there'd rarely been secrets between them. Dorian, slightly built, barely 110 pounds, with short-cropped black hair, oversized, black-framed glasses, pulled off the androgynous look with style, always coming to work dressed in a black button-down collared shirt, black jeans, and black sneakers with white, rubber soles. Less politically correct visitors would often whisper a question to Miles, wanting to know whether his assistant was male or female.

38

Invariably, he would answer, 'Does it make a difference?'

In all the time she'd worked for him, Dorian had offered very little information about her private life, and Miles had learned not to ask.

Miles said, eyeing the Coke can, 'It's personal.'

'No shit,' Dorian said. 'You ask me to stalk your brother, and grab something he's touched, something that he's put to his mouth, and bring it to you. You're right, that's very personal, and you've brought me into it. I can think of only one reason why you would want me to do that. You want a sample of his DNA. So I ask myself, why would you want that?'

'Dorian, just—'

'Maybe it's that you don't really think he's your brother? Or maybe someone broke into your place and did a dump on your living room rug and you're wondering if it was him?'

'Why would you even—'

'Just blue-skying.' Dorian shrugged, but then gave him a steely glare. 'And while we're on the topic of strange behavior, what's been going on with you lately? Gone half the time, jumping out of planes, drinking. You think I don't notice this stuff?'

Miles nodded slowly, aware that as he did so, his head was moving at an odd angle. Early signs of chorea. He could see the troubled look on Dorian's face. It was hard to get anything past Dorian.

39

'You're right about the DNA. I want you to send that to the lab we've worked with before. A rush job. I know they can do that if you throw enough money at them.'

Dorian nodded with some satisfaction. 'And what should they be looking for?'

Miles swallowed. 'Huntington's.'

That wiped the smugness from her face. 'Jesus,' Dorian said. 'Your brother thinks he has Huntington's? No, wait, if you're doing this behind his back, *you* think he has Huntington's? What the hell makes you think he has Huntington's?'

Miles looked at her, waiting for her to put it together.

'Oh, fuck,' Dorian said, and dropped into one of the two Eames leather chairs on the other side of Miles's desk. 'How long have you known?'

'A week.'

'Oh, Miles. I'm so sorry. But why . . . wait, you haven't told Gilbert yet.'

'No.'

'You're waiting for *his* genetic test to come back. To find out if he has it.'

'Yes.'

'Is this ethical?'

'Probably not,' Miles said, 'but I think it's the right thing to do. Given that I've been diagnosed with it, there's a very good chance he has it, as well. When I tell him about my diagnosis, it won't be long before he thinks about the implications for himself. And for his daughter. I want to be

40

able to tell him, then and there, whether he has anything to worry about.'

Dorian melted into the chair, overwhelmed. 'Oh, man. I'm so sorry. It's so . . . fucking unfair.' She shook her head slowly. 'I'll get the DNA test done. What else do you need?'

He ignored the question, going quiet for several seconds. 'You know that group that came through here day before yesterday? From that new streaming service?'

'Yeah?'

'I got talking to one of them. Oscar, his name was. He was blind.'

'Yeah. Black guy, sunglasses.'

'He went blind, like, overnight. When he was only thirty. Detached retinas in both eyes. Very rare. So we got talking, and he said, if only he'd known it was coming. There were all these things he wanted to see someday. The Taj Mahal. The Great Wall. Victoria Falls.' Miles had to stop for a second. 'His son.'

Dorian nodded. 'I get it. You're thinking of the things you want to do . . . while you can.'

Miles looked at Dorian reproachfully, as though she had missed his point entirely. 'No, that's not what I was thinking at all.'

'Okay,' she said. 'Then what?'

'Never mind,' Miles said. 'Just get my brother's DNA tested.'

CHAPTER 4

Providence, RI

Chloe Swanson found her mother, Gillian, hunting for something in her Camry. She had the driver's door, and the driver's-side back door, open, and was on her knees, on the driveway, looking under the front seat.

'Mom?' Chloe said.

'It's got to be here somewhere,' Gillian said. She pulled up the rear floor mat, ran her hand over the carpeting.

'What are you looking for?' her daughter asked.

'My goddamn Visa card. I used it to get out of that parking garage? You swipe it going in, then coming out, and—' She had her hand so far up beneath the driver's seat that Chloe could see her fingers wiggling out from under the front.

'And what?'

'So I take the card out, and the gate goes up to let me out, and I want to take a second to put the card back in my wallet, but I've got some asshole behind me honking his horn for me to get going, so when I drive out I put the card on the passenger

42

seat, and you know how you have to drive up the ramp out of that garage, like a winding staircase or a corkscrew or something, and when I get home the card's not on the seat. It slipped. Why can't they have parking attendants like they used to? Someone in an actual booth?'

Chloe went around to the car and opened the front passenger door. 'I'll look on this side.'

While they were both digging their fingers into crevices and under floor mats, unable to look directly at each other, Chloe said, 'I'm going to be gone for a couple days.'

'What?'

'Taking a drive up to Massachusetts. Around Springfield somewhere.'

Gillian was moving the driver's seat forward and digging into the narrow space between it and the center console. 'Well, I've found a straw and two quarters. You said a couple days?'

'Yeah.'

'You cleared it at work?'

'My weekend's Tuesday, Wednesday. So I'm going to drive up Tuesday morning, first thing.'

'So what's in Springfield?'

'I'm going up there to meet someone.'

Gillian raised her head, peered at Chloe between the two front seats. 'To meet someone? Like, for the first time? Or someone you've met before?'

'Someone I've never met before. Someone I met online.'

Now Gillian extracted herself from the car and

stood next to it, peering across the roof as Chloe did the same. She had something in her hand. A credit card.

'I found it,' Chloe said. 'It must have slid off the seat and was tucked down by the door.'

She slid it across the roof, her mom slapping her hand on it before it slid down the slope of the rear window. If Chloe was expecting to be thanked, it did not happen.

'Someone you met on the internet?' Chloe's mother said. 'Jesus, do you need your head read? The internet? Home of perverts, sickos, and predators?'

'It's not like that.'

'Was it some sort of dating site? You don't have enough guys hitting on you in the diner?'

'Yeah, they're a prime bunch, Mom. Thanks for thinking that's the gene pool I need to choose from.'

'So it was a dating site? You know people just lie about themselves online. You think you're going to meet George Clooney and it turns out to be Danny DeVito.'

'It's not a dating site.' Chloe bit her lip, looked away briefly. When she turned her eyes back on her mother, she said, 'You have to promise not to be mad.'

'Mad about what?'

'Your face. It looks like it's getting ready to be mad.'

Gillian struggled to compose herself. She placed

her hands flat on the roof, then raised all her fingers for a second, a signal to proceed.

'I sent away,' Chloe said slowly, reaching into her pocket for her phone, 'for one of those tests.'

Gillian's face paled. 'What . . . test?'

'I bet you can guess.' She raised the phone, opened the camera, and set it to record video. 'Jesus Christ, Chloe, you know—'

'You promised.'

Gillian struggled to calm herself. 'You know how I feel about this. And for God's sake stop recording this!'

'I'm documenting,' Chloe said.

'Stop it!'

Chloe lowered the phone and picked up where she'd left off. 'I have a *right*—'

'What *right*? Show me where it's written that—'

Chloe exploded. 'I have a right to know who I am!'

Her mother took her hands off the roof and took a step back, as though blown by a gust of wind. When she spoke, her voice was little more than a whisper.

'When did you—'

'I had the test mailed to the nursing home, to Grandpa. I knew if it showed up here you'd freak out. Or if it arrived when I wasn't here you'd just throw it out and never even tell me.'

Gillian said nothing to that. She knew it was true.

'I spit into this little tube and mailed it off. First

they emailed and told me my heritage. Like, 30 percent Scottish, 20 percent something else. That kind of shit, which I didn't care about all that much. And you could have them test you for like illnesses and stuff, but I figured at my age, who cares, right? But it also said, if there were others who'd taken the test who had a, like, partial DNA match, and they were willing to get in touch, they'd do that, you know?'

Gillian was barely able to mouth the words. 'You've found out who your father is. Chloe, not even I know that.'

'No,' she said emphatically. 'I *didn't* find that out. I still have no fucking idea. So if *that's* what you were worried about, you can rest easy.'

Gillian's look bordered on disappointment.

'Holy shit,' Chloe said. 'Part of you actually wanted to know.'

'I – I won't lie. I've wondered. But I've told you, and I'm telling you now, some things are not worth knowing. Some guy, going into a little room with a dirty magazine, putting a sample in a cup – that's not a father. That's not a *parent*. What – what if at some point in your life you had a blood transfusion? Like, if you were in an accident? And that blood saved you? Would you be hunting all over the world trying to find out whose blood it was?'

'This is different and you know it,' Chloe said. 'A blood donation hardly compares to a sperm donation.'

'So, if it's not your father that you've found . . .'

'It's like, a brother,' she said quietly. 'A half brother. Someone conceived from the same sperm.'

Gillian put her hand to her mouth.

'Chloe,' she said.

'He gave his contact info to WhatsMyStory and I got in touch. I emailed him first, and then we talked on the phone.' Chloe began to tear up. 'There was something, in his voice . . . I don't know how to describe it, but he sounded like me. I mean, not *like* me, but the way he pauses, thinks about what he's going to say, it reminded me . . . of me.'

Gillian looked stricken.

'So I'm going to drive up and see him. I'm going to drive up to fucking Massachusetts and meet my brother. I don't know how it's going to go. Maybe it'll be a disaster.'

'Don't,' Gillian whispered. 'We're good. You and I. We're good. We don't *need* other people. We don't need more family. You don't know anything about him. Just because he's somehow related—'

'He's not *somehow related*, Mom. He's a *brother*.' Chloe looked at her mom with sympathy. 'I get why you're afraid. It's new. It's scary. *I'm* scared. But I just . . . I just have to do this.'

Gillian dug into her pocket for a tissue, dabbed the corner of her eye.

'What's his name?' she asked.

'Todd,' Chloe said. 'Todd Cox.'

47

CHAPTER 5

New Haven, CT

As an adult, Miles had always lived alone. Not only had he never married, he'd never had a live-in girlfriend. Sure, plenty of women had slept over through the years, but rarely more than two nights in a row. Miles didn't encourage that kind of thing. Never give a woman the chance to get comfortable under this roof. He valued his privacy. He liked things just so. Living a solitary existence, at least on the home front, was not a problem.

But since the diagnosis, something in him had changed. Not physically, but emotionally.

He was lonely.

Miles found himself having conversations, out loud, with himself, if only to hear someone's voice. Not when the housekeeper was there, of course. No sense having her think he was losing his marbles.

Unless he was.

No, no, he wasn't. Miles was sure of that. Whatever cognitive issues awaited him, they were

48

not present yet. Maybe, he thought, it'd be better if they were. Perhaps he'd be less tormented than he was now.

'What are you going to do about them?' he said aloud, standing in the kitchen, making himself another vodka and soda water. 'What *should* you do about them?'

He knocked back the drink. 'It's not my responsibility. It's not my fault. There was no way I could have known. It's fucking life, right? It's all a throw of the dice.'

What was different tonight was that this conversation with himself was escalating into an argument.

'What do you mean you don't have any fucking responsibility? If you didn't know, that'd be one thing, but you *do* know. You did the right thing where your brother is concerned, testing his DNA, but you don't give a fuck about the rest?'

And then he threw his tumbler hard enough at the stainless steel door of his Sub-Zero fridge to put a dent into it. The glass shattered across the floor.

Miles turned his back on the mess and headed for his bedroom, not bothering to turn off lights along the way, putting his hand on the hallway walls every few steps to maintain his balance. He stripped down to his boxers and collapsed onto the bed, atop the covers, rolling onto his back and staring, briefly, at the slowly rotating ceiling fan before he fell asleep.

He'd been asleep for only a few minutes when he sensed someone in the room. Miles opened his eyes and felt his heart do a somersault. There was more than *someone* in the room.

There was a *crowd*.

Perhaps as many as twenty or thirty people. All standing around the bed, arms at their sides, staring down at him, rigid as statues. About a fifty-fifty split between men and women, and most of them appeared to be in their twenties. The faces were indistinct, as if Miles were viewing them through frosted glass.

'Who the fuck are you?' Miles asked.

One of them, a young woman, said, 'You don't know?'

One of the men said, 'Typical.'

'If you really do care, do something,' another woman said. 'If you don't, then stop thinking about us.'

Together, they raised their arms to the ceiling and waved them about frantically, as though they were those inflatable people one found out front of used car dealers. But then their waving arms morphed into flames, and their bodies began to burn.

A chorus of screams erupted from their blurred mouths.

Miles woke up.

'Jesus,' he said.

Miles was not the type of person to read much into nightmares. He did not make major life decisions based on the advice of ghostly figures from his subconscious. But those strange people in his dream had at least accomplished one thing. They'd given him a pounding headache. Of course, he could also be hungover.

He pulled back the covers, got out of bed, and padded on bare feet into the kitchen. He ran some water into a glass, rummaged about in one of the cabinets for the container of Tylenol, and when he turned back around, there they were.

Miles's mother and father. Perched on stools on the other side of the kitchen island, watching him.

He could tell it was them, even though large chunks of flesh were hanging from their faces. What skin hadn't peeled away was peppered with granules of windshield glass. Their clothes were drenched in blood.

Miles's father was holding an empty vodka bottle in his hand, holding it up to the light to see whether there might still be a drop or two in it. 'Hello, son,' he said.

Miles's mother looked at him and smiled. 'If we had known,' she said, 'we'd have told you.'

Miles began to scream. And then he woke up, this time for real.

The next morning, Miles asked Dorian to take a walk with him. Once outside the building, she said, 'I don't have the DNA test back yet.'

'That's not what I want to talk to you about.'

'Okay.'

51

'You know I don't have that many people I can talk to,' he said. 'Gilbert, yeah, he's my brother, but there are issues there.'

Again, Dorian said, 'Okay.'

'I want to know whether he's got the disease because there's a high probability. Fifty percent chance that it gets passed down. So if one of our parents had it, then there's just as much chance he's got it as I do.'

'Yeah, I Googled it.'

They'd reached a small park that bordered a creek. Miles steered them onto the grass and headed for a bench.

'My brother's not the only one I've been thinking about,' he said.

They reached the bench and sat. Dorian studied her boss and nodded slowly. Miles could almost see the light bulb come on over her head.

'You have a kid,' she said. 'I mean, you've never mentioned it, but . . . did you just find out? Some girlfriend from years ago?'

'Not like that,' Miles said. 'And it's not just one kid.'

'You have a *couple* of kids,' Dorian said, unable to hold back a wry grin.

'The thing is,' Miles said, 'I have no idea how many there might be.'

Dorian blinked. 'Say again?'

Miles laid it all out for her. That nearly twenty-four years ago, desperate for cash, he went to a fertility clinic.

'It wasn't like they paid a fortune for donations. A few hundred. But back then, when I was broke, that was a lot of money. And you had to meet all sorts of criteria. Couldn't smoke, good lifestyle choices, college education. You couldn't just walk in off the street, go into a cubicle and—'

'I get the picture,' Dorian said. 'So there could be a hundred little Mileses or Millies out there today?'

Miles said he'd been told by the clinic that they wouldn't use his sperm more than, say, a dozen times. But had they kept their word? Might there be more? And even if they'd kept that promise, someone might have had twins, or even triplets.

Which was why Miles had no idea how many biological children of his might be out there.

Miles told her about how that morning he'd been sitting at a red light, watching the pedestrians who crossed past the front of his car. A guy in his twenties wearing a Boston College sweatshirt, a backpack slung over his shoulder. *What if he's my son?* A young woman jogged past, buds in her ears, listening to music while she did her run. *What about her?*

It was not the kind of thing he'd thought much about before. It had barely crossed his mind over the last two decades that there could be people out there with half his genetic makeup.

'But now I can't stop thinking about them. And what, if anything, I owe them.'

What if he were one of his biological children? Would he want to know there was a 50 percent chance that he might be carrying the gene that might be the end of him?

Had he known what the future held for him, he'd never have gone to that fertility clinic. He'd have found another way to get the money for that new computer he'd needed.

But hey, Miles said, everybody eventually gets something, right? Something's got to kill you, sooner or later. It wasn't his fault, was it? There was no way he could have known. Was there even a test at the time that could have told him he had Huntington's?

'Right,' Dorian said. 'There's no way you could know. There's no way anyone could know. I mean, maybe *now*, maybe *today*, they could test someone who goes to a clinic like that. I don't know. But not back then.'

If he'd known, at the age of twenty, what awaited him, would he have lived his life differently? Would he have spent those two years backpacking around Europe, or would he have stayed home and gotten serious about his career sooner? For sure, he wouldn't have spent much of his twenty-first year partying. Maybe, if he'd known the future, he'd have accelerated his efforts to reach the upper echelons of the tech world. Maybe he'd have made his first million from designing apps ten or twelve years ago instead of five.

Or maybe he'd have figured, what's the point?

Why not spend the rest of his life traveling, drinking, and whoring?

'The question is,' Dorian said, 'if you *could* have known, would you have *wanted* to know?'

'That's the question,' Miles said.

'Or maybe the question is, would you have at least wanted to be able to make that choice?' she asked.

Miles had no immediate answer.

'You know what app we should have invented?' he said finally. 'One where I can go back in time and never go to that goddamn clinic.'

'Look,' Dorian said, putting her hand on his, 'you can't change the past. You have to deal with the here and now. Get this other shit out of your system. Jumping out of planes, drinking too much. Then figure out what you want to do. Figure out what you're capable of doing. The resources that you have.'

'What I have,' Miles said, 'is money.'

Dorian said, 'I'm . . . aware.'

'I'll never be able to spend it all,' he said.

'Yeah,' Dorian said, smiling. 'We should all have such problems.'

He had a will. He wasn't an idiot. His legal advisers insisted that someone with a successful tech company and a sizable personal portfolio had to plan for the unexpected. Even before his diagnosis he was willing to concede that one day he might step in front of a bus while looking at his phone. He'd chosen a few charities and foundations

55

to leave his money to. Now, he'd probably want to rethink that, maybe leave a big chunk of his estate to Huntington's research.

But his current will left nothing of significance to any one individual.

There was no spouse. There'd been a couple of girlfriends at UConn, a couple of romances right after college, and he'd had a few meaningless flings in the past decade. But if Miles was honest with himself, he'd only ever had one real love: computers. There'd been some women who might have been happy to share a life with him despite all that, but he'd seen, firsthand, what a marriage could descend into. The only thing that had kept his parents together, at least until they'd driven into that bridge abutment, was their mutual hatred for each other. It was a kind of sick, twisted energy that kept them both alive. Miles had always wondered if his father had driven deliberately into the abutment, or if his mother had reached over and grabbed the wheel to make it happen.

How could you endure an upbringing like that and want it for yourself? Not Miles. His brother, Gilbert, had believed he could beat the odds, but the woman he'd found and committed himself to – the one Miles thought of as Cruella but whose actual name was Caroline – had as many issues as their mother, if not more. She was a controlling, narcissistic woman. She could put on a smile when she needed to, charm you from here to

Cleveland, but the moment your back was turned, watch out.

And from everything Miles could tell, Gilbert's daughter, Samantha, had come under the mother's spell, or at least been cowed by her mood swings. Go along to get along, as they say. Maybe Gilbert put up with the daily tension and anxiety because he didn't know it could be any other way. When you grew up in a dysfunctional family, you assumed all families were that way. You could walk out on the one you had and trade it for one that was even more fucked up. Miles guessed that was how Gilbert saw the world. As bad as it was, it could be worse.

Miles had been reluctant to leave his brother a large part of his estate because he feared Caroline would get her hands on it. And he'd felt no small measure of guilt because of that. Gilbert was forty-five, the older brother by three years. He'd looked out for Miles when they were younger. Ran interference for him, protected him from their parents' tirades. Like the time Miles, too young to have a driver's license, took out the father's Oldsmobile for a joyride and backed into a fire hydrant, knocking the bumper right off and sending a geyser of water into the sky. Gilbert knew their father would kill him, so he confessed to the crime. Gilbert was nearly six feet tall at age fifteen, and had enough weight on him that their father would never dare take a belt to him the way he might have when Gilbert was younger.

But Gilbert bore the brunt of his anger, which was considerable.

It was interesting how Gilbert was better at standing up to their father back then than he was at standing up to Caroline now.

Miles had set up a trust for Gilbert, without his knowledge, that would pay him twenty thousand dollars a month once he'd passed. Given what Miles had, it was a token amount, and there was nothing he could do, in death, to stop Gilbert from handing it over to his wife, but at least it would keep Caroline from getting her hands on a massive inheritance.

But now, there were other people to consider.

'I have to sort some things out,' he told Dorian, 'while I'm still able.'

'Go on.'

'This disease isn't going to kill me overnight. It may be long and drawn out and pretty fucking horrible. If I'm going to leave money to my children, whoever they are, I need to do it now. Give it to them while they have time to enjoy it.'

'That's what you want to do,' Dorian said, seeking clarification. 'Distribute your wealth . . . now . . . to these biological children, whoever and wherever they may be.'

He nodded.

'I see,' Dorian said. 'No others you'd want to consider?'

'I'll still allocate some to charities,' he said.

58

The look on Dorian's face suggested she had been hoping for a different answer.

Miles said, 'I need to find out who they are. My children. How *many* there are. Names, addresses.'

'Jesus, Miles, think about this a minute,' Dorian said. 'What if they don't even know they owe their existence to a fertility clinic? That their father isn't their *real* father? You gonna send them an email with "Guess what?" in the subject line? Call them up and say, "Hey, I'm your dad. I donated sperm at a clinic more than two decades ago, your mom got it, and here you are! *And* you're about to become a multimillionaire! Wanna grab a beer? Oh, and by the way? I've got a fatal genetic disease, and there's a chance – nothing to get alarmed about – you might develop it, too. So whaddaya say about that beer?" Miles, there's a lot to consider here.'

Miles closed his eyes briefly. 'Shit,' he said.

'Exactly.'

He opened his eyes. 'They're entitled to know.'

CHAPTER 6

New York, NY

The police had closed off Seventieth Street at Park. A massive crane truck sat dead center in the street about halfway between Park and Lexington, and not a car, not a cab, not even a cyclist, was going to get through here for the next few hours.

Parked on the street, just behind the crane truck, was a Winnebago, a mid-1970s recreation vehicle from the company's Brave series. Eighteen feet long, as aerodynamic as a box car, with that distinctive W painted down the side. The RV was wrapped in an assortment of straps and braces, and the man in the small, glass-enclosed cockpit was moving the crane's hook into position above the vehicle.

The sidewalk in front of three brownstones had been blocked off, and up on the third floor of the one on the right was a gaping hole about twenty feet wide and twelve feet high. Two large panes of glass that would have filled that space were hung

60

on either side of the opening from straps that came down from the roof.

A large crowd had formed in the street to watch. It wasn't every day one got to see an RV placed on the third floor of a New York brownstone. But as everyone knew, this was where Jeremy Pritkin lived, and if Jeremy Pritkin wanted a Winnebago in the top floor of his residence, that was exactly what Jeremy Pritkin was going to get.

Several news crews were there to cover the event, and a reporter from NY1 had managed to pull Pritkin away from supervising the project to ask him a few questions. Pritkin, six feet tall, trim, looked at least a decade younger than his sixty-five years. He stepped well away from the crane for the interview and took off his yellow hard hat, revealing short, salt-and-pepper hair. He had not chosen the rest of his outfit with an engineering project in mind. He was in his trademark midnight blue suit, crisp white shirt, and dark blue tie decorated with hundreds of minuscule golden dollar signs.

'Angie Warren here on East Seventieth,' the reporter said, 'talking to New York notable Jeremy Pritkin about a somewhat outlandish decorating project. Are you really putting a Winnebago inside your house?'

Pritkin smiled, showing off a set of Hollywood-perfect teeth. 'It's going into my office, up on the third floor.'

'That's kind of where you allow your eccentricities to run free,' Angie said.

'Well, I don't know about that. We all have our idiosyncrasies, don't we?'

'Why a Winnebago?'

'First of all, it's an iconic American design, a symbol of exploration. Thousands of Americans got into these vehicles and set forth on adventures of exploration, a little like early settlers who moved westward across the nation. They're beautiful machines, in an ugly kind of way.' He chuckled.

'But there's something personal about them for you, isn't there?'

Pritkin nodded. 'When I was in my teens, my parents bought one of these – a slightly longer model – and when my dad got his summer holidays, we'd hit the road. Saw everything from Niagara Falls to the Grand Canyon. I think it was those trips that really sparked my interest in national infrastructure, highways and bridges and the like.'

'And prompted you, eventually, to create a multi-billion-dollar highway engineering firm.'

'Which I sold fifteen years ago, which allows me certain indulgences such as this,' Pritkin said, grinning. 'The Winnebago will be a mini-office within my much larger study. A little retreat, if you will.' He pointed to the open space that had been created in the side of the building. 'And with any luck, in a few hours, it will be in place, the windows back on, all in time for tonight's party.'

62

'Will you be giving tours of the new addition?'

Pritkin shook his head. 'The third floor is my private place.'

'While we've got you, Mr Pritkin, you wrote an op-ed in the *Times* yesterday very critical of the mayor's budget cutbacks, suggesting he doesn't have a clue what he's doing.'

Pritkin shrugged. 'I'm not sure that he does. But I don't imagine my opinion will stop him from coming to my party.'

Angie smirked. 'You have so many strings to your bow. Industrialist, author, opinion columnist, philanthropist, financier – can we now add interior decorator?'

'Yeah, I'm sure this will start a trend. Everyone's going to want an RV in their living room. I can imagine one now being added to Frank Lloyd Wright's Fallingwater.' He chuckled again.

Pritkin saw that the crane had hooked onto the Winnebago, and the vehicle's tires were losing their grip on the pavement as it began its ascent.

'Must end things there,' he said, put the hard hat back on, and headed back to the operation, standing almost under the RV as it was lifted off the street. Pritkin was joined by another man in an orange hard hat and matching orange safety vest. He had a tag on his vest that read: BERT: SUPERVISOR.

'I hear some sloshing,' Bert said. 'Is there still fuel in the tank?'

'We'll siphon it out later,' Pritkin said. 'Not to worry.'

'Moved a few grand pianos in my day, but nothing like this,' Bert said. 'I can't believe the city let you do this.'

Pritkin looked at him and winked. 'It helps to know people.'

He watched with awe and wonder as the vehicle rose higher. Within a few minutes it was level with the third-floor opening. Half a dozen workers stood at the edge, ready to guide it into the building and put it into position.

'Love to keep watching, but I've a party to get ready for,' Pritkin said, giving Bert a pat on the shoulder and heading into the brownstone.

As it turned out, the mayor did not come. Jeremy Pritkin figured his feelings were hurt, the big baby. But the guests who did arrive that evening still made an impressive list. Anybody who was anybody was here, wandering the first two floors of the joined brownstones, drinking, laughing, dancing, mingling, nibbling. And the nibbling was not restricted to the hors d'oeuvres. Ears and necks were evidently just as tasty. If you saw a bathroom door closed for a long time, it wasn't because someone was suffering from indigestion.

Jeremy liked his guests to have a good time.

If ever there was a party house, this was it. And shouldn't it be, for a place that was listed for $60 million when he bought it four years ago? There were movie stars here, Grammy winners, failed presidential candidates, a former governor, a famous lawyer who offered his expertise on CNN or Fox or MSNBC nearly every night, a composer who'd won a Tony fifteen years before and had been dining out on it ever since, even a sheik from one of the Emirates, dressed not in his traditional Kandura white robe but a pair of thousand-dollar jeans and a silk shirt with the top three buttons undone.

Jeremy had acquired a who's who of interesting friends and acquaintances over the years. When you were something of a Renaissance man, who'd dabbled in more fields than Hershey's had kisses, and had a problem, chances were you already knew someone who could help you solve it.

No matter how serious.

Also sprinkled throughout the crowd were a few less-than-famous faces, although what they lacked in notoriety they made up for in beauty. Young, gorgeous women, some younger than others. Aspiring starlets, models, stewardesses, dancers, many looking to make some cash while they waited for their Broadway careers to blossom. Jeremy liked to have at least half a dozen here to serve drinks, gather up coats, tend to the guests' needs.

Some were more needy than others.

Jeremy worked the crowd. Lots of hugs, plenty of thank-yous.

A silver-haired woman in her seventies, dressed in a glittering floor-length gown, sidled up to him, slipping her arm into his.

She whispered, 'On behalf of the Met's board

of directors, I would like to thank you for your generous support.'

'It was nothing,' he said modestly. 'Glad to do it.'

'Two million is *not* nothing,' she said. 'I just wanted to show my gratitude.'

He grinned slyly. 'But Gretchen, your husband is right over there.'

She laughed, slapped his upper arm. 'You're too much!' And then, whispering again, 'If I thought I could get away with it, and if only you had a thing for older women . . .'

Now it was his turn to laugh. He gave her hand a squeeze and moved deeper into the crowd.

'Thanks for that tip!' someone outside his field of vision said to him. 'The stock has doubled!'

Jeremy gave a general thumbs-up and kept moving. He had his eyes on a round-shouldered man who had to be pushing eighty, looking down the dress of one of the young women hired to work the room.

'Judge Corliss,' he said, getting the man's attention. 'How are we doing tonight?'

The man's head snapped up as he eyed the host. He nodded and extended a hand. 'Great party,' he said. 'Special occasion?'

Jeremy shook his head. 'Do you need an excuse to get together with friends?'

'Course not.'

'I understand you're going to be presiding over our case,' Jeremy said. 'Just found out, in fact.'

'Before or after you sent my invitation?' The judge laughed at his own joke.

'After. Look, I know you have to call it the way you see it. I know you'll be fair.'

'Without question,' the judge said, but there was something exchanged between them at that moment. A look. An understanding.

Jeremy shook the man's hand again and was about to strike up a conversation with the anchor for one of the Big Three networks' early morning shows and a director who'd been up for an Oscar three years ago – how he'd been nominated in the first place was a mystery to Jeremy; the film was utter shit – when someone tapped him on the back.

He turned and came face-to-face with his personal assistant, Roberta Bennington. Fiftyish, shapely, and tall with jet-black hair that she always swept over to rest on her right shoulder. She might not have been able to look him directly in the eye were it not for the four-inch stilettos she wore whenever here at work. Jeremy had a thing that none of the female staff in his employ could wear flats. Not a fetish, he insisted, although not one of the women who worked for him believed that for a minute.

'She's waiting for you in your office,' Roberta told him.

Jeremy nodded, turned, and departed.

He walked up the two broad flights of stairs to the third floor. Given that his home was three

67

brownstones stitched together, some areas of the third floor were open to wanderers, but to enter the long, wide hallway that led to his office, one had to enter a four-digit code to open the double doors.

He keyed in the numbers, opened the door, and proceeded down the hallway, lined on one side with massive windows made of one-way glass that looked down onto East Seventieth, and on the other, large, framed black-and-white photographs.

These pictures were unlike the Picassos or Pollocks or Pissarros one might find elsewhere in his expansive home. These photos were neither abstract nor landscapes. These were works by Helmut Newton and Robert Mapplethorpe and others. Erotic photographs. Men with women, men with men, women with women. Men alone, women alone. Imaginative couplings and solitary pleasures, many with close-ups of genitalia.

When he reached the end of this gallery, he reached a second set of doors, but there was no keypad this time. He opened the doors and went inside.

It was, if not quite the size of a tennis court, close. One wall, the glass one that had been dismantled earlier in the day and then put back in place, afforded a broad view of East Seventieth Street, but anyone gazing up from the sidewalk, or hoping to get a peek into Jeremy Pritkin's world from the brownstone across the street, would have been disappointed. This glass, like that in the hallway, was one-way. From the street, this window gave the appearance of a massive mirror.

The angular, boxy Winnebago was parked up against the far wall, the front end pointed toward the street, close to the window. Shelves stocked with art books lined another wall, and more graphically sexual art was displayed on the one behind the expansive desk that dominated the room.

Well, that dominated the room *before* the RV was put in place.

As Jeremy closed the second set of doors, he heard the crying, even before he saw the girl.

The large leather chair in which she sat enveloped her. With its oversized arms and towering seatback, the chair dwarfed her, like some novelty piece of furniture at a state fair that visitors needed a ladder to crawl into to have their picture taken.

The girl was not waiting to have her picture taken.

Dressed in fashionably ragged jeans and a sweatshirt emblazoned with the letters NYPD, she sat with her knees drawn up to her chest, her skinny arms wrapped around them to hold them in place. Her hair, blond with streaks of pink, hung over her eyes, partly obscuring the tears that ran down her cheeks. When Jeremy entered she drew in on herself, tightened the grip on her knees.

She did not look more than fifteen.

'Oh, Nicky, Nicky, Nicky,' Jeremy said softly. 'Nicky Bondurant. Look at you.'

He sat in a matching leather chair next to hers and turned so that he could address her more directly. He drew out the folded silk handkerchief that was tucked into the front pocket of his suit jacket and handed it to her.

'Dry those eyes, darling,' he said.

Tentatively, she reached out for the handkerchief, dabbed away the tears, and wiped her nose. When she went to hand it back, Jeremy raised a hand.

'It's yours,' he said. He waited, wondering whether she would speak, and when she did not, he said, 'You hurt me, Nicky.'

She said nothing.

'After all the things I've done for you, this is how you repay me.'

Nicky sniffed. She was studying a frayed opening in her jeans that allowed a peek at her knee.

'Has there ever been anything I denied you? When you needed a new phone, who got that for you? Tickets to *Hamilton*? No problem. Who got you in to see *Saturday Night Live*? You even got to meet some of the cast, after. Remember that?'

Nicky spoke for the first time. 'Yes.'

'Do you remember what it was like when you first came to New York? How hard it was for you to get by?'

'I know.'

'Who's shown more interest in your welfare? Me, or your mother in Norfolk who couldn't have cared less when you left home?'

Nicky sniffed. 'You.'

'And who set you up with your own little apartment so you didn't have to keep living with that family in Brooklyn?'

'You.'

'I understand how hard it can be for a young girl on her own. The challenges, the troubles, all the obstacles. I've taken you under my wing and what kind of thanks do I get?'

'I'm really sorry,' she whispered. 'I wasn't going to do anything.'

'You're not like so many of the others, you know. You're special. Despite coming from a tough background, where you were neglected and taken for granted, you've got compassion. Empathy. You could have ended up as one of those kids on the street, looking through Dumpsters for scraps of food, begging for change. But you're better than that. I see things in you. I've always imagined a future for you with me, with my organization, in any number of roles.'

Nicky said nothing.

'I've been happy to help you and the other girls. But lately, they've been the ones showing more gratitude, more loyalty.'

Nicky forced herself to look Jeremy in the eye. 'It's not . . . right.'

71

'What's not right, Nicky? How I've provided for you? How I've looked after you? I'll tell you what's not right. Considering, even for a moment, of going behind my back and telling outsiders about matters that are nobody else's business.'

'Do your friends know . . . how old I am? Do they even care?'

Jeremy frowned. 'Age is just a number, Nicky. An artificial construct. You're a very mature young lady. Why else would I have anything to do with you? But I was dismayed when one of the girls came to me and told me what you were thinking of doing. That's why I wanted to take this opportunity to speak to you before you did anything foolish. Not for my sake, but for yours.'

Nicky whispered, 'What do you mean?'

Jeremy smiled. 'Do you know who's here, right now? At my party?'

The girl shrugged. 'Lots of people, I guess.'

'Yes, lots of people. Important people. Lawyers. Politicians. Judges. Prosecutors. Movie stars. You know what all those people have in common, Nicky?'

She shook her head.

'They run the world,' he said. 'They make the rules. Fuck Santa. They know who's been naughty and nice. And you know what the important thing is that they have in common?'

Nicky waited for the answer.

'They are all my *friends*,' he said. 'No, more than friends. Many of them are beholden to me. They owe me. I've made many of them rich. I've come to the rescue of their charities and foundations. They have a hospital wing named after me in Queens. Did you know that? I've made dreams come true for more of them than I can count.' He paused. 'All manner of dreams.'

He smiled.

'So who, exactly, do you think you might go to with some wild stories about what's gone on here? Maybe that prosecuting attorney who shows up on MSNBC all the time who loves a good spanking from Leanne? Or that judge who likes to pontificate on Fox News who always asks for Sheena when he comes here because he likes the way she ties knots? Would it be one of them you want to go to?'

Slowly, Nicky shook her head.

'Nicky, what you need to understand, and I say this in all kindness, is that you are *nothing*.' Jeremy let that sink in for a moment. Her eyes began to well up again with tears. 'You are as insignificant as an ant. You are a bug on the bottom of a shoe. You are a discarded condom, my dear. No one will ever listen to you, no one will give you the slightest attention. You will be dismissed. Oh, someone might nod sympathetically, might say they'll look into it. But then your statement will go into the trash and you will never hear from anyone again.'

He smiled, touched her cheek, and caught a tear on the edge of his index finger. 'I'm telling you this to spare you the pain. The shame and the embarrassment. Do you understand what I'm saying to you?'

Nicky nodded.

'That's good. That's very good, Nicky. You're a good girl. You really are. Now, although I've been hurt by what you were thinking of doing, I know you can find a way to make it up to me.'

'Yes?' she whispered.

He nodded in the direction of the Winnebago.

'You can be the first to try out the new playroom.'

Nicky released her grip on her knees, put her feet on the floor, and stood. She turned and walked toward the door to the Winnebago.

'I'll be along shortly,' Jeremy said as she reached the door, opened it, stepped in, and closed the door behind her.

Jeremy sighed. Personnel matters were always the most trying.

He got out of the chair, glanced at his watch. He figured he could be back at the party in five minutes. He took a step in the RV's direction when the phone on his desk rang.

His personal line. Only a few people knew it.

Before he picked up, he saw that the caller was his older sister, Marissa, from Seattle. What could she want? They hadn't spoken in months. A family emergency, perhaps? The last time he'd heard from her, their mother had dropped dead of a heart attack. The funeral had been the last time he'd seen his sister.

74

Jeremy grabbed the receiver and put it to his ear.

'Marissa.'

'Hey, Jer,' she said.

No one else called him that. He hated that name.

'What's happened?'

'Why do you assume something happened?'

'You don't usually call just to say hello.'

'Nothing's happened,' she said. 'I mean, no one's died or anything, this time.'

'Walter's fine?'

'He had a little heart flutter a few weeks back but it turned out to be nothing. At least that's what we think.'

'Good to know. Listen, Marissa, if this is a social call to catch up – and if it is, I couldn't be more delighted to hear from you – but it's not a good time.' He glanced at the RV. 'I'm hosting a party at the moment.'

'When *aren't* you hosting a party?' she asked.

'Good point. But why don't I get back to you tomorrow? Would that—'

'The thing is,' Marissa said, 'I found out something that doesn't make any sense at all, and I thought maybe you could shed some light on the situation.'

'What would that be?'

'Is it possible we have relatives we've never even heard of?'

Jeremy said, 'What?'

'It's like, it came back with a 25 percent match,'

75

Marissa said. 'I think that's what you get between uncles and aunts and nieces and nephews.'

'"It"?' he said.

Jeremy dropped into the chair behind his desk. Nicky was going to have to wait.

CHAPTER 7

New Rochelle, NY

Miles arrived ten minutes early for his appointment at the ReproGold Clinic. He hadn't had much in the way of involuntary muscle movements, so he decided to take the Porsche. Every drive, he believed, might be his last. Might as well have some fun while he still could. Even picked up another speeding ticket along the way.

As if he gave a fuck.

When he entered the waiting room, he found himself joining two young women sitting together on one side of the room, and on the other, a man and woman Miles guessed to be in their late thirties. The woman, who looked as though she might have been crying earlier, was quietly shredding a tissue in her hands.

As Miles approached the reception counter, he could hear the man whispering to her, 'It's going to work this time. I know it. Third time's a charm.'

A woman wearing a JULIE name tag was on the phone at the reception desk.

'What do you mean the insurance doesn't cover it?' she said quietly. 'Look at your files again. It's Harkin. Julie Harkin. What's the point of paying for insurance if when you need it you don't have it? Where am I supposed to get ten thousand dollars to fix that kind of water damage? How—'

At this point, she noticed that Miles was standing there. She raised a *just a second* finger in his direction and went back to her conversation.

'This is not over,' she said. 'You people haven't heard the last of this.' Julie hung up the phone and looked apologetically at Miles. 'Sorry.'

'It's okay,' he said. 'Hope you get that sorted out.'

'Insurance companies,' she said, shaking her head.

'You're in good hands,' Miles said, cupping his palms, as though they were full of water. Then he opened them. 'Until you're not.'

'No kidding. How can I help you?'

'Miles Cookson. I have an appointment.'

She consulted her book. 'Yes, right. This wasn't a referral?'

'No. Not a referral. It's another matter.'

She gave him a brief, quizzical look, then said, 'Have a seat.'

Miles sat. The two other couples went in ahead of him. After nearly forty-five minutes his name was called and he was directed to a door at the end of a short hallway. The door, with the name DR MARTIN GOLD printed on it, was ajar. Miles pushed it open and stepped in.

78

A balding man in his late sixties sat behind a desk. He took off a pair of reading glasses, set them down, and looked up.

'Mr Cookson?'

'That's right.'

'Please sit.'

Gold didn't look as though he would top out at five-five once he stood up out of that chair. His face and hands looked soft and doughy.

The walls were decorated not with the usual framed degrees but half a dozen photographs of bridges. Miles didn't know what they all were, but he recognized the Golden Gate Bridge and the Sydney Harbour Bridge.

Gold scanned his desktop and frowned. 'I'm afraid you have me at some disadvantage. I usually have some sort of file, perhaps something from a family doctor, but I don't have anything here related to your case. So, I guess I'm starting from scratch. What can I help you with? I'm going to guess, you're married? You and your wife have been trying for some time to have a child, without success?'

'No,' Miles said. 'It's not like that. I wouldn't expect you to remember me. And chances are, any files you have on me are before you switched over to computer. Probably tucked in an office box somewhere. It was a long time ago.'

'Okay,' he said. 'Go on.'

'More than twenty years ago, I came to this clinic. I was a donor.' And then, as if clarification were needed in a place like this, he added, 'A sperm donor.'

'Oh, okay.' He smiled. 'Was that back in the day when we gave away a free toaster with every new deposit?' He laughed. 'Sorry. An old joke.'

Miles managed a crooked smile. 'You may not have been giving away toasters, but what you paid donors allowed me to upgrade my computer. I desperately needed a more powerful one, and you helped make that happen.'

'Glad to be of help.'

'In fact,' Miles said, 'that computer ended up being a real breakthrough for me. Got me headed in the right direction. I'm in the tech industry. Apps. You might have heard of my company. Cookson?'

Gold shook his head. 'Sorry. But I'm glad we were able to give you the financial boost at the right time. I hope you'll forgive me. I don't actually recall your earlier visit with us. As you can imagine, we get a great many people through here. And we try to help them all as best we can, and are grateful to men like yourself who make our work possible.'

'Sure. And I don't think we met, anyway. Someone else guided me through the process back then.' He pointed to one of the photographs. 'What bridge is that?'

'Confederation Bridge,' he said. 'Not that spectacular to look at, but amazing just the same. Links

Prince Edward Island to the mainland. Opened in 1997.' He smiled. 'Bridges are kind of my thing.'

Miles nodded, cleared his throat. 'Anyway, I should explain why I'm here. It's a long story, but I'll try to make it short.' He paused. 'The thing is, I've been diagnosed with Huntington's.'

Gold's face dropped. 'I'm sorry. That's . . . a tough one.'

'Yeah,' he said. 'I find myself having to make some big decisions.'

'I'm sure.'

'One of the things I've been thinking about is the children that may be out there that are . . . I don't know that "mine" is the right word because they are not my children, but they are the children I fathered. These children that exist, that are out there in the world, living and breathing, because of the donation I made at this clinic many years ago.'

Gold nodded thoughtfully.

'I think those children – I suppose they would all be adults now – are entitled to know what their future may include. As you may know, there's a 50 percent chance of a child developing Huntington's if a parent has it.'

'Yes,' Gold said. 'I am aware.'

'I've been . . . very successful in my field and have a substantial estate, and I would like to start dispersing it sooner rather than later. After considerable thought, and no small amount of soul

81

searching, I have decided I want to distribute a large part of my . . . fortune . . . among these adult children. If they should ever develop the disease, they'll have the resources to look after themselves, and in the meantime have the means to do things they might otherwise not have been able to afford. Travel, buy a place in Spain. Or do nothing with it. Pass it on to their own children, if they have any. It'd be up to them.'

'And if it turns out they don't have the disease?' Gold asked.

'They get the money anyway,' Miles said.

The doctor tented his fingers and leaned back in his chair. 'I see. Your heart is certainly in the right place, and I understand your position, but I should point out to you that I don't see any legal responsibility here for you. This isn't exactly medical jargon I'm about to impart to you, but life is a crapshoot. The sperm from any donor carries the potential for troubling consequences. Any couple having a child faces the same issues, including couples who don't avail themselves of the services we provide. We all bring our genetic makeup to the table. It's life.'

'Still.'

'And besides, it's all rather moot,' the doctor said. 'You don't know who these children are.'

Miles said, 'But you do.'

'Excuse me?'

'The names of the women impregnated with my sperm. You must have that information.'

82

Gold shook his head and smiled sadly. 'I'm afraid that's impossible. Those files of ours are completely confidential. It's not negotiable.'

'There must be a way. What if you were to contact these women, urge them to get in touch with me?'

Gold was shaking his head. 'No, it's out of the question. Mr Cookson, I am not without sympathy. You have a tough road ahead. And your intentions are noble. Generous. But you came here, years ago, with the understanding that you would never know how your donation would be used, and the recipients came here with the understanding that their privacy would not be violated. My hands are tied.'

Miles sat there, making fists of frustration. 'I think they – these children – would want to know.'

'They very well might. If they truly *do* want to know, there are steps they can take, and may have already taken. It's a different world now. Maybe some of the people you hope to find have taken advantage of the services that are available today. They provide a DNA sample, learn about their ancestry, and are connected with family they didn't know they had. You could take the same route. Who knows where that might lead?'

'That's a shot in the dark,' Miles countered. 'Too many variables. I could be dead before anyone I need to connect with does that.'

Gold's shoulders briefly went up a quarter of an inch. 'I don't know what to say.'

He stood, signaling that the meeting was over, and extended a hand, which Miles took with little enthusiasm.

'Good luck,' the doctor said.

Miles said nothing on his way out. As he passed reception, he glanced at Julie, on the phone again. She had her head down and turned away, a hand partially covering the mouthpiece so that she could not be heard.

But Miles caught some of what she was saying.

'I don't know, sweetheart. When's the tuition payment due, again? Christ, can you get some kind of delay on that?'

On his way home, Miles got another ticket.

CHAPTER 8

Springfield, MA

'Oh, my God, did you see what you just did there?' Todd Cox asked.

'What?' Chloe said. 'What are you talking about?'

'The way you put your hand on your forehead.' He demonstrated, slamming the heel of his hand into his head, fingers splayed upward. A *duh* gesture. 'I do that all the time.'

'Bullshit,' she said. 'You do not. You're just saying that, looking for things. Seriously.'

'No, I'm not fucking kidding. I do that all the time.' He gave his head a shake. 'This is unbelievable. I've got an honest-to-God sister.'

'Half.'

'Huh?'

'*Half* sister,' Chloe pointed out.

'It still beats *no* sister.'

They were sitting in a McDonald's, around the corner from the ordering counter, a few steps from the washrooms. It was after the lunch hour rush, and they figured they could sit there for a while

85

without anyone asking them to leave. They'd already polished off their burgers and fries, but Todd was still working on the last few drops of his vanilla milkshake. Chloe had gone back for a coffee.

'What made you do it?' she asked. 'Send in a sample?'

'Okay, so, it wasn't my idea. I wasn't really all that interested. I never really thought much about who my biological dad might be or whether I had any half brothers or half sisters. I guess I'm not what you'd call a big thinker. I kind of live for the moment, you know? Like, what does it matter what happened in the past? I'm here now. And that's the only shit I really have to deal with. But—'

'Hang on,' Chloe said. 'I should be getting this.'

'Huh?'

Chloe put her smartphone on the table. 'I'm making a kind of video journal. About my family. Putting it all together. Documenting it.'

'Oh, okay.'

'You mind?'

'No. It's cool.' He ran his fingers through his hair. 'Do I look okay?'

'You look fine.'

'I got this one spot where my hair sticks up.'

'It's good.'

'Is this an okay place to shoot? In a McDonald's?'

'It's more authentic. I want to get you when you tell this story for the first time.' She raised the phone, framed Todd on the screen. 'Okay, so, you

86

weren't thinking about sending in your DNA, but you did. How'd that happen?'

'Okay, so, like I was saying, it wasn't my idea. But my mom, she's real interested in this stuff, and I think she's been kind of wondering whose, you know, donation was used so that she could get pregnant.'

'So she's told you all about this. It's never been a secret.'

'Well, she didn't tell me until I was like ten? I think it was? I mean. I had a dad. She was already married so I always assumed my dad was my dad. Right? But then, like, when I was nine, he got killed in this accident. He was an arborist.'

'A what?'

'Arborist. Tree guy. He cut down trees and shit. So one day, he's chainsawing this huge tree, has it all figured out which way it was going to fall, but he kind of fucked it up. It went the other way and he couldn't get out of the way in time and he got crushed to death.'

'Jeez, I'm sorry.'

Todd shrugged. 'So, after that, my mom thought I should know that while he was still my dad, there was something she'd never told me. That when they were trying to have a kid, they couldn't. My dad . . . he had like a low count or whatever they call it. So they went to this clinic outside New York and they did whatever they do and along came me and we all lived happily ever after until, you know, he got crushed.'

Chloe had already said sorry once, so she said nothing.

'So, we don't have a whole lot of relatives or anything. My dad didn't have any brothers or sisters and the same's more or less the case with my mom. And she's been worried that I don't have any kind of extended family, and she knew there had to be some out there. So she ordered two tests – one for herself and one for me – and the next time I was over there she sprung it on me. Spit in this, she says.' He shrugged. 'No big deal, so I did it. And she wanted me to say it was okay for anyone to get in touch. And *you* did.' Another shake of the head. 'Mind blown.'

'My mom was the exact opposite. She didn't want me to do it. She doesn't think I need to know.'

'Everybody's different, I guess.'

Chloe tapped the phone to stop recording. 'Good stuff.'

'So let me ask about you, then. What do you do?'

'Oh, I have a magnificent career. I wait tables in a shitty diner. I was going to school to study photojournalism but didn't have enough money for the tuition. My mom chipped in what she could but she's not exactly swimming in cash. If I had any money, you think I'd be driving a 1977 Pacer?'

Todd glanced out the window into the parking lot at Chloe's car, which looked more like a rusted fishbowl than something someone might drive.

'When I have time,' she said, 'I go to the old folks home where my grandfather lives.'

'Oh?' The comment got Todd's attention. 'Like, to visit?'

'Yeah, and also, I've been interviewing him. About his life, like I was just doing with you. There's been this, I don't know, void, not knowing who I really am. So I try to find out as much as I can about the stuff I *am* able to find out about. Does that make sense?'

'Sure.'

'Don't you wonder about your biological father? Like, WhatsMyStory was able to connect us, but now we have this shared mystery. Who's our daddy?'

That made Todd laugh. 'Who's your daddy?' he said quickly, as though it were a rap lyric. 'Who's my daddy? Ever-body wants to know, who's your daddy?'

'But seriously, don't you wonder?'

Todd shrugged. 'I guess. But even if I knew, what difference would it make?'

'Doesn't it make a difference knowing about me?'

He nodded. 'Yeah, but you're, like, pretty much my own age. My dad, whoever it is, would just be some old guy.'

Chloe drove the heel of her hand into her forehead. 'Well, duh. Parents are always older.'

He pointed to her head. 'You did it again. So, tell me some more about your grandfather.'

'He's a veteran. Served in Vietnam. He wrote a book about his time there that he self-published. It's really good. I mean, I'm no book critic, but I thought it was terrific. And he saw some awful shit, you know? Came back from that, got a job at Sears, spent the rest of his working life there. But talking to him, learning his story, it's got me interested in talking to the other residents. They've all got stories. You think they're these old people just sitting around waiting to die, but they've done things. They've *seen* things. Attention must be paid.'

'Attention what?'

'"Attention must be paid." It's from *Death of a Salesman*.'

Todd looked at her blankly.

'The play? *Death of a Salesman*?'

'I don't go to a lot of plays. Concerts, sometimes. I saw Metallica one time. They were awesome.'

'I haven't seen the actual play, either,' Chloe said. 'But I read it. In school. And it's been made into a movie a few times.'

'I like the *Avengers* movies. All the Marvel ones.'

A brief look of disappointment crossed Chloe's face. Just because you were related to someone didn't necessarily mean you were going to have similar interests. But she wasn't going to stop looking for common ground.

'You still got grandparents?'

'They've passed. I never really got to know them. They all died before I was, like, five years old. My mom's got an old aunt. We used to visit her every year. My mom still does, but when I got a bit older I found some excuse to get out of it. And now, well, I moved out a couple of years ago. I've got a trailer, which sounds kind of shitty, but it's nice. I like having my own place.' He grinned. 'And I'm right next to the fire station, so if it blows up or anything, they'll be there in no time.'

'You in one of those parks, with a bunch of retired people?'

'No, I got my trailer on its own lot. Just me. No old people.'

'Oh.'

Todd sensed some disapproval in Chloe's tone, so he added, 'But I talk to them on the phone.'

'Who?'

'Old people.' He forced a grin. 'Sort of like sales calls. Talk to them all the time.'

CHAPTER 9

Seattle, WA

Marissa Pritkin thought her brother would be excited about her news. Instead, he lost his shit.

After all, it wasn't every day you discovered new relatives. Wasn't that something to celebrate? Or, at the very least, be somewhat curious about? He didn't even ask her who she'd connected with.

Maybe, she told herself, she'd caught him at a bad time. He did tell her he was in the middle of throwing a party. For anybody else, that would be like interrupting someone when they were watching TV. Her brother was always hosting one event or another. Some fundraiser with Bill Gates to fight malaria, an opening-night celebration for a Broadway show he'd invested in, or a bash to raise money for some political candidate – didn't matter which party; her brother was always looking to make friends on both sides of the aisle. Jeremy always had something going on. She Googled him about once a week to see what he'd been up to, what TV show he might have appeared on, what think piece he might have written for the *Times* or the *Post*.

They'd kept in touch, Marissa and Jeremy, even if they didn't see each other all that often. If work took him to Seattle, he might invite her and Walter, her husband, out to an expensive dinner, if time allowed. He did all the talking, dropping names like geese dropped turds. There wasn't a president, prime minister, king or queen, or famous entertainer Jeremy hadn't met at some point.

Marissa would wait all through dinner, wondering, will he ask me even *one* question about our lives? How *we're* doing? Where *we* went on vacation last year? What show *we're* binge-watching these days?

The closest Jeremy got to being inquisitive about their lives was when he asked how their portfolio was doing. Because that was really a question about himself, and whether all the insider tips he'd passed along to them had paid off.

Of course, they almost always had. Often, big-time. Marissa had to admit she and Walter wouldn't be in the house they were in now, in Seattle's North Beach neighborhood with a drop-dead-amazing view of Puget Sound, if it weren't for some of the tips Jeremy had passed along. And, to be fair, he had been more than generous where she and Walter and the kids were concerned. Not that Marissa and her husband didn't do okay. She ran an insurance brokerage and Walter was an orthodontist. But even with a good income, sometimes your children's interests could cost you more than you'd budgeted for, like when their son Zachary became obsessed with everything horse related.

Well, Jeremy had always loved horses, too, so what did he do? Bought Zachary a horse, paid to board it at a stable, and even covered the cost of all the riding lessons. You didn't have to ask Zachary who his favorite uncle was.

So, when Marissa got her results back from WhatsMyStory, she felt she owed it to her brother to call him first with the news.

'According to this,' she said, 'I share about 25 percent of my DNA with this other person, which suggests it's a niece or a nephew. Now this other person and I just have to agree to disclose our identities and we can connect. A niece or nephew? How is that even possible?'

Of course, Marissa had already considered the fact that Jeremy might have gotten someone pregnant years ago and that this person had never disclosed this fact to him. All the more reason to tell him, she figured, and all the more reason why she figured he would be curious.

Jeremy had not responded well.

Accused his sister of meddling in his affairs. How could she do something like this without consulting him first?

And then he'd said he couldn't discuss it any further, that he would be in touch later. Later turned out to be the following night, after Walter got home from work. They were both on the deck, sitting down in their comfortable chairs, each with

94

a glass of wine, looking out over the sound, when Marissa's cell rang.

Jeremy was only a minute into his rant when Marissa put the phone on speaker so that Walter could hear how upset her brother was.

'What were you thinking?' he asked her.

'I don't know what you mean,' she said, keeping her voice level and controlled. 'Lots of people have done this. *Millions* of people have done this.'

'Well, now you're as foolish as the rest of them.'

'I don't understand what's foolish about wanting to know where you came from, who you are, what other relatives you might—'

'Jesus, Marissa, don't the relatives we already have give us enough grief? Why ask for more?'

At this point, Walter could no longer remain silent. He didn't much care for the way his brother-in-law was speaking to his wife.

'Jeremy,' he said. 'Walter here.'

Silence from the other end of the line for a moment. 'Hello, Walter.'

'Do you think maybe you're overreacting to this a bit? Marissa meant no harm.'

This time, Jeremy was quiet for so long they thought the connection had been lost.

'Jer?' Marissa asked. 'Did we lose you?'

'I'm here,' he said coolly. 'Walter, could I talk to you a second, off speaker?'

Walter glanced at his wife, as though looking for permission. This was *her* brother, after all. She shrugged, allowing Walter to pick up her phone, hit the button turning off the speaker, and put the phone to his ear.

'I'm here, Jeremy.' Walter got out of his chair, stood at the railing, watching what looked like a whale breaking the surface of the water.

'Good. Walter, listen closely, and try not to give away anything by acting shocked or startled.'

'What? What are you talking—'

'See? You're already acting shocked and startled. So put your game face on and listen to what I have to say.'

Walter took a moment to compose himself. 'Okay, then,' he said.

'I know where the money's going.'

Walter suddenly felt a shiver run the length of his spine, and he nearly blurted out a *What?* but instead managed to remain calm and said slowly, 'Go on.'

'You may be doing your best to hide it from my sister, but I'm aware of the addiction.'

'I'm sorry, I don't—'

'Walter, please, don't interrupt. You have a problem. You should talk to someone. Gamblers Anonymous, maybe. The only reason Marissa hasn't noticed a cash flow problem is because I've been helping you out when I can. But the online gambling, hitting the casinos, you need to get a handle on that.'

'Yes, yes, that's very interesting,' Walter said.

Marissa looked at her husband and mouthed, *What's he saying?* Walter held up his index finger.

96

'You're probably wondering, how could I possibly know this?' Jeremy continued. 'How could I have learned that my brother-in-law is throwing his money away? It's my job to know things, Walter. Information is my currency, whether it's about you, or Marissa, the New York Stock Exchange, or the fucking king of Siam. So this is what's going to happen. You're going to tell Marissa to stop researching her family tree. I'm not going to get into why, but you can tell her that this course of action she's taken could open me up to strangers harassing me, making claims against me. I'm in the public eye, and vulnerable to all sorts of charlatans. How does that sound?'

'That sounds good.'

'And the reason I'm having you persuade her is because I'm only her stupid brother and she's never wanted to listen to me before, so why would she listen to me now? How about that?'

'Absolutely,' Walter said.

'So we're clear. You're going to make sure she abandons this new little hobby of hers, or I am going to tell her all about yours.'

'I understand,' he said. 'I totally see your point.'

'Now put Marissa on so I can say goodbye.'

Walter slowly took the phone from his ear and handed it to his wife. 'He, he wants to say goodbye.'

Marissa took the phone. 'Jeremy?'

'You take care,' he said. 'Let me know, next time you're coming to New York, we'll all go to a show.

97

Just tell me what you want to see. I can get tickets to anything.'

'Okay, but—'

'Gotta go,' he said, and ended the call.

Marissa put down the phone and said, 'What the hell did he say to you?'

Walter had an answer ready. 'Well, first he apologized for his outburst. I think he was genuinely sorry about how he spoke to you. And then he calmed down and said – and I may have lost some of the details here about how it all works – but that he has so many people trying to make some kind of claim against him, that any sort of loose connection to him could lead to all sorts of legal entanglements.'

Marissa made an *oh, I never thought of that* kind of face. 'Gee,' she said. 'He's probably got a point.'

'So he's hoping you'll drop it. And you know, it's totally up to you. It's your life. But—' and he stepped forward and encircled her in his arms '—I don't think it would kill us to honor his wishes. Let's face it. He's been awfully good to us.'

'Okay,' she said, returning his hug. 'I think he's overreacting, but if that's what he wants, then fine. I won't take it any further.'

'Probably for the best.'

'I'm still pissed,' Marissa said, 'but you're right. He's been pretty good at watching over us over the years.'

And I had no idea until now, Walter thought, *just how closely.*

CHAPTER 10

New Rochelle, NY

Even in good times, Julie Harkin didn't have the money to go out for lunch. Every morning, before she left home to go to her receptionist job at the ReproGold Clinic, Julie would make herself something. A simple sandwich, or a salad. A few crackers and some sliced cheddar. A handful of grapes. She shopped carefully, bought items on sale, sometimes went from one grocery store to the next to take advantage of weekly specials. She figured her homemade lunch probably cost her less than two dollars a day – a peanut butter sandwich was only pennies – while even the cheapest meal at a fast-food place would set her back at least five or six. And she never, ever, bought bottled water. What sort of fool paid for something you could get out of the tap for free?

Julie had always been careful about her spending, but never more so than after her divorce ten years ago. She hadn't seen anything from her ex since they'd split, and it wasn't worth the time or money to track him down to try and squeeze a few nickels and dimes out of him to help raise their daughter, Sophie. Chances were, even if she could find him, he'd be out of work, or spending, in local bars, what little he made from digging ditches or putting up drywall. Even if she had to struggle to get by, she was better off without him.

Now, with Sophie in her second year at Monroe, they were cutting it pretty fine. Thank God Sophie was attending a college close enough that she could still live at home. There was no way Julie could pay to board her someplace. And God bless her, Sophie was doing everything she could to make it easier for her mom. She'd spent the summer working every night in the kitchen of an Italian restaurant, often bringing home lasagna and tortellini and salad that the manager might otherwise have pitched at the end of the day. Sophie was soaking up everything she could on how a place like that operated. Dovetailed perfectly with the culinary degree she was going after. Everything Sophie made she put toward her school year. But it wasn't enough. Julie had to dip into her savings to make up the difference.

And then the flood hit.

One of those torrential rainstorms, the kind the weather experts called a 'hundred-year storm' but which seemed in more recent times to happen annually. Those black clouds, heavy with moisture, hung over Julie's neighborhood for hours. The storm drains on the city streets couldn't keep up.

Water rose above the curbs. And then the front lawn of Julie's modest one-story was underwater.

The shallow, ground-level windows that allowed some light into the basement caved in, and water cascaded into the house.

The mess was unbelievable. Basement furniture floated upward until it hit the ceiling. The circuit breaker panel became submerged. Once the storm was over, the water receded, and the basement had been pumped out, the extent of the devastation could be seen. Twenty, thirty thousand in damage, the insurance company said. Too bad you're not covered for this kind of thing. Go ahead, look at your policy. Read the fine print. Oh, you didn't? Is that *our* fault?

Despite how desperate things were, today Julie went out for lunch. Because, she figured, what the hell. She was in a hole so deep she was never going to crawl out.

She couldn't afford to fix her house. She might have to sell it, at an enormous loss, and find some cheap apartment to live in.

Sophie owed the college an installment on her tuition, and she had drained every last cent out of her own account. Julie didn't know how she would make up the difference.

She had told Dr Gold about her dilemma. Julie had too much pride to ask him, outright, to help her. But if he were to offer, well, that'd be different. She hoped to appeal to his better angels, that upon hearing her tale of woe, he would reach into his desk and pull out his checkbook. It didn't have to be a gift, she'd tell him. She would pay him back. He could take it out of her pay, a small sum each week until it was totally paid off. Just something to help her get through this difficult period.

Dr Gold had listened as she brought him up to date on her misfortunes. He had nodded sympathetically.

And he'd said, 'That's just awful, Julie. I hope you're able to work out things with the insurance company.'

At which point he went back to reading something on his computer screen.

The weasel.

So today, Julie treated herself. At the Winslow Diner, a block from the ReproGold Clinic. She ordered an egg salad sandwich and a coffee. Seven dollars and thirty-five cents, not counting tip.

It was delicious.

But she found herself unable to enjoy it. She felt guilty. She could have brought her own lunch and been up five dollars. And somewhere around her fourth bite, Julie believed she might start crying.

Hold it together, she told herself.

She put down her sandwich, dabbed the corners of her eyes with her paper napkin, and took a sip of coffee from the chunky, ceramic mug. There were only half a dozen customers in the diner, although it could probably hold close to thirty. Julie had chosen to come shortly after eleven, before it became crowded, and when there were no appointments scheduled at the clinic. Rather than sit on a counter stool, Julie had taken a table for two and sat so that she could watch people walk past outside.

A woman entered the diner.

Fiftyish, Julie thought. A bit frumpy, plump, gray hair that she'd pulled back into a ponytail. Gave her a kind of aging-hippie look. She was wearing a jacket that was frayed at the edges and clutching a much-scuffed purse large enough to hold a sleeping bag. She had a somewhat distracted look, as though she was not quite sure why she'd come in here.

But then the woman scanned the restaurant and her gaze seemed to stop when it landed on Julie. Slowly, she worked her way through the tables until she reached Julie's. She smiled and said, 'May I join you?'

There were plenty of places to sit, Julie thought. Couldn't she take one of the other tables? Maybe sit at the counter?

'Um,' Julie said, 'I'm about to leave in a minute.'

'Okay,' the woman said, and flopped down into the seat across from her. She made it into something of a production, letting out a big sigh, adjusting her coat so it wasn't bunched up under her, then lugging her large purse up into her lap. She glanced around, as if looking for a server.

'How's the coffee here?' the woman asked.

'It's . . . okay.'

'Looks like a good sandwich. Egg salad?'

Julie nodded. Was this woman homeless? Should she offer her the rest of her lunch?

'You're Julie Harkin,' the woman said, smiling.

That got Julie's attention. In a fraction of a second, she realized this was not a random event. This woman had sought her out.

'Yes. Have we – do I know you?'

The woman smiled. 'No. My name is Heather.'

'Heather . . .?'

'Last name's not important.'

Julie glanced about nervously. None of this felt right. Should she get up and walk out?

'It's okay,' Heather said. 'I'm not here to deliver bad news. I'm here to make a proposal.'

'A proposal?'

'Yes. I represent someone sympathetic to your current situation.'

'My current situation?' Julie leaned in closer. 'What do you mean, you represent someone?'

'I have a client who believes you can help him. And he's prepared to reward you for your efforts.'

'I have no idea what you're talking about.'

'You make thirty-three thousand dollars a year. Your home has sustained damages that amount to more than that annual salary, and your insurance company is denying coverage. You have a daughter in college who needs financial help. Your car, a 1998 Civic, hasn't been serviced in three years and three out of the four tires are

104

bald. That's not safe. You should do something about that.'

'Who the hell *are* you?'

'Let me show you something,' Heather said. She dug down into her purse and came out with a plain, letter-sized envelope. She set it on the table, but rested her arm on top of it so it was barely visible. In the glimpse she'd had of it, Julie noticed that it was very thick, and sealed.

'This envelope contains fifty thousand dollars,' Heather said. 'It's for you.'

Julie could find no words. She wasn't even sure this was really happening. She could not stop looking at the envelope under Heather's arm.

'Fifty thousand dollars would go a long way to solving your current problems. You could get your house repaired, cover your daughter's educational costs, and even have enough left over for some new tires.' Heather smiled. 'I'm kind of partial to Michelins, but that's totally up to you. I understand your daughter is interested in pursuing a career in the culinary arts. That's wonderful. You must be very proud of her.'

Julie managed to get out a sentence. 'I don't understand.'

'I want to make it very clear that there is no threat here,' Heather said. 'If you do not wish to help my client, I'll leave, and take that envelope with me. You won't hear from me again. This will be the end of it. But if you do wish to help my client, these funds constitute a thank-you. Simple as that.'

'What does your . . . client want?'

'Information.'

'What . . . does he want to know?'

Heather spelled it out.

CHAPTER 11

New Haven, CT

M iles believed the time had come to bring his brother into the loop. He owed him that. Plus, he had a little something for him.

He wouldn't have to go far to find Gilbert.

Gilbert was down the hall, in the accounting division of Cookson Tech. Miles had acquired this two-story industrial building five years ago. At one time, long ago, dog biscuits had been manufactured here. After that company went bankrupt, the building sat empty for nearly two decades and had fallen into disrepair. Squatters fought with rats and raccoons for territorial dominance.

Miles acquired the building, and the land it sat on, at a city auction. A steal. All he had to do was spend another $20 million to make the building usable. He'd taken a lead from other tech companies and done his best to make the workplace *fun*. Open spaces, pool tables, foosball, places to gather for coffee and conversation. A small theater.

Even the accounting department had pinball

machines, ones that didn't have to be fed coins to operate.

Miles found Gilbert taking a break at one of them. He was pushing the buttons furiously, making the paddles jump. He missed catching a pinball on the rebound and it dropped away back into the machine.

'Shit,' Gilbert said.

His brother had never been very good at video games, Miles mused. Back in the early nineties, Miles could whip his older brother's ass at every Nintendo game.

'At least you didn't have to put a quarter in,' Miles said.

'Hey,' Gilbert said. 'What's up?'

'When you finish your game.'

'One ball left,' Gilbert said. He managed to keep it in play for another minute before it slipped between the paddles and the game was finished.

'Nice,' Miles said.

Gilbert rolled his eyes. 'Oh, please.'

'Got a minute?'

Gilbert's face fell. 'Is there a problem?'

'No problem.'

'Because I was actually going to come and see you.'

'About?'

'The invoices from Excel Point Enterprises.'

'What about them?' Miles asked.

'I don't remember seeing that company name before.'

Miles shrugged. 'Probably something to do with the ardees.' His nickname for the people in research and development. 'Don't worry about it. Let's get some air.'

They descended a set of Lucite steps and exited the building. The neighborhood had been in decline when Miles first bought the building, but Cookson Tech had revitalized the area. There were other tech buildings, coffee shops, a Thai restaurant. Parked at the curb was Miles's Porsche.

Miles reached into his pocket for the car-shaped key fob, but for a moment had some difficulty getting his fingers to close around it. But once it was out, and in his palm, he held it out to Gilbert.

'Here,' he said.

'Seriously?' Gilbert said. 'You're actually going to let me drive your precious baby?'

'Why not. Let's take a spin.'

Gilbert, agog, was not convinced. 'I don't believe it.'

'For Christ's sake, get in the car.'

Gilbert's face broke into a smile. A kid getting his first ride on a pony. Miles dropped the key into his hand.

'Not that you need it,' Miles said. 'It's keyless. As long as one of us has it, the car will start. But, you know, symbolically, you should have it in your possession if you're behind the wheel.'

Gilbert closed his fist around the key, walked around to the driver's door, and got in. Miles got into the passenger side.

Gilbert was searching the dash for a start button. 'Switch is to the left of the wheel,' Miles said.

Gilbert found it, put his foot on the brake, and turned it. The car rumbled to life.

'Wow,' he said, looking more than a little intimidated. He ran his hands around the wheel, getting used to the feel of it. 'Where are we going?'

'Anywhere you want,' Miles said. 'Maybe take it out onto the highway.'

Gilbert put his hand on the shifter. 'I was expecting a stick.'

Miles shook his head. 'Pretty much all the Porsches are coming with the PDK.'

'The what?'

'Never mind. Let's just go.'

Gilbert put the car in Drive and pulled out into the street. 'It feels so tight,' he said. He feathered the gas and the car leapt forward. 'Christ, it doesn't take much.'

Miles nodded. 'Yeah, a light touch is recommended until you get the hang of it.'

'Yeah, well, a spin may not make me an expert.' He glanced over at his brother. 'So how'd I manage this privilege? Getting behind the wheel of your baby?'

'Think of it as a test drive.'

'What?'

'Nobody gets a new car without taking it out for a test drive.'

Gilbert shot him another look. 'What are you talking about?'

'It's yours.'

Gilbert looked dumbfounded. 'What do you mean, "it's yours"? What are you talking about?'

'It means that when we get out, you keep that key in your pocket. The car is yours. I'm giving it to you. I don't need it anymore.'

Gilbert blinked. 'You're kidding me.'

'I'll sign it over to you. I want you to have it. There's a few speeding tickets in the glove box. Actually, more than a few. I'll take care of those.'

'This is . . . I don't know what to say.' Gilbert forced a laugh. 'I don't get it. You're either getting something even faster, or you're dying.'

'Yeah, one of those,' Miles said.

Gilbert's face turned serious. 'Tell me it's the first one.'

Miles shook his head slowly, then pointed forward, encouraging Gilbert to keep his eyes on the road.

'Talk to me,' Gilbert said quietly.

'So, yeah, I'm dying. Not right away. At least, probably not right away. It may take a few years. But it's coming. I'm giving up driving. I could probably keep doing it for a while longer, but if I'm going to have to give it up, I might as well do it now. I'm having some . . . muscle control issues. Surely you've noticed.'

'Not . . . really.'

'My awkward limb movements at times. My head rolling around on top of my shoulders.'

'I thought you were just stretching . . . or

111

something. Okay, I've noticed. But I didn't really think it was anything, and it was none of my business, anyway.' He shook his head. 'I can't drive and have this talk. I have to pull over.'

'Sure.'

Gilbert saw a wide shoulder up ahead, put on the blinker, steered the car over onto the gravel, put the car in Park, and killed the engine. 'Okay,' he said. 'From the beginning.'

Miles told him. The problems he'd been having trying to focus. Unable to remember things that had just happened. Increasingly irritable, prone to outbursts.

'Those, you probably didn't notice so much,' Miles said, 'given that I've always been kind of an asshole.'

What really got him worried, Miles said, was the clumsiness. Dropping things. Tripping over his own feet.

'I knew something was wrong, so I went to see Alexandra. She ordered a bunch of tests.'

'Parkinson's?' Gilbert asked.

Miles shook his head. 'That would have been good news.' He took a breath. 'Huntington's.'

Gilbert stared at him blankly, as though shell-shocked.

'God, Miles, I'm so sorry.'

And then Miles could see something happening behind Gilbert's eyes, and he knew what he had to be thinking.

'It's okay,' Miles said.

'What's okay?'

'You probably already know the odds, so let me put your mind at ease. You're thinking if I've got this, maybe you've got it, too. And if you've got it, will Samantha get it?'

Gilbert said nothing, but looked at his brother as though awaiting news of his death sentence.

'You're fine,' Miles said. 'You don't have it.'

'How can you possibly know whether—'

Miles raised a hand. 'Don't go apeshit on me, but I had your DNA sampled.'

'When did you—'

'Dorian took your Coke can. When I broke the news to you about myself, I didn't want you to have to wait to find out what your own situation was. You're in the clear.'

Gilbert looked as though he might begin to weep. 'I feel a little overwhelmed.'

'Sure.'

And then Gilbert did something Miles wasn't expecting. He leaned over, as best he could in the cramped cabin of the Porsche, and put his arms around his brother, burying his face in his neck.

'I'm so sorry,' Gilbert said. 'This is so goddamn fucking unfair.'

He held on to Miles for nearly fifteen seconds. 'It's okay,' Miles said, starting to disentangle himself from Gilbert. 'It's okay.'

Gilbert settled himself back into position behind the wheel, slowly shaking his head as a tear rolled down his cheek. 'Whatever you need, if there's anything I can do, all you have to do is ask.'

Miles smiled and tapped the dash. 'Take care of my baby.'

Gilbert sighed. 'I don't give a shit about the car.'

'Well, if you *don't* want it, then—'

'I didn't say *that.*'

Which prompted them both to laugh to the point that they both had tears running down their faces.

'I haven't laughed like that since I got the news,' Miles said.

'Oh, jeez,' Gilbert said, wiping his tears.

Once they'd calmed down, Miles said, 'There's something else.'

'Something else? Jesus, you've already given me one heart attack. You want to go for two?'

'This part may be even harder to tell you.'

Gilbert said nothing, steeling himself.

'You're an uncle.'

'I'm . . . what?'

'You're an uncle,' Miles repeated. 'Several times over.'

'I don't understand what you're talking about.'

Miles was about to speak when his eyes widened and his head weaved slightly.

'Miles, are you okay?'

'Just . . . a little woozy for a second there. I'm okay. So, more than twenty years ago, I was looking for some extra cash. I made some money in kind of an unconventional way.'

Miles told him about going to the ReproGold Clinic, the sperm donation. Gilbert listened intently, mouth open, attempting to process so many family-related developments in such a short time.

'So,' Gilbert said, letting it all sink in, 'you could have all kinds of kids out there.'

'As it turns out, just nine,' Miles said. He reached into an inside jacket pocket and pulled out a folded sheet of paper. 'And here they are.' With some dramatic flair, he unfolded the sheet and handed it to his brother.

'Ta-da.' Gilbert looked at the words on the page. A list of names, with addresses and brief biographical details next to them.

Nina Allman, Todd Cox, Katie Gleave, Jason Hamlin, Dixon Hawley, Colin Neaseman, Barbara Redmond, Chloe Swanson, Travis Roben.

None of the names meant anything to Gilbert. Slowly, he said, 'I thought – I didn't think – how did you get these? I thought this information is confidential.'

'It is,' Miles said. 'But someone with access to the relevant files was having some financial troubles. As the Godfather would say, I had someone make her an offer she couldn't refuse.'

'Christ, I hope she didn't have a horse.'

Miles smiled. 'Nothing like that. I sent Heather, you know, who does our security work. Investigative stuff. She's pretty remarkable. She says there's no one more invisible in this world than a

115

middle-aged woman. She works it to her advantage. Anyway, her efforts definitely expedited the process of finding out who my biological kids might be.'

Gilbert, still looking at the names, shook his head. 'This is unbelievable.' He looked at Miles and said, 'Why?'

'Why?'

'Why'd you go to all this effort to find out who they are?'

'Think about it,' Miles said. 'Think about what they need to know.'

'Oh God, of course. There's a high probability that . . . oh man. You've been in touch? They all know?'

'No,' he said. 'Not yet. None of them know. I've been thinking about how to make the connections. It's possible some of them aren't even aware they weren't conceived the good old-fashioned way. But I'm going to have to tell them. They're going to have to know. They deserve to know.'

Miles started to feel light-headed again. He closed his eyes briefly, took a few breaths. 'I'm okay,' he said without being asked.

Gilbert's brow was wrinkled. 'Why? Why do they have to know? I mean, you got to this point in life without knowing. Things happen when they happen. Why do you feel you have to tell them? What's driving this? I mean, okay, I know you're sick. You've explained that. You have only so much time left. But why disrupt their lives this way?'

'I'd imagine some would want to know more about who they are, what they might be facing in the future.'

Gilbert did not appear convinced.

'But let me get to something else first,' Miles said. 'I've set up something for you, for when I'm gone. A trust.'

'A trust? What do you mean, a trust? Don't you set those up for kids before they come of age?'

'In a lot of cases, yes. But they can be used for more than that. You'll get twenty thousand a month, or nearly a quarter million a year. And this car, of course, which you can sell if you want. It's up to you.'

'Jesus, Miles, that's . . . generous of you, but why . . . why parcel it out that way? I'm your brother. You're worth . . . millions. You think I can't handle . . . I mean, considering I'm . . . your only real family.'

Miles couldn't look his brother in the eye. He stared, briefly, out the window, then looked down into his lap.

'Oh,' Gilbert said, his focus sharpening. 'I get it.'

'Gilbert, please understand that—'

'It's Caroline. This is all about Caroline.'

Miles caught his eye briefly. 'Yes, it's about Caroline.'

'Christ, Miles. I don't know who should be more insulted. Her or me.'

'I don't mean to insult you,' he said. 'But . . . I think I have to be frank here, Gil. I know you, and I know Caroline. I've observed the . . . dynamic of your relationship from its outset. Anything I were to leave to you I'd really be leaving to Caroline. She'd be on that windfall like rats on a discarded pizza.'

'That's not . . . that's not fair. And could you have picked a more disgusting analogy?'

Miles hesitated, unsure whether to proceed. 'I've never told you this story. I kept it to myself because I blamed myself. I have to hand it to Caroline. She's enterprising. Remember when we had that reception here for that team from Google?'

Gilbert nodded. 'It was a big event. With the tent set up at your place, lots of food and drink. You even got Chicago to play the gig.'

'Right. And Caroline came. She made a few contacts. Later, she approached one of the team, made a proposal to him for an app. Something that would allow a regular person, for free and with ease, to instantly check a person's criminal record, credit history, everything. Perfect for checking out potential hires, or some guy you just met. Not the worst idea in the world, actually.'

'What are you talking about?'

Miles raised a hand, asking him to just wait. 'She wanted a hundred thousand to put the idea into development.'

'Caroline has no tech experience. That's crazy. She never mentioned a word of this to me. I mean, she works in the court system, so I can see where she might have gotten the idea, but she hasn't any skills to bring it to fruition.'

The hand went up again. 'That's why she told the Google rep the project had my backing. That I'd already chipped in a hundred grand. She showed him a letter, signed by me, endorsing the plan.'

Gilbert looked as though he might have a stroke. 'Miles, I swear, I never knew anything about this. I have no idea what she did with that money.'

'She never got it.'

'What?'

'The Google guy, before he cut her a check, he called me to clarify one or two points. I was caught off guard there for a moment. I didn't want to expose what she'd done, not to him, so I said I'd reconsidered my support of the project based on my own assessment of its merits. Privacy issues, getting access to literally millions of court records. So he pulled out. And then I called Caroline. It was a very simple call. I said, "I know what you did and don't do it again." She apologized and asked me not to tell you. I never promised her I wouldn't.'

'I can't – what was she thinking? How did she think she'd get away with that? How did she think you wouldn't find out? How the hell was she going to invent something she had no idea how to invent?'

Miles gave the question some thought. 'I'm not sure Caroline thinks that far ahead. She comes up with a plan that has an immediate payoff, but doesn't have a plan for the fallout.'

'What she did . . . it's misrepresentation, or fraud, or both.'

Miles didn't agree or disagree. 'But I give her credit where credit's due. It was a pretty audacious scheme. Anyway, that's why I'm not leaving the bulk of my estate to you, Gilbert. I don't trust Caroline, and I'm not confident you could stop her from taking it all away from you. I'm sorry. And up until recently, I'm not really sure where I would have directed it. But now, I have a plan.'

It only took Gilbert a moment to figure it out. 'You're leaving it to these nine.'

'Yes. But I'm not going to make them wait. I want to start distributing it to them now. At first I thought, find out who they are and put them in my will. But say I hold on for ten, fifteen years. That's a long time before they come into the money. And they might have a need for it long before then.'

Gilbert said, 'You've given this a lot of thought.'

'I have.'

Gilbert was silent.

'You feel betrayed,' Miles said.

Gilbert's mouth had gone dry. He moved his tongue around, trying to moisten it. Finally, he said, 'I'm your brother.'

'I know.' Miles paused.

Gilbert's cheeks began to flush. 'Just so I understand, you're divvying up your fortune to all the relatives you don't actually know, and not recognizing the only one you do.'

'I suppose I'd be angry, too,' Miles said.

'Look, I can't excuse what Caroline did. I'm deeply sorry about that, but . . .' And he started to shake his head angrily. 'If you weren't dying I'd kick your ass.'

'Don't let that stop you.'

Gilbert tossed the sheet of paper back to his brother and gripped the wheel so hard his fingers went white. 'I always looked out for you.'

'That's true,' Miles said. 'Why do you think I brought you into the company?'

'I've thought about that. And so has Caroline, for that matter. You didn't hire me out of any brotherly loyalty. No, you did it so you could show me, every day, how much more successful you are than I am. I work for *you*. That's the message.'

'That's not true. That has never been true.'

'And now you're coming to the rescue of a bunch of mystery kids. This isn't about helping them. It's about making yourself look good. Going out on a high note.'

'No,' Miles said. 'Getting news that your time is running out, it changes you.' His eyelids fluttered. 'I think I'm going to be sick. I need some air.' He set the piece of paper with the names on it on top of the dashboard, opened the door, and got out. A brief wind gust took the page and dropped it into the passenger's-side footwell.

Miles took a few steps away from the car into

121

the tall grasses beyond the shoulder and leaned over, putting his hands on his knees, waiting to see whether he was going to be sick to his stomach.

Gilbert looked down into the footwell at the piece of paper with the list of names. He reached down for it, held it in his hand.

Stared at the nine names.

And then he reached into his pocket for his phone, opened the camera app, held it away from the page until it was properly focused, and fired off several pictures.

Then Gilbert let the page flutter back to the floor.

Miles came back, opened the door, and settled into the passenger seat.

'I'm ready to go back,' he said, reaching down for the piece of paper, then folding it and tucking it into his jacket.

CHAPTER 12

Springfield, MA

The second time Chloe went to visit Todd, ten days after their first meeting, she went to his place. She wanted to get some video of him in his home environment, and see if his mother would be okay with answering a few questions for the minidoc she was putting together.

She entered his address into the map app on her phone. Her Pacer, not surprisingly, was not equipped with a navigational system. Nor, for that matter, was it equipped with air-conditioning, a working radio, or a windshield that did not have a huge crack in it. He had told her his place was immediately past a fire station, behind a line of trees. There was no name on the mailbox, but Todd had told her to look for the one that was totally covered in rust. Turned out there were a few of those, but eventually she found it.

Chloe turned into the first driveway after spotting the fire station, and very soon the trees opened up to reveal a mobile home. Parked out front were a small Hyundai and a Volkswagen Golf. At the sound of her approach, the front door of the trailer – well, there were actually two, but the one closest to the hitch apparatus – opened and Todd stepped out, waving. He was followed out the door by a woman in her fifties.

'Hey!' Todd said, bounding down the cinder block steps and rushing over to give Chloe a hug as she got out of her car. She was a little taken aback by the gesture, but responded in kind, putting her arms around him and giving him a squeeze.

Todd pointed to the woman, who was limping toward them, a smile on her face. 'Chloe, this is my mom. Mom, this is Chloe.'

'I'm Madeline,' she said, and gave Chloe her second hug. Madeline had tears in her eyes. 'I can't believe it. It's just a miracle. I'm so happy to meet you.'

'Yeah, it's pretty neat,' Chloe agreed.

'Excuse my hobbling,' Madeline said. 'I did something to my ankle, but I'm okay.'

'Let's go inside,' Todd said. 'You want a beer or something?'

Chloe shrugged. 'Yeah, sure.'

Todd ran back to the trailer. Chloe took her time so that she could walk alongside Madeline, who wasn't moving as quickly.

'He's so excited,' Todd's mother said. 'Well, so am I. How was the drive?'

'Good. It was good.'

Madeline struggled with the steps up to the

trailer door, but made it without complaint. Once inside, Chloe looked about. Dishes in the sink, takeout food containers scattered about. In her head, she was saying, *I hope you didn't go to any trouble*, but kept her sarcasm to herself, this time.

Todd had taken three cans of beer from the fridge, handed one to his mom first, then one to Chloe.

'Let's sit down,' Madeline said. 'This ankle is killing me.'

'What happened?' Chloe asked.

Madeline laughed. 'I was stepping out of the tub and I don't know what I did. Turned it the wrong way. Who knows!' She cackled. 'You get to a certain age you can throw your back out just wiping your ass.'

'Mom, Jesus,' Todd said, cracking his own beer and taking a swig.

They all sat at the small kitchen table. Chloe dropped into a chair by an open laptop and two cell phones, one of them a really cheap flip one like she hadn't seen in a decade. When her elbow bumped the table the screen came life. She glanced at it and noticed, quickly, it opened onto a webpage listing various senior citizen facilities in New Hampshire.

'Let me get that out of your way,' Todd said, folding the screen down and shoving the laptop to the end of the table. 'How about this, huh? We're like a family.'

Madeline reached out and squeezed Chloe's

125

hand. 'I'm already thinking of you as the daughter I never had.'

Chloe said, 'Uh-huh.'

'I'm really looking forward to us getting to know each other.'

Chloe smiled awkwardly. 'Me too. Did Todd tell you I wanted to ask you some questions, like, on video? I'm kind of doing my own little documentary about this – what should I call it? Journey of self-discovery? I don't know if anyone will ever see it, but it's something I feel I need to do.'

'Oh, yeah, sure,' Madeline said. She ran her fingers through her ratty hair, which looked not unlike an oversized bird's nest. 'How do I look?'

'Great,' Chloe said. She got out her phone. She'd decided to do everything handheld, and not use her minitripod.

'Is the lighting okay?' Todd asked. A single bulb hung over the table.

'Perfect,' she said.

Madeline smiled, getting ready for her close-up. Todd said, 'I guess you don't need me for this part.'

'Not really,' Chloe said.

Todd stood, scooped up the laptop and the two phones, and disappeared down the hallway that led to a room at the back of the trailer. Madeline and Chloe heard a door close.

'Can I talk to you about something?' Madeline said, leaning in closer and whispering. 'I mean, before you start filming?'

Chloe lowered the phone. 'Okay.'

'I'm worried about him.'

'Oh.'

'He doesn't listen to me. But he might listen to you. He's been doing some things he shouldn't.'

'Like?'

'I'm not sure. But you should ask him where he gets enough money to live like this. A place of his own.'

Chloe cast her eye about the debris-strewn kitchen. 'Right.'

'He's got some job at a computer store but I know they don't pay him much. I know he's up to something.'

Chloe thought about what she'd seen on the computer. 'Why would Todd be looking up old-age homes? He told me his grandparents are all passed on, right?'

Madeline nodded. 'Yup. All passed on. Why would you ask that?'

'It was on his computer,' she said.

Madeline thought about that. 'I guess you should ask him.'

'I should ask him?'

'You're his sister,' Todd's mother said.

'I've only been his sister for a couple of weeks.'

'That's not true. You've always been his sister. You only just found out recently. That's different.'

'Still, you know him a lot better than I do. I think if anyone's going to talk to him it should—'

'No, no, I think you came into our life for a

reason.' Her eyes seemed to drift skyward for a second. 'I think you came into our life to help Todd find his way. He can't stop talking about you.' She laughed. 'If you weren't his sister, well, I think he'd be very interested in you in a *different* way.'

Chloe shivered. 'Yeah, well, thanks for that. I'm really glad to have connected with Todd, too. And, you know, if he ever needs someone to talk to . . .'

'That's wonderful. I'm so glad you feel that way. Okay, let's do your little movie.' She sat back in her chair and flashed Chloe a Hollywood smile.

Madeline was sitting on the couch in front of Todd's TV, watching *Family Feud*, her right leg resting on a plastic milk crate, an ice pack under her ankle, when it came time to say goodbye.

'You okay if I don't get up?' she said.

'No problem,' Chloe said, standing at the door.

'Give us a kiss before you go,' she demanded. Chloe bent over to give the woman a peck on the cheek, but got pulled into another hug. 'Don't be a stranger. And don't forget what I asked you.'

'Sure thing,' Chloe said.

'Walk you to your car,' Todd said.

Once outside, he said to her, 'She can be a bit much sometimes. But she's really happy to meet you. Did she give you a good interview?'

'Yeah.' Chloe paused, wondering whether to get into it. 'She's worried about you.'

128

'What else is new?'

'She says you're getting into some bad shit, but she doesn't exactly know what.'

'She imagines things,' Todd said.

'Why did you have a list of old folks homes on your computer screen?'

'Huh?'

'I saw it. Before you closed your laptop. Why would you be researching those kinds of places?'

'I might have gotten on the page by mistake.'

'Why'd you have two cell phones?'

Todd blinked. 'Who says I have two cell phones?'

'They were sitting right there.'

He shrugged. 'Just a backup. You know, in case one dies.'

They'd reached Chloe's Pacer. 'Let me tell you a story,' she said. 'I go visit my grandfather a lot.'

'Yeah, you said.'

'One time I was there, sitting in the dining hall, and there was this one old lady, in a wheel-chair, and she wouldn't stop crying. Sometimes, you know, you hear them moaning and stuff because they're old and shit hurts. But she was just crying and crying. I thought maybe someone had died. So I asked my grandfather, did he know what happened with her?'

'Okay.'

'And he says, that day was her son's birthday. She had this grown-up son, like forty or fifty years old. But anyway, it was his birthday, and he was going to come and visit her, but she had nothing

129

for him. She'd always get one of the staff to go out and pick him up a gift card for Burger King. Her son loved Whoppers, and I think I saw him one time, and I gotta say, I believe it. She'd get him a card with fifty bucks loaded on it. But she didn't have any money in the bank. She couldn't do it. She'd lost almost everything. Not a fortune. Around three thousand or something, although if I actually had that much in the bank I'd feel like the richest person on Earth. But anyway, she had all this money but she got scammed out of it.'

'Scammed?'

'Yeah. I don't know all the exact details but she gets this random call one day, and it's someone pretending to be a relative or something, and they're in some kind of trouble and need money right away. Like, for an operation or bail, or something. And she falls for it, and wires all this money to someone. And that was the last she saw of it.'

'Jeez,' he said. Hesitantly, he asked, 'What's the name of this old folks place?'

'Providence Valley.'

Todd nodded slowly. 'Oh.'

'Heard of it?'

He shook his head.

'Anyway, it was the saddest crying I ever heard,' Chloe said. 'What kind of person would do something like that?'

'I don't know,' Todd said. 'Someone kind of shitty, I guess.'

'Yeah,' Chloe said. 'Someone kind of shitty.'

CHAPTER 13

New Haven, CT

'It's not true,' Caroline Cookson said evenly. 'None of it. I never talked to anyone at Google or Apple or Netflix or anyone about some app.'

'You didn't say something to one of the Google representatives that could have been interpreted as a request for money, and that you had Miles's blessing?' Gilbert asked his wife that evening as they got ready for bed.

Caroline laughed. 'Wow. That's just . . . I don't know what to say. You think I'd forget saying something like that?'

Gilbert had been cautious with his tone, trying not to sound overly accusatory. More like he was just hoping to clear up a misunderstanding, trying to give her the benefit of the doubt. Maybe there was a simple explanation for what Miles had disclosed to him. Dealing with Caroline could be like walking on proverbial eggshells. You had to be careful because she could become very defensive in a hurry, and when that happened, watch out.

But Caroline, who gave every indication of being shocked by what Miles had told Gilbert, remained relatively calm. To Gilbert's surprise, her response bordered on sympathetic.

Caroline blinked her blue eyes at him and slowly shook her head. 'I just feel so badly for him. What a terrible thing for Miles to go through. And you. You must be devastated. But honestly, what he told you, it simply did not happen.'

'Why would he lie about that?' Gilbert said.

Caroline, pulling her long blond hair back behind her head and securing it with an elastic, just as she did every night before crawling into bed, thought about that. 'Maybe he's not lying,' she said.

'What?'

'Maybe he believes what he's saying. After you got home, and told me about Miles's diagnosis, and went upstairs to give Samantha the news, I did some online research. You know that Huntington's will affect his mental capacity. That dementia is part of what he's going to go through. Maybe he's confused, misinterpreting things, misremembering things, believing certain events happened that never did. For some reason he believes I did this awful thing, when the truth is I did not.'

Gilbert thought about that. It didn't strike him that Miles was anything less than fully engaged. He had to admit Caroline was convincing in her denials, but then again, that was the sort of thing she was good at.

'I mean, okay, I *did* talk to some of the Google people at that party,' Caroline said. 'But nothing along the lines of what Miles suggested. Let me ask you this.'

'What?'

'Did he show you any proof?'

'Proof?'

'Any documents? Any emails? Recordings of me talking to someone at Google? Anything at all like that?'

'No.'

Caroline nodded with satisfaction. 'Well, there you go. Don't you think, if he'd had any evidence, he would have shown it to you?'

'I . . . don't know. Maybe.'

'What Miles is alleging, why, that's just criminal. Why didn't Miles call the police?'

'Well, for one, you're his sister-in-law.'

'Oh, please. You really think that would have stopped him? You know he's never cared much for me. But seriously, how would I think I could get away with something like that?'

But there was something going on there, behind those eyes. Gilbert could tell.

The thing was, Caroline had plenty of insight into people who got on the wrong side of the law. She worked in the court system, as a court reporter, or stenographer, as the job was also called. Sitting through trials and depositions, listening to thousands of hours of testimony, getting it all down for future reference.

She never failed to come home with a story. People who'd committed murder, tax fraud, kidnapping. A favorite was the story of the hit man on trial for killing some guy's wife, but he got off when the star witness failed to show up. And not just for his court appearance. He failed to show up anywhere, ever again.

The accused, he actually looked over at me and winked, Caroline had said. *Like he was putting the moves on me right in the middle of the trial.* When she told that story, she'd actually shiver, although Gilbert could never quite tell whether it was with fear or excitement.

But most of Caroline's stories were about people who did not get away with it. *You know why so many criminals get caught?* she would ask. *Because they're stupid.*

She would often cite some of her favorite examples. The guy who bragged on Facebook about the goods he'd stolen. The man who'd fatally stabbed his girlfriend, then used a dry paper towel to get the blood off the knife, missing much of it, and not bothering to wipe his fingerprints off the handle. The bank robber who went on a spending spree. The woman who said she couldn't have killed her husband because she was visiting an aunt in Cleveland, but turned out not to have an aunt in Cleveland.

Gilbert sometimes thought his wife was a classic example of someone who could see in others the faults she could not see in herself. Case in point: that time she backed her car into another at JCPenney, left the scene, and denied ever having been there. She even persuaded Samantha to back her story, to say the two of them had been together at a different mall on the other side of town. When the other car owner managed to obtain, from mall security cameras, video that showed crystal clear images of Caroline causing the damage, she had *still* continued to deny it.

Which was why Gilbert didn't believe her denials about the Google encounter for a second.

But he had raised it with her for a reason. It might help her better appreciate Miles's decision about his estate and his decision to start divvying up his fortune among his biological children, once he had been in touch with them.

The discussions surrounding that had happened earlier, after Gilbert had come home behind the wheel of the Porsche.

Once he'd filled her in on why he had the car, as well as the news about the nine children who had come into the world because Miles had visited a fertility clinic more than two decades ago – he had shown her the picture of the list of names he had taken with his phone – she had not responded well.

'This car is supposed to make things right? You could buy a thousand of these with what he should be leaving to you when he's gone. After all you've done for him?'

Gilbert was conflicted. On some level, he agreed with his wife. But at the same time, he wanted to defend his brother, which led him to relate the Google story. There was a look on Caroline's face, if only for a second, that persuaded him Miles had not lied. That glimmer of *I've been caught* in her eyes, but she had recovered quickly.

The thing was, he'd found Miles's story convincing, and Caroline's denials much less so, because it fit a pattern. How many times over the years had Caroline lamented her husband's lack of success, at least when compared to his brother? Oh sure, he had a good job in the accounting division and was paid well enough, but it wasn't like he *owned* the company. It wasn't like he was in *charge*. Gilbert could imagine a scenario in which Caroline might try to dip into her brother-in-law's pocket, a way of evening the score, if only a little.

It was a case of the old you-reap-what-you-sow, Gilbert figured. You tried to cash in on my brother's reputation, and now it's bitten you in the ass.

Maybe this would be a lesson to her. Gilbert was hopeful that her subdued response to all these developments was evidence of some introspection.

Not that he was foolish enough to get his hopes up too high.

There were times when Gilbert thought about

136

finding a way out of this marriage. He knew, in his heart, that while he could pretend to be, he was not a happy man. He tried to love this woman, even though he was not at all certain she loved him. And besides, there was Samantha to think about. True, she was closing in on the end of her teen years. It wouldn't be like splitting up when she was still in diapers.

But Gilbert didn't believe he could face the trauma of a divorce. The acrimony, the ugly scenes. Selling the house, finding a new place to live. And he knew Caroline would find a way to persuade Samantha it was his fault. She'd drive a wedge between them. Samantha, desperate for her mother's respect, was always looking for ways to please her, and if that meant shutting her father out of her life, she might just do it.

Maybe this was what marriage was, Gilbert mused. Unrelenting unhappiness, but at least you had someone to talk to.

He was thinking all these things as he and Caroline got into bed and turned out the light. She reached under the covers and gave his hand a squeeze and whispered, 'I'm sorry about your brother. I truly am.'

He was nearly asleep when three words suddenly came to him.

Excel Point Enterprises.

Those invoices from a firm he wasn't familiar with.

No, he thought. *She wouldn't.*

And very quickly dismissed the thought, and drifted off.

When Caroline heard his breathing deepen and she was sure he was asleep, she quietly got up, went to his side of the bed, and picked up the phone that was charging on his nightstand.

She knew his four-digit password, and within seconds was into his photo app. She pulled up the shot of the list of names, emailed it to herself, put the phone back down, and exited the bedroom.

Caroline went down to the kitchen, where they kept a desktop and a printer on a small desk off to one side. She sat down, opened up her mail program, and printed off the picture, confident that the grinding noise of the printer would not wake her husband upstairs.

But Samantha did happen to stroll into the kitchen. She was more of a night owl, often going to bed two or more hours after her parents. She opened the refrigerator and took out a can of diet cola, and spotted her mother.

'Hey, what are you doing?' Samantha asked.

Caroline said, 'Come sit.'

CHAPTER 14

New Haven, CT

*S*ure, *I may be dying,* Miles thought, *but I still have a company to run.*

But his next thought was often, *Yeah, but for how long?*

While the progression of his disease would not disable him overnight, he needed to think about the future of Cookson Tech. There were times, since his diagnosis, when he wondered if he even wanted to run it anymore. He'd made his millions, made his mark in the tech world. Apps designed by Cookson Tech were on as many as a billion phones. What was left to prove?

If word got out that he was interested in selling, he'd have every tech company in the world, at least those with deep pockets, beating down his door in minutes.

It wasn't something he had to make his mind up about right now, but it was worth thinking about. Maybe it was time for a change. Write a book. Get involved in the movement to find a cure for Huntington's. Give them a whack of money, and set out to raise more.

Or, maybe, go to Hawaii and get stoned.

So many choices. And who was to say he couldn't do all of them?

But while he considered his options, Cookson Tech had to continue to move forward, develop new and innovative products in a highly competitive market. If he didn't sell out, there needed to be a succession plan. Who would run the joint when he handed over the reins?

In his heart, he would have liked to hand it all over to Gilbert. But as long as Caroline was in the picture, that was off the table.

At some point soon, Miles would have to assemble the board of directors and inform them of his diagnosis. His occasional uncontrolled movements were going to become more pronounced over time. People would suspect something was wrong. A whispering campaign would begin. Miles would have to bring the public relations department into the loop so they could start formulating a strategy for when his condition became public. They might recommend getting ahead of it, maybe call a news conference, arrange a *60 Minutes* interview, do a spot on one of the morning shows. Tell his tale to Gayle King or Wolf Blitzer. He'd met both of them over the years.

But it was probably best to put all those things on hold until he had connected with his biological children, the Nine, as he had come to think of them. He was still trying to figure out the best way to approach them. A few days earlier he had called Dorian into his office.

'With Heather's help, you're going to need to pull together—'

'Profiles on the Nine, yeah. She's already on it.'

'Okay, good,' Miles said. 'But we're going to need more than just basic information on these individuals. We'll need—'

'Family and educational background.'

'Yes,' Miles said. 'But the important thing is, these inquiries need to be—'

'Discreet. Under the radar. Figured that.'

Miles sat back in his chair and grinned. 'Where would I be without you?'

'Nowhere,' Dorian said.

He nodded with bemused resignation. 'Okay, well, when this information starts to actually come in—'

'We have it,' Dorian said.

Miles threw his hands in the air. 'I'm gonna shut up now. Just hit me with it.'

Dorian, who had walked in carrying an iPad, raised it in her hands and started tapping and scrolling on the screen.

'Okay, so, not surprisingly, they're scattered all over the place. One's up in Massachusetts, we've got one going to college in Maine, another on an extended vacation in Paris. One's in Fort Wayne, another in Scottsdale. Closest one is in Providence.'

Miles felt a kind of excitement surging through him.

'What . . . do they do?' He'd been thinking, if there was anything to inherited talent, maybe one of them was a software developer or something else in the tech world.

'We've got an art gallery employee, a waitress who's an aspiring documentarian – she's the one in Providence – a guy who works part-time in a computer store.'

Miles said, 'Hmm.'

'That's just three. I can send this to you. It's reasonably comprehensive. It's not all that hard to find out things about people. Like I need to tell you that. So many people putting their lives out there on social media. And Heather's got a hundred tricks up her sleeve to go beyond the easy stuff. Oh, and this is cool. Every one of them has one or more Cookson apps on their phones.'

That prompted a chuckle from Miles, but his expression quickly turned anxious.

'Now it's all about the approach.'

Dorian, deadpan, said, 'Maybe one of those emails that says they've got a few million dollars coming their way and all they have to do is provide their bank details so that the transfer can be made.'

Miles smiled. 'I'd have to get a fake email address.'

'We could figure that out.'

'Okay, so email is out. Maybe the old-fashioned way. A personal letter? Registered?'

Dorian quickly shook her head. 'Suppose it goes

142

to the wrong person, or gets to the right house but is *opened* by the wrong person? Say you think you're some kid's dad and this letter comes along saying it's someone else. Your wife never told you. It's freak-out time.'

Dorian put the iPad aside, sat down, put one leg over the other and leaned forward.

'You know what you have to do,' she said.

'Have someone approach them in person, on my behalf?'

'You're close,' she said.

Miles furrowed his brow. 'What?'

She sighed. 'It should be you.'

'Me?'

'I know you're used to delegating pretty much everything, but there are some things you can't fob off on someone else. If someone's going to come out of the blue to tell me who my real father is, well, I think maybe it ought to be my real fucking father.'

Miles appeared thoughtful. 'Yeah.'

'Yeah?'

'Yeah, you're right. I can't ask someone else to do this.'

Dorian nodded. 'Good. Because if you were going to ask me, I'd have said no.'

'I guess to do that you'd need to be in a higher pay grade,' Miles said, and let loose a short laugh.

Dorian said nothing.

'Anyway,' Miles said, 'if I'm going to go face-to-face with them, I'm not sure approaching them

143

on their home turf is best. There might be other family there. Away from home would be better. Maybe at work, or catch them on a lunch break?'

'I think you'll have to play each one by ear. And there's going to be some travel involved. There's that one woman in Paris. I can charter a private jet for those.'

'Sure.'

'And the closer ones, I can get Charise, seeing as how you handed the Porsche off to Gilbert.'

'He told you?'

'I saw him come to work in it. If you've got any other Porsches you're giving away, I'd be willing to help you with that.'

'Okay, get in touch with Charise. And of course you've got pictures of them all?'

Dorian gave him a *duh* look.

'If it was me,' she said, 'I'd start with Chloe Swanson, the one in Providence. She's the closest. Good way to get your feet wet. If the personal approach goes south, you fine-tune your approach before you go on to the next one.'

'Chloe Swanson,' Miles said, more to himself than Dorian. 'Have I got a surprise for you.'

CHAPTER 15

New Haven, CT

The funny thing was, Caroline had actually run into that alleged hit man one day, several months after the trial where he was found not guilty, and a few weeks before she learned about Miles's diagnosis.

She was at a Starbucks, paying for her caramel latte, when she turned around and bumped into a man waiting for his hot chocolate. He was tall with short brown hair, high cheekbones, a strong jaw. He was wearing a long cashmere coat and a pair of dark brown leather gloves. He looked, at a glance, like someone out of a Hugo Boss ad.

'Sorry,' she said. 'God, I nearly got some foam on you.'

'It's okay,' he said, rearing back, looking down at his coat. 'No harm done.' He reached around her for his hot chocolate. Caroline noticed the name PETE written on the side of the paper cup.

Pete was about to turn and head for the door when he stopped and gave Caroline another look.

'Have we met?' he asked.

She said, 'I don't think so,' but that was before she gave him a closer look. 'Wait a minute. I think . . .' And then her face broke into a nervous grin. 'Oh my, I do remember.'

He grinned slyly at her. 'Okay, maybe you should fill me in.'

But she shook her head, as though she suddenly realized she was wrong. 'No, no, I'm mistaken,' she said. 'We haven't met.'

'Maybe not met, officially, but I do recognize you,' he said.

'No, really, I—'

He snapped his fingers with his free hand. 'I know now.' He smiled. 'At my trial. You're the court stenographer.'

Caroline swallowed, hard. 'Um, that's, I think that's possible.' She laughed nervously. 'I do believe I remember you.'

She remembered *everything* about him. Especially the part where he had winked at her during the proceedings. The small, electric thrill it had given her.

But Caroline wasn't quite feeling that now. Right now she was feeling more like she might lose control of her bladder.

This man was a killer.

'I'm sorry,' the man said as if reading her thoughts. 'I've made you ill at ease. That wasn't my intention.'

'It's okay,' she said. 'It's just not every day you meet—'

She stopped herself.

The man smiled. 'A hired killer? You do recall that I was acquitted, don't you?'

'Of course, yes, I remember,' Caroline said. 'I suppose I should offer congratulations? I mean, it's a little late, and it really wouldn't have been appropriate to say anything at the time.'

He said, 'There's a void for Hallmark to fill. "Congratulations on Your Acquittal." Or, in your case, belated congratulations.'

Caroline's eyes were fixed on his. There was an almost hypnotic quality about them. No, that was pushing it. But the man did have a certain charm. How did you make conversation with someone who, allegedly, had been hired to kill another man's wife? The charges were dismissed, of course. Didn't she have to give him the benefit of the doubt? But what about that star witness who never showed up? Did Pete here have a coworker somewhere out there who'd made that person disappear?

And by the way, her recollection was not that his name was Pete, but something else. Was it Paul? Patrick? No, wait, it was something altogether different. Something French or Italian? No, not something foreign, but it was longer than most names. A name with a hard edge to it. Something like—

Broderick!

She was sure of it. So why was he telling the Starbucks barista that his name was Pete?

All those thoughts ran through her head while she pondered what to say, but it was Pete/Broderick who came to the rescue.

'Would you like to sit down?' he asked her.

'Would I what?'

'Would you like to join me?'

Before she could think of a reason to say no, she said, 'Sure. Why not.'

He found them an empty table in the corner, very delicately cleared away some dirty cups and, with a napkin, swept some muffin crumbs off it.

As Caroline sat down, she could feel her heart racing. *What the hell am I doing?* she asked herself. *This is not a good idea.*

'It makes me crazy when people leave the table a mess,' he said. Having cleared away the crumbs, he was now wiping up a small coffee spill with a paper napkin. 'That's better.' He balled up the napkin and pitched it in a nearby garbage can.

He sat down across from her and smiled. 'It's nice to see you again.'

'I don't remember your name being Pete,' she said. 'It's Broderick.'

He smiled, pointed a finger at her. 'Very good. Especially given all the names you must hear in any given week.'

'So why . . .' She pointed to the cup.

'Oh,' Broderick said, and grinned. 'You're suspecting something sinister. That I go around using a fake name. You know how much trouble baristas have with the name Broderick? Trying to write it on the paper cup? First, they're not sure they heard you right and ask you to repeat it or spell it. Or they just scribble "Broad Bricks" or, one time, "Broad Dick." I swear.'

Caroline found herself giggling.

'The other thing is, there's not enough room on the cup to write my real name. Hence, Pete.'

Caroline nodded, satisfied. 'That makes perfect sense.'

'You're still with the courts, I assume? Writing everything down that the judge and the lawyers and the bad guys say?'

'Yes.' Her voice was barely above a whisper.

'Interesting work, I'll bet.'

'Some cases more so than others.' She paused. 'Like yours.'

'Mine was a good one?'

'Uh, yeah. It sure beat the guy being sued for selling defective siding.'

He nodded knowingly. 'I guess murder is slightly more titillating.'

'I didn't mean it that way,' she said. Or did she?

Broderick leaned in close and whispered, 'If you ever get charged with murder, I highly recommend my lawyer.' He gave her arm a little squeeze.

Caroline's heart was jackhammering. Was it excitement, or fear? She picked up her cup and said, 'I really should be going.'

Broderick put his hand on her arm again and held it gently. 'I'm sorry. Please stay. I apologize.

I sometimes joke about what I was accused of when there's nothing funny about it at all. A terrible thing, being accused of such a horrible crime.'

Tentatively, she said, 'I guess it was lucky that that witness . . . changed his mind about testifying.'

'Yes,' Broderick said. 'I guess he had second thoughts about lying on the stand. Perjury's a serious offense.'

A question about what happened to that witness was on the tip of her tongue, but she decided against asking it. Instead, she asked, 'So, what . . . what do you do now?' She laughed nervously. 'I don't mean *now*, as opposed to what you were accused of doing *then*. I mean, what do you do? What's your job?'

'I'm a problem solver,' Broderick said.

'What does that mean?'

'Exactly what I said. If you come to me with a problem, I'll do my best to solve it for you.'

Caroline circled the rim of her cup with her index finger. 'Kind of like Denzel Washington in *The Equalizer*?'

Broderick grinned, waved the question away, and asked, 'You ever have problems?'

'Sure.'

'Name one.'

She had to think. She got as far as 'Uh, well' and then started to laugh. 'It's too silly.'

'Go ahead.'

'The dealership won't fix this thing that's wrong with my car, even though it should be under warranty. The engine's making this funny noise, and it's stalling half the time. They say I missed a scheduled maintenance by about a hundred miles or something, which means whatever's wrong with the car is on me. That it's not their fault.'

'Where'd you get the car?' he asked.

She told him, and added, 'But that's probably not the kind of problem you're talking about, is it? Give me an example of a problem you'd solve.'

Broderick thought for a moment, took a sip of his hot chocolate. 'I helped in a labor negotiation one time. A furniture company, all the workers were looking to unionize and the employer felt he was being very generous with his latest offer, but the union leadership was not receptive. They were heading toward a strike, which would have been very crippling for the company. Would have hurt the workers, too. The company asked if I could intercede. I did, and everything got sorted out.'

'How did you do it?' Caroline asked.

Broderick smiled. 'I simply talked to the interested parties. I find that people are actually quite reasonable when you present realistic alternatives to them. If you do *this*, this thing will happen. If you do *that*, that thing will happen. It helps when one of those choices comes with a level of . . . inconvenience. And if that doesn't work, I employ other strategies.'

Caroline was going to ask, then decided against

151

it. She believed there were some things she was better off not knowing.

Broderick had glanced down at her hand more than once. 'I see you're married. What does your husband do?'

'He's an accountant,' she said, unable to hide the disappointment in her voice. 'For a tech firm his brother owns.'

'Oh,' he said. 'That sounds interesting.'

'Not particularly. So, this work you do, are there others who do this, too?'

'I know others,' he said. 'We have our own network. Sometimes we team up if the job is challenging.'

Caroline thought again about that missing witness.

'And what are you working on right now?'

'As it turns out,' he said, smiling, 'I'm between jobs and have some free time.'

Two days later, the service manager at the dealership where Caroline had bought her car phoned to say they were going to replace the entire engine, no charge, and they were tossing in one free car detailing per month for the next two years. It was also the first time Caroline could ever remember a car dealership sending flowers.

CHAPTER 16

New York, NY

Jeremy Pritkin never did join Nicky Bondurant in the Winnebago that night. She'd done as he'd asked and gone inside, figuring he would be along shortly and they would do what they always did, or at least some variation of it. But then he'd gotten that phone call and forgot all about her.

The windows of the RV were cranked open, so she was able to hear the conversation, although she didn't really have any idea what it was about. But it was clear Jeremy was upset about something, and she had the sense he was talking to a sister or a brother. She thought she'd heard the name Marissa.

When he was done with the call, Pritkin left the office and, presumably, returned to his party.

Nicky thought the smart thing to do was wait, at least for a little while, in case he came back. The last thing she wanted to do was make him even more disappointed with her.

It was never a good idea to disappoint Mr Pritkin.

She waited for the better part of thirty minutes before deciding it was safe to leave, more than enough time to check out this new addition to Jeremy's headquarters. What a crazy thing, putting an RV in your third-floor office. The man came across, in public, like a pretty normal guy. Well, if you defined *normal* as unbelievably rich and connected, outspoken and opinionated, someone who had the ear of decision makers around the globe.

But the outside world also had glimpses of his eccentric side. The Winnebago event was only the most recent.

Jeremy let *Architectural Digest* do a spread on his place in Spain, where he had a swimming pool shaped like the grill of a Rolls-Royce. And he'd once spent hundreds of thousands of dollars to buy some custom-made car from a TV show in the sixties – the Black Beauty or a Monkeemobile or a junky truck some hillbillies drove around in. She couldn't remember which because she had no idea what the shows were. But when Jeremy bought it at an auction, it made the news. So now that he had it, he'd tucked it away in a garage somewhere. It wasn't like he could actually drive the thing down Park Avenue. He spent God knew how much on a sports jacket Steve McQueen wore while driving a Mustang in some famous movie chase in San Francisco. Couldn't wear it. Wasn't even his size.

So those were some of the things the public knew.

But Jeremy Pritkin also had secrets, his love for erotic photography one of the less notable ones. Much bigger was his passion for having young girls like her available to him in his palatial New York residence.

Nicky was not the only one. Over the years, plenty of young women had moved through here. Entertained the man of the house and his friends, then moved on to other things when they got a little older.

She'd found it surprising, at first, that this had not become well known beyond the walls of this place, but having now spent time here, she understood. Pritkin liked to offer some of his more influential friends the fringe benefits that came with knowing him, with being part of his club of influencers. Young, shapely fringe benefits.

Membership has its privileges.

And once those friends had partaken of the pleasures here, the last thing they wanted to do was blab about it. They didn't want to put themselves at risk of exposure. But they did more than that for good ol' Jeremy. They ran interference for him, protected him.

Like that old fart of a judge.

Eeewwww.

And the girls who'd been through here kept quiet, too. From what Nicky'd been told, several

155

had leveraged the connections made here to go on to better things. Hotel management, personal assistants to CEOs, internships for political types in Washington. At least, those were the ones Roberta liked to talk about. Nicky'd also heard gossip about at least one who'd become a junkie and ended up on the streets of Newark, and another who just, well, one day she was there and one day she was gone. No one ever heard another thing about her.

Nicky felt badly that she had disappointed Jeremy by raising, with a couple of the other girls here, the issue about whether what went on here was, you know, *right*. True, Jeremy had been good to her in many ways. He'd pulled strings to get her enrolled in a local high school even though she had no roots in the community, no family in the Big Apple.

In the beginning, Nicky thought he'd done this out of the goodness of his heart, but it wasn't long before he was asking her to invite friends to the brownstone. Young girls who might need a hand up, a little financial assistance, were willing to learn about the 'service industry.' The services, Nicky soon realized, more often than not included keeping Mr Pritkin and his wealthy, male friends entertained behind closed doors.

Jeremy made it clear she needed to find just the right girls. At first, she'd thought that meant *pretty*. And of course, Jeremy did want her recruits to be attractive. But what he really was implying

156

was girls who were vulnerable. Girls from low-income households, one-parent families. Girls not connected to people with any kind of pull or influence. Girls with no one to turn to for support. Girls who would be amenable to the needs of Jeremy and his acolytes in return for a life that was better than the one they currently had.

Runaways, for example, like Nicky.

She'd left her Norfolk home seven months earlier. Her mom had found a new boyfriend – the fourth in twelve months – and this one had moved in with them. If there was any good news, it was that this guy wasn't an ass-grabber or anything. He left Nicky alone where that was concerned. But he ordered her around like he was her goddamn father. Pick up your room, clean the house, make dinner. Do your homework. Turn down the TV. Stop being on your phone all the time. Take those buds out of your ears.

Nicky complained to her mother, but that got her nowhere. 'He's taking an interest,' her mom said.

The previous summer, hanging out at Virginia Beach, Nicky became fast friends with a girl from Brooklyn who was on vacation with her family. Nicky even got to know the parents in the week that they were there. Super laid-back. The dad was an artist, the mother a music producer. Artsy types. Nicky hit it off with them.

'If you ever come to New York . . .'

So Nicky went to New York. Got in touch with

157

her friend from Brooklyn. Bunked in with them for a week.

Then two.

The parents finally went, 'Uh, you moving in?'

Her friend pleaded her case. There was trouble at home. Could Nicky stay a little longer? The parents said okay. And then, when it looked as though their patience was wearing thin, one of their daughter's friends told Nicky she knew of a rich guy in Manhattan who was looking for some help and maybe she should go check him out?

And now, here she was.

At school, Nicky found it difficult paying attention. How did you focus on algebra and chemistry when one of the richest men in the country was pissed off with you because you weren't crazy about giving hand jobs to UN officials, B-list actors, and museum board members? If only her teachers knew what was troubling her, the things she had on her mind. What an idiot she was, confiding in one of the other girls that she was coming around to the conclusion that Pritkin was kind of a sicko, that the things that went on in this fancy New York brownstone were very, very wrong. Against the law, even.

'What law?' asked her friend, who wanted everyone to call her Winona, like the actress, even though her real name was Barb.

'I don't know, exactly,' Nicky said. 'Pervert laws.'

Nicky said it would be creepy enough, the stuff Jeremy asked them to do. But when he pushed them to do it with his friends, these other important people, didn't that kind of cross a line?

Winona was not convinced. 'He treats us good,' she said. 'You think you'd get this kind of money working at Arby's? Anytime I need some cash, he gives it to me. And look at the people we get to meet! You know that director? Who was here last week? He told me I could be an actress. That I had what he called *the look*. He's going to keep me in mind, case anything comes up that I might be good for.'

'He's feeding you a line of bullshit.'

'I don't think so. Look at me.' Winona tipped her head back, turned her face to the light. 'Come on, check me out.'

'Maybe.'

'And the thing is, Mr Pritkin is very special. He's not like regular people, so the regular rules don't apply to him.'

Nicky had heard all this before, and not only from Winona. Jeremy enjoyed talking about how he had been born with a superior genetic makeup. Just as some people could develop genetic diseases, there were others who could develop superior genetic characteristics. People like Michelangelo or Einstein or Gershwin or Lincoln. Gifted people.

Jeremy believed himself to be one of them, and allowances had to be made for particularly gifted people. The standard rules were not applicable.

'What makes him so special?' Nicky asked.

'Uh, look around?' Winona said. 'This house? The people he knows? The things he's done for them? You think an ordinary person could do all that?' Winona shook her head disapprovingly. 'You better not be thinking of telling on Mr Pritkin. That'd be really stupid. If you don't like it here, leave. No one's forcing you to stay. But don't mess it up for the rest of us.'

After Jeremy had his little sit-down with Nicky, reminding her of her place in the power structure, she knew it was Winona who'd ratted her out.

Now Winona would be in his good books. Nicky needed to get back in there, too. What else was she going to do? She would tell him she'd made a mistake, that she was grateful for the lifestyle he'd given her.

Not that she really was sorry. But sometimes, there was shit you had to do to get by. This was one of those times. She knew that what Jeremy had said was true. She was a nothing. He had rich and powerful friends. If she ever decided to speak out, no one would believe her. Or if they did, they wouldn't care.

Nicky had a plan. She would sneak up to his office – one time, when he'd had her accompany him up there, she had spotted the four-digit code he entered to unlock the door – and wait for him inside the Winnebago. Surprise him. Wear her highest heels. Jeremy had a thing about high heels, insisting all the women who worked in the house wear them. Like it was a Playboy club, said one of the kitchen staff, with Hugh Hefner in charge.

Nicky had no idea who Hugh Hefner was.

But she did know one interesting tidbit. Jeremy's professed reason for installing the Winnebago, that he had taken family trips in one as a boy, was only partly true. The real reason was, he'd lost his virginity in one when he was fifteen. The RV was a way of commemorating that blessed event.

Jeremy was in the residence today. He wasn't jetting off to Europe or Asia or Africa. Sooner or later, he'd be coming up to the third floor. It was where he spent much of his day. So, without being seen by any of the staff, she got up to the third floor and got into the RV.

Twenty minutes later, he showed up.

She was peeking out the window, and while she was relieved at first to see him, his expression gave her pause. His face looked like thunder.

Oh-oh.

Jeremy went straight to his desk and picked up the phone. In case he looked her way, she dropped down below the window. But she could still hear his side of the conversation.

'I've been trying to get you all day. This is serious.'

A pause.

'Don't tell me to calm down. This is a whole new ball game. Twenty years ago no one could have predicted this. I've been giving this a lot

161

of thought and I can't see but one way to contain it.'

Another pause.

'Look, so far, it doesn't appear that many of them have done it. But more might. And the more people who do, the more likely this will all lead back to me. That can't happen. You can't afford to let it happen, either.'

Pause.

'Shut up. Stop blathering. There's no point rehashing what was done. It happened. We have to deal with things as they are now. Things are already under way.'

Pause.

'No. Money can solve a lot of problems. But not this time. Too many variables. Tentacles reaching out in too many directions. That's why I'm going at this another way.'

Pause.

'I don't think you really want to know.'

Pause.

'I suppose the only upside is, I've formed no attachments. If I had, this might have been more difficult. But based on the latest reports, there aren't exactly any standouts. Not a great loss.'

And then he said something else, prompting a chill that ran the length of Nicky's spine.

I did not hear that. Forget you heard that.

Jeremy was finishing up his conversation. A couple more grunts, an 'uh-huh,' and then, finally, 'Fine.'

At which point he put the phone back onto its cradle.

'Sweet Jesus,' he muttered to himself.

Nicky raised her head high enough to peek out the window again. Jeremy didn't look any happier now than he did when he'd walked in. Her plan to put things right would have to be postponed to some later date.

She ducked her head back down, figured she would hide here until he left for another part of the house. Nicky sat down on the floor, resting her back against the cabinet door under the sink. Her movement set off the tiniest, almost imperceptible squeak from the springs in the recreational vehicle's undercarriage.

'Who is it?' Jeremy called out.

Shit, Nicky thought.

Should she step out, reveal herself? Shout 'Surprise!' and see if she could bring a smile to his face, pretend she hadn't heard a thing? Or hold her breath, not move, make him think there was no one there?

But again, he called out, 'If there's someone in there, you better come out. Now.'

There was a small bed at the back end of the vehicle, with horizontal cabinetry doors underneath it instead of open space. Not exactly a place to hide there.

Nicky heard a drawer in Jeremy's desk slide open. Some rustling.

She peeked through the window. He was tossing

items from the drawer onto the top of the desk. A notepad, some scraps of paper, a set of keys with a silver *W* attached to them, some pens.

Finally, he found what he was looking for.

A gun.

'Last chance,' he said. 'I've every right to shoot an intruder, and I will do it.'

If he entered the Winnebago, he might shoot before he realized it was her.

'It's me!' she cried. 'It's Nicky!'

'Nicky?'

She got to her feet and opened the door. There were already tears coming down her cheeks. 'I wanted to surprise you. Make things right.'

Jeremy stared, dumbfounded. At least, Nicky thought, the gun was pointed at the floor.

'Christ, you're lucky I didn't load this. I could have shot you.' For a moment, he had looked relieved. But now his face was awash with worry.

'You were listening.'

Nicky shook her head. 'No. No, I wasn't. I didn't hear anything.'

'How could you not?'

She tried to think of something to say, some lie that would be convincing, but she couldn't come up with anything.

'Oh, Nicky,' Jeremy said sadly. 'Oh dear, dear Nicky.'

CHAPTER 17

Lewiston, ME

Before there was Todd Cox, there was Jason Hamlin.

They had decided to do him first.

Kendra Collins, again posing as a police detective, and Rhys Mills, who was also carrying a very authentic-looking police badge, knew that Jason went for a jog very early in the morning. Most young men his age, particularly those attending college, liked to sleep in, but Jason was different. He was a sports-oriented individual. Not so much football. That had never been his game. Jason was more a winter sports kind of guy. Skiing, snowboarding. And attending school up in Maine afforded plenty of opportunities through the winter months for him to engage in his favorite activities.

But before the snow fell, Jason liked to stay in shape with jogging. He set his iPhone to wake him at six, although he usually woke up on his own minutes before that and turned the alarm off so as not to bother any of his housemates. He

165

would slip on some shorts, a T-shirt, and a pair of Nikes, and then leave the old house a few blocks from the campus and do a four-mile route that took him through the town.

This was usually a time when he could clear his head. Breathe in that cool, crisp morning air through his nose, feel it filling his lungs. Slip the buds into his ears and listen to Garth Brooks. (Jason wasn't a big country-western fan, but there was something about this Brooks guy that spoke to him.) On this morning, however, Jason was unable to appreciate the freshness of the dawn or Garth singing 'The Night I Called the Old Man Out,' which always had a place in Jason's heart, reminding him of the shouting matches he'd had with his own old man, or, more accurately, the old man who'd *raised* him. And that was because he could not stop thinking about what had happened the night before, when he was with Jenny, this girl he'd been seeing pretty seriously for the better part of two weeks.

She was from Kingston, Ontario, on the other side of the border. She'd picked Bates College because her mother had gone there, and her grandfather had gone there, so it was kind of a family tradition. She'd actually have been glad to go to Queen's, in her hometown, and saved her family a fortune, but hey, you couldn't fight tradition.

Jason hailed from Baltimore, and he'd been wrestling with whether to find a job here in Lewiston for the summer, and hang on to his off-campus

166

accommodation, or head home. Jenny planned to go back to Canada once school ended. So Jason had been thinking, if he wanted to visit her through the summer, was it better to be in Lewiston or Baltimore? He'd checked Google Maps and saw that either way it was an eight- to nine-hour drive. How could you visit someone for the weekend when it took two whole days just to get there and back?

But that was not what he was thinking about as he went for his run this morning.

What was on his mind was something Jenny's friend Denise had said the night before when a bunch of them had gone across the bridge into Auburn to have a few drinks at Gritty's. Clearly, Denise wasn't aware that Jason and Jenny had been a thing in the last month, that Jenny had even slept over at Jason's three times, because if she'd been aware of that, she probably wouldn't have asked Jenny if she'd slept with Carson yet.

It wasn't like she'd shouted the question. She'd asked it when she was sitting to Jenny's left, and Jason was sitting on Jenny's right, but Denise had asked it loudly enough that Jason heard it loud and clear.

Carson? Who the fuck was Carson?

So the second they were outside Gritty's, heading home, he'd asked her. She'd shrugged it off. Denise was kidding around, she said. Or confused. She'd known a guy named Carson once, but that was a long time ago.

But Jenny hadn't been able to look him in the eye.

Jason got this very sick feeling in the pit of his stomach. When he got back to his place – a century-old house about four blocks from the campus that he shared with three other guys – he went online to see if he could track down this Carson dude.

He'd had no luck, but as he ran down Main Street, heading for the footpaths that ran along the banks of the Androscoggin River, he promised himself he'd do more research when he got back.

Maybe if he hadn't been so preoccupied with his love life, and if Garth hadn't been crooning in his ears, he would have noticed the black four-door sedan that had been riding along about fifty feet behind him.

The car suddenly sped up, then pulled over to the curb ahead of Jason, brakes squealing. The car hadn't finished rebounding from the sudden stop when the passenger door opened and Rhys leapt out, flashing a badge in the palm of his hand just long enough for it to register with Jason.

'Jason Hamlin?' Rhys said.

Jason stopped, yanked the buds out of his ears, and said, panting, 'What?'

'Are you Jason Hamlin?' he asked again.

He chose to nod instead of speak, still catching his breath. He saw a woman getting out now from behind the wheel. She flashed her badge, too, as she came around the back of the car.

'Is this Mr Hamlin?' Kendra asked her partner.

'Yeah,' he said.

Now less winded, Jason said, 'What's this about?'

Kendra said, 'This is Detective Mills and I'm Detective Collins. I'm afraid we have some bad news for you, Mr Hamlin.'

'What?'

'Am I correct that Margaret and Charles Hamlin, of Baltimore, are your parents?'

That sick feeling he'd had in his stomach the night before was nothing compared to what he felt now.

In the distance, they could hear sirens.

'Yes?' he said weakly, glancing for a half a second over his shoulder, where the sirens were coming from.

'We were asked to track you down. If you come with us we can give you a ride back to your residence.'

'Why? What's happened?'

Rhys said, 'We're guessing you're going to want to go back there.'

'Just tell me,' he said.

'There was a car accident,' Rhys said. 'We don't have all the details.'

Kendra walked over to the car and opened the back door. An invitation. Jason, his legs rubbery, got into the back of the car. Kendra closed it, went around, and got back in behind the wheel. Rhys went around to the driver's side but opened the back door, taking a seat next to a visibly distraught Jason. He closed the door.

They sat there for several seconds, the car not moving. Jason was not so overwhelmed by the distressing news that he failed to notice they weren't going anywhere.

'Um, what are we waiting for?'

As Kendra shifted around in her seat, Rhys pressed himself up against his door and quickly put his arm over his own face. Kendra raised her hand above the seatback. In it was a small tube, not much bigger than a lipstick, with a button on top. She aimed it at Jason's face and pressed the button with her index finger.

A misty spray enveloped Jason's face.

'The fu—'

But then he started to cough and gag. His eyes began to sting, and he closed them. That was when Rhys jabbed the needle into his neck.

A fire truck went racing up the street in the opposite direction.

Kendra glanced in the rearview mirror.

'I can see the smoke,' she said.

Jason drifted into unconsciousness almost immediately, slumping in the seat. Rhys adjusted the man's body to move his head below the windows, then powered his window down to bring in some fresh air.

Kendra put the car in Drive and slowly pulled away from the curb. She'd already consulted her map app to find the quickest way out of town. They'd set up a disposal site about ten miles out of Lewiston.

She glanced in her mirror one more time, not to check on the smoke or whether Jason was dead yet, but to look at Rhys. He had his head half out the window, face to the wind, like a dog enjoying all the scents the world had to offer.

The house Jason shared with his friends burned to the ground. Some sort of gas leak, followed by an explosion. Jason's three friends survived, although one spent two weeks in the hospital with serious burns to his arms and upper torso.

Jason usually jogged in the morning, but the fact that he was missing had led authorities to speculate he could have been in the home when it exploded, and that the subsequent inferno had incinerated him. They were still looking through the ashes for any trace of him, however, and until they did find something, his where-abouts was treated as an open question.

And a week later, in what was seen as a tragic coincidence, Jason's family's home in Baltimore burned to the ground. An electrical fault was blamed.

CHAPTER 18

Providence, RI

Chloe usually worked the evening shift at the Paradise Diner, but today she was filling in for one of the other girls, who was sick – Chloe had a theory she was pregnant and experiencing the first indications – so she'd started at seven in the morning and was going to work through the crazy breakfast hours, have something of a lull between nine and half past eleven, and then do her best to survive the lunchtime madness. With any luck, she could hang up her apron and walk out the back door shortly after one.

So things weren't too crazy around ten when, glancing out the window, she saw the black limo pull into the lot. Didn't get a lot of limos stopping by the Paradise, she mused, and turned her attention to clearing off some tables.

Seconds later, the bell on the door jingled. A guy came in and looked about, as if waiting to be shown to a table.

'Wherever you want,' Chloe said.

He nodded and slipped into one of the booths by the window. If it had been a busier time, Chloe might have steered him to a stool at the counter, or maybe a table for two, but this time of day, if he wanted a whole booth to himself, that was fine.

He didn't exactly look like someone who'd be chauffeured around in a limo. But then again, what did she know about people who took limos? But this guy was what she thought of as 'professor casual.' Jeans, sports jacket, collared shirt. Couple of decades ago, that jacket would have had patches on the elbows.

The Paradise didn't exactly appeal to a high-end clientele. You could get three eggs, toast, and home fries, as well as a choice of bacon, ham, or sausage, for $6.99, and that included coffee. A BLT at lunch was $5.99, or $7.99 if you wanted a side of fries. Most of the folks who ate here arrived in pickup trucks, a few outfitted with a set of truck nuts dangling off the back bumper.

Who showed up in a limo?

Okay, maybe it wasn't a *limo* limo. It wasn't half a block long and the windows weren't all blacked out. She could see the driver, at least. A heavyset woman, looking at her phone. It looked like one of those cars that people who didn't have to bum rides from their friends took to the airport.

She approached the man, now scanning the menu he had taken out from between the paper napkin dispenser and a ketchup bottle.

'Coffee?'

'Um, yeah,' the man said, smiling.

He seemed to be looking at her chest. That would hardly make him unique. Half the men she served could never get their eyes above the tit line.

'Chloe?' he said.

Oh, okay, he was reading her name tag. Once he'd read it, he looked her in the face.

'At your service,' she said. 'I'll get your coffee.'

He looked like he was about to say something else but she'd already turned on her heel. Within a minute she was back with a white ceramic mug of coffee.

'Put enough cream and sugar in it and it's even drinkable,' she said. 'Know what you want?'

'How are the pancakes?'

'Flat.'

The man chuckled. 'Just the way I like them. I'll have those and a side of bacon.'

'Okay,' she said.

'Thank you, Chloe,' he said.

A little too much emphasis on her name, she thought, walking away. Like he enjoyed saying the word. Was that weird?

She thought of Anthony Hopkins saying *Clarice*. Yeah, kinda like that. Making your name sound like it was coming out of a sewer grate.

She put in the order, turned her attention to a single mom who brought along her toddler for a late breakfast once a week, then cleared dishes from another table.

Before the pancakes were ready, she delivered a

174

bottle of syrup and some extra pats of butter, each in their own sealed container, to the guy. Before she could turn away, he cleared his throat again to get her attention.

'Do you have a second?' he asked.

'You wanna change your order?'

'No. I just wanted to ask, have you worked here long?'

'About a year.'

'Like it?'

'I'm just here till some big-time movie director comes in and discovers me. I'm gonna go check on your—'

He reached out and grabbed her arm before she could walk away. 'Hang on a second,' he said.

She looked at the hand on her arm and quickly wrenched it away. 'Hands off, mister.'

'Sorry,' he said. 'But I was wondering—'

This dude was creeping her out. Shoot him a lie and shut this down. 'Let me help you out here. I have a boyfriend, and even if I didn't, you're old enough to be my daddy.'

The man chuckled. 'I don't know about that.'

Chloe departed before he could say anything else. She'd been hit on before – like, maybe every single fucking day – but it was usually by guys closer to her age. Sure, you had some dirty old men, guys who probably couldn't get it up if you rubbed your boobs right in their face, but that didn't stop them from pinching your ass as you walked by.

The other waitresses, who'd been at it longer than her, said things were better than they once were. The message was slowly getting through, even to the Neanderthals, that you couldn't pull that kind of shit.

She sidled up next to Vivian, who was working the cash register and had been at Paradise for pretty close to twenty years now, and said, 'Seen that guy in here before?'

Vivian shot him a look. 'Maybe. Might be a professor from Brown, wanting to mix it up with the common folk. Could be we're part of a research project.'

'You seen the black car out front?'

Vivian took a step away from the register to get a better look. 'Hmm,' she said. 'Forget the professor thing. I say he's a reviewer from the Michelin guide. This is the big break we've been waiting for. Hey, you find a credit card the other day? Someone phoned, was asking.'

Chloe said no.

The pancakes were up. As she was heading to the table something outside caught her eye. The limo driver was outside the car, and opening the back door for someone. So maybe this guy wasn't—

'Looks delicious,' the man said as Chloe set the plate in front of him.

'Can I get you anything else? Need a refill on your coffee?'

'Maybe in a second.' He looked into his mug.

'Still got half a cup. Warm it up in a couple minutes.'

'Sure.'

Behind her, she heard the bell on the door jingle again.

The man tipped his head back, looked her square in the face, and said, 'I hope I didn't get off on the wrong foot before.'

'Don't worry about it.'

'I was here before but you didn't wait on me. I'm glad it was you this time.'

That was when he ran his hand up her leg.

'Jesus!' Chloe shrieked, jumping back.

And then she screamed because something very horrible happened to the man's face. It appeared to explode, to erupt in blood.

Except it wasn't blood. It was ketchup, streaming at him from a squeeze bottle being held by another man who seemed to have come out of nowhere.

'What the fuck!' said the man in the booth, wiping ketchup from his eyes.

Chloe whirled around, saw someone else standing there, the man who had seconds earlier gotten out of the limo. He was holding the ketchup container, ready to take another shot if need be. There was something slightly off about him. His head was rocking slightly on his neck, like he had some sort of palsy or something.

'Leave her the fuck alone,' he said.

'Get out,' Chloe added.

The man in the booth grabbed a wad of paper

napkins from the chrome dispenser and wiped his face as he shifted his butt to the end of the bench and exited the booth. He looked ready to fight back, but then he caught sight of Vivian, closing the distance between them, an iron skillet in her hand. She had it raised, like it weighed no more than a balloon.

Holding up his hands in a gesture of peace, ketchup-smeared napkins clutched in his fingers, he said, 'Okay, okay, I'm going.'

Once he was out the door, he made a sharp left, and did not head toward the black limo. He got into a Civic parked just beyond it and drove off.

Chloe, rattled, took the ketchup bottle from the second man's hand and set it back on the table he'd grabbed it from.

'Thanks,' she said.

'No problem,' he said.

'Who the hell are you?'

The man hesitated before replying. 'My name is Miles,' he blurted, 'and I think I'm your dad.'

CHAPTER 19

New Rochelle, NY

Something was not right with Dr Martin Gold.

His assistant, Julie Harkin, noticed he'd been acting strangely for several days. Showing up late to the office, leaving early. Canceling appointments with almost no notice, yet not leaving the building. He'd just sit behind his desk, staring at his computer screen.

Julie knew he was drinking more. She believed he was keeping a bottle of something in his desk, because more than once, when he'd come out to ask her a question or hand her something to be filed, she could smell alcohol on his breath. And he was glassy-eyed. One morning, she'd been able to smell booze on him when he first arrived, like he was skipping coffee and having vodka shots with his bacon and eggs.

Gold had always enjoyed a drink, but in all the years Julie had worked for him she had never seen him this way. Good thing he wasn't a surgeon, she thought. You wouldn't want this guy cutting into you.

At first, she was worried that somehow his erratic behavior had something to do with her.

Maybe he'd figured out what she'd done.

The first few days after she'd given those files to that Heather woman, the one who'd approached her in the coffee shop with fifty thousand in cash in her purse, Julie was terrified she'd be found out. She'd tried to be careful, believed she'd covered her tracks. One day while Gold was out for lunch with a friend, she'd found in his desk the key to the storage unit a few blocks away where the clinic stored all the paper files from decades past. She also knew the keypad code to enter the facility – 1825, which just happened to be the length of the Brooklyn Bridge, in meters. That night she went to the storage place, entered the code, then found Gold's locker. There were no light switches that she could find. Everything was motion sensitive. You walked down a hall, the lights came on. She located Gold's locker, used the key to open it, and rolled up the door.

The information Heather wanted was most likely to be found in one of the many cardboard business boxes. The time period she was interested in was about a year before the ReproGold Clinic made the transition from paper to computer filing.

The locker was about half filled, and not just with boxes of files. About five years ago Gold had refurbished the office, buying new furniture for the waiting room. Rather than throw out the old stuff, he'd stored it here, probably thinking someday he might be able to sell it.

She found the files pertaining to Miles Cookson and the women who'd been the recipients of his contribution. She gathered them up, stuffed them into her bag, and went home, where she immediately made copies of everything on her home printer. And then she got back in her car and returned the files to their proper places in their proper boxes.

It was as she was leaving the facility the second time that she noticed the security cameras.

Well, *of course* there would be security cameras. How could she not have thought of this? The storage company had set up cameras in every hallway, at every entry and exit point. So both of her visits were recorded, monitored. Saved.

She returned to the coffee shop the next day, handing over to Heather a thick envelope of the papers she'd photocopied.

'I'm scared,' she'd said, telling her about the cameras.

'Don't worry,' Heather told her. 'As long as Dr Gold has no idea you did this, there's no reason for him to ask the storage people for a review of the surveillance video. Most companies keep the video for two weeks to a month. You'll be okay. I trust you left everything as you found it?'

'Yes.'

'I'm sure you'll be fine.'

Easy for her to say. She wasn't the one sneaking around behind her boss's back. But as each day went by and the issue didn't come up, Julie became more confident that she was going to get away with this.

Julie hid the cash in the back of her bathroom closet, behind the towels and the extra rolls of toilet paper. She got back in touch with the various contractors who'd stopped working on her house when she could no longer pay them. 'Can you come back?' she asked. 'And is cash okay?'

It was.

But she hadn't mentioned anything to Dr Gold about work resuming on her house. She didn't want to raise any questions about where she'd found the money. She became increasingly confident he did not suspect her, or anyone, of getting into the storage unit.

So something else was bothering him.

Finally, she asked, 'Dr Gold, is everything okay?'

She put the question to him shortly before noon when he announced, without warning, that he was not coming back after lunch, that she would have to cancel the afternoon appointments.

'I'm fine,' he said without conviction. 'Just do it.'

Women and their partners trying so hard to start, or enlarge, their families did not respond well to these cancellations. Some of these people, desperate for the clinic's help, had scheduled their appointments weeks earlier. They'd taken time off from work. Some had driven long distances.

Gold seemed not to care.

If the man didn't pull himself together, the clinic's future would be in jeopardy. Julie would have to find herself another job.

She was starting to think she might have to rein in the contractors again. She might need that fifty grand to live on.

CHAPTER 20

Providence, RI

Miles had actually spent quite some time in the back of the limo before working up the courage to go into the diner. Going over in his head what he was going to say. He thought back to when he was in high school, the butterflies he had in his stomach while he worked up the courage to ask a girl to the prom. That, in retrospect, was nothing compared to telling a young woman that she was your biological daughter.

It had taken a little more than two hours to make the drive here from New Haven, and he'd spent much of it in quiet contemplation. His frequent driver, Charise, had noticed.

'Hope you'll forgive the intrusion, Mr Cookson,' she'd said, 'but you seem a little preoccupied today.'

He had told her more times than he could remember to call him Miles, but Charise was a stickler for protocol. When you drove someone around, you wore a white shirt, jacket, and tie, no matter how warm it got outside. You opened the door for your passengers. You addressed them formally. You didn't take personal calls in your employer's presence.

'Yeah, a little preoccupied,' he'd said.

'Would you like the radio on?' Her finger had been ready to bring in the Sirius station of his choice. 'Beatles?'

'No, that's okay,' he'd said. 'I'm happy with quiet.'

He had not necessarily meant that she, personally, should zip her lip, but she had almost nothing to say for the rest of the trip.

As per Dorian's suggestion, Miles was beginning this process with Chloe Swanson. Much was riding on the encounter. If it went well, he'd feel encouraged about getting in touch with the others. If it went badly, well, he might have to rethink everything.

He had settled on a go-slow approach. Head into the Paradise Diner, find a place to sit away from other patrons, order a cup of coffee, hope Chloe Swanson would wait on him, and if she did, engage her in conversation. Get a feel for her before asking if he might speak to her privately.

Heather had found out for him that Chloe would be working the morning shift. She'd called the diner, pretending to be someone who'd lost a credit card. Chloe had been her waitress, Heather said, and maybe she'd found it? Come by in the morning, she was told. Chloe was covering someone else's shift.

And so here he was.

Miles was going to meet his biological daughter.

He took a deep breath, got out of the car, walked into the diner, and right into a nasty situation between Chloe and some asshole customer.

It was at that moment a hint of the Huntington's made its presence known. A sudden flash of irritation, anger. He grabbed the ketchup from the next booth over and shot it all over the guy's face. Like throwing water on a dog in heat.

And then he'd just come out with it.

My name is Miles and I think I'm your dad.

God, talk about smooth.

The look on her face. Stunned, dumbfounded, gobsmacked. Just stood there, staring at him for several seconds before finally saying, 'What?'

There was no way to ease into it at that point. The proverbial cat was out of the bag.

He said, 'That didn't come out the way I'd planned. I—'

'Jesus,' she said, now looking at the table, which was covered with rivulets of ketchup that crisscrossed the pancake order. 'What a fucking mess.'

'I'm sorry. I saw him grabbing you and—'

'Yeah, you're a hero. Like I don't know how to deal with handsy dickheads.'

It was like she hadn't even heard, or comprehended, what he'd told her.

'Is there someplace we could talk?' he asked her.

186

She grabbed the cloth tucked into the waistband of her uniform, took a preliminary run at wiping up the ketchup, saw that some of it had hit the vinyl-covered bench, and said, 'Shit.'

She took the untouched plate of food and the mug of coffee and walked them over to a nearby station filled with other dirty dishes, Miles following her.

'Did you hear what I said?' he asked.

'Whatever it was, it didn't make any sense to me,' she said dismissively.

'It's true.'

Chloe stopped momentarily. 'Seriously. Well, I have no dad. Never have.'

She'd grabbed another cloth and went back to wipe down the bench.

'I know,' Miles said quietly. 'You have two moms. Gillian and Annette. I'm sorry about Annette. I know you lost her when you were very young.'

Chloe stopped cleaning, turned, and looked at him.

'You're freaking me out. Who the hell are you?'

He introduced himself again. 'Miles. Miles Cookson. I came up today from New Haven.' The words were catching in his throat. 'To see you.'

Chloe wavered slightly, as if struck by a spell of dizziness.

'Why don't you sit,' Miles said, and Chloe slid onto the bench of the booth she'd just wiped down.

187

Miles, awkwardly – one of his legs was slow in getting the message that he wanted to sit down – settled in across from her.

Vivian, the skillet still in her hand but hanging, nonthreateningly, at her side, approached and said to Chloe, 'You okay, sweetheart?'

Chloe gave her a dazed look. 'Um . . . is it okay if I take a break?'

Vivian looked at Miles and then Chloe, realized there was something going on, even if she had no idea what it was, and said, 'Sure. You need something, just holler.'

'I wouldn't mind a coffee,' Miles said.

Vivian shot him a look, suggesting she hadn't been talking to him. 'Comin' right up,' she said and walked off.

Miles smiled at Chloe and said, 'She looks like someone you don't mess with.'

Chloe said, 'How do you know about me? How do you know about my moms?'

'I've had to do my homework,' Miles said. 'Or had people do it for me.'

'I don't understand.'

'I know you have a hundred questions, and this is all a lot to take in in just a few seconds, but let me start by asking you one. What do you know, what have you been told, about your biological father?'

'Nothing. My mom went to a fertility clinic. Got pregnant. Had me. End of story.'

'You must have wondered.'

She nodded slowly. 'I don't know that I should be telling you this.'

'I understand. If you ask me to leave, I'll leave. But I hope you won't. I'm legit. I'm who I say I am. I swear.'

'I did the WhatsMyStory thing.' She paused. 'But it didn't connect me to you.'

'I haven't sent them my DNA. I could have, but there was no guarantee it would accomplish what I wanted, in the time I have.'

'What's that mean?'

'I'll come back to that. I got the names of everyone who was implanted with my sperm. Doesn't matter how. And from there, I was able to learn the names of the issues from those donations.'

'Issues? I'm an issue?'

Miles shrugged. 'I still don't know the language to use.'

Vivian returned with coffee and a handful of tiny, sealed creams. 'Everything okay here?' she asked, noticing that Chloe's eyes were misting.

She grabbed a napkin, dabbed her eyes. 'We're good, Viv.'

'Okay.'

Once she was gone, Chloe asked Miles, 'You found all of them?'

Miles nodded.

'How many?'

'Nine.'

'Nine? I thought they could use a sperm bank donation like dozens and dozens of times.'

189

'In my case, I guess they didn't. I was a little surprised, too.'

'Nine,' she said, again, more to herself. 'I've found one of them.'

Miles's eyebrows went up. 'You have?'

'A half brother. Todd Cox.'

'Yeah, that's one of the names on my list.'

'Do you *have* it? Can I *see* it?'

Miles looked down at the table and shook his head. 'Once I've tracked everyone down, had a chance to talk to them, see how they feel about this, then I can arrange for everyone to meet each other. Bring everyone together.' He cracked a grin. 'I guess *reunion* would be the wrong word. An introduction.'

'Yeah, well, I guess. But they could be all over the place. Anywhere in the world.'

'I can cover that,' he said.

'Why? You rich or something?'

'Yes,' he said plainly.

'Oh,' Chloe said. She waved her arm at her surroundings. 'I'm working on my first million here.' She shook her head wonderingly. 'This is all so weird. And yeah, it's a lot to take in. Here you are, just sitting there. I'm not sure I actually believe it.'

'Why would I lie?'

'I don't know. I'm not saying you are. But it's kind of hard to get my head around. All my life I've wondered who my honest-to-God father is, and now you're here, and I think, shouldn't I feel different? Is my life changed?'

'Maybe not yet,' he said.

Her face became serious. 'So, why?'

'Why?'

'Why are you here? Why find me?'

'Why'd *you* get in touch with WhatsMyStory? There are things *you* wanted to know.'

'Okay, but I'm thinking, with you, there's got to me more to it than that.'

This was going to be the hard part. 'I had some tests done recently,' he said.

'Tests?'

'I was noticing some changes. Muscle-type things. Short-term memory lapses. Involuntary movements.'

'You seem okay.'

'It's early days. Anyway, they checked me out, to see what might be wrong.'

And then he thought, *I can't tell her.*

If she knew anything about Huntington's, she'd immediately know she was at risk. He couldn't drop a bomb like that on her. Not this fast. Tell her he had something that presented with similar symptoms. Something that wasn't as likely to be passed on.

'I've got ALS,' he said. 'Sometimes it's called Lou Gehrig's disease. That's—'

'I know what it is. I visit my grandfather all the time at his seniors home. There's someone there who has it. It's a bad fucker.'

Miles smiled. 'Yeah, it is. So, the clock's ticking. Although I don't know how fast. I'm considering

. . . my legacy. I want to find the people I'd be leaving behind that I didn't even know I had.'

'Okay.' This time, a tear escaped and ran down her cheek. 'So, after all these years, in one hour, I find out who my dad is, *and* that I'm going to lose him.'

'Well, not right away.'

'Fuck,' Chloe said, grabbing another napkin and wiping the tear away. 'I'm sorry. I'm making it sound like this is all about me. You're the one who's sick.'

There was so much more to tell. About what he intended to give her and the others. About how she would become very, very rich. And, eventually, the health threat she might face.

But that could come later.

Chloe sniffed a couple of times, pulled herself together.

'You know what I think I should do?' she said, attempting a smile.

'What?'

'Introduce you to Todd. You don't have to show me your list. I know about him. I could kind of pave the way, ease him into it.'

Miles considered it.

'It's a long way to go.'

'That's okay. And you could send your driver home.' Chloe took a phone from her pocket, set it on the table. 'I've got my Pacer parked out around back.'

'A Pacer?' Miles said, incredulous.

She flashed him a smile. 'One of the wagon models. The radio doesn't work and all the wood paneling has peeled off, but it gets the job done. You don't have to get all snobby. What do you drive? A fucking Porsche?'

Miles started to tell her he'd just given it away, but held his tongue.

Chloe was tapping away on the phone, sending a text. 'Todd always gets right back to me,' she said. 'He's kinda . . . strange? And his mom? She's something else.' She laughed. 'Like *I'm* normal. She's the one who's really into this whole trace-your-DNA thing and got Todd to do his.'

Chloe looked down at her phone again, the absence of a response.

'Huh,' she said. 'He's not answering. That's weird.'

CHAPTER 21

New Haven, CT

The day after Gilbert had shown her the list, Caroline found herself in a room at the Omni Hotel in the Yale University neighborhood. She was in one of the luxury units, on an upper floor, standing at the window with a view of the Yale campus. She could see the Sterling Memorial Library, the Law School Towers, the High Street Arch. Well, she could have seen those things had it not been for the black, silk Hermès scarf covering her eyes and knotted tightly at the back of her head.

She had followed his instructions explicitly.

Caroline was to go to the hotel desk at four in the afternoon – not one minute before and not one minute after – and ask for the room key that would be waiting for her.

She was then to go to the room, let herself in.

There would be a recently opened bottle of champagne, chilling, and two flutes. She was to fill one, have a drink, unwind.

A tub would already have been run for her. Caroline was to strip down, have a relaxing bath. She had mixed feelings about this part. Did he think she wasn't *clean* enough? But she had to admit, he got the water temperature just right, and it *was* relaxing.

At half past four, she was to get out, dry off. When she came out of the bathroom, she was to slip into the intimate apparel laid out for her on the bed. Lingerie from Agent Provocateur, Bordelle, other high-end brands she'd seen in magazines but never felt she could afford.

And the scarf.

She was to go to the window, fold the scarf into a four-inch-wide band, and tie it around her head, blindfolding herself.

And then she was to wait.

It might be no more than a minute. It might be ten. When she heard the door open, sensed someone coming into the room, she was not to move. He would approach silently, moving across the carpet as stealthily as a cat. She wouldn't know he was there until she could feel his breath on her neck.

And then things would really start to get interesting.

This was their routine. This was how Broderick liked to find her. He'd been very specific about his desires, right from the first time. That had been months earlier, a week or so after he'd used his powers of persuasion with the service manager who had refused to do the necessary repairs on Caroline's car for free.

It only seemed right to find a way to show her gratitude.

She had researched the court records to learn more about Broderick, starting with a last name. Broderick Stiles, forty-three years old. There had been an address attached to his name, but when she went to look for it, she found a vacant lot. She could find no phone record for him, and he certainly didn't have a Facebook page or a Twitter handle.

So she kept going back to the coffee shop where they'd first met, hoping they'd cross paths again. She tried to go at the same time of day as when she had first met him, but after a week she became discouraged, and more than a little over-caffeinated. It was on the eighth day, while paying for her latte, when she heard someone behind her say, 'Car running okay?'

'Oh!' she said, whirling around.

They sat at the same table where they'd first chatted. She said, 'I don't know what you said, but they fixed the car and they were very, very nice about it.'

'I'm so glad to hear that,' Broderick said.

'So what *did* you say?'

He had smiled. 'Does it really matter?'

The thing was, she didn't want to know. It was more fun *not* knowing. It was more fun imagining what he might have said, or done, to get her service manager to see reason.

She had leaned across the table, nearly touching her forehead to his, and said, 'I would like to find a way to thank you.'

He said, 'I have just the idea.'

The next afternoon was her first trip to the Omni. A week later there was another, and the week after that, another. And so on.

There had been occasions when Broderick was away, doing work for clients out of town. But whenever he was in New Haven, he would arrange a rendezvous.

It was not Caroline's first affair, but it was certainly her most exciting. When it came to the bedroom, Gilbert had never been particularly imaginative. Everything was by the numbers, no accountant puns intended. Spend a little time here, spend a little time there, then hop aboard and get it done. Really, what could you say about a man who liked to keep his socks on when having sex? But it was more than that. It was not easy to work up enthusiasm for a man who, at some level, you could not bring yourself to respect.

But wait, she would sometimes ask herself. Could you respect what Broderick Stiles did for a living? (If he did what she *believed* he did.) She could find ways to rationalize it. He was a man who performed a service. Perhaps it was outside the bounds of what was, technically speaking, legal. But the world was an increasingly complicated place. Some problems called for unconventional solutions.

And holy fucking Christ, the sex was something else.

On this particular day, not yet twenty-four hours since Gilbert had told her about Miles's illness, how her brother-in-law was leaving next to nothing to Gilbert except for that Porsche, that he intended to give away his fortune to a bunch of biological children he'd never so much as sent a birthday card to, Caroline had been wondering whether there was anything she could do.

Should she talk to Miles herself? Try to get him to change his mind? Would he even agree to meet with her? Could she tell him how sorry she was that she'd traded on his name with that Google exec? Tell him she wasn't that person anymore, that she had learned her lesson?

Maybe she could remind him what a good brother Gilbert had been to him. Guilt Miles into doing what was right.

No, Miles would never listen to her. He was a selfish man. Totally self-consumed.

But she had another idea, one that was, to use one of her daughter Samantha's favorite phrases, 'pretty out there.' It was a long-term approach, and not something she could do alone. There were any number of ways it could go wrong. But, oh, if it worked . . . the payoff would be huge.

She wondered what Broderick would think.

So this afternoon, stretched out on the bed, and after Broderick had given her permission to take off the silk blindfold, she decided to broach the subject.

'The first time I met you,' she said, 'you described yourself as a problem solver.'

'And I solved one for you,' he said.

'You certainly did.'

She paused.

Finally, he asked her, 'Do you have a new problem?'

'I do. But it's a little more complicated than the one I had with my car.'

199

CHAPTER 22

Providence, RI

An hour had gone by and Todd had not responded to Chloe's texts or emails. Finally, she had just phoned him, which, Miles mused, always seemed to be the last option among younger people.

Todd did not pick up. Chloe had left a voice mail: 'Hey, dipshit half brother, call me the second you get this because I have got news that will blow your mind.'

And still, no call back.

'So maybe he's busy,' Miles had said.

Chloe admitted that was possible, but was unconvinced. 'It's not like him.'

'How long have you actually known him?'

'Okay, not that long. But the guy lives with a phone in his hand.' She thought a moment. 'I say we go.'

Miles was less sure. 'Could be a long way to go to find him not there.'

'What else you got to do?' She cocked her head. 'What *do* you actually do, anyway?'

'I run a tech company.'

'So what's that mean?'

'Hand me your phone.'

'What?'

'Just . . . give it to me.'

With some reluctance, she passed it across the table to him. He glanced at all the apps she had on it. The usual ones were there. Facebook, Twitter, iTunes, Instagram, Waze, some games. He thumbed over to the second page of apps, smiled.

'See this one?' he said, tapping on it.

The screen filled with the word SHOPSAW.

'Yeah?' she said.

'This is the one, you take a picture of something you saw somebody wearing, it tells you where you can buy it.'

'I know how it works.'

'That's one of ours.'

'You're shittin' me. Your company *invented* that app?'

Miles nodded.

'Fuck me,' she said, taking back the phone. 'I'm impressed. I use this all the time. Sneak shots of people wearing shit I wish I could buy. It's always from some place I could never afford to shop. Hang on.'

She aimed the phone at Miles, tapped the screen, looked at it. 'You got your jacket from Nordstrom?'

'Yup.'

Chloe shook her head admiringly. 'And that's how come you're rich.'

'Yup.'

'Anything pressing back at the office, or you want to take a run up to Todd's place?'

He shrugged. 'Why the hell not. Charise can take us.'

'You call your car Charise? Like, *Christine*?'

'Charise is my driver.'

'Of course she is,' Chloe said. 'Look, no offense, but I still don't know for sure that you're the real deal, that you're who you say you are. So the last thing I'm doing is getting in some strange car with you. It's probably got doors you can't open from the inside and a glass partition thing and the driver hits a button and sleeping gas fills up the back seat.'

Miles said, 'That's my other car.'

'I'll tell Vivian I gotta go, gonna lose the apron, and I'll pull around up front.'

'Okay if I have Charise follow us? Then, later, she can take me straight home.'

'You can't just call up your private chopper or something?'

'I think if she followed, it'd be easier.'

She gave that a moment, said, 'Okay,' then slipped out of the booth.

Miles was briefing Charise about the change in plans when Chloe's Pacer appeared from around the back of the diner. They heard the car before they saw it. It was a a minisymphony of rattles and groans and squeaks, as well as a deep-throated rumbling from a busted muffler.

'You're going in that, sir?' Charise asked.

'Evidently.'

'Would you like me to drive – what is that, Mr Cookson? It looks like a goldfish bowl.'

'A Pacer.'

'Would you like me to drive that, and the young lady could drive this car? You'd be more comfortable.'

Miles smiled. 'No, but thank you.'

Chloe brought her car to a stop, brakes squealing, next to the limo. 'Hop in,' she said, her window rolled down. Charise gave the car a visual appraisal and did not appear pleased.

'This thing pass a safety test?' Miles asked.

'I make up for its deficiencies by being a great driver,' Chloe said. 'Been driving since I was four-teen, legally since sixteen. I even drove a delivery truck when I was seventeen. It was a FedEx van, and I kind of took it for a joyride without permission, but once I got behind the wheel it was a piece of cake. When I was nineteen my mom rented a motor home thing and we did a trip to D.C.'

Miles went around to the passenger side, where he encountered the biggest car door he had ever seen. And then he remembered that the Pacer had been designed with a longer right-side door to allow easier access to the rear seat. The door sagged when he opened it, as if too heavy for the hinges.

'When you get in,' Chloe said, 'you have to pull really hard to get it back in place.'

'Noted,' Miles said, getting both hands on the armrest and pulling with everything he had.

'Okay, let's hit the road. But first . . .' She took out her phone. 'You got some sort of ID?'

'Huh?'

'Driver's license or something?'

Miles blinked, took out his wallet, and dug out his license. Chloe took it in one hand and took a picture of it with the other.

'What are you—'

'Hang on,' she said. She handed back the license and did some swift tapping, followed by a *whoosh*. 'Emailed it to Viv, at the diner. In case you're actually a strangler-rapist-serial-killer guy.'

'Understood.'

Still holding the phone, she said, 'I've been documenting all these encounters, you know, relating to my family history, my background. I've been doing video of my grandfather, and Todd, and I should have recorded our whole meeting just now.'

'That's okay.'

'No, no, it's not. I really want this stuff. It's important. You hold this and shoot while I'm driving, okay? 'Cause I can't exactly film and drive at the same time. If I'm talking, shoot me, and if you're talking, do the selfie thing. Can you do that?'

'I suppose. So we'll use the time to tell each other a little more about ourselves?'

'Exactly,' she said, cranking the wheel and hitting

the gas. The back wheels kicked up gravel. She glanced in the rearview mirror, saw the black limo falling in behind. 'Hope I didn't chip her paint.'

Miles asked her to tell her story first. She said she didn't need him to record much of that, since she already knew it. But she told him about her upbringing, about having two mothers, the teasing and the abuse she got from other kids growing up, and how that wasn't entirely a bad thing because it had toughened her up, taught her not to give a shit about what other people think.

She told him about the video interviews she had done with her grandfather. 'You never know how much time he's got left, so you want to find out as much as you can, while you can.'

'I understand.'

She glanced over at him, grimaced. 'Sorry. That came out sounding a little insensitive.'

'That's okay.'

'My mom's going to be pissed,' she said.

'Why?'

'She thinks this is a bad idea.'

'You told her we were driving up to see your half brother?'

'Not that. This whole thing about finding out who you are. I don't mean *you*. I mean, like *me*. She didn't want me sending my DNA to WhatsMyStory. She was furious about it. And now, out of the blue, you getting in touch, me finding out who you are, that just might push her over the edge.'

'Why do you think that is?'

'She feels threatened. For so long it's just been me and her. We were this tiny contained unit, you know? But me finding out about half siblings, it's like, what's that phrase? They're going to breach the ramparts?'

'Yeah.'

'What the fuck *is* a rampart?'

'It's like a castle wall.'

She nodded, eyes on the road ahead. 'Okay, point the phone at yourself. It's twenty questions time.'

'What?'

'I'm gonna ask you some shit, see if we really have stuff in common.'

'Okay,' he said, holding up the phone and aiming it at himself.

'Favorite movie?'

Miles thought for a moment. 'I have a couple. *The Godfather*, the second one. *Rear Window*.'

'Rear what?'

'*Rear Window*. A Hitchcock classic.'

'The fat bald guy?'

'Yeah. The fat bald guy. You?'

'*Lady Bird*,' she said.

'I never got to that one.'

'Okay, so that was a miss. Favorite ice cream?'

'Butter pecan,' he said, and instantly saw the disappointment on her face.

'Rocky road,' she said.

'They both have nuts in them,' Miles said, but Chloe did not look encouraged.

'Favorite TV show,' she said. 'Of all time.'

'*The Wire?*'

'Oh, come on, that's everybody's go-to answer. Be a little original.'

Miles had to think again. 'I guess maybe *Six Feet Under*, about the family that ran the funeral home. Although, given the theme, I might not enjoy it as much today. You?'

'Don't laugh.'

'I won't,' he said, now aiming the phone at her.

'Mister Rogers. He died around the time I was born and so they weren't making any new shows. But my mom found tons of episodes at a flea market that someone recorded on videocassette. Remember VCRs?'

'I do.'

'So I had about fifty episodes that, when I was little, I'd watch over and over again.' She bit her lower lip for a second. 'I used to imagine he was my dad.' She glanced over at Miles. 'I bet you don't even own a cardigan.'

'I don't.'

'Okay, gonna give this one last try. Favorite fast food.'

'Pizza.'

'God damn it,' Chloe said, banging her fist on the steering wheel. 'Tacos.' She shook her head and looked at him sorrowfully. 'No way you're my dad.'

'I guess there's no point even doing a DNA test,' he said. 'Can I put the phone down now?'

'Hell no. Keep shooting. Tell me your story.'

He told her about growing up in Stamford. His father, an insurance salesman, was an alcoholic. His mother dealt with her husband's addiction by taking pills. Despite their addictions, they managed to get through each and every day, doing their best to fool the world into thinking they were a happy couple when in fact they were barely holding it together. For Miles and his older brother, Gilbert, home life was akin to walking on eggshells. His father was consistently abusive emotionally and, occasionally, physically. When Gilbert left to go to college, Miles knew he couldn't survive in that house if no one was there to have his back, so he left, too. Not officially. But he bounced around from one friend's house to another until he finished high school, and then he was gone for good.

'Are your parents still alive?'

'No. After my brother and I left the nest, they were in a car accident.'

'Do you miss them?'

'Yes,' he said.

That surprised her. Her eyebrows shot up for a second. 'Really?'

'They're my mom and dad,' he said.

'You and your brother – shit, I just realized I have an uncle – are you close?'

Miles considered the question. 'We have been. He works for me. But I think this would be the wrong week to ask him if he feels close to me. My arm's getting tired holding this phone.'

'Suck it up. What's the deal with your brother? Why's he pissed with you?'

Was he ready to get into it? About how he planned to disperse his estate? He'd made it clear to Chloe he was well fixed, but if it had occurred to her some money might be coming her way, she gave no indication.

'Long story,' he said, finally, putting down the phone and turning off the video function.

They made a stop at a fast-food burger place – they hadn't passed any place advertising pizza or tacos – and Miles invited Charise to join them.

Charise, a large woman who tipped the scales at 225, said she was trying to eat more healthily, but one whiff of all that grease weakened her resolve.

While the three of them ate, Chloe, her mouth full of fries, said to Charise, 'This is my first meal in my entire life with my dad.'

Charise's eyebrows rose a notch. 'Oh?'

'This doesn't look like the kind of place that has champagne,' Chloe said, grinning.

'I don't think so,' Miles said. 'Maybe later.'

Charise looked across the table at Miles, her expression an unspoken question. Miles was about to offer a short explanation, but Chloe cut him off.

'Save it for later. No one wants to hear the word "sperm" while they're eating.'

They were back on the road in twenty minutes. Bringing Charise up to speed would have to wait, given that she was in the trailing car. About an hour after they'd left the burger place, Chloe pointed ahead and said, 'This is it, up here. Just past the fire station.'

She slowed the Pacer, hit the blinker, and turned off the main road onto a gravel driveway. She made a turn around a copse of trees, and there was the trailer. Charise stayed on the main road, pulling over onto the gravel shoulder to wait.

'So this is it,' Miles said, scanning the trailer from one end to the other.

'I don't see his car,' Chloe said. 'Let me try him again.'

She got out her phone, tapped the screen, put it to her ear. She waited for several seconds before it went to voice mail.

'Hey, Todd,' she said. 'We're at your place. Where are you? Wherever it is, you need to get your ass back here ASAP. I brought someone you need to meet.'

She ended the call, tucked the phone back into the front pocket of her jeans.

'I heard it inside,' Miles said.

'Heard what?'

'When you called him, I heard a phone ring inside the trailer.'

CHAPTER 23

Worcester, MA

The plan had been, once Kendra Collins and Rhys Mills got to the funeral home about an hour's drive from Springfield – one of several across the country with whom they had a standing arrangement for body disposal – they would search Todd Cox's body for a second cell phone before they put him on the conveyor belt and sent him on his final journey, right into the crematorium. They'd realized there had to be a second phone after recalling the Verizon bill they'd seen on the trailer's kitchen table. They were hoping to find it in Todd's pocket.

They hauled the body bag up onto a table, unzipped it, and Kendra, pulling on some latex gloves and holding her breath, dug down into the front pockets of the dead man's jeans, but came up empty.

'Maybe it's in one of his back pockets,' Rhys suggested, turning away, trying not to gag.

'Help me turn him on his side.'

'Shit,' Rhys said, holding his breath as he rolled

the body onto its side so Kendra could check the back pockets.

'Nothing,' she said, stripping off the gloves with two declarative snaps. 'Where else could he have it?'

Her partner shook his head as he let the body settle onto its back again. 'Nowhere else *for* him to carry it.'

'Maybe it fell out and it's in the bag somewhere,' Kendra said, looking at Rhys.

'What?'

'Feel around.'

He met his partner's look with one of disdain. 'You've already been digging around in there. You do it.'

'I just took off my gloves.

Why don't we just call the number and listen for the ring?'

'I don't have a number for his personal cell phone. Do you?'

'No. Come on,' she said. 'Snap on a pair and give it a go.'

He didn't miss her double meaning. She knew he was squeamish about bodily fluids – other than blood – and the bag was swimming in it.

Fuck it.

He pulled on the gloves and felt around inside the bag, right into all four corners, under Cox's lifeless legs, around his head. He withdrew his hands, carefully peeled off the gloves, saying, 'Nothing.'

'Son of a bitch,' Kendra said.

'Yeah,' Rhys said.

'Could it be in any of the garbage bags?'

The bags of material removed from the trailer were still in their van and Todd's Hyundai, outside. Their next stop was to be a nearby junkyard, where the car would be crushed into a cube, never to be found again.

'We would have noticed it, wouldn't we?' he said.

She briefly closed her eyes, as though seeking some sort of divine guidance. 'I think we would, but we need to check.'

'We leave the bags in the car, let it get crushed with everything else, does it matter?'

'We'll never know,' she said. 'We have to know. The phone matters. It's something he handled. There's more traces of him on that than just about anything else.'

He knew she was right.

Confident now that the phone was not in the body bag with Todd, they could at least proceed with this stage of their duties. They moved the bag and its contents onto the platform in front of the door to the furnace. Rhys fired it up, and they waited for it to reach the desired temperature, then watched as the body was conveyed into the raging furnace.

That done, they went back outside to the Hyundai, parked in back of the funeral home, and hauled out all the bags.

'There's no easy way to do this,' she said.

They dumped everything out onto the parking lot. Cleaning rags, clothing, bedding, the laptop, all of Todd's most personal items, like his tooth-brush and comb. They spread the items out on the pavement. They found the cheap flip phone that had been on the kitchen table in the trailer, but that was it.

Rather than put everything back into bags, they tossed it all, loose, into the trunk and the back seat.

Kendra said, 'We have to go back.'

Rhys leaned up against the Hyundai and hung his head. 'I'm so fucking tired.'

'I know. Let's get rid of the car, get some break-fast, mainline some caffeine, we'll go back.'

Wearily, he nodded. 'You take the car, I'll follow.'

They went to the junkyard, asked for 'Harry,' who was happy to put the car into the crusher after Rhys slipped a thousand in twenties into his greasy palm. They stayed until they saw the Hyundai go into the crusher and be reduced to a small cube of mangled metal and plastic.

They found a nearby Denny's and demanded coffee immediately. Kendra ordered a veggie omelette, Rhys went for the steak and eggs.

'You know, I usually work alone,' Rhys said as he sipped on his first cup.

'Same,' she said. 'But the client was right, figuring this was a two-person job.'

'Yeah,' he said. 'Different.'

'So, *Rhys*, you got a real name?'

'I do. But how do you know it isn't Rhys?'

'No one would really want to be named Rhys. If it was your name, you'd change it.'

'How about Kendra? Sounds like you walked out of a Chanel ad.'

'Okay, so I'm not Kendra and you're not Rhys.'

Rhys raised his mug and smiled. 'To us, whoever we are.'

She raised her mug and clinked his, as if they were wineglasses.

Their waitress arrived with the food, and even before the plate had been set down in front of her, Kendra had her fork in her hand. She speared some home fries, shoveled them into her mouth. While chewing, she said, 'This one is a weird gig.'

'Gig? What are we, a band?' he asked, cutting into his steak, checking to see whether it was rare, as he'd ordered.

'Everything's a gig to me,' she said. 'You don't have questions?'

He shrugged and chewed. 'Everything's a job, a task to be completed.'

'This list, though,' she said. 'What's the connection? Why the special instructions about cleaning the scene? The fires?'

Rhys slowly shook his head. 'Only know what you need to know.'

They ate hurriedly and soon were back in the van, heading to Todd's trailer outside Springfield. Nearly an hour later, when they were within a mile of their destination, Kendra yawned and said, 'I should've had one more coffee.'

'Did you see that place we passed about two miles back?'

'Yeah.'

'Why don't you let me out, I'll look for the phone, you go back and get us a couple more coffees, come back. If I haven't found it by then, you can help me.'

Kendra nodded. She saw the driveway up ahead.

'Don't bother pulling in. Just drop me,' Rhys said.

The van slowed and came to a stop at the end of the driveway. Before he opened the door, Rhys hit the button on the glove compartment and opened it, then removed a silencer-equipped Ruger and tucked it into a deep, inside jacket pocket.

'Expecting trouble?' she asked.

He smiled. 'Like the Boy Scouts say.' He opened the door. 'Maybe get a donut or something, too, if they've got it.'

He slammed the door and started walking up the driveway while Kendra waited for the traffic to clear so she could do a U-turn.

Rhys approached the trailer, mounted the cinder block steps to reach the door, and went inside. The place still smelled of bleach. He closed the door, behind him and immediately got to his knees, peering under chairs and the living room couch. He worked his way to the kitchen and, using the flashlight app on his phone, peered into the cracks between the stove and fridge and cabinetry.

'If I were a phone, where would I be?' he said under his breath.

He stood, briefly, to walk down the hallway to the bedroom at the trailer's tail end, then went down on his knees again.

That was when he heard the approach of a vehicle.

It was too soon for Kendra to be back with the coffee, and besides, this did not sound like the van, which was a well-tuned machine. Whatever was coming down the driveway sounded like the proverbial bucket of bolts. Rattles, squeaky springs, perforated muffler.

He crept to the closest window, went up on his knees, and peeked outside.

It was an old piece of American Motors shit. A Pacer. A young woman was driving, a middle-aged guy in the passenger seat.

'Fuck.'

He moved away from the window and considered his options.

The trailer had a so-called back door, but it was on the same side as the front door. He couldn't slip out without being seen.

He heard the car's two doors slam shut. Voices. The man and the woman were having a conversation as they got closer.

And then, from the front end of the trailer, the ringing of a cell phone. *Inside* the trailer. Terrific.

217

Now he knew where to look, but couldn't do a damn thing about it.

He had to hide.

Where did you hide in a mobile home? It wasn't like there was a basement to scurry down into. No attic to crawl up into.

He figured he could squeeze himself under the bed. He'd cleared the space out only hours earlier. He flattened himself on the floor and edged his way under.

But not before taking the Ruger out of his pocket and gripping it firmly in his right hand.

CHAPTER 24

Springfield, MA

Chloe, standing outside the trailer, phone in hand, said, 'That dumbass. No wonder I can't reach him. Left without taking his phone with him.'

'You said it never leaves his hand.'

She shrugged. 'I haven't known him *that* long. Maybe sometimes he has something *else* in his hand. You'd know a little something about that, wouldn't you, Mr Sperm Donor?'

Miles gave her a disappointed look. 'Is that any way to talk to your dad?'

She took a step toward the trailer. 'If he's left it unlocked, we can wait inside.'

'We can't just walk in.'

Chloe waved him off. 'He's family.'

She mounted the cinder block steps and tried the door. 'Here we go,' she said, pulling the door open. She stepped inside. Miles followed her.

Once inside, Chloe screwed up her face. 'Jesus, what's that smell?'

'Some kind of cleaner?' Miles said. 'Maybe bleach? Call his phone again and I'll try to track it down.'

Chloe dug out her cell one more time and a moment later they could hear a ring near the front end of the trailer. Miles walked over to a couch, looked down, and saw the edge of the phone tucked down in between two cushions.

'Must've slipped out of his pocket,' Miles said, picking up the phone and displaying it. 'Maybe he tried to find it, but had somewhere to go and had to give up looking. There's some texts here, and not just from you. There's a Madeline?'

'His mom.'

'Can't access them. Know his password?'

'No.'

Chloe had stepped into the kitchen area. 'What the . . .' She took her phone, still in hand, tapped the camera app, and set it to video. 'I'm getting a record of this shit. This is crazy. I mean, look at the place.'

'What? The place looks fine.'

'That's the point. The place is fucking spotless.'

'So Todd's a neat freak.'

'No, he *isn't*.'

She walked slowly over to the sink, looked down. 'I can see my reflection.'

Miles bent over, putting his nose to a countertop. 'I can smell the bleach here. Maybe Todd hired the world's best cleaning lady.'

'It's more than that,' she said, nodding toward the kitchen table. 'Where's his laptop? Where's his stuff? I'm telling you, the guy's like totally messy. And the thing is, I don't think he even *knows* he's messy. It'd never occur to him that he needed to spruce the place up or bring in a cleaning lady or anything.' She pondered a moment. 'Maybe his mom did it? She was here the other day, would have seen how messy it was. Except she was limping. Can't see her doing all this hobbling around on one foot.'

She struck off down the hallway, raising the phone to record her journey. As she headed toward the back of the trailer, Miles held back, in the kitchen, standing at the hallway's end. He felt like more of a stranger here than Chloe did – an interloper – and that he didn't have the right to start nosing around. But when she reached the end of the hall, she looked back at him and waved at him to join her.

She was starting into the bathroom when he came up alongside her.

'Whoa,' she said, stepping in for a closer inspection.

'What?'

'You could eat off this toilet,' she said. 'Not that I plan to.'

Miles followed her into the bathroom. Not large, but large enough for the toilet, small built-in cabinets with drawers and a sink, and a bathtub that doubled as a shower. Chloe, with her free hand,

221

opened the cupboard doors, then each of the drawers, all of which were completely empty and scrubbed clean.

'Do you believe this?' she asked.

'Did Todd rent this trailer?' Miles asked.

'What? Why?'

'If he decided to leave, to move on, his landlord could have had this place cleaned.'

Chloe shook her head. 'He told me he owned the trailer, had it brought in here, but he paid some guy to rent the land it's sittin' on. But the trailer, it's his.'

'Maybe he was going to sell it. To whoever owns the property.'

Chloe edged around him and went into the bedroom at the back of the trailer, continuing to film. Again, Miles followed. Chloe opened a set of folding doors that revealed a wide closet. Except for a few wire hangers, it was empty.

'This is like, nuts,' she said.

A built-in set of drawers that spanned the rear wall was her next target. She wanted both hands to open them more quickly, so she stopped recording and put her phone back into her pocket. Every drawer was empty.

'No way,' she said.

Miles, feeling weary, plopped down on the bare mattress.

'Nothing?' he said.

'Not so much as a sock with a hole in it.' Chloe sat down on the bed beside him, ran her hand across the surface of the mattress. 'There's not even any sheets here. What do you make of *that*?'

'Looks like he's cleared out.'

Chloe glared at him. 'You think?' She slowly shook her head. 'So, okay, let's say you're right, and he decides to take off. What's with how clean the place is? Why would he leave without telling me? None of this makes any sense.' Then she looked at him, sharply. 'Unless . . .'

'Unless what?'

She hesitated, as though weighing how much to tell Miles. 'I think Todd's into something he shouldn't be.'

'Like what?'

'Conning old people,' she said. 'I tried to ask him about it, but he just clammed up. Like, some kind of phone scam, where you call people in retirement homes and try to trick them into buying something or giving you their money. Something like that.'

'The computer virus scam.'

'The what?'

'Just one of many. You call someone up, say that you're from Microsoft or Apple and say you've detected a virus on their computer but you can send a fix. All they have to do is provide a credit card number or send some money to Western Union.'

'I can't believe people do that. Take advantage of oldsters. I'm gonna kick Todd's ass if I find out he's really pulling that kind of shit.'

'If you can find him.'

'Yeah, if I – did you hear that?'

'Hear what?'

'Shush,' she said, putting her index finger to her lips. 'I thought I heard something. Like, in the wall or the floor.'

'I didn't hear any—'

'Just *shut up* for a second.'

Miles shut up. For several seconds, neither of them breathed. Finally, Chloe exhaled.

'Maybe it was a mouse or something,' she said.

'Can I talk now?'

'Sure.'

'You mentioned Todd's mom?'

'Yeah.'

'You got a way to get in touch with her?'

'Right there,' she said, pointing to the cell in Miles's hand.

'Told you. It's password or thumbprint protected.'

'You're the tech guy. Can't you get into it?'

'I've got some people at the office who might be able to. But maybe we could just look her up online, find an address. Maybe she knows where he's gone.'

'I guess. I don't know why—'

She was interrupted by the sound of brakes squealing, tires ripping across pavement, like a driver in panic trying to avoid a crash.

'What the hell was that?' Miles said.

'Up on the road,' she said.

Charise, so far as they still knew, remained parked at the end of the driveway.

'Let's go, Chloe,' Miles said, springing to his feet, leaving Todd's phone on the mattress. They went out the back door, steps from the bedroom. Once on the ground, they both ran past the Pacer for the main road, but Chloe instantly had the lead. Miles felt resistance in his legs, like they didn't want to do what was being asked of them.

But he soon caught up to her at the roadside, where he found Charise and Chloe helping a woman out of a van that had veered off partway into the ditch about twenty yards behind the parked limo.

'I nearly hit it!' the woman screamed, sliding out from behind the wheel.

'Are you okay, ma'am?' Charise asked her as she went around to the front of the van, leaving the driver's door open, to see how far she was into the ditch.

'Nearly hit what?' Chloe asked.

'You didn't see it?' the woman said. 'A goddamn deer!'

'A deer?' Miles said, catching his breath.

'Thing came out of nowhere!' the woman said. 'Came shooting across the road, went running into the woods there!' She pointed. 'I came this close to hitting the son of a bitch!' She held up a hand, spacing her thumb and index finger an inch apart. She looked at Charise. 'You must have seen it.'

Charise shook her head. 'Was looking in the rearview when I heard you hit the brakes. You

225

nearly plowed into the back of me. Nice maneu-
vering. Are you sure you're okay?'

'I'm fine,' she said.

The woman looked down and noticed, seemingly
for the first time, that the front of her blouse and
pants were wet. 'Yikes, that smarts,' she said, as
two empty paper cups rolled out of the open van
door, dropped onto the shoulder, and were swept
under the vehicle by the wind. 'That coffee was
fuckin' hot when it hit me and now it's gettin'
cold.'

She ran her hands across the front of her clothes,
as if she could somehow brush the spilled coffee
away.

'Where you headed?' Miles asked.

The woman eyed him for the first time, blinked,
and said, 'Driving to Rochester to see my sister.'

'You've still got your back wheels on the gravel
there,' Charise said. 'I'm betting, you take it slow,
you can back out without needing a tow.'

'Let's give it a whirl,' she said, getting back into
the van. She put it in reverse, feathered the gas
so as not to send the back wheels into a spin, and
slowly pulled the van back onto level ground.

'Nicely done,' Charise said.

Through the open driver's window, the woman
said, 'Sorry for all the commotion. You see that
deer, give it a piece of my mind.'

She steered the van back on the pavement and
drove off. Charise kept watching it until it
disappeared.

'Huh,' Charise said.

'What?' Miles said.

'Nothing, sir.' She paused. 'Will you be wanting a drive back soon, Mr Cookson?'

'Not sure,' he said, and glanced at Chloe.

She shrugged. 'I guess you might as well. I can try to get in touch with Todd's mom, let you know what I find out.'

'Let me go back and get his phone,' Miles said. 'Might have someone who could break into it.'

He and Chloe walked back down the driveway and mounted the cinder block steps to the front door again. Together, they walked to the bedroom at the back of the mobile home.

Miles stared at the bare mattress.

'Where is it?' he said.

'The phone?' Chloe said.

'I left it right there.'

'Maybe it slid off. We kind of took off in a hurry. It could've fallen onto the floor.'

Chloe dropped to her knees and looked under the bed.

'Nothing here,' she said, and got to her feet again. 'You sure you didn't have it in your hand?'

He shook his head adamantly. 'No, I mean yes, I'm sure. Hang on.' He patted his pockets, wondering whether he'd slipped the phone into one of them without thinking. But he came up with nothing. 'No, I left it on the bed. I'm certain.'

Chloe said, 'Maybe you had it in your hand and dropped it when we ran to the road.'

'No,' he said with certainty. 'No. *I left it right here.*'

'Well,' Chloe said, 'it didn't sprout legs and walk out of here on its own, unless you've designed an app which does *that.*'

Miles felt a sense of uneasiness wash over him. 'Maybe it was your mouse,' he said.

Chloe eyed him skeptically, shook her head. 'It has to be *somewhere.*'

She got down on her knees again to take a second look under the bed. 'I'm telling you, it's not here.'

Miles's own cell phone rang. He took it from his pocket, looked at the screen.

'It's Charise,' he said. 'Yes, Charise?'

'Mr Cookson, something doesn't feel right. It's probably nothing. But you know, I never saw any deer.'

'Okay.'

'That woman. Said she was driving to Rochester to see her sister.'

'Yeah, I remember.'

'She's got a few hours ahead of her. Kind of early to be picking up a coffee for her.'

Miles shook his head, not understanding. 'What's that, Charise?'

Charise said, 'Why'd she have *two* cups of coffee? I mean, sure, you're on a long trip and want to be well supplied, but it's not like she can pull over to the side of the road and step into the bushes, if you get my meaning.'

CHAPTER 25

East Seventieth Street, Manhattan

There was a knock on the door of Nicky's room.

She was sitting cross-legged on her bed, in her pajamas, mindlessly playing *Angry Birds* on an iPad, not able to do much else with it but play games as the Wi-Fi was disabled in this part of the house. It was like the room was cocooned with lead or something. There was a window, but it was a small one, two feet square, and all it did was look out to the alley. About five feet away, a wall of brick.

Her phone had been taken from her, so she'd been unable to text with anyone since she'd been put in here nearly a week ago. No phone calls, either, and she couldn't send or receive emails. It was weird, not having any communication with anyone from the outside world.

She couldn't even use having to go to the bathroom as an excuse to be let out once in a while. This guest suite had its own bathroom – and what a bathroom it was, too. Everything marble. A huge

229

whirlpool tub and a walk-in shower. One of those things next to the toilet that shot water up your ass. And they were bringing meals to her three times a day. One thing you had to say about this place: the food was fantastic. Jeremy Pritkin had some pretty talented people working in the basement kitchen. The head chef had supposedly been lured away from a Four Seasons somewhere. And the room itself was better than decent. A huge king bed, thick-pile rug that felt wonderful on bare toes, a flat-screen that got about two hundred channels. If you had to be under house arrest, this was the house to be in.

When the knock came, she didn't bother to get up and go to the door. She couldn't open it from the inside. So she shouted, 'Come in!'

She heard a deadbolt turn, and then the door swung wide open. It was Roberta Bennington, Jeremy's assistant. Pretty hot looking, Nicky thought, for someone pushing fifty. Black hair, lots of curves, and nearly six feet tall with her four-inch heels. She'd apparently been with Jeremy for fifteen years, and was the first person Chloe met when she was drawn into this place by her Brooklyn friend's acquaintance.

Roberta had made hanging out at Jeremy's place sound like the opportunity of a lifetime. Nicky, Roberta said, would be part of 'the Pritkin Experience.' She would make real money mingling with movie stars, movers and shakers, important people from all walks of life, and the most important person of all, of course: Jeremy. Nicky would be part of a team of young girls who'd help make a visit to the brownstone one that no one would ever forget. Think of the advantages! The things she would learn! These people could advance their careers, get them into the best schools, find them placements at some of the richest firms in the country.

Hadn't quite worked out that way so far for Nicky.

Oh, Nicky had made some good money, no question about it. And it had come at the right time, when she had hardly any at all. It wasn't like her mom and her new boyfriend were transferring anything to her account. But as for all the things she would learn, probably the most important one around here was, especially where Jeremy Pritkin was concerned, the only good massage was one with a happy ending.

'How are we doing today?' Roberta asked.

Not far beyond her, a short way down the hall at the second-floor landing, stood one of Jeremy's security detail. Heavyset, well dressed, the guy looked like a refrigerator in a suit and tie. Nicky knew he was there in case she decided to make a run for it when the door opened. She knew because she had tried it once. The guy grabbed her, carried her back to her room, and tossed her inside like she was a misbehaving puppy.

Roberta was carrying a small tray.

'Look what we have here,' she said. 'Just about

the best lunch ever. We hosted a little dinner last night for the Peruvian ambassador, and there was some beef Wellington left over. And a piece of chocolate almond cake that is to die for.'

Roberta set the tray down on the desk in the corner. Then she pulled out a chair, inviting Nicky to leave the bed and take a seat.

'I'm not hungry right now,' she said.

'I see,' Roberta said, unable to hide the hurt in her voice. 'Antoine went to a lot of trouble to make this for you.'

'I'll eat it in a bit,' she said.

Roberta painted on a smile and took a seat in a plush, leather chair that faced the bed. 'You didn't answer my question.'

'What question?'

'How are we doing today?'

'I want to leave,' Nicky said flatly. 'I want to go to school.'

'Well, of course you do,' Roberta said, almost cheerfully.

'How long is my punishment going to be? I mean, I've heard of someone being sent to their room, but this is getting kind of ridiculous.'

'I totally understand that. I promise you, I'm going to speak to Mr Pritkin about it. I guess a lot of it will depend on whether he feels you've learned your lesson.'

'I have, I really have.'

'That's good. That's good to hear.'

'Is he still mad at me?'

'Oh, Nicky, I wouldn't say he's mad at you. Unhappy, yes. Disappointed, for sure. But not mad.'

'I haven't seen him since it happened.'

'He's very busy. Did you see him last night on CNN?'

'I was watching something else, I guess,' Nicky said.

'He was talking to Chris Cuomo about the federal infrastructure plans. Jeremy knows a lot about that kind of thing. Not enough is being done.'

'If you say so. Listen, if I could talk to him for a minute, tell him again I didn't hear anything, then maybe you could let me go?'

'I'll certainly deliver that message. But surely you understand, hiding in his office, spying on him, so soon after you were thinking about talking to . . . others . . . about our life here inside this building—'

'I wasn't spying.'

'It certainly looked that way, Nicky. And appearances mean everything. Mr Pritkin is a great and powerful man, and he doesn't take kindly to efforts to undermine him.'

'Honest, I didn't mean anything by it.' Her shoulders sank. 'Are you still texting the school and my friends, pretending to be me?'

'They all send their best wishes. Everyone wants to let you rest. That's what they suggest for mono. They all know it can take several weeks to recover from that. So they're not alarmed by your absence. I've spoken directly with the school administrators. Everything's under control. Meanwhile, we're trying to make things as pleasant for you as we can.'

'This is kidnapping,' Nicky said.

'Don't be ridiculous. You're a sick girl. We're looking after you.'

Nicky felt tears coming, but she fought them. She would not cry in front of this woman.

Roberta stood, headed for the door. 'I'll send someone back for the tray later,' she said. 'You really must try it. It'd be a shame to waste it. Would you mind if I told Antoine that you loved it? Because he's going to ask.'

'Sure,' Nicky said. 'The last thing I would want to do is hurt anyone's feelings.'

Roberta smiled broadly. 'That's the spirit.' She went to the door and rapped on it twice, quickly. Seconds later, it was opened by the security guy. Roberta was halfway into the hall when Nicky called out to her.

'Roberta.'

Roberta stopped. 'Yes, child?'

'What's the plan? I mean, you can't keep me a prisoner here forever.'

'No,' said Roberta. 'No, I don't suppose we can.'

CHAPTER 26

Paris, France

It took Bonnie Trumble a while to figure out where she should go to report a missing person.

She was living in the Third Arrondissement, in the Marais district, around the corner from the Picasso museum. She and her bestie had found a place through Airbnb, had been saving their money for three years so they could come over here for a couple of months. Growing up in Lackawanna, just outside Buffalo, it was hard to imagine a place more exotic than Paris, although, when you lived in Lackawanna, the bar was not set all that high. All the way back to the ninth grade, shortly after they had become fast friends in their first year of high school, they had talked about going to the City of Lights someday.

When they finished high school, instead of going straight to college – their parents' choice for them, of course – they decided this was their chance. They would rent a place, right in Paris, and spend two months there. Soak it up, live like the locals.

And when the two months were over, they would go back to their boring Lackawanna lives.

And it had been going great. They did all the touristy things the first week they were here. The Eiffel Tower, the Louvre, Notre Dame Cathedral, although at that last one all they could do was walk around it, what with the fire and all a couple of years ago. Once they had the sightseeing stuff out of their system, they settled into more of a routine. Making meals at home – they were going to wipe out their savings pretty fast eating in the cafés every day – and going out to shop every day to get what they needed. Oh, man, the bread! Who could have guessed something as simple as bread could be that good? And you had to shop every day, because everything over here was smaller. The cupboards were small. You put a couple of containers of yogurt in the fridge and it was full. You didn't exactly take out the car and go to Costco and bring home a six-gallon jug of olives.

Things were going so well.

And then her friend Katie disappeared.

While they were best friends, there were days when they wanted to do their own thing. On this particular Wednesday, Bonnie wanted to spend the day wandering the Pompidou Centre. She was into modern art, stuff that was more offbeat, but Katie had had enough of museums. 'Knock yourself out,' she told Bonnie. 'I'm gonna take my book and go someplace and get a latte and take three hours to drink it. I'll find us something for dinner and get it ready for when you get back.'

When Bonnie returned shortly before six, Katie was not there.

That was not necessarily alarming. Katie could have decided to leave her shopping duties until late afternoon. Then it got to be seven, and then eight, and with each passing hour Bonnie's anxiety level increased exponentially.

But it was more than Katie being missing.

She had discovered something very weird about the apartment. Something so weird she felt she needed to talk to the police about it tonight. Not tomorrow morning. Right fucking now.

It had never occurred to Bonnie that she might need to get in touch with the police while she was in Paris. What were they even called? Gendarmes? Policier? Where was the station? And if she could find one, would she be able to find a police officer who knew English really well? Because, let's face it, her French was pretty basic.

It turned out that every arrondissement had its own police headquarters, so Bonnie was going to have to find the one for the third. The building where she and Katie were living had two other rental units. She banged on the door of the first one, found no one home, but got lucky with the second, which was occupied by an elderly couple from Toronto who took the place for half the year. They were fluent in French, and offered to go with Bonnie to the police station in case she had any trouble communicating with the authorities.

Once the Canadian couple had paved the way for her, a police officer in his fifties, named Henri and dressed plainly in jeans, a white dress shirt, and a sports jacket, offered to sit down with Bonnie and hear her story. She wondered, given that he was not wearing a traditional uniform, whether he was some kind of detective, but whatever. She wanted someone who would listen, and fortunately, he spoke English.

Henri: What is your friend's name?
Bonnie: Katie Gleave. Um, Katie Frances Gleave. We're both from Lackawanna, New York. It's near Buffalo? We're both nineteen.
Henri: And what brings you to Paris?
Bonnie: We wanted to experience it, you know? Living here?
Henri: Of course.
Bonnie: She's gone.
Henri: Tell me when this happened.
Bonnie: I went to the Pompidou for the day. Katie just wanted to hang out. She was going to get something for our dinner. But she wasn't there when I got home and she hasn't come back.
Henri: She has not been gone very long. Not even overnight. Did you try calling her?
Bonnie: I texted her, phoned her. Nothing.
Henri: Perhaps . . . she has found a boyfriend?

Bonnie: No, no way. That's not what happened. And even if it did, she would let me know. She wouldn't make me worry like this. But there's more.

Henri: Okay.

Bonnie: Her stuff is all gone.

Henri: Her stuff?

Bonnie: Her clothes.

Henri: Ah, I see. Maybe she has decided to go home, to go back to America. Maybe things were not working out between the two of you?

Bonnie: And the sheets from her bed.

Henri: The sheets?

Bonnie: Why would she take the sheets off her bed? What sense does that make? They weren't hers. They belong to the people who own the apartment.

Henri: That is strange.

Bonnie: And everything in the bathroom. Not just her stuff. All of mine, too. I mean, if she was going to take off, which I don't think she did, I could see her taking her own toothbrush, but why would she take mine?

Henri: That . . . is curious.

Bonnie: But here's the weirdest thing of all. The place has been cleaned.

Henri: Cleaned?

Bonnie: It's like, cleaner than the first day we got the place. Everything's sparkling. I mean, we're not pigs, okay, but we're not the tidiest people in the world, either. We'd kind of let things go for a while. I was thinking, later this week, I'd clean the bathroom and maybe run through the place with the Dyson, but now the place isn't just clean, it's been disinfected.

Henri: Disinfected?

Bonnie: Bleach. The place reeks of bleach.

CHAPTER 27

Springfield, MA

The Pacer, with Chloe at the wheel and Miles sitting beside her, stopped at the end of the driveway. Charise was out of the limo and leaning up against the door, arms crossed, but when Miles got out of Chloe's car, she straightened up.

'Mr Cookson?'

Miles said, 'Todd – Chloe's half brother – wasn't here. We're going to try and find Todd's mom. Chloe found an address for her online.'

'I'll stay on your tail. When you need me, I'll be there.'

'That's great.'

'Mr Cookson?'

'Yes?'

'I hope I wasn't overreacting about the coffee thing.'

'Not at all.'

'It didn't feel right. But maybe it's nothing.'

'I always say, go with your instincts. Charise, I'm guessing you haven't always been a driver for hire.'

241

'No, sir. I've done a few other things. A 911 operator, a cook, wrestler.'

'I'm sorry, wrestler?'

Charise smiled. 'In my younger days. Big shows, the fights all choreographed. Wore a costume. I was "the Ebony Nightmare." Did that for three years. I suppose that's where I learned to spot fakers. We were all fakers, back in the day.'

Miles smiled with admiration, and no small measure of astonishment. 'I won't cross you. Don't want to be tossed across the hood of your car.'

Charise smiled. 'I wouldn't do that to you, sir. But I could.'

Miles returned to the Pacer. It took him three tries to get the passenger door to close all the way and latch.

'Let's go meet the mother of my son,' he said grimly.

'You don't sound too happy about it,' Chloe said. 'Is that how you're going to be when you meet *my* mom?'

'I'm sorry,' he said. 'I'm a little on edge. Meeting the mothers first wasn't part of my game plan. And from what you've said, your mom won't be thrilled to meet *me*.'

'Yeah, but I'd give a lot to see the look on her face when I introduce you.'

She glanced over, expecting some reaction from Miles. But he was just sitting there, looking straight ahead. Sullen.

'Hey,' she said. 'What's going on?'

'Nothing.'

'Come on, *Pops*. What's wrong? The missing phone freaking you out?'

'Yeah. That's part of it.'

'But it's something else?'

He looked plaintively at her. 'What I have, this disease . . .'

'Yeah, you told me. ALS. So?'

'I'd like you to take a test.'

'What kind of test?'

'A genetic test.'

'Like DNA?'

'Sort of. I'd pay for it. And any subsequent medical expenses.'

'So this *isn't* about who I am? Because you got the information from the clinic, right? That says you're my biological father? So this is a different test?'

'Yes.' Miles was silent for several seconds. 'I was going to get to this later, but it goes to the heart of why I wanted to find you. And Todd. And the others.'

She waited.

'I've told you I have . . . a disease. I'm going to get a lot worse. The good news, if there's any, is that I have the money I'll need for special care when I'm less able to look after my needs. And it's going to cost a lot.'

'Okay,' Chloe said slowly.

He turned in his seat to look at her more directly. 'There is a chance, only a chance, not a certainty—'

and at this point he winced inwardly because the likelihood of her developing Huntington's was much greater than just a chance '—that what I have might not just be the ALS, that it could be more serious than that. And, maybe, at some point in your life, you might get this disease, too.'

'Are you kidding me?' She adopted a sarcastic tone. '"Hey, guess what, not *only* am I your dad, but by the way, you might die!"'

'It's not as bad as that. I just – fuck, maybe this has all been a mistake.' He turned back straight into his seat, looked out his window. 'The test would show whether you'd develop the disease.'

'So, I could take it, find out I'm *not* going to get it, but then they'll find out I'm going to get something totally different,' she said.

'I hadn't thought of that. But yes, I suppose that's true.'

'We're all going to get *something*,' she said. 'It's not like any of us are going to live forever. So what's the point?'

'The point is . . . I have money.'

'So?'

'A lot of it. I don't have any children from, you know, a marriage. No children that I've raised myself.'

'You never got married?'

'No.'

'Never lived with a woman?'

'No.'

'You gay?'

'No.'

'But, like, you've done it with something *other* than a cup.'

'Yes,' he said. 'I've had relationships over the years, but none that led to anything.'

'Why's that?'

'We're getting a little off topic here.'

'Yeah, well, forgive me for not wanting to talk about my getting a fatal disease. How come you never hooked up permanently with someone?'

'Maybe because I'm kind of an asshole,' he said.

'Really?'

'I like how you sound surprised.'

'That wasn't meant to be sarcastic.'

'I was always more interested *in* work than *making* it work with anyone in particular.'

'Lots of women would put up with that. Especially if you're loaded.'

'I wasn't loaded at the time. That came later.'

'So then, why not find someone *later*?'

'You ask a lot of questions.'

She sighed, rolled her eyes, focused on the road again. 'Gee, why would that be? You show up a few hours ago, tell me you're my dad, tell me I should get this test to find out if maybe, just maybe, I have some fatal disease, and you think it's weird that I have questions.'

Miles said nothing.

'Huh?' she said. 'Well?'

'The thing is, if, and it's just an *if*, but if it turns

245

out you do, someday, have this . . . condition . . . you'll be able to afford whatever kind of care you need.'

Chloe's face turned serious. 'What do you mean?'

'This is one of the reasons why I'm looking for you and . . . the others. My plan is to divide what I have between all of you.'

'You're leaving me money?'

'Yes.'

'What if I don't get sick? Do I have to give it back?'

'No.'

'How much money we talking here?'

'A lot.'

She set her jaw firmly, thinking. A moment later, she said, 'I don't need your money.'

'Excuse me?'

'I don't need your money. I don't *want* your money.'

'It'll change your life,' Miles said.

'For better? Or maybe for worse.'

'Better.'

'You've got shitloads of money. Are you happy?'

'Of course I'm not happy. I'm dying.'

'How about before? Before you found out you were dying. Were you happy then?'

The question caught Miles off guard. 'I don't know that I ever thought about that.'

'It's a simple question. Were you happy before your diagnosis? Yes or no?'

'I guess . . . no.'

'Well, there you go. You can take your money and shove it.' She paused, and then added, '*Dad*.'

Miles started to grin. It broadened, and then he started to laugh.

'You're something else,' he said.

'You bet your ass I am,' Chloe shot back.

Chloe brought the Pacer to a brake-squealing halt in front of a modest two-story brick house. A Volkswagen Golf was parked in the driveway.

'That's her car,' she said.

She killed the engine, which uttered a few death rattles even after she had the key in her hand. 'I gotta get that looked at,' she said as she opened her door. Charise, in the limo, pulled up behind them and sat, awaiting further instructions.

Madeline was opening the front door before they'd reached it. She stepped out, tentatively at first, but when she saw Chloe her face brightened and she limped toward her, arms outstretched.

'Oh my God, it's you!' she said, giving Chloe a hug. Chloe responded with a less enthusiastic return.

'Where's Todd?' Madeline asked, once she'd separated herself from Chloe. 'Is he with you?'

'No,' Chloe said.

'I was going to drive out there. I've been trying him all day.'

'When'd you last talk to him?' Miles asked.

Madeline Cox turned her head. 'Who are you?'

Chloe said, 'This is Miles Cookson. He's—'

247

Miles shot Chloe a stern *not yet* stare.

'—he's a friend,' she said.

Miles extended a hand, which Madeline took with some hesitation. Her eyes narrowed as she took him in. 'Do I know you?' she asked.

'No ma'am,' he said.

'Because you look a little familiar to me, like maybe we've met before.'

And that was when Chloe, figuring that Madeline must have seen something of Todd in Miles, studied his face in a way she hadn't before. She quipped, 'I don't see it.'

'Excuse me?' Madeline said.

Chloe realized she had been thinking out loud and said, 'Nothing. Listen, we were hoping to find Todd here, but—'

'You've been to his place?'

Chloe nodded worriedly. Miles, thinking back to how the trailer had been stripped of anything personal, asked, 'How long has it been since Todd lived here, Ms Cox?'

'Almost a year,' she said dispiritedly. 'He had it pretty good here, getting waited on hand and foot, but he wanted to be out on his own.' She turned to Chloe and dropped her voice to a whisper. 'Did you talk to him? About what he was up to?'

'I haven't really had that much of chance,' she said.

Now Madeline turned back to Miles. 'Did she tell you how she and Todd found each other? It's quite a story.'

248

Miles nodded. 'I've heard some of it.'

'Where do you think he got off to?' Todd's mother asked. 'It's not like he hasn't disappeared before for a day or two, but I could always get hold of him.'

'Can you think of any place he might have gone?' Chloe asked. 'Someplace he's always wanted to go?'

She thought a moment. 'Africa. He's always wanted to see giraffes and stuff.'

Miles shook his head. No one stripped their bed clean and bleached the kitchen before going to Africa.

'Well, if you're talking to him, or hear from him, would you have him get in touch with me?' Chloe asked.

Madeline nodded. 'You all want to come in or anything?'

Chloe caught Miles's eye, as if looking for a signal. His look said *not now*. Madeline noticed the shiny black vehicle parked behind the Pacer. 'Whose limo is that?'

'She's with me,' Miles said. 'Chloe, a minute?'

He led her back to the Pacer, and they got in. Chloe had her phone out, as if hoping Todd would get in touch, even though they knew he'd left his phone behind. She tapped, absently, on the camera app and started up some video she'd shot at Todd's trailer.

'That's kind of distracting,' Miles said.

'I want to get a shot of Todd's house. For my

doc. But I just wanted to look at this again.' Miles could hear his own voice and Chloe's coming out of the phone. It was the video she'd shot when they were in the trailer. She muted it. 'So what did you want to talk about in secret?'

'Something's off about all of this,' he said.

'Yeah, I kinda was coming to that conclusion, too,' she said, glancing occasionally at the video.

'It might be time to bring in the police, report Todd missing,' he said. 'But I didn't want to mention that in front of his mom. She doesn't know yet about how his place was cleared out. I can't figure out why he'd do that.'

Chloe, still looking at her phone, said, 'Neither can – *SHIT!*'

She screamed so loud Miles felt his heart skip a beat.

'*Holy fucking shit!*' she said, staring at the screen.

'What?'

'Look!'

She turned the phone in his direction so he could get a good look at it. 'This is from the trailer.'

'Yeah, I know.'

'Fucking look at this.'

It was video Chloe took, walking down the hall, stopping at the bathroom, and finally, going into Todd's bedroom.

'You see it?' she asked.

'See what?'

'Christ,' she said, using her finger to move the video back a few seconds. When it reached the part where she was entering the bedroom, she paused it, freezing the image.

'Now do you see it?'

'What am I looking at?'

'Right here,' she said, and pointed to the gap between the bed and the floor.

Miles squinted. When he saw it, his eyes went wide.

'Oh my God,' he said, his voice barely above a whisper.

It was a hand.

CHAPTER 28

San Francisco, CA

Cheryl Howson, president and CEO of WhatsMyStory, author of the number one best seller *Finding My Own Story* – six weeks in the top spot on the *New York Times* nonfiction list – strolled into the office of her fashionable Mission District home before heading down to breakfast.

She could smell bacon.

Cheryl was strictly vegan, and breakfast for her was usually fruit and fiber, sometimes all-in-one in a smoothie, but her husband, Clifton, home this week from traveling around the world making business deals, was not, and neither was their seven-year-old daughter, Tina. So when Daddy finally had time at home, it was bacon at breakfast, burgers at lunch, and probably a T-bone for dinner. And what with Pauline, their full-time cook and housekeeper, taking a couple of days off, there was no stopping him.

Cheryl took a seat in her office and shook the mouse. The screen lit up, and she saw that she had more than a dozen emails, far too many to deal with before having her first coffee of the day. Most of them were from her assistant, who ran interference for Cheryl so she could actually do the job of running the company. But there was a request from the *Wall Street Journal* for a profile, a proposal from a competing firm that they share data, and some reports from her legal team about law enforcement requests to use DNA data from WhatsMyStory's files to compare against DNA recovered from crime scenes across the country.

God, the headaches. You started an enterprise with one simple idea – *find out who you are* – and before you knew it you were buried under a mountain of shit. Moral and ethical issues and lawsuits coming out your ass. Look at Zuckerberg. Started off with a site that would rate college girls as 'hot or not' and now he was accused of undermining democracy on a global scale. Which he was, of course, but that was his cross to bear, not hers.

She padded downstairs in her slippers, still wearing her silk pajamas and a robe, her cell tucked into the pocket. She entered the kitchen, saw Clifton blotting the grease from the rashers of bacon, and outside, on the deck, Tina watering the flowers with a small plastic watering can.

'Good morning, Tina baby!' Cheryl said through the open door. Tina waved and went back to watering.

There was a beelike buzzing noise outside.

'What is that?' Cheryl asked.

253

'Someone's playing with another one of those damn drones,' her husband said.

Cheryl looked at the bacon and inhaled. 'God, that smell.'

Clifton waved a slice of bacon in the air. 'You know you want it.'

She snatched the bacon from his fingers, folded it over once, and shoved it into her mouth. 'Oh, sweet Jesus,' she said. 'I feel like a criminal.'

'Pancakes?' Clifton asked.

'Seriously?'

'She asked and I'm delivering.'

Cheryl raised a hand, crooked her index finger, as if holding an invisible mug, and said, 'What's missing in this picture?'

Clifton grabbed a special mug with a picture of her book emblazoned on the side, filled it with black coffee, and handed it to her. Cheryl took a sip.

The outdoor buzzing persisted.

'Remind me when you fly out again?'

'Tomorrow night. Dubai.'

She sighed as she settled onto a stool at the island. 'Maybe I'll come with you. I could take up residence in the mall.'

He grinned. 'You could use the break.'

'Let me think about it.'

'Don't think long. We'll need to get you a ticket.'

'I know, I know. There's a few things I'd have to – oh shit.'

There was the ping of an incoming text. She

reached into the pocket of her robe, pulled out her phone, thumbed the Home button. 'Must be . . . what the . . .'

She suddenly looked up, then to the outside, and screamed: 'Get Tina!'

Clifton said, 'What?'

Cheryl pointed. 'Get her! Get her inside!'

'What the hell—'

Do it!

Clifton ran from the house, scooped his arm around their daughter, lifting her into the air so quickly that her watering can went flying, landing in a grouping of flowers, snapping stems.

'Daddy! Stop—'

He practically threw her into the kitchen. As he let go of her she stumbled.

'The door!' Cheryl said.

Clifton slid the glass door into place and locked it without having to be told.

'You hurt my knee!' Tina said to her father.

'I'm sorry, sweetheart, I'm sorry. Your mom – your mom thought—' At which point he looked at his wife, hoping she would offer a reason for what had just happened.

'Go upstairs, Tina,' she said.

Tina was on her feet now. 'I didn't do anything wrong! Daddy made me spill—'

'Go to your room!' her mother screamed.

Tina looked ready to burst into tears as she ran from the kitchen and thumped her way up the stairs.

Clifton glared at his wife. 'What the fuck is wrong with—'

She extended her arm, holding the phone so he could see. A few seconds of video was playing on the screen.

Of their house. Shot from above.

The focus was on Tina, playing in their backyard, moments earlier.

Clifton took the phone from his wife's hand. 'What the hell?'

He slid open the kitchen door again, took one step out, looked into the sky for the drone. But the buzzing had become distant. Whatever had been up there was gone.

When he stepped back inside, he looked at the phone.

'What's this number? Who is this from?'

'I don't know,' Cheryl whispered. 'Read below the video.'

Clifton slid the picture up and saw a block of text, all caps. It read:

YOU WILL RECEIVE A LIST OF NAMES. YOU WILL SEARCH THE WHATS-MYSTORY DATABASE FOR THEM. IF YOU FIND ANY OF THEM YOU WILL PERMANENTLY DELETE THEM AS WELL AS ANY DNA SAMPLES FROM THESE INDIVIDUALS. DO NOT TELL ANYONE. YOUR DAUGHTER IS VERY CUTE.

Clifton looked up.

'What the hell?' he asked.

Cheryl, her hands shaking, shook her head.

'We have to call the police,' he said, reaching for his own cell that was on the counter, next to the sink. 'We've got to—'

Cheryl's phone dinged again. Clifton's eyes went down to it.

THAT WOULD BE A BAD IDEA.

His face paled. He handed the phone back to Cheryl. When she saw the words, a tiny squeak came from her throat. They scanned the kitchen, as if they might be able to spot whatever device was picking up their conversation.

'We can't call the police,' she said, her voice down to a whisper. 'They got my private number. They're listening to us. They're *watching*.'

For several seconds, neither of them spoke. Clifton broke the silence, leaning in close, his voice barely audible.

'What do you think it's about? Who are these people they want deleted? Why would they want that? *Who* wants it?'

'How the fuck would I know?' she snapped.

'Hey, it's not *my* company this is about. *I* didn't get the text.'

She gave him a hateful stare. 'You're blaming me?'

'No, no, fuck.' He put his hands on her shoulders

257

and brought her in close to him. He put his mouth to her ear and whispered, 'What are we going to do?'

Cheryl broke free of him, picked up her phone, and hit the button to reply. She typed four words:

SEND ME THE NAMES

And hit Send.

CHAPTER 29

Fort Wayne, IN

Travis Roben visited Super Duper Comics pretty much every week, usually on his day off from restocking shelves at Walmart, but he didn't spend much time in the superhero section. He didn't care about any of that Avengers Marvel shit or Spider-Man or any of the Justice League crowd. He had no time for Superman, Batman, Green Lantern, Wonder Woman (okay, maybe Wonder Woman, who was pretty fucking hot), or Flash. That stuff bored him.

He preferred offbeat graphic novels, ones where the main characters hadn't been bitten by radioactive spiders or blasted by gamma rays or were sent to Earth to escape a planet that was about to blow up.

Travis liked stories about real people dealing with real situations. Like that epic *Clyde Fans*, by that Canadian graphic novelist Seth. Good old-fashioned noir stories, like the Nick Travers books by writer Ace Atkins and artist Marco Finnegan, or *Louise Brooks: Detective* by Rick Geary. There was that really amazing memoir, from a decade ago – which he definitely had not read at the time, when he was ten years old – about using the services of prostitutes. *Paying for It*, it was called, by Chester Brown. Amazing. That one hit home for Travis. While he'd never been to a hooker, he had to admit the idea had crossed his mind. To be twenty and never have had sex, and to have no *likelihood* of having sex, well, you wanted to at least fantasize about your options, even if you knew you'd never go that route.

Sure, he'd kissed two girls over the years. One was his cousin, and that was at her mother's funeral. You can't expect a lot of tongue in a situation like that. The other was when he was nine, and some bullies had pushed him and Wendy Bettelheim together behind the school and threatened them with a beating if they didn't pucker up and kiss each other on the lips. They had never spoken of it again.

Travis knew he was a bit different. It was more than just a nerdy interest in comic books. Lots of guys were interested in comic books and still got some action. But Travis was on the shy side, had few friends, and liked to spend most of his free time – at his parents' home; he hadn't quite made the leap yet – working on a graphic novel of his own.

The glasses didn't help much, either. God, talk about going full nerd cliché. He'd asked his mom to at least get him some cooler glasses, ones that didn't have big heavy frames that made him look like his name should be Poindexter or something. She'd said his glasses were just fine. He could see, couldn't he? And if he wasn't happy with his glasses, she'd told him, he could take some of his Walmart money and buy some on his own, if he had any left after his latest trip to Super Duper Comics.

Yeah, well, she had a point there, he supposed.

When he wasn't reading his latest purchases, or working on his own graphic novel, which just happened to be about a lonely guy who still lived at home and felt belittled by his parents ('Write what you know!' all the books told him), or maybe jerking off to some online porn, he was finding out about this 'incel' movement, which was pretty fucked up, but still, kind of interesting.

There were all these posts from guys who described themselves as being 'involuntary celibates,' which meant that they wanted to get laid, but no women were willing to go to bed with them. Okay, so on first reading, it sounded like these guys were simply a bunch of losers, but the more Travis read about them, the better he could see their point. Suppose you did everything you could to be nice to some woman? Brought her flowers, complimented her on her appearance, asked her out for a drink. And no matter what you did, she kept saying no, she didn't want to go out with you? Whose fault was it then? Certainly not yours. *You* were making the effort. If this was the kind of reaction you were getting from every woman, you had to ask yourself one question: What the hell was wrong with these women?

It made you think.

But some of these incel guys had taken it too far. Like, getting violent. Attacking women. Running down strangers with a car. That was wrong. Guys like that, they were spoiling it for the rest of the movement, giving it a bad name. Kind of like when—

'Excuse me, do you work here?'

Travis turned.

Holy shit.

It was a girl. Standing right next to him. Okay, not a girl. This was a young woman, probably his age, a year older or younger maybe. And she was a good-looking young woman, blond hair down to her shoulders, slim, jeans with ragged little holes around the knee. She smelled nice, too. He had no idea what the smell was – something flowery, *duh* – but he liked it. He was taken aback for several reasons. One, she was an actual female in the comic shop. Okay, you didn't want to make a sexist generalization, but the fact was, the ratio of males to females in this shop was about ten to one. Sure, you saw a few. Often, they came in with their boyfriends. And once in a while, there'd be a girl in here who was generally interested. Like, say, an art student whose interest was more curriculum related.

'Well, do you?' she asked.

Travis realized that since she had first asked him if he worked here, he had done nothing but stare at her.

He blinked, cleared his throat, and said, 'No, no, I don't.'

'Oh,' she said, looking disappointed. 'I didn't see anyone on the cash register, so I thought maybe you were in charge.'

Travis, his stomach fluttering, glanced over at the counter by the front door. 'Oh yeah. I guess Danny ran out to get a sandwich or something. He should be back in a second.'

'Okay,' she said, turned away briefly, then turned back. 'Maybe you can help me anyway.'

Travis's mouth suddenly felt very dry. 'Um, okay.'

'I don't really know all that much about comics and stuff, but I wanted to get something for my nephew, who's going to be twelve next week and I wanted to get him something for his birthday.'

'Okay.'

'I know he likes Batman, so I was thinking maybe a Batman comic.'

'There's only a million of them,' Travis said. 'There's like, classic stuff from the fifties and sixties and seventies, and then it started getting all serious in the eighties with Frank Miller and the Dark Knight stuff. And then there's the Elseworlds series, and—'

'Elseworlds?'

'Like, totally alternate timelines or universes. Like, if Batman lived over a hundred years ago

263

and was in London instead of Gotham City and was hunting for Jack the Ripper. That'd be an Elseworlds kind of thing.'

'I don't know if that would be appropriate for a twelve-year-old,' she said.

'Oh, sure,' Travis said. 'By age twelve I'd read *The Killing Joke* and the Arkham Asylum stuff and it's all pretty intense and violent and kind of sick, but I turned out okay. They're really good. If he hasn't read those, I bet he'd like them. Do you know what Batman books he's already got?'

'Not really.'

Travis swallowed hard, working up his courage. He hoped he could be heard over the beating of his heart. 'Let's go over where the Batman stuff is,' he said, leading the way, brushing up against her ever so slightly as he moved around her.

'Okay, here,' he said, waving his arm at an entire section devoted to Batman graphic novels.

'Wow,' she said. 'I had no idea. There's like hundreds of titles.'

'Yeah,' he said. 'I used to read Batman like crazy but not so much anymore.'

'Why not?'

'I'm not so into superheroes. I mean, they're okay, but not my thing.' He had turned his head slightly sideways so that it was easier to read the spines. 'Here's a good one.' The comic was so jammed in between other editions that he struggled to extract it. He lost his grip once because his fingers were sweating. But once he freed the book, he handed it to her. His fingertips left small, sweaty marks on the cover that slowly evaporated.

'*The Long Halloween*?' she said.

'A classic. Written by Jeph Loeb, who produced stuff like *Smallville* and *Lost*.'

'Oh my God, *Lost*,' she said. 'I binge-watched it last year. I loved it, well, except maybe the ending. I'm not even sure what happened.'

'Same here. But it was a great ride.'

'I loved that episode where you thought it was a flashback, but it was actually a flash-forward, and—'

They heard a bell jingle and both looked in the direction of the door. Danny, the store proprietor, clutching a Subway bag, found his way back behind the counter.

'So, uh, Danny's back,' Travis said. 'You should probably pay for that before he gets too far into that sandwich. He usually gets double onions and could drop you dead from ten feet away.'

That made her laugh. Travis could not remember the last time he'd made a girl laugh. At least, not in a good way.

The woman held up the comic and smiled. 'So, like, thanks for this. And all your advice.'

'Yeah, sure, okay,' he said.

'What's your name, anyway?' she asked.

'Travis,' he said, and then, just to be sure, added, 'Travis.'

'I'm Sandy,' she said, flashed a smile, and walked away.

Just in time, too, because Travis could feel this huge woody growing in his pants and was afraid if she'd stayed any longer she might have caught a glimpse of it under his jeans. Christ, if it popped out, he'd be knocking books off the shelves.

He went back to where she'd found him, just as Danny called out, loud enough for anyone in the store to hear him, 'Hey everybody, just a heads-up. If you got any doobies in your pocket be aware there's a couple of narc-y, cop-looking types across the street.'

That didn't worry Travis. He didn't do drugs.

His heart rate was getting back to normal, the bulge in his pants was diminishing, and his hands were not nearly as clammy as they'd been only a minute earlier.

He should have asked her last name. He should have asked where she lived, or worked. No, no, that would have been a terrible idea, because then he would have had to endure the embarrassment of her struggling with some excuse for not divulging any personal information.

Okay, fine, be one of those types. Maybe those crazy incel guys were on to—

'Can I thank you by buying you a cup of coffee or something?'

Travis almost sprained his neck turning his head so quickly. 'What?'

'There's a place like two doors down,' Sandy said. 'Interested?'

CHAPTER 30

Springfield, MA

Miles was as freaked out as Chloe was by the hand under Todd's bed. She'd paused the image and expanded it to get a closer look. It appeared to be a man's right hand, and the fifth finger, the smallest one, was unusually short, as though it had been cut off at the first knuckle.

'Was he there the whole time, while we were sitting there?' she asked as the two of them sat in the Pacer in front of Todd's mother's house.

'Had to be,' Miles said. 'But then we heard that van up on the road, the brakes squealing. When we came back and I was trying to find the phone—'

'—I got down on my hands and knees and looked under the bed,' Chloe said, and started hyperventilating. 'Holy shit, if he'd been there then—'

Miles placed a comforting hand on her arm. 'But he wasn't.'

'What the fuck is going on?' she asked, her eyes pleading for an answer as she looked at him.

267

'I don't know. Whoever it was, he wanted that phone. I *knew* I hadn't lost it.'

Chloe's eyes widened. 'Maybe it was Todd!'

Miles considered her theory, which, judging by her hopeful expression, she wanted to believe. It was a less creepy possibility than some stranger hiding under the bed.

'Does that make any sense?' he said. 'You know Todd. Wouldn't he have been happy to talk to you? And his car wasn't there. His stuff all gone . . .'

'I know, I know. And anyway, Todd's not missing part of a finger.'

'And there's the business with the woman in the van,' Miles said.

'What about the woman in the van?'

'She came along at just the right time, didn't she? Charise thought there was something funny about her.'

Chloe's eyelids fluttered. 'Like what?'

Miles was thinking. 'We hear what sounds like an accident, we run out to see what's happened. Our guy under the bed takes that opportunity to get out, with the phone. By the time we get back, he's gone. That woman, who said she was trying not to hit a deer, that might have been a distraction.'

'But how . . .'

'Guy hears us come in, he hides under the bed, he mutes his phone, sends her a text. Tells her to do something that will draw us outside.'

'Oh my God,' Chloe said.

Miles, more to himself, said, 'There was no deer. Charise didn't see a deer.'

'Okay.'

'It was a distraction. Hitting the brakes. It got us out of the trailer. We'd arrived there right in the middle of whatever it was they were up to.'

'The scam,' Chloe said.

Miles nodded, figuring out where she was going. 'Yeah, maybe.'

'Whatever phone scam Todd was doing, maybe he wasn't in on it alone. Maybe he was working with, you know, like, some organized-crime types or something. Maybe he double-crossed them.'

Miles ran his hand over the top of his head, thinking. He looked back at the house.

'We have to tell her,' he said. 'We need to tell her that something might have happened to her son. She needs to call the police.'

'Shit, seriously?' Chloe said. 'Because if she does, then the cops will find out what Todd's been doing, *whatever* it is, and then if it turns out he's okay, he's gonna be up to his ass in trouble.'

'She has to know,' Miles said firmly. 'You said she already knows he might be up to something illegal. Bring her up to speed, let her make the call. She's his mother.'

'You're his father,' Chloe said.

The words hung there.

Miles was about to say it wasn't the same, but couldn't bring himself to utter the words. To

269

downplay his relationship to Todd was to downplay his relationship to Chloe.

'Yeah,' he said. 'Should we tell her together?'

'You gonna tell her your connection?'

'Let's play that part by ear,' he said.

As he put his hand on the door handle, his cell rang. He took it from his jacket, looked to see who it was from, then put the phone to his ear.

'Yeah, hello,' he said. 'Dorian.'

'How's it going, boss?' his personal assistant asked.

'That's kind of a long story. What's up?'

'Okay, so, couple of things. The gamers want to set up a second meeting, maybe in—'

'Just set it up, whenever they want. What's the other thing?'

'So . . . can you talk?'

'Yeah. What is it?'

'I'm following up on that list, getting more information on all the people on it, building up even more detailed profiles so when you approach them, you're up to speed, you know.'

'Sure.'

'So, I've run into something kind of weird with a couple of them.'

'What do you mean, weird?'

'Let's start with Jason Hamlin.'

'Okay, right. The one in Maine.'

'Right. The college student. He's missing.'

Miles suddenly felt light-headed. 'Missing?'

'Well, maybe not technically. He may have died

in the fire. They're looking for his body in the wreckage.'

'Dorian, start at the beginning.'

'I'll email you a link to the story. Hamlin was living in a house off campus that he shared with some other guys. There was a gas leak and an explosion. The others made it out, but not Hamlin. They haven't found his body but they're thinking it has to be in the ashes. The thing is, though, he usually went out for an early-morning run, but he must not have done it that day, because, well, if he had, he'd have showed up. Right?'

Chloe was giving him a *what's going on?* look. Miles raised a hand.

'Send me the stories,' he said.

'And this Katie Gleave? From outside Buffalo? Lackawanna?'

'Right.'

'She's been in Paris, posting stuff on Instagram pretty regularly. She's over there with a friend, and now the friend is asking if anyone knows where she is, to get in touch. She's disappeared. Police issued a release and everything.'

Miles's light-headedness was getting worse.

'Miles, you there?' Dorian asked.

'What . . . what about the others? Dixon Hawley, and . . . and . . .' He knew every name on the list by heart, but now he couldn't remember them. 'Um, the one in Fort Wayne, Travis, what's the name, Travis Roben. What about him? And Nina—'

'That's all I got so far,' Dorian said. 'But I

thought you'd want to know. Did you find the Swanson girl? Chloe?'

'Yes,' he said slowly. 'Dorian, I'll have to call you back.'

He ended the call, put the phone away, and stared straight ahead, shell-shocked. He tried to get his head around Dorian's news. He contemplated the odds that three connected individuals might, seemingly at random, suddenly encounter misadventure.

'What was that all about?' Chloe asked. 'You okay? You look like shit. Was that your doctor? Bad news?'

'Not . . . my doctor.'

'Yeah, well, whatever it was, we have to figure out what to do right now about Madeline. She's looking out the window at us. We gonna tell her about Todd or what?'

Miles tried to draw some moisture into his dry mouth.

'It might just be a hell of a coincidence,' he said, 'but your theory about Todd? About whatever it is he's into?'

Chloe nodded.

'There might be something totally different going on.'

When Dorian was finished with her call to Miles, she saw that Gilbert was standing outside her door.

'Gil?' she said.

Miles's brother entered hesitantly.

'Do you have a minute?'

'Sure,' she said. Gilbert took a seat and Dorian came out from behind her desk and perched herself on the edge of a coffee table. 'What's up?'

'Where's Miles?'

'He's . . . on the road.'

'You know about his diagnosis, of course.'

She nodded. 'I know. It's awful. He doesn't deserve what's happened to him.'

'I . . . I need to ask you about something and I don't want you to share it with Miles. I know that puts you in a difficult position.'

'Yeah, it kinda does, Gilbert.'

Gilbert bit his lower lip, considering whether to proceed. 'Miles told me something about Caroline. Something she tried to do, and got caught.'

'Oh,' Dorian said. 'Okay. You want to tell me what that was?'

He shook his head slowly. 'Not really. But she tried to take advantage. Financially. And I'm worried she might be trying to do it again.'

'What are you talking about?'

'I mentioned it to Miles the other day, but he had so much else on his mind, he kind of brushed it off.'

Dorian was growing impatient. 'Gilbert.'

He sighed. 'Excel Point. It's showed up several times in the accounts. We've paid them about $198,000. I've been through all the departments, talked to our people in research and development, and no one knows what it is.'

Dorian did not immediately look concerned. 'We pay a lot of people a lot of money around here.'

'I know,' Gilbert said. 'That's why I think it would be so easy for someone to bill us for something they never did. I looked up Excel Point and I can't find a thing about them online.'

'Maybe they don't have a website.'

It was Gilbert's turn to be impatient. 'A tech firm with no online presence?'

'Okay, point taken,' Dorian said. 'What would you like me to do?'

'Can you check into it? And if it leads back to Caroline, can you give me a heads-up? I want to try and get ahead of this. If she's done this, I'll make her pay it all back.'

'I'm on it,' Dorian said.

'And you won't tell Miles?'

She paused before answering. 'Don't make me promise that, Gil. But I'll see what I can do. And you know what? Maybe it's legit. Maybe it's something you missed.'

Gilbert sighed with relief and stood. 'Thank you. I owe you one.'

'It's okay,' she said.

'At first, I was going to ask Heather, but that felt like making it too official,' Gilbert said.

Dorian shook her head. 'No need. Leave it with me. If I find out anything, I'll let you know ASAP.'

CHAPTER 31

Boston, MA

They were sitting in a bar at Logan International, waiting for their flight to Phoenix, going over the events earlier in the day.

It had been, Rhys Mills conceded, a close one.

Hiding under the bed while the girl and the older guy were in the front end of the trailer, Rhys, his gun in one hand, had managed to extract his phone from his pocket with his other one and text a message to Kendra.

PEOPLE HERE, he had tapped. HIDING IN TRAILER. CREATE DISTRACTION.

He could, of course, have simply shot and killed his visitors. But there'd been little sense in making this any more difficult than it already was. He'd had no idea who the man and the girl were, but as they'd approached the tail end of the trailer and he was able to more clearly hear their conversation, it had sounded like the girl knew Todd.

Well, *duh*. She was in his trailer.

The girl had gone through the closet, the drawers,

275

found them all empty. She and the man had speculated about why Todd might have taken off. That had encouraged Rhys. They weren't even tossing around the idea that he'd been killed. And then the girl said something about this Todd character being involved in some shady shit. Rhys remembered Todd being very nervous when he and Kendra had shown up, posing as police. That was encouraging, too. When and if the real police became involved, they'd be looking in that direction.

Moments after sending the text, he heard the screeching of brakes.

Once the girl and the man had split, Rhys had crawled out from under the bed and seen the phone sitting on top of it. The very one he'd come here to find. He'd left the trailer, unseen, run through the woods, and rendezvoused with Kendra half a mile up the road after she'd put on her little show about nearly hitting a deer.

Got in the van, had the nerve to ask, 'Where's my coffee?'

She'd pointed to her damp lap. 'If you want to suck on that . . .'

And now, here they were at the airport, heading to their next assignment.

Kendra was on her second glass of chardonnay when she received a text. PARIS DONE, it said. She told Rhys, who was on his third Heineken.

'Wouldn't have minded doing that one,' he said. 'Been to Paris?'

'Couple of times,' she said.

The Katie Gleave job had been outsourced. Better to assign that one to a local, someone who knew the territory.

'Wouldn't have made any sense, having us do it,' Kendra added.

'Eight-hour flights there and back.'

'Yeah, still, would have been nice.'

She rolled her eyes. 'Your life that tough?'

'You think this isn't work?'

'Sure, but think of the interesting people you get to meet.'

He looked at his watch, glanced up at the arrivals/departures board. 'Still half an hour to board.'

'Can't believe we're in a cattle car. Where's the respect?' She looked down into her glass, as if the answer to one of life's mysteries were there. 'Anyway, Phoenix is nice. I like a dry heat. Too bad there's not time to drive up to Sonoma.'

Rhys shook his head. 'Then we could lay back for a bit.'

'What's this "we" stuff? When we're done, I'm gone.'

'I wasn't implying anything.'

'Running back and forth across the country, it's not very efficient. What about that one in Indiana? Wouldn't it make sense to hit that one on the way? All this flying. Think of the carbon.'

'Never took you for an environmentalist.'

They would have to do their prep all over again once they got there. Buy the cleaning supplies they needed, rent a vehicle, connect with someone local – a funeral home, a wrecking yard – who was used to assisting folks in their line of work.

'Was never my goal to be a cleaning lady,' Kendra said.

'Right back atya,' he said. 'Torching a place is easier.'

She caught the waitress's eye, ordered another glass of chardonnay, then said to her partner, 'What do we know about the next one?'

Mills got out his phone, opened a file.

'Dixon Hawley. Works in an art gallery.'

'Dixon. That a man or a woman?'

Mills flashed a thumbnail headshot on his phone. 'Guy.'

She nodded approvingly. 'I'm okay with guys. I don't like doing women. There's too much violence against women in today's society. And after Phoenix?'

'That's *Indiana*. Fort Wayne. Got us booked on a flight there out of Phoenix morning after next. Hoping we can do Phoenix in a day.'

'Huh.'

Rhys was back to looking at his phone. His eyes widened.

'Hmm,' he said.

'What?'

'Just remembered something he said.'

'Who?'

'The man who came into the trailer, with the girl. There was a lot going on. You'd started the distraction. They were sitting on the bed. Lots of noise, bed creaking, them heading for the door.'

'What are you talking about? What did he say?'

'He called her Chloe. I'm sure of it.' He looked back to his phone again. 'There's a Chloe on the list.'

CHAPTER 32

New Rochelle, NY

Sitting at his desk at the ReproGold Clinic, Dr Martin Gold considered his options.

He could do nothing, of course. He could keep quiet and hope none of this ever came back on him. Ride it out.

But what if it did come out? What if there was blowback, and it came his way? How could it not? Was there anything to be gained by getting out ahead of this? Going to the authorities? Telling them what he'd done, what he knew? That was a high-risk choice. A major toss of the dice.

And of course, there was always . . . as a doctor, he had access to any number of pharmacological solutions. Take the right thing, feel no pain, never wake up again.

Tempting.

He'd been online, read about Jason Hamlin. There was a Facebook post from Katie Gleave's family in Lackawanna asking for help in finding her in Paris. Gold's searches on other names had so far turned up nothing of note, but that had not put him at ease.

Gold picked up his cell, started to make a call, changed his mind. His mouth was dry. He moved his tongue around, trying to create some saliva. He opened the bottom drawer of his desk, pulled out a bottle of scotch and a shot glass, poured himself a drink, knocked it back, then put the bottle and glass away.

He picked up the cell phone again. This time, he found the inner resolve to make the call. After the sixth ring, someone picked up.

'It's Dr Gold,' he said. 'I need to speak with—'

The person who'd picked up cut him off midsentence. He waited for a pause, then said, 'It's urgent. We need to speak.'

The person at the other end hung up.

Gold was about to pour himself another drink when there was a soft rapping at the door.

'What?' he barked.

The door opened and his assistant, Julie, poked her head in. 'Dr Gold, the Caseys have been waiting for twenty minutes.'

Gold looked blankly at her, trying to remember who the Caseys were. All these people, trying to have kids, there were days when he just wanted to say to them, *For Christ's sake, go adopt.* And some of them, God, by the look of them, they really shouldn't reproduce. Do the world a favor and spare us your progeny.

'The Caseys,' he said.

'From Greenwich? It's their initial appointment. You haven't seen them but you have the file.'

'I do?'

'Yes.'

At which point Julie strode into the room and came around his desk with the intention of pulling it up onto his screen. As she was reaching for the mouse, Gold noticed that a story about a fire up in Maine was on his screen.

'Stop!' he said, and then did something he'd never done before. He grabbed Julie by the wrist and pushed her away, hard enough that when she hit the wall she sent the doctor's framed picture of the Golden Gate Bridge swaying on its hook.

She yelped in pain and said, 'What's the matter—'

Gold leapt to his feet, his face full of apology. He couldn't believe what he'd done.

'I'm sorry, Julie, I'm so sorry. My God, I don't know what came over me.'

Julie, massaging her wrist, locked eyes with the doctor. It wasn't a look of fear she gave him but contempt. Then she looked at the screen, wondering what the doctor had not wanted her to see.

The headline read: BATES STUDENT FEARED DEAD IN FIRE. It was accompanied by a headshot of a young man, the name JASON HAMLIN printed underneath.

Gold used the mouse to make the page disappear.

'What was that?' she asked.

'Nothing,' he said. 'Personal. Julie, honestly, I'm very sorry.'

'I don't know what's going on with you, Dr Gold, but it's something bad. Canceling appointments, drinking. You think I don't see, but I do. *I'm* the one who has to deal with the angry patients, the ones who've been counting on you to help them.'

'I know, I know.'

'Tell me what's wrong. Maybe I can help.'

'Just . . . send them in. The . . .'

'Caseys,' Julie reminded him. 'Do you want me to bring up the file or not?'

Gold moved out of the way so Julie could access his computer more easily. She hit a few keys and up came a file labeled 'Casey, Katerina and Matthew.'

'There,' she said.

'Are you hurt?' he asked. 'Please tell me I didn't hurt you.'

She didn't answer. She went back to her desk and told the Caseys the doctor would now see them.

Gold put on a cheerful face and came around the desk to greet them. 'A pleasure to meet you,' he said. 'Katerina and Matthew?'

They nodded. Katerina, midthirties, tiny, with short black hair streaked with silver highlights, said, 'We've heard so much about you.'

Her husband, Matthew, who looked like he might have played college football at one time but

283

had not kept himself in shape since, extended a hand and said, 'We feel real lucky to be able to see you. You're our last hope.'

'Oh, well, never give up hope,' the doctor said with feigned enthusiasm as he went back to his seat. 'I've got your file here, but maybe you'd like to tell me your story.'

'Well,' Katerina said, 'we've been together ten years, got married five years ago, and a year after that we started trying.' Tears welled up and she reached for a tissue from a box on the doctor's desk. 'God, I can't even get started without losing it.'

'It's okay,' he said. 'Take your time.'

'I feel like it's all my fault,' she said.

Matthew put his arms around her, nearly swallowing her up in the embrace. 'I've told her it's no one's fault. It's just what it is. And it could just as easily be me, true? That's one of the things that we have to look into, right?'

Gold was nodding. 'That's very true. First, that it could be either one of you, or both of you, and second, that this is not a question of finding fault.'

'I have some . . . questions,' Katerina said.

'Of course. Ask anything.'

She hesitated. Her husband said, 'She's a little embarrassed.' He looked at her and asked, 'Want me to do it?'

She nodded.

'When they talk about artificial insemination, she doesn't actually have to do it with—'

284

'No, no, of course not,' Gold said. 'It's a procedure, conducted here in the office. There are many examples, of course, of couples who engaged the services of someone – a family friend, a brother, perhaps, of the husband with very similar DNA – to complete the act with the woman, but that can lead to a lot of emotional complications. That is definitely not recommended. There can be legal complications, as well.'

'So it's better not to know who the donor is.'

'You want to know everything you can about the donor, short of a name. Anonymity is guaranteed if that is what the parties wish. But today, there are many avenues to discover the identity of a donor, or for the donor, his offspring. Provided everyone is agreeable.'

Katerina cleared her throat. 'I have another question, and I don't want to offend you in any way, but—'

'Please go ahead.'

'I read a story in the *New York Times* about a fertility clinic where women thought they were choosing from a wide selection of profiles, but in fact, everyone was being inseminated by . . . someone *at* the clinic.' She paused. 'Like, the doctor. He was donating his own sperm. To everyone.'

Gold's face flushed.

'I'm not suggesting anything like that would ever happen here, but how do we actually know? How do we know what we're, you know, getting?'

Gold pressed his lips together, as though trying to hold back some kind of emotional explosion. Finally, he said, 'That would be an outrageous breach of trust between patient and doctor for something like that to occur.'

'But it has happened,' Matthew said. 'Right? Just like, sometimes surgeons make a mistake and, you know, amputate the wrong leg or something.'

Gold, simmering, said, 'Contributing one's own sperm would hardly be an *accident*. That would be a willful act.' He took a moment to compose himself.

'I *have* offended you,' Katerina said. 'I'm so sorry.'

'It's fine,' Gold said. 'Let's see if we can get things back on track here and—'

His cell phone rang. His head snapped downward to see the screen, and the number that came up.

'Um, I'm sorry,' he said. 'I have to take this.'

He grabbed the cell and put it to his ear. He swiveled around in the chair, turning his back on the Caseys, who were looking at each other uncomfortably, wondering whether they should excuse themselves.

'Tell me you're not really doing this,' Gold whispered angrily. 'Tell me it's not you.'

He hunched over, as if somehow this would give him more privacy from the Caseys. Katerina had stood, but her husband shook his head, giving her a *wait and see* look.

'You can't . . . you can't expect me to just stand by while this goes on,' the doctor said. 'I've countenanced a lot of things, things I'm not proud of, things I've allowed you to talk me into, but this is going too far.'

Matthew's eyebrows went up, and he stood, nodding to his wife that yes, they really *should* leave the room until the doctor was finished with this call. Katerina took a step toward the desk, leaned in slightly, and whispered, 'We'll just wait—'

Gold turned and glared at them over his shoulder. 'Get out,' he said.

Katerina recoiled, as if slapped. Her husband appeared ready to leap across the desk, or at the very least say something, but she shook her head vigorously, warning him off doing anything. Besides, Gold had already turned his back on them again and resumed his conversation. She guided her husband to the exit and pulled the door closed behind them as they left.

'Just someone in the office,' Gold said. 'They left. No, no, they didn't. Stop. Stop. Listen to me. I'll tell everyone what I did. I will. I'm past caring. I can't do my job. I'm a disaster. I can't sleep. I spend half the time wondering whether to kill myself. No, God no, I haven't said anything to my wife. You think I'm crazy? But yes, she's noticed I'm on edge. I've told her the clinic . . . that we're having a slight cash flow problem, that it can be resolved.'

He listened to the other person talk for the better

part of a minute, by which time Gold appeared to be calmed, slightly.

'Okay,' he said. 'Okay, okay.'

And then one more 'Okay.'

Gold ended the call, turned around in his chair, and put the phone on his desk. He looked at the two empty chairs across from him and blinked a couple of times, as though trying to remember who had been there only a moment earlier.

Before the Caseys emerged from the doctor's office, Julie Harkin had been at her desk, opening a browser on her desktop and entering the headline she'd seen atop the news story on the doctor's computer.

She found the story almost instantly, read it from top to bottom. A house where several Bates College students lived off campus had burned down. One man, Jason Hamlin, had not been found, and authorities were now starting to believe he'd not been in the house when the fire began. But if he hadn't been there, where was he?

Why, Julie wondered, was this story of interest to the doctor?

The story had a link to another one: FAMILY HIT WITH DOUBLE TRAGEDY. Julie clicked on it. The Hamlin family home in Baltimore had burned down not long after the Lewiston tragedy.

As if the family had not suffered enough, Julie thought.

And then she read the names of Jason's parents: Margaret and Charles Hamlin.

'Oh my God,' she whispered to herself.

One of the couples whose names, along with their children's, she gave to that woman in the coffee shop.

CHAPTER 33

Springfield, MA

'What do you mean, something else might be going on?'

Chloe asked Miles as he sat next to her in the Pacer.

Miles hesitated. He needed another moment to digest the information he'd received from Dorian. Could it be coincidence that three of the people he was hoping to connect with – Todd Cox, Jason Hamlin, and Katie Gleave – were missing or presumed dead? That they had gone missing, or died, in such a short period of time?

And all since Miles had started his hunt for them?

It was possible, he supposed. Bad things did happen to people. Houses caught on fire. Young people visiting foreign countries, where they were unfamiliar with local customs or the language, could find themselves in trouble. And there was a possible explanation for Todd's disappearance: he was into something illegal and had made a run for it.

And yet.

Why was Todd's trailer so spotlessly clean? Why had every trace of him been erased? Who'd been hiding under the bed? Not Todd. And who was the woman in the van that had screeched to a stop out on the main road?

He thought back to what Dorian had told him about Jason Hamlin. A house fire. The other students who lived there survived, but not Jason. Surely, eventually, his body would have been found among the ashes. So if he hadn't been in the house when the fire broke out, where was he? What had happened to him?

'You gonna answer me or what?' Chloe asked.

Miles said, 'I'm trying to put it together.'

'Put *what* together? I'm right here. What the fuck is going on?'

Slowly, he said, 'The list, the nine people that I – Jesus, am I allowed to call them my children? Is that too . . . presumptuous?'

Miles, feeling overwhelmed, was losing his focus. This emotional tidal wave washing over him was making it increasingly difficult to direct his thoughts logically. It wasn't that long ago that Miles could picture lines of computer code in his head like they were right there on a billboard, in front of him. Intricate, complex concepts were as easy to visualize as a sunset.

But now, all this information and events coming at him at once – finding Chloe, *not* finding Todd, news about the others on the list – was starting to feel like too much. Dorian's call was like someone dumping onto the table several hundred pieces of a jigsaw puzzle and demanding they be put together in ten seconds.

'Fuck, fuck, fuck,' he said, bending over, making his hands into fists and pressing them against his forehead.

'Miles?'

'I . . . need a minute,' he said.

He took his fists from his forehead and looked at Chloe.

'Can I call *you* that? Can I call you my child? Can I call you my daughter? Because . . . to be able to do that, to have the right to do that, don't I have to be more than just a sperm donor?'

He was afraid he might cry. *Fight this*, he told himself. *It's a symptom. Don't let it control you. Okay, one of your* daughters *is missing. Two of your* sons *are unaccounted for.*

He hadn't had a chance to so much as say *hello* to them yet.

'Miles, are you okay?' Chloe asked, reaching out and touching his arm.

He swallowed hard, as if that would tamp down the emotional storm. Then he attempted a nod. 'Yeah.'

'I *am* your daughter,' she said. 'You're allowed to call me that.'

'Being a parent is a lot more than just biology,' he said.

'Yeah, well, now you've got a chance to make

up for the other part,' she said, giving his arm a squeeze. 'You need to get back on track here, okay?'

'Okay.'

'Can you answer my question?'

'Try me again.'

'The phone call. What was the phone call about?'

'It was my assistant,' he said. 'She's been gathering information for me on . . . the others.'

'Okay.'

Without giving her the names, he told her about the missing woman in Paris and the student believed to have perished in a fire.

The news hit Chloe harder than he expected.

'So . . . I've lost a brother and a sister? On top of Todd going missing?'

'I'm sorry,' Miles said.

'What's happening?'

'I don't know.'

'I mean, is it all connected? Is that what's going on?'

'Chloe, I don't know.'

She took her hand off his arm and her empathetic look turned severe. 'So wait. Around the time you start trying to find me and my half brothers and sisters, shit starts happening?'

'It . . . it looks that way.'

'Nothing happens for years to any of these people, and then when you start nosing around bad stuff happens. You think that's a coincidence?'

'I swear, Chloe, I don't know.'

'Like, what did you do, tweet out all their names so somebody could go after them?'

He gave her a sharp look. 'Don't be ridiculous. I haven't even told *you* their names. And why would anyone go after them?'

'Hey, you're the rich, techie genius. You might be able to figure this out faster than I could. Okay, so it's not you, but you're not the only person who knows who all your little kidlets are, right?'

Miles considered the question. 'No.'

'Who knows what you know?'

'Dorian. My assistant. She's worked for me for years. And then there's Heather, who does investigative work when we need it. There's the doctor from the clinic. There could be any number of people who have the information. What are you suggesting? What if someone *did* know the names of the people I'm trying to make contact with? How does that connect to someone going missing, or being in a fire?'

'Hey, you're the one who seems freaked out by it, so there's got to be something going on in the back of your mind.'

'It's . . . maybe it's all nothing.'

'Yeah, well, *I* don't think it's nothing. And you want to know why?'

'Why?'

'Because I'm one of them. You've got nine people you're trying to find. Two are missing and one's maybe dead. That's a third of your list, right there. So if – *if* – someone is going around and

294

deliberately making this happen, when's it going to be my turn?'

Miles gave her a look that suggested the idea had not occurred to him until she'd said it. 'Christ.'

'To put it fucking mildly,' she said. 'Look, you're supposedly the guy with the big brain here, but let me toss this out.'

'Go ahead.'

'You're planning to divide up all your money and shit between the nine of us. And like I said, I don't need your money, but let's put that aside. So these nine people, they all get, well, a ninth of the pot. Am I right so far?'

'Yes.'

'So, when nine goes down to six, those six end up getting way more. Right?'

'Right,' Miles said slowly.

'And if nine goes down to five, then those five end up getting more. You see where I'm going with this?'

'Chloe, you're making huge leaps here.'

'Well, that's easy for you to say,' she said.

'What do you mean?'

'You're not one of the nine.'

The words hit him hard. Miles felt the emotions welling up again. He didn't want to lose it again. He struggled to stay on track.

'What you're talking about,' he said, trying to keep his voice even, 'is murder. You're talking about someone going around murdering my . . . progeny. There's no evidence, at least not in what

295

I heard from Dorian, that suggests any of these
. . . occurrences . . . are homicides.'

'That's only because they haven't found the
bodies,' Chloe countered, almost casually.

Miles looked out his window. 'What you're saying
. . . it's unthinkable. But if it's somehow true . . .
have I somehow set the wheels in motion?'

Chloe said nothing.

'The whole reason . . . I set out to do this to
help all of you, not to bring *harm* to you. Who –
who would do this?'

'Oh, that's easy,' Chloe said.

Miles turned away from the window, wanting to
look her in the eye as she presented her theory.

She shrugged, smiled goofily, and said, 'One of
us.'

'What?'

'One of the nine,' she said. 'You want the whole
pie, you knock off your half brothers and sisters.'

'No,' Miles said under his breath.

'One of your kids already knows about the others
and is taking us out,' she said, almost cheerily.
'Makes sense to me.'

'No,' he said again.

'Just so you know,' she said, reaching out and
touching his arm again, 'it's not me.' She paused.
'Of course, that's what I *would* say, isn't it?'

And then Miles did something neither of them
expected. He laughed.

'This is the very definition of a clusterfuck,' he
said. 'Maybe it *is* you. You're like the girl in *Hanna*.'

Now Chloe smiled. 'I saw that movie. About the sixteen-year-old girl who's an assassin. Yeah, okay. One of your kids just happens to have been raised to be an international killer, and now she's killing all her half siblings. I could pull that off.'

Now they were both laughing.

Miles placed a hand on the dash to steady himself. The laughs subsided. 'Oh, man, nothing about this is funny.'

Chloe shrugged. 'You have to laugh sometimes.'

Once he'd composed himself, Miles took a deep breath and said, 'We should get you home, and I should get back to New Haven and try to make some sense of this mess.'

'Yeah, like that's fucking happening. If there's a chance in a thousand that I'm right about this, you think I'm gonna go home and wait for someone to make me disappear? You may not be much of a bodyguard, but I'm sticking right by you.'

She paused, and then added, '*Pops.*'

Wearily, Miles nodded and said, 'Got it.'

CHAPTER 34

New York, NY

Nicky, increasingly, believed there was only one way this could end.

When she'd said to Roberta that Jeremy couldn't keep her locked up in this multi-million-dollar brownstone forever, Roberta had conceded the point. What was Nicky supposed to take from that?

Was Roberta going to show up in her room one day to announce Nicky was free to go? That Jeremy'd had a change of heart, that her punishment was over, that he was no longer concerned about what she might have overheard?

Yeah, that was going to happen.

For a while there, Nicky thought they'd try to buy her off. Offer her money, or gifts, to make her forget what she'd heard. She imagined Jeremy coming to see her and saying this whole thing had been a terrible misunderstanding, that he'd like to make it right by giving her a good-paying job in the organization, preferably someplace overseas where she'd be far, far away from any New York authorities.

And she'd go along with it, happily.

Sure, she was just a kid, but she was mature for her age, very attractive, and smarter than most girls her age. She could pass for nineteen or twenty if she had to. Old enough to be put on the payroll somewhere. Maybe train her as a future Roberta. Someone who could find more young girls to entertain Jeremy and his important friends.

But she didn't think that was going to happen. She feared Jeremy was considering a more permanent solution. How would they do it? Put some slow-acting poison in those wonderful meals Antoine made? But she hadn't felt even the slightest bit ill, so she'd ruled that out for now. Good thing, too, because the food was the best thing about being imprisoned here.

So, if they were going to kill her, why not just get it done? Maybe they were working up the nerve to do it. They had to figure out not only how to do it, but how to cover it up.

If Jeremy Pritkin was anything, he was a meticulous planner.

So Nicky had been thinking, *I have to get the fuck out of here.*

Her second-floor room was maybe twenty feet from the wide landing between two broad sets of stairs, one going down and one going up. One of Pritkin's security goons was always there, just like there was that one day when she tried to make a break for it.

Nicky's visitors were invariably Roberta or one of the staff bringing her a meal, or fresh bed linen or clean towels or rolls of toilet paper. Nicky was expected to change her sheets herself. She'd been instructed to strip the bed every second day and leave the sheets, along with the towels from the bathroom, piled up by the door.

Sometimes, if Roberta was feeling kindly, she'd bring Nicky a stack of reading material – *Vogue*, *Vanity Fair*, the most recent Sunday *New York Times* – which Nicky would devour, even the articles she wasn't all that interested in. It helped to pass the time. She had TV, but the Wi-Fi continued to be disabled in this part of the building. That iPad they'd given her was only good for games.

One day, Nicky had tried to enlist the help of one of the housekeepers when she came to drop off sheets. The woman, named Teresa, was in her fifties, and Nicky had asked her one time where she was from – Hidalgo, in Mexico – and whether she had kids.

'Girl and a boy,' Teresa had said after she had kicked off her heels. When there was no chance they could be seen by the master of the house, the help went around in stocking feet.

Nicky asked, 'How old are they? Are they in New York?'

Teresa's daughter, who was twenty, worked in a dry cleaner's in California. Her son was twenty-three and worked in construction in Arizona and New Mexico. Nicky had the sense no one in Teresa's family was in America legally.

'If somebody was holding your daughter prisoner,' Nicky said, 'wouldn't you want someone to help her?'

Teresa pretended not to hear the question.

'All I'm asking you to do,' Nicky said, 'is tell the police I'm here. Tell them I'm being held here against my will. Make an anonymous call.'

Teresa was putting fresh towels in the bathroom and would not look at Nicky.

'Please? I'm begging you.'

Teresa finished her duties and left without saying another word. Later that day, Roberta came and had a little chat with Nicky.

'Never put the staff in that kind of position again,' Roberta said. 'Anyway, the people who work for Mr Pritkin are very loyal.'

Not loyal, Nicky thought. More like scared shitless.

That was when Nicky upped her strategizing about how she could, on her own, draw the police or the fire department to the Pritkin brownstone. She considered starting a fire in her room, but she didn't have any matches or a lighter or even two sticks to rub together. There was a hair dryer in the bathroom, and one day Nicky tried to heat up some shredded toilet paper to the point that it would burst into flame, but had no success. Then she thought about stuffing towels into the drains of the tub or sink and opening up the taps. But what good would a flood do, beyond pissing off Jeremy and Roberta about all the water damage she'd cause?

The room had only that one window, about two feet square, that looked out to a brick wall across the narrow alley. Some view. And this was no cheap pane of glass, either. It was thick, and embedded with what looked like chicken wire, the kind of glass they used in doors in schools. So, breaking it wasn't an option. And even if she could smash it, what then? Could she even fit through it? And if she could, did she think she was Spider-Man? Was she going to scale the wall down to street level?

One day, while standing by the glass and straining to get a glimpse of Seventieth Street, she happened to glance down at the iPad in her hand.

She was getting a weak Wi-Fi signal.

It had to be coming from behind the brick wall on the other side of the alley.

Oh my God, she thought. *If I can piggyback onto that Wi-Fi I can get a message to someone.*

The Wi-Fi was tagged LOLITASPLACE. Someone named Lolita, Nicky guessed – *duh* – was right across the way there, behind that wall. The only problem was, Nicky needed a password to get onto Lolita's network.

Well, gee, how hard could that be?

She tried the obvious passwords that people too stupid to remember them used. Like PASSWORD, or ABCDEFG, or 123456789, or, given that this was Lolita's Wi-Fi, LOLITASWIFI, and LOLITASPAD. Nicky must have tried more than a hundred variations over the next couple of hours.

No joy.

'Shit, shit, shit,' she said to herself. She was about to give up when she decided to give it one more shot.

She typed in ATILOL. The name of the presumed occupant, spelled backward.

The password was accepted.

'Yes!' Nicky shrieked under her breath.

She immediately opened up Safari, Googled the home page for the New York Police Department. There was an email address! But was this iPad set up for email? Not a problem. All Nicky had to do now was set one up. Gmail, or Hotmail. She could do that in seconds, then send an email to the NYPD and help would be on the—

The door to her room burst open.

Roberta strode in, her face aflame. She ripped the iPad from Nicky's hands, tossed it onto the carpeted floor, then drove her four-inch heel into the screen – not once but three times – shattering it.

Nicky babbled, 'I wasn't doing anything! I was just—'

And that was when Roberta slapped her across the face. No, this was more than a slap. This was an open-handed punch, and it sent Nicky reeling.

She threw out a hand to brace herself as she hit the floor.

'You think we don't know?' Roberta shrieked. 'You little fucking slut!'

Nicky was on her knees, struggling to stand, when Roberta hit her again. Not across the face, but the side of her head. Harder this time. Nicky saw stars as she landed on the carpet. She burst into tears, repeatedly shouted that she was sorry, begged Roberta to stop.

That was when she realized there had to be a camera somewhere in the room. They'd been watching her all this time. Seen her excitement when she piggybacked onto someone else's Wi-Fi.

Through her tears, Nicky saw the door was still open, and standing there was Jeremy Pritkin.

Watching.

His face was blank. Not smiling, not laughing. No indication he enjoyed watching Roberta beat Nicky, but no expression of disapproval or disappointment, either. He watched impassively, the way someone might watch another person in an act as uneventful as vacuuming or reading a book.

Pritkin looked at Nicky as though she were nothing.

Finally, he spoke.

'Roberta,' he said.

Roberta gave Nicky one last withering look, then turned and left. Nicky could hear, above her own whimpering, the sound of the door's lock being driven home.

She could hear them talking in the hall.

Nicky crawled across the carpet until she reached the door, then leaned up against it. Maybe, if Roberta was in the hall, she wasn't, at that moment, watching Nicky on some surveillance feed.

Roberta was saying, '. . . indefinitely . . . have to do something . . .'

And then Pritkin replying, '. . . limited number of people I trust do this kind of work . . . currently in the field.'

'. . . much longer?'

'. . . hope not . . . first thing as soon as they return.'

Their voices faded away as they walked down the hall.

So, Nicky thought, there really was only one way this could end. She found little comfort in the fact that she had called it right.

CHAPTER 35

Fort Wayne, IN

It was pretty unbelievable.

Travis Roben had a girlfriend. Travis Roben had a goddamn girlfriend, and her name was Sandy, and she was a real, honest-to-God female of the human species. Not a picture in a magazine, not some blow-up doll, not a video on some pornographic website, but a living, breathing person.

They'd gone for that coffee after their initial meeting in the comic book store, where Sandy had sought advice about what to get for her twelve-year-old nephew. Sandy ordered a decaf cappuccino and a biscotti while Travis went for a plain old coffee with a ton of cream and half a dozen spoonfuls of sugar because he really had no idea what the difference was between what Sandy was getting and a latte and an Americano and all those fancy coffee drinks. The truth was, Travis mostly drank Mountain Dew, and his idea of a sophistic-ated snack was a Hostess Sno Ball.

And he'd made a huge social blunder right from

the get-go – letting Sandy pay for her own drink. *Stupid stupid stupid,* he told himself once they'd sat down. *Smooth move, idiot.*

But if Sandy had been offended, she didn't show it. She sat right down and started talking.

About herself.

Where she was from (Spokane) and what she had taken at school (veterinarian science) and what she hoped to do with her life (not, as it turned out, become a veterinarian but teach music) and how her parents moved to Fort Wayne when she was fifteen because her dad got transferred (he was with an insurance company) and how she moved out early because her parents were not getting along and were probably going to get a divorce (oh, well, what can you do, saw it coming for years) and that she had been going out with this guy who was big into sports (hockey, mostly) but she'd kind of had it with jock types because they were so into themselves and had no idea what was going on in the world and what about you?

'Me?' Travis said. He shrugged. 'Not much to tell.'

Which was the truth. But he told her about how he was working on his own graphic novel, which she found pretty interesting, or at least pretended to find pretty interesting. Either way, Travis was okay with it. After about five minutes of talking about his interests, she was back to talking about herself.

God, who cares? She's so hot.

307

The entire time they'd been sitting together, Travis had been thinking about one thing. Well, two. The first was, he needed to get some control over how aroused he was. When they finished their coffees and got up, Travis did not want people to think he was smuggling a fire extinguisher in his pants. But the main thing he was thinking was, if he were to ask her out, would she say yes? Maybe to go to the multiplex? And not to see some stupid Marvel or DC or Star Wars or James Bond thing, but a nonfranchise, original, not-based-on-something-else film. She struck him as a girl who'd be into an indie.

But Travis had never asked a girl out before. What did you say? Something along the lines of *Would you like to go on a date with me?* No, that sounded overly formal, outdated, nerdish. Maybe something more casual, off the cuff, like *Hey, wanna hang out tomorrow night? Like, see a movie or something?* Yeah, something like that.

And then Sandy said, 'What are you doing this weekend?'

So here they were, on a Saturday afternoon, at – get this – a bowling alley. Travis hadn't been to a bowling alley since attending a friend's seventh birthday party. He didn't even know there still *were* bowling alleys. Aside from going to the batting cages occasionally, Travis had never been particularly sports minded. All through school, he was the one who always got picked last when teams were being assembled. Even baseball, as obvious a team sport if there ever was one, was something Travis basically played alone.

This outing to the bowling alley wasn't even their second get-together, but their fourth. The day after they had coffee, they met up for lunch at a local McDonald's (Travis felt somewhat uncomfortable about having ordered a Big Mac when Sandy then went for a more sensible salad, but seriously, who even stepped foot into a McDonald's to order a salad?), and it was over lunch that Sandy had said she wanted to make what she knew was an inappropriate proposal.

OhmyGodohmyGodohmyGod, Travis had thought.

She had said, 'You know your glasses?'

And he'd said, 'Huh?'

'Your glasses are really – I don't know how to say this without sounding all judgy and everything, but your glasses are kind of nerdy.'

'What?'

'I mean, just because some of your interests are nerdy – and I have no problem with that, because I think comics and graphic novels are a true art form and you have nothing to be ashamed about – but just because your interests are a bit, you know, like that, you don't have to *look* like that. And your glasses . . . is there some reason why the frames are so thick and the lenses so oversized?'

Travis's face had flushed with embarrassment.

'Oh, shit, shit, I'm sorry,' Sandy had said. 'I really over-stepped, didn't I?'

'No, no, it's okay,' he'd said. 'I guess, they're just what I've always worn. I asked my parents once for some nicer ones and they said these were fine. But, yeah, maybe they're a bit on the geeky side. I look like a professor in one of those sixties puppet adventure shows like *Thunderbirds*.'

Sandy had looked at him blankly, not getting the reference.

'Anyway, yeah. I've thought about getting different ones, but anytime I have some money, I spend it on something else.'

'Let's get you some new glasses. We'll do it tomorrow.'

'Gee, I don't know. They could be expensive and—'

'They could be my treat,' she'd said. 'And after that, we could, you know, and tell me if I'm way over the line here again, go to the Gap or something and get you some clothes.'

'Clothes?'

'No offense, but you could use a slight upgrade in the wardrobe department.'

'Oh.'

Sandy had given him a light kick under the table. 'Listen to me, you idiot. I don't think you have any idea, but right under the surface here' – and she'd spun her index finger in the air in front of his face – 'is a sexy guy waiting to burst out.'

'You think?'

'I know.'

The thing was, Travis actually did have some

money saved up – pretty close to a thousand dollars – so the next day he went to the ATM and took out a couple hundred in cash and allowed Sandy to take him to the mall for a mini-makeover. It wasn't a lot of money, but it went pretty far at the Gap. Sandy picked out some shirts that were on sale, and a pair of stylish jeans. It was when she suggested Travis get some new boxers that he nearly lost his mind.

They'd only known each other a couple of days, and they hadn't done anything but kissed a few times – that's right, Travis had finally put his lips on a girl's in a circumstance that was not a family funeral or under duress – but Travis couldn't stop thinking about the possibility that even better things were coming. The fact that Sandy would actually have a suggestion about an item of apparel that touched his boys was pretty much the most amazing thing that had ever happened to him in his entire life.

The trip to the Gap didn't leave Travis any money for new glasses, but Sandy insisted that she would help him with that. He could always pay her back later. So they went to the eyeglass place in the mall and found an over-the-counter pair that were every bit as good as the prescription ones he'd been wearing for years and didn't even cost very much.

So by the time they got to the bowling alley, Travis felt like a new man. Sandy had remade him, and all it took was a pair of glasses and a new outfit. Oh sure, Travis still had something of a nerd vibe going on, and he knew it, but Sandy didn't seem to mind. He guessed it went back to what she'd said about her former boyfriend, the jock, a subject she had expanded on in subsequent conversations. She didn't like guys who were full of themselves, who thought they were hot shit, who were narcissistic assholes who believed the world revolved around them.

Hey, Travis thought, if Sandy's tastes now ran to guys with low self-esteem who couldn't throw a football if their lives depended on it, she had found her perfect man.

After their game – Travis shot an astonishingly bad score of 80, but Sandy wasn't much better at 95 – they went for a burger, and for a change Sandy didn't talk exclusively about herself.

'No offense,' she said jokingly, 'but you are not the best bowler I ever saw.'

'Right back atya,' he said. 'Bowling's not really my game.'

'What *is* your game?'

He rolled his eyes. 'Not really anything. I take my little Louisville Slugger to those batting cages once in a while, but that's about it.'

'I used to do that,' Sandy said.

'Do what?'

'I was on a girls' softball team.' She smiled proudly. 'I wasn't half bad, either. Next time, we'll do the cages thing.'

'Sure.'

'So,' she said, easing into a different subject, 'tell me more about your parents.'

He shrugged. 'I don't know. They're just normal, I guess.' He paused, looked down. 'They don't really think much of me.'

'What do you mean by that?'

'They're always telling me how to change my life. Get out more, meet people, stop being so wrapped up in my own world.'

Sandy smiled. 'Aren't you kinda doing that?'

He looked up and met her gaze. 'Seems like it. I guess they want the best for me, but it always feels like they're putting me down.'

'Do you have a picture of them?' she asked.

'On my phone.'

'Let me see.'

He got out his phone and opened the photo app. 'I don't have that many of them. Oh, wait. Here's one. It's from my mom's birthday, like, last year, I think.'

He handed the phone to her and she studied the shot. Travis's parents had their arms around each other, both wearing paper party hats and looking cheerful or a little drunk, or both. The woman had pale, white skin and graying hair, while her husband was darker, but not from a tan.

'Your dad, he looks . . . what's the word? Swarthy? That's not a racist word or anything, is it?'

'I don't think so. My dad's roots, they go back to Armenia or something.'

'So, Roben is an Armenian name?'

'Yeah, but my first name comes from the detective.'

'Detective?'

'Travis McGee. My dad, when he was younger, was a big John D. MacDonald fan.'

Sandy did not know who that was. She took one last look at the picture and handed Travis back his phone. 'He's really handsome. But you look more like your mom. She's pretty. You've kind of got her eyes and cheekbones and stuff.'

'Yeah, well, no surprise there,' he said.

Sandy blinked. 'What's that mean?'

He shrugged again. 'It's not something I really talk about.'

Sandy's face softened. 'I don't understand.' Then, as if a light bulb went off, her eyes widened and she said, 'Oh, I get it. So, like your mom was married before? Another guy is your real dad?'

'You're half right,' he said. 'The first part, you're wrong. My mom's always been married to him. They've been married for thirty years, and they really love each other and all.' He winced. 'No offense, like, about your own parents, splitting up and all.'

'That's okay. But what about him not being your real dad? What did you mean by that? Oh my God, did your mom have an affair?' She put her hand to her mouth.

Travis laughed. '*No*. God, your mind.'

'Sorry.'

'When I got to be around thirteen, my parents

314

sat me down and said they had something to tell me, that I was entitled to know the truth, about who I was and everything. My parents – well, my dad – couldn't have kids. Like, the natural way? They'd tried for a long time. So they ended up going to this place, like, near New York, because they used to live in Newark, so it wasn't that far. A clinic, you know?'

'Like a fertility clinic?'

'Yeah, like that. So, they had this stuff from another guy—'

'Stuff?'

Travis's face went red. 'Sperm.'

'Oh, yeah, sure,' Sandy said casually. 'You can stop right there. Your dad had a low sperm count, so your mom used a donor. And you're the kid from that donation.'

'Yeah.'

'Wow, that's pretty cool,' Sandy said.

'I don't know if I'd call it that.'

'No, I think that's really amazing. So, do you know who your biological father is?'

He shook his head. 'Nope.'

'Have you tried to find out?'

'Nope.'

'Aren't you curious?'

'Nope.'

She shook her head in wonder. 'If it was me, that would drive me crazy. That'd be something I'd have to know. You haven't done one of those tests? I see the ads on TV all the time.'

'No.'

'You should,' she said. 'You should find out.'

For the first time, Travis bristled at Sandy's interference. 'I think that's a pretty personal decision.'

Sandy said, 'You're right. I'm sorry. Forgive me. I stick my nose in where it doesn't belong.'

'It's okay.'

'Well, here's another question, and it's not super personal.'

'Shoot,' he said.

'I'm gonna say something, but don't look. Not until I say.'

'What are you talking about?' Travis said.

'There's this couple, over past where we got the bowling shoes? A man and a woman, like in their forties? They're not bowling or getting something to eat. They're just hanging around, and they keep looking this way.'

'Can I look?'

'Okay, but be casual like?'

He stood, stretched, slowly turned around, like he was taking in things, not looking at anything in particular.

'Oh, smooth,' Sandy whispered.

Travis saw them. Standing right where Sandy said, but they were looking the other way now. He sat back down.

'Maybe they're waiting for somebody,' he said.

'I bet they're cops,' Sandy said. 'Maybe there's been some drug dealing or something here.'

'At the bowling alley?'

Sandy shrugged.

'So what now?' Travis asked.

Sandy smiled. 'You wanna do it?'

CHAPTER 36

New Haven, CT

Miles agreed with Chloe that, whatever was going on with her other half brothers and sisters – if there was actually anything going on at *all* – it made sense that she come back with him to New Haven. But he did not want to ride all the way in her dilapidated Pacer, nor did he want to take the time for her to return the car to her home in Providence. He persuaded her to leave the car in Springfield – promising to have it brought back to her, one way or another, as soon as possible – and head to his place in the limo.

Chloe had called her mother and told her not to expect her back because she was staying over at Todd's place. A lie, of course, but Chloe was not yet ready to tell her the father of her child had wandered into the diner and turned her life upside down.

It was dark by the time they got to his place, a modern, stunning architectural wonder on a wooded lot just outside of New Haven. As the

318

limo rounded the last corner of the long, paved drive, the house came into view. It was a broad, one-story structure with walls of glass, interrupted at regular intervals with rust-colored steel beams, giving it a high-tech yet industrial look.

'Whoa,' said Chloe. 'This is a house? It's not, like, some secret military installation?'

'I've got a guest room, with its own bathroom,' Miles said. 'It's fully stocked. Toothbrush, toothpaste, shampoo, whatever you need.'

'Tampons?' she asked.

Miles shot her an awkward look.

'Just messin' with ya,' she said.

'I can send Dorian out first thing in the morning to get anything else you might need, including some fresh clothes. And there's a housekeeper if you want to wash your things.'

'Yeah, well, with all those glass walls, I hope you've got an extra bathrobe.'

'The glass can be tinted dark enough to afford complete privacy. No need for curtains or blinds.'

'Get out.'

'Really.'

As they got out of the limo, Miles asked Charise to be on call for the following day. At the front door, Miles touched his thumb to a pad. The security system read the print, turned back the deadbolt, and this was followed by a beep inside the house, indicating the alarm system had been disengaged.

'Come on in,' Miles said.

Chloe was agog as she crossed the threshold. The spacious entryway was decorated with leafy shrubs growing from planters built into the walls. A rock formation along one side of the room featured a waterfall that lent a sense of tranquility to the surroundings.

'You gotta be kidding me,' Chloe said.

'Kitchen's this way,' Miles said.

As Chloe followed Miles, her head moved from side to side, taking the place in. 'What'd it cost you to buy this joint?' she asked.

'I had it built,' Miles said as they reached the kitchen. He pulled on a handle that appeared to be attached to a panel in the wall, but it was actually the door to a massive refrigerator.

'I could park my Pacer in there,' Chloe said.

Miles grabbed two bottles of water and handed one to Chloe.

'So what did it cost you to build this place?'

'Just under eleven million,' he said.

Chloe put her water bottle on the counter and walked into an adjoining room. 'Fuck me,' she said.

Miles followed to see what she was looking at. She was standing in the media room, looking at a screen that covered one entire wall.

'You can watch something if you want,' Miles said. 'I'm probably gonna pack it in soon. It's been a long day. Remote's right there. It does everything.'

'You got some beer in that fridge?' she asked, looking at him.

'Uh, yeah.'

Chloe went back to the kitchen, used both hands on the refrigerator handle and pulled it open as though it were a bank vault. She peered inside, grabbed a can.

'Bud Light? Seriously? You got an eleven-million-dollar house and the fridge is full of Bud Light? I thought you'd have some fancy-shmancy craft beer or something.'

Miles shrugged. 'I like it. But if you look in the back I think I have some of the fancy-shmancy stuff.'

'No, no. I like this. I'm just surprised.'

Miles set down his water bottle. 'Grab me one.'

She reached into the fridge for another one and tossed it his way, but the can bounced off his chest, hit the floor, and rolled under the edge of the counter.

'Sorry!' Chloe said.

'Shit,' Miles said. 'Shit shit shit.'

She bent over to retrieve the can and set it on the counter. 'Better not open that one for a while. What happened?'

'I don't have the coordination I once did,' he said. 'I saw the can coming, but my arms didn't get the message from my brain fast enough to catch it.' But he was moving his arms now, looking at them with a mix of wonder, bafflement, and disappointment. 'Jesus.'

'Let me get you another one,' Chloe said, going back to the fridge. This time, she cracked the can

321

open and held it out to Miles. He reached for it tentatively, and once he had his hand firmly around it, he nodded and Chloe let go.

He took a sip.

'This is why I want you to take a test.'

Chloe, trying to make light of what had just happened, said, 'Written or oral?'

Miles sighed. 'We talked about this. A genetic sample. You don't even have to go anywhere. They'll come to the house, it'll take two seconds.'

'I've *done* that. When I sent in my DNA sample to WhatsMyStory I had to spit into a tube.'

'But they weren't necessarily looking for – look, if we compare your sample to mine, there are certain genetic markers that'll show whether you'll develop what I've got, at some point in the future.'

'Who really needs to know this the most?' she asked. 'Me, or you? Why do I even need this information right now, especially if there's not a damn thing I can do with it? I think this is about you. If I test positive, then – wait. Is positive if you have it, or is positive if you don't have it, because that kind of news would be positive?'

'Positive is if you have it.'

'Okay, so if I test negative, then you don't have to feel all guilty that you've passed something on to me. Is that what this is about?'

Miles looked down.

'We all got to die from something, right? So I take this test, we get the result, and we find out, hey, good news, no signs of whatever it is, but guess what? I've got some rare kind of cancer. Something you weren't even looking for. And then I got that shit to worry about for who knows how many years when if I didn't know I'd be a lot happier. You following me?'

'Yes,' Miles said. 'I do. But—'

'How will I be better off knowing?'

'You could . . . prepare.'

'Prepare,' she said, nodding. 'Okay, let's say, twenty years ago, you knew what was going to happen to you. What would you have done differently?'

He had to think about that. 'I'm not sure. I think I would have taken things a little more seriously. I wouldn't have wasted my time.'

'How did you waste your time?'

God, she could be infuriating, he thought. 'I would have applied myself more.'

'So you could get a house like this a couple of years sooner? Would that have made you happy? And didn't we already have the *happy* discussion? You know what? There's a lot to be said for wasting time. You can't spend your whole life on a treadmill. Sometimes you have to jump off and go sit on the beach. Sometimes you have to pick up a good book and sit in a hammock and fall asleep. And don't forget getting actually *wasted*. I'm something of an expert on that.'

Miles sighed. 'How'd you get to be so goddamn wise so young?'

'Maybe I'm not all that wise, I just look that way compared to you.'

Miles glared at her.

'Please don't tell me that's no way to talk to my father,' Chloe said.

Miles turned away, exhausted. Chloe, sensing it was time to offer a concession, said, 'What about this? I'll do your dumb test, but I don't want to know the result. You can know it, and whatever it is, whatever it finds I'm going to die from, you can keep that to yourself because I don't need to know. That a deal?'

Miles thought about that. He said, 'Deal.' Chloe extended a hand and they shook on it. 'I'll set it up. We can get it done tomorrow.'

'How long for the results?'

'I have connections with a private lab that can expedite things. Maybe even the same day.'

Chloe nodded cynically. 'With enough money, you can get whatever you want as fast as you want it.'

'Pretty much.'

'Does that apply to pizza, too? Because I'm so hungry I could eat a bucket of deep-fried beaks.'

'I thought you were a taco person.'

Forty minutes later they had a large pizza delivered to the door. Double cheese, pepperoni, black olives, green peppers. Chloe found two plates, put three slices on each of them, and set everything down on a coffee table in the media room.

She went back into the kitchen for two more cans of beer.

Miles dimmed the lights before they got comfortable on the enormous black leather sectional. Chloe, sitting to his right, reached for the remote and said, 'I've never seen anything on a screen this big, except in a theater.'

She hit some buttons and a streaming service filled the screen with movie thumbnails.

'Pick anything you want,' Miles said, biting into his first slice.

Chloe, with one hand holding a slice and the other wielding the remote, wandered through a screen filled with selections. 'Seen it, seen it, seen it, liked it, don't want to see it, saw it and hated it, didn't see it – oh, what about this?'

'*Little Women?*'

'Yeah. Did you see it?'

'No,' Miles said.

'Because you thought it would be a stupid chick flick?'

'No. I just didn't get to it.'

'You should see it. I've watched it twice.'

'Fine. I'll watch it one day.'

'No, you should see it now.'

'I'm pretty beat, but go ahead.'

Chloe hit the button to download the movie. She settled back into the cushions, holding the plate up close to her chin so she wouldn't drop crust crumbs or tomato sauce on herself. She downed two of the three slices, put the plate back on the table, and worked on her beer.

'My God, it's so clear you can see right up Meryl Streep's nose,' Chloe said.

About half an hour into the movie, Miles said, 'This is really good.'

Chloe said nothing.

As Miles turned to see why she'd not responded, her head slowly drifted toward him until it came to rest on his shoulder. He carefully pried the half-empty beer can from her fingers, set it on the wide leather arm of the couch, then took the remote from Chloe's lap and muted the movie.

He listened to her soft, sleepy breathing, felt the warmth of her next to him.

When he'd made the decision to go looking for his biological children, it had been because he believed it to be the right thing to do. He felt he owed them something – a future. Accepting that his own was limited, it felt appropriate to make a better one for those he was leaving behind.

What he hadn't anticipated was this. That he would forge a connection.

That he would find someone he could very possibly care about.

A daughter.

And there were others out there. Not as many as he'd originally come to believe, but there were others. Three unaccounted for – Todd Cox and Katie Gleave and Jason Hamlin – but, so far, according to Dorian, none of the others on his list

– Nina Allman, Colin Neaseman, Barbara Redmond, Travis Roben, Dixon Hawley – had met with misadventure.

That said, he felt an urgency to find them. But at least, for now, he'd found one.

He rested his head against Chloe's and, despite all the turmoil of the last couple of weeks, felt, at least in this moment, a sense of contentment. No, it was more than that. It was a sense of closeness.

As he allowed his eyelids to shut, as he permitted himself to let go and fall into a much-needed sleep, a thought came to him:

This is good.

And, even more incredibly:

I'm happy.

CHAPTER 37

Scottsdale, AZ

Dixon Hawley turned out to be, as the saying goes, a piece of cake.

Rhys and Kendra followed him after he finished closing up the art gallery where he worked late one evening. Dixon didn't have a car, and he lived close enough to his job that he walked to and from work. He did not, like many his age, live at home with his parents, but in a small apartment complex. Yes, there would be some cleaning involved, as any attempt to set his residence on fire was going to be met with limited success. The building was equipped with automatic sprinklers and only a couple of blocks from the closest fire station.

But for the most part, everything was going their way on this one.

To reach the entrance to his apartment building, Dixon had to walk down a narrow, dimly lit passageway lined with vines and bushes. At one end was the street; in the middle, the entrance to the building; and at the other end, the parking lot.

He was almost to the door, had the key in his hand, when Kendra, who was near the end by the parking lot, called out to him.

'Excuse me?'

Dixon stopped, looked, and said, 'Yes?'

'Do you live here?'

'Yeah?'

'Okay, so, I'm visiting, and I was backing out, and I hit someone's car and I wonder if you know whose it is.'

'Won't be mine,' he said. 'I don't have a car.'

'If you know whose it is, I can see if I can find them in the building, give them my name and number.'

Dixon smiled. How often did you meet people that honest?

So he tucked his key back into his pocket and walked to the end of the passageway, where Rhys was hiding behind a bush with a landscape rock in his hand, which he brought crashing down on poor Dixon Hawley's head.

They quickly bundled him into a body bag and then into the back of their rented van, where Rhys whomped Dixon one more time on the head, through the bag, just to be sure. They closed and locked the van and then, with Hawley's key, let themselves into the building, bringing along several empty garbage bags and cleaning materials, including, of course, the bleach.

Aware that the building had security cameras,

they both wore ball caps with large visors and kept their heads down as they made their way.

'Oh, I love this guy,' Kendra said upon entering the young man's second-floor apartment. 'He's a neat freak.'

It was true. The unit was small but immaculate. The stainless steel kitchen sink was empty, and glistening. The dishwasher was empty, all the dishes and glasses put away. The bathroom, even before they'd broken out the cleaning kit, smelled of Lysol. A single toothbrush stood propped up in a crystal clear glass. Not that they still didn't have their work cut out for them. Bagging the man's clothes, his bedding, toiletries. Hairs removed from bathroom drains, then drain cleaner poured in for good measure. Surfaces Dixon was most likely to have touched were wiped down with bleach. Kendra ran through with a vacuum, emptied its contents into the garbage bag. And even though the glasses and dishes were clean, Dixon would have touched them when he emptied the dishwasher, so Rhys put them all back into the machine and set it to run.

What they were doing, of course, was not fool-proof. Their employer had told them to do the best they could, and that was what they set out to do.

This time they remembered to make sure they had Dixon's phone – it was with him, in his pocket, in the body bag out in the van. And they bagged the laptop that was sitting on the coffee table in the living room, even the remotes lined up in front of the TV.

You did what you could.

The apartment had a small balcony that over-looked the parking area, so when they were done, Rhys went outside and collected the garbage bags as Kendra dumped them over the railing.

Then all that was left was to drive out in the desert, find a nice, secluded spot away from the main road, bring out the body bag, soak it with unleaded, and put a match to it.

The following morning, they were on a plane headed for Fort Wayne.

Now, standing in the bowling alley, they assessed the situation.

They'd been following Travis Roben around for the better part of a day and had concluded this one was going to be more difficult than Dixon Hawley. The young man lived at home with his parents – always more problematic when there were other people on the scene – and when he wasn't at home he was in the company of this blond chick.

This was looking more and more like a collateral damage situation. To get to Roben, they were going to have to risk exposing themselves to the girl. So they might have to take her out, too. At least, where she was concerned, there was not the added business of cleanup. So what if her body was found? So what if someone got her toothbrush or extricated some hairs from her shower drain? Their client was not concerned about any DNA test on her. They had concluded, on the flight to Phoenix, that the mandated cleanups were to erase DNA evidence, although they still had no idea why that mattered.

Kendra said, 'She's gonna do him.'

Rhys was skeptical. 'What are you talking about? You got some sort of sixth sense? You a student of body language?'

'I can read lips,' she said. 'She just asked him if he wanted to do it. I can't tell you what he said because his back's to me.'

'I can tell you what he said. He said yes.'

'Oh. Do *you* have some sort of sixth sense? Are *you* a student of body language?'

'No. But there isn't a guy on the planet who'd say no to her.'

'You like her?'

'She's cute. A little young for me, but if I was twenty again? It's not rocket science. Look at him. Ever since she asked him, he looks like he's got the fidgets.' He smiled. 'I think he's new at this.'

Kendra leaned up against the wall, crossed her arms. 'They'll have to go somewhere. Somewhere private. Could present an opportunity.'

Rhys nodded thoughtfully. 'But a short one. Got a feeling this guy's gonna come before he's even got his pants off.'

CHAPTER 38

New Haven, CT

Around one in the morning Chloe, her head still tucked into Miles's shoulder, stirred, waking him. They struggled off the couch, leaving their plates of pizza crusts on the coffee table. Miles showed Chloe to a guest room, where she flopped down onto the bed without even turning back the covers, and Miles went off to his own bedroom.

He was up shortly after six, having slept fitfully in his own bed. He'd gotten more of a rest when they'd fallen asleep on the couch. He kept asking himself one question: Who knew the names?

Dorian and Heather.

His brother, Gilbert, although he had shown him a printout of the names for only a second.

There was the woman at the ReproGold Clinic who had provided the names of the women who'd been artificially inseminated with Miles's donation.

There was Dr Gold himself.

Maybe Gold was worth visiting again. Go back

333

to the source, except this time don't settle for noncooperation. Lay it out for him, if possible without exposing his assistant as the source of the information. Miles might be able to bluff his way through that part, persuade Gold he'd made some headway through the services of WhatsMyStory. Or, given his own background, maybe Miles could persuade him he'd hacked into some database somewhere to get the information.

The other matter weighing heavily on Miles was the need to get in touch with the rest of his biological children. If there really was a chance they were in danger, he needed to alert them. But as of today, as of right now, what would he tell them?

It was enough of a shock to have someone walk up to you and announce he was your father. Even more of a shock to then be told that one day you might come down with a crippling disease. Now, on top of all that, imagine adding, *Oh, and by the way, something really, really terrible might be about to happen to you.*

Jesus.

Having stared at the ceiling long enough, he got up, wandering into the kitchen at 6:15 A.M. He dropped a pod into his Nespresso, and while he drank his coffee, he made yet another list – a mental one – of what needed to happen today.

Miles got out his phone and texted Dorian.

COME TO THE HOUSE INSTEAD OF OFFICE. ASAP.

He hit Send.

Before he could put the phone back down on the countertop, he saw the three dancing dots indicating that Dorian was already getting back to him.

NEARLY TO YOUR PLACE.

It was barely light out and Dorian was coming to the house? He debated asking why, then figured he'd find out when Dorian arrived. He typed:

OK.

He walked down the hall to the guest room. The door was open a crack and he peeked inside. At some point during the night, Chloe had crawled under the covers. She was asleep, her hair splayed out across the pillow. Miles watched her for several seconds before gently and noiselessly closing the door.

When he got back to the kitchen, he saw a set of headlights coming up the driveway. Dorian's Prius. He went to the door so she wouldn't have to ring the bell and possibly wake Chloe.

'Hey,' Miles said as Dorian got out of the car and approached. 'And here I was worried my text would wake you.'

'I'm your personal 911,' Dorian said.

Dorian came into the house and accepted Miles's offer of a coffee.

'If you were already headed here, you must have news.'

'Well, you texted at the crack of dawn, so I'm guessing you've got something urgent on your mind, too. You go first.'

'Can we get same-day test results?' he asked.

'What kind?'

Miles tipped his head toward the back of the house. 'Genetic. I have a guest. Chloe Swanson.'

'First on the list,' Dorian said, and smiled. 'How's that going?'

Miles took a moment. 'Good, I think.' He paused, appeared on the verge of being misty-eyed. 'I like her. She's her own person. Doesn't take any shit. Single-minded. Smart.'

Dorian nodded. 'Like my mom used to say, the apple doesn't fall far from the tree.'

'I've been feeling pretty stressed.'

'Who wouldn't be? This is a crazy situation.'

'It's not just that. It's the Huntington's. It's clouding my brain at times. And everything that's happened in the last few days, it's like it's accelerating some of the symptoms. Short-tempered, frustrated, unable to concentrate. Not to mention that I feel like I'm wobbling around all over the place. I'm feeling this sense of urgency. That we need to find these people, that Chloe needs to get tested.'

'Don't worry. We can get all these things done. How's Chloe feel about the test?'

'Not great, but she'll go along with it. She has

a somewhat fatalistic view of life. Maybe I did at that age, too. She says I can keep the results to myself. She doesn't want to know. I don't know why, but I *need* to know.'

'I've got the lab that did the test of Gilbert primed and ready to go,' Dorian said. 'I make the call, someone's here right away to retrieve the sample. We'll pay through the nose, but what do you care, right?'

'Yeah.'

'Then they should be able to tell us something before the end of the day. I've seen it done. Worst case, tomorrow.'

'And we need to set up another meeting with Heather. I don't exactly know what to do next, but she may have some ideas. I want to know more about the woman from the ReproGold Clinic.'

'Sure.' Dorian pulled out a phone. 'I'll text her now. She'll be up.'

'Okay, your turn,' he said.

'Hmm?'

'You were already on your way here. What was so important that you couldn't text me or tell me over the phone?'

Dorian put the phone down and looked at Miles, grim-faced.

'There's another one,' she said.

'What?'

'I've got all the names on your list set up on Google Alerts. Anything anywhere pops up about them, I get a notification.'

The color drained from Miles's face. 'Tell me.'

'Dixon Hawley is missing.'

Miles blinked. 'Scottsdale.'

Dorian nodded. 'Didn't show up yesterday morning at his place of work. An art gallery. When he didn't show, they tried calling him. No luck. So they sent someone around to his place and there was no sign of him. He's just . . . gone.'

'This can't be happening,' Miles said.

'I'm still trying to get more details, but there was something funny on the release that was on the police department website.'

'Which was?'

'His apartment had been stripped clean. Every personal item gone. Clothes, bed linen, toiletries. More than what you'd take if you were hitting the road.'

Miles wavered.

'You okay?' Dorian asked.

'I feel a bit . . . dizzy,' he said.

Dorian rushed to his side and steered him onto a nearby stool at the kitchen island.

'What's happening?' Dorian asked. 'Is this a symptom? Do I need to get a doctor?'

'No, no,' he said quietly. 'It's not that . . .'

'I know it's a shock, this Hawley guy going missing, but it's only been a day and—'

'It's the same.'

'What?'

'It's the same as what happened at Todd's place.'

Miles told Dorian about the spotless condition

338

of Todd's trailer when he and Chloe arrived. Then he filled her in about someone hiding under the bed, and the woman in the van who'd hit the brakes, creating a diversion.

'This is nuts,' Dorian said.

Miles placed his palms firmly on the counter, as though getting his bearings. 'These aren't coincidences.' He fixed Dorian with a hard glare. 'Who else could know?'

'Know what?'

'The names. You know. Heather knows. The doctor and his assistant know. Who else?'

Dorian shrugged.

'You haven't told anyone?' Miles asked.

'Of course not.'

'Is there any way anyone could have gotten the names from you? Hacked your computer? Listened in on your calls?'

'No. You know we do security sweeps all the time. Jesus, Miles, you think I'm some sort of mole or something?'

'No, of course not,' he said. 'I'm sorry. But somehow . . . somehow it's gotten out.' He took a moment to think. 'Get the test done on Chloe. Then organize a plane. I need to connect with those that are left. That's Nina Allman, Colin Neaseman, Barbara Redmond, and Travis Roben. Four stops, four days. Like I'm Drake on tour.'

'Yeah, like you're Drake,' she snickered.

'Can you do that?'

'Yeah. I'll take care of it.'

Miles put his elbows on the counter and rested his face in his hands.

'It's going to be okay,' Dorian said. 'We'll get this sorted out.'

They heard the padding of feet on the floor and turned to see Chloe walking into the kitchen wearing a white robe she would have found in her bathroom. She looked sleepy-eyed and her hair was a tangled mess.

'Do I smell coffee?' she asked.

CHAPTER 39

Fort Wayne, IN

Kendra Collins and Rhys Mills were still waiting for the right opportunity to deal with Travis Roben.

When Travis wasn't with the girl, he was at home with his parents, or on the road in his van, or at the comic shop. There hadn't been a moment when they could get to him without being seen by others. They were facing the prospect of taking out more than one person in order to get the target.

After observing Travis's interactions with the girl in the bowling alley, Rhys believed some sort of sexual rendezvous was in the offing, but it hadn't happened yet. They'd spent more of that day together, but hadn't checked into a motel or gone back to her place, wherever that was, and Travis had gone back that evening to the house where he lived with his mother and father.

Once it was dark, they attached a tracker to his van – a shitty old Chrysler job that was rusting around the wheel wells – so they wouldn't have

341

to sit on his house all night long. They checked in to a local motel, renting rooms side by side, confident that if Travis decided to head out on a midnight drive, they'd know about it. Kendra had an alert set up on her phone.

So when there was a knock on Rhys's door at one in the morning, he jumped out of bed, wearing nothing but a pair of boxers, and opened it to find Kendra standing there. He believed Travis had to be on the move, that an opportunity had presented itself.

Such was not the case.

Kendra placed her cold palm on him, entangling her fingers in the hairs on his chest, and pushed him back into the room until he was standing at the side of the bed, at which point she gave him a gentle shove. His butt dropped onto the mattress, placing him eye level with her breasts. Kendra placed her hands on his head and pulled him toward her.

'We're going to be unprofessional,' she said. 'I've been on the road too long.'

Rhys was willing to oblige. When they were finished, and Kendra had come three times, Rhys was expecting she'd spend the rest of the night with him. But she'd hopped off the bed, pulled on just enough clothes to get back to her room, and went for the door.

'See you in the morning,' she said, and left.

Several hours later, at a nearby diner, Rhys

looked across the table at his partner and said, 'About last—'

She performed a mini karate chop over her mug of coffee. 'Stop right there.'

'All I was going to say is—'

'You're going to say fuck all, that's what you're going to say.' She leaned forward and whispered, 'You ever find yourself just going along, and out of the blue, you think, "I'd kill for a hot dog." You know they're not good for you, but suddenly you're craving one, and you've got to have one, so you go to some hot dog stand and you get one, and you eat it, and it's good, and you kind of hate yourself, but it's over.'

'I'm a hot dog,' Rhys said.

'There you go.' She took a sip of her coffee.

Rhys said, 'Nothing on the phone?'

Her cell rested on the table next to her plate of corned beef hash. 'Nothing.'

'Can't see going into the house. Parents there. Too many variables.'

Kendra slowly shook her head in frustration. 'This one's taking too long. I'm getting sick of this.'

'You won't feel that way when you get paid.'

'Something I've learned over the years is, doesn't matter how much you're getting, it won't make you enjoy the work any more. It might make you tolerate it, but it doesn't make you like it.'

'Agreed. But—'

Her phone dinged.

'Hang on,' Kendra said, picking up the phone. 'Our boy's going for a drive.'

Rhys threw a twenty on the table. Kendra was already headed for the door.

Sandy had told Travis to pick her up in front of the Dunkin Donuts. And she was right where she said she'd be, looking pretty hot in a pair of jeans, some Ugg boots (how someone could wear these when it was not winter was a mystery to Travis, but what the hell), and a pullover top that fit her very snugly. He had made one stop along the way, at a CVS, which should have been a quick stop, but it took him a while to work up the nerve to go to the counter with his purchase.

He swerved the van over to the curb, holding his foot on the brake instead of putting it into Park, and Sandy opened the door. She was carrying a bag and a cardboard tray with two drinks tucked into it. One, in a paper cup, looked like a coffee, but the other, in a clear plastic container, looked more like a milkshake, topped with whipped cream and chocolate drizzle.

'I thought you might like one of these,' she said, dropping into the passenger seat. 'And I got donuts.'

Travis was still mentally pinching himself. A girl who wanted to have sex with him, *and* she brought donuts? Had he died? Was this heaven? And if it was, couldn't he have been provided with a ride that was cooler than a rusted minivan?

'Awesome,' he said.

'Needless to say,' she said, holding up the drink topped with whipped cream, 'this is yours. I just got a regular coffee.'

She transferred the drinks to the van's cup holders, then tossed the tray back to the middle row of seats where it found a home next to other discarded fast-food detritus, a baseball bat, some comic books in clear plastic sleeves, a pair of boots, and a snow brush that had been there since last winter. She pried back the opening on her coffee cup lid and took a sip.

'Yikes, it's hot,' she said.

'Like you,' he said, instantly wishing he could recall the two words. Talk about *lame-o*.

Sandy opened the top of the bag. 'I got half a dozen. Chocolate dip, cream-filled, a—'

'Surprise me.'

She dug out a chocolate and handed it over, but he was checking his side mirror as he pulled out into traffic. Once he was moving, he took the donut and bit into it.

'Mmmm,' he said.

'So where's this place?'

'Not too far. It's like, still within the city, but it's kind of isolated? A whaddaya-call-it, an industrial park but the place went out of business. You can drive around back. And it's right next to these woods, so it's pretty private.'

'You're sure?'

'Yeah, it'll be good. I wish we could go to, like,

an actual place. But my mom's home all the time, and if we went to a motel or something then you have to use a credit card and all that. That's why I used cash for the clothes. My mom looks at all my statements that come in the mail and I don't want her asking a whole bunch of questions.'

'Okay,' Sandy said. 'And my place is no good because my landlord's always snooping around, watching my every move.' She glanced again into the back seat, where she'd tossed the takeout tray. 'So, it's gonna be *here*?'

'Is that a problem?'

'You couldn't have tidied?'

'Sorry,' he said. 'I can clear off the seat when we get there. And I brought a blanket, in the back.'

Sandy looked skeptical, maybe even a little repulsed. 'I guess,' she said. 'Sorry if I got your motor running yesterday when I, you know, suggested this. Sorry yesterday didn't work out.'

'It's okay,' he said. 'I guess . . . I guess I was thinking you'd changed your mind.'

'No,' she said quickly. 'Nothing like that.' She paused, then asked, 'Did you get the things?'

He smiled, patted his pocket. 'Sure did.'

Fifteen minutes later, they were driving through an area of factories and warehouses. Travis turned the van into the lot of a building covered in pale blue metal siding, the windows all boarded over. A chain-link gate blocked the path to the rear of the structure. Travis stopped the van a foot ahead of the gate.

'Not to worry,' he said, getting out of the van and leaving the door open as he went to the gate, unlooped some chain, and pushed it open. He got in behind the wheel and said, 'Lock's been gone for ages.'

Once he had pulled past it, he jumped out again, swung the gate back to its original position, and got behind the wheel.

He pointed ahead through the windshield. 'Just back around here.'

The location was as he had described it. The lot was deserted save for a couple of rusted shipping containers and general debris, and was bordered on two sides by a wooded area. There were no other homes or buildings within view.

'See?' he said. 'Private.'

He got out of the van, went around to the back, opened the tailgate, and grabbed a folded pink blanket he'd tucked away there. He slid both side doors back on their tracks, cleared off everything that had been on the seat, then spread the blanket onto it. All this time, Sandy stayed in the passenger seat.

Travis went to her door, opened it, and extended his arm gracefully, a regular hotel concierge showing her to her room.

Sandy got out slowly, first putting her feet on the cracked pavement, taking half a step, and then getting into the middle seat. She shuffled over, leaving room for Travis to settle in next to her. They turned to face each other, and then Travis slipped his arms around her and planted his lips on hers.

He eased his fingers under her top, just above the waist, feeling bare skin. Slowly, he started to move his hands upward.

Suddenly, Sandy pushed him away.

'What?' he said. 'What is it?'

'I can't do this,' she said.

'What do you mean? I thought—'

'I'm not – I'm not ready.'

'What did I do?' Travis asked. 'Did I do something wrong?'

'No, no, you didn't,' she said, breaking away from him and sliding a few inches away, closer to the open door on the other side of the van. 'I need – I need some space. I need to think about this. I mean, I like you, I do, but—'

'Okay, okay,' Travis said. 'Whatever you need.'

She swung her legs out the door and slid out until her feet touched the pavement. She started walking.

'Where are you going?' he said, scooting across the seat and getting out, dragging the pink blanket along with him.

Sandy kept on walking, her back to him. Without turning, she said, 'I need a minute, okay?'

He watched her until she turned the corner of the building. He ran ahead, saw her headed for the gate.

'Shit,' he said to himself. 'What did I do?'

★ ★ ★

348

'And there it is,' Rhys said. 'Our opportunity.'

They had tracked Travis's van down to an abandoned warehouse in an industrial district. The entire area had fallen on hard times, as there were other abandoned businesses on either side of the warehouse. Kendra steered their rental into one of those lots. They got out and worked their way along a fence dividing one property from the other, and found a hiding spot behind a stack of empty wood cable reels that afforded them a partial view of the van.

'She's getting out,' Rhys whispered. 'They've had an argument or something.'

They held their position as the girl walked speedily along the side of the building, passing within a few feet of them as she headed toward the gate. She unhooked the chain, opened the gate a couple of feet, and slipped out without bothering to reclose it.

Rhys tapped Kendra on the shoulder, pointed to a gap in the fence, and motioned for her to follow. They pried back the chain-link, squeezed through without getting their clothes caught, and walked quietly toward the back of the building.

When they rounded the corner, they found Travis sitting dejectedly on the side-door rocker panel. When he saw them walking his way, his eyes went wide as he leapt to his feet.

'Hold it right there,' Kendra said.

They each flashed their bogus badge as they

closed the distance. Travis looked ready to wet his pants.

'I'm not doing anything!' he said.

'This is private property,' Rhys said, drawing his weapon. 'What do you think you're doing here?'

'Nothing!' he said, seeing the gun and throwing his hands into the air. 'Honest to God. I drove back here with my girlfriend and we kind of had a fight or something and she walked off and I only drove back here because it's private and I'm not stealing anything.' He lowered one hand, waved it. 'What would I take? There's nothing here!'

Rhys and Kendra had discussed earlier that in a spot like this, in back of a deserted warehouse, they might be able to get away with slightly less caution. They could shoot him, then go back to the rental for the body bag and other supplies. So what if some blood spilled onto the pavement? No one was ever going to know it happened here. They'd be taking the van elsewhere to burn it, along with the body. Or, if that didn't work out, taking it to a wrecking yard and having it crushed.

Still, Rhys was thinking, it might be better for the execution to happen around back of those cargo containers.

'What's your name?' he asked, even though he knew.

'Travis!' he said, his voice squeaking. 'Travis Roben.'

'You been in trouble with the law before?' Kendra asked, glancing at Rhys, the corner of her mouth going up a fraction of inch, giving him a look that said *I shouldn't be enjoying this, but I am*.

'Never!' he said.

'I need you to step over here,' he said, and motioned for Travis to walk toward the containers.

'Okay, okay,' he said. 'Can I put my hands down?'

'I never asked you to put them up,' Rhys said. 'But . . . no.'

When they reached the rusted containers – two of them, one labeled MAERSK was stacked on another marked EVERGREEN – Rhys gave Travis a little shove, pushing him around to the other side.

'Why do I have to go back here? Jesus, all I did was a little trespassing! You don't have to shoot me!'

'Maybe I do,' Rhys said.

Kendra was standing a few feet in back of her partner, taking in the show.

'No, please!' Travis said.

'Turn around,' Rhys said.

Travis, hands skyward, burst into tears as he turned his back to Rhys and Kendra.

'You have no idea, do you?' Rhys said.

'What?' he said.

'No idea why this is happening.'

'I told you, I'm sorry! I'll never step foot on this property again. I swear.'

351

Rhys raised his arm, aimed directly at Travis Roben's head.

That was when Kendra thought she heard something behind her, and started to turn around to see what it was.

A millisecond later, Sandy swung Travis's Louisville Slugger into Kendra's face, making her nose blow up like a tomato.

CHAPTER 40

New Haven, CT

Dorian, whose phone contained the digital equivalent of the world's biggest Rolodex, and who could find anyone, anywhere, to do just about anything, had someone from the DNA testing lab at Miles's house by nine. Chloe hadn't even had breakfast yet, unless one counted flavored coffee pods. So far she had tried a caramel espresso, a vanilla espresso, and something with the word *Guatemala* in it, and was pretty close to bouncing off the walls when it came time to provide a DNA sample.

'Will this hurt?' Chloe asked the technician, an East Indian woman in her early thirties. At Ferrari speed, she added, 'Because if it does hurt I'm okay with that because I have a pretty good tolerance where pain is concerned unless you know someone is hitting you in the head with a hammer or something and then, whoa, that's kind of my limit, not that anyone has ever hit me in the head with a hammer.'

'It'll only take a second,' the woman said. 'And

it's not a blood sample. I'm not sticking a needle into you. I'm just taking a swab and putting it into your mouth.'

'Okay,' Chloe said.

She put the sample in a small vial, sealed it in a plastic bag, labeled it, and put it into a pouch.

Dorian asked, 'How long?'

'We'll put a rush on it,' the woman said. As she headed for the front door, Chloe called out to her, 'After all this coffee, don't be surprised if my DNA shows I'm Ethiopian!'

Dorian said, 'Maybe your next one should be a decaf.'

Chloe said, 'Where's Miles?'

'He was feeling tired and went to lie down for a bit. He didn't sleep well.'

'Yeah, well, there's a lot of shit going down, isn't there?'

'Yes,' Dorian said.

'I need to eat something before I go totally buggy. Gotta soak up this caffeine. Has Miles got something like that thing in *Star Trek*? I tell it what I want to eat and a little door opens and it's there?'

'Sadly, no. The closest thing Miles has to that is a housekeeper, and she doesn't arrive until ten. But help yourself to anything. See that door? That's a pantry. All kinds of stuff in there.'

Chloe looked, marveling at the shelves lined with canned items, boxes of cereal and pastas and rices, a dozen kinds of olive oil, veggie chips, potato chips, corn chips. There was an extra freezer in there as well, where Chloe found half a dozen flavors of Ben & Jerry's, steaks and chops and whole chickens.

'Miles is definitely a meat-a-tarian,' she said, loudly enough for Dorian to hear.

'Yes.'

Chloe popped her head out, pointed a finger at Dorian. 'I'm betting you're vegan. You've got this vibe about you.'

'And what kind of vibe is that?' Dorian asked.

'Vegan goes along with the whole androgynous thing.'

'I like my steak rare,' Dorian said, adding, 'And bloody.'

'Well, there you go. So much for stereotypes.' She glanced back into the pantry. 'There's more food here than where I work.'

'And where's that?'

'The Paradise Diner in Providence. I wait tables.'

'Oh.'

Chloe came back into the main part of the kitchen, went into the fridge, and came out with a container of eggs and a bag of shredded cheddar cheese.

'I don't work in the kitchen, but I still know my way around,' Chloe said. 'I'm gonna scramble some of these. You in?'

'I'm good.'

'Would Miles want some?'

'He ate.'

'Okay.' Chloe found a bowl and a frying pan. She cracked four eggs into the bowl, tossed in a handful of cheese, beat it, then put the pan on the stove. She turned on the burner, dropped a pat of butter in, poured in the eggs, and stirred them around with a wooden spatula. The entire process took less than five minutes. When the eggs were ready, she slid them onto a plate, salted them, and perched herself on a stool on the other side of the island from Dorian.

'So what's your story?' she asked.

'My story?'

'How long have you been Miles's assistant?'

'About ten years,' Dorian said.

'Good guy to work for?'

Dorian hesitated. 'Sure.'

'Whoa, hard to read between the lines when it's just one word, but that doesn't sound great.'

'I'm sorry. That came out wrong. He's demanding. Often short-tempered. Irritable. But I wouldn't have given him a decade of my life if I didn't believe he was, ultimately, fair. And a decent person.' Dorian paused. 'These last few weeks have changed him. He knows what's coming and he's dealing with it. And . . .'

With a mouthful of eggs, Chloe said, 'And?'

'And I see a difference in him even today. He's stressed, but there's a softer side coming out. I wonder if that has something to do with you.'

Chloe said, 'Me?'

'I think finding you, and his quest to find the

others, has given his life some renewed meaning. However long that life may be.'

Chloe said nothing.

'Do you have any idea?'

'Any idea about what?'

'What this will mean to you? How your life will change? I mean, look around.'

'I don't care about this.'

'Really? You look like you're settling right in.'

Chloe shrugged. 'So I'm impressed. That's all.'

'You and the others will share millions.' Dorian couldn't hide a look of some disdain. 'And done nothing for it.'

'What's that supposed to mean?'

'What have you done to deserve it?' Dorian asked.

'Sweet fuck all,' Chloe said. 'Not arguing with you there. Shit, you deserve it way more than I do. Working for him for the last ten years. You must be getting a cut, right?'

Dorian did not respond.

'Oh,' said Chloe. 'Maybe he's leaving you something but hasn't told you.'

'Miles has been very forthcoming about how his portfolio will be distributed. I've seen the documents. Every piece of paper and email and text that goes to Miles goes through me first.'

'Huh,' Chloe said. 'That's gotta burn a little bit.'

'I'm an employee,' Dorian said. 'It's very simple. Eventually, Miles will have to work out a succession plan, choose someone to take over. Maybe he'll even sell. I might be kept on, but maybe not. I'll manage.'

They heard footsteps. Miles walked into the kitchen, gave Dorian a nod, then turned his attention to Chloe.

'Eat up and get dressed. We've got places to go, people to see.'

CHAPTER 41

Fort Wayne, IN

It wasn't clear which sound made Rhys spin around first.

It could have been Kendra's scream as the bat caught her square in the face. It could have been the sound of the bat striking flesh and bone. It might have been the scuffling of shoes on pavement as Kendra lost her footing. And it might have been the girl herself, the one wielding the bat, who let loose a scream of her own when she took the swing.

Given that all these various sounds happened within a millisecond of one another, it might not have been any one sound but their combined effect. Rhys heard a minisymphony of chaos behind him, and regardless of how focused he might have been on his current task, which was to shoot Travis Roben in the back of the head, he could not stop himself from whirling around to see what had happened.

It took another millisecond for him to assess what had happened.

The girl – he did not know her name was Sandy, as they'd not been properly introduced – had returned, observed that the two of them were about to kill her boyfriend, grabbed a bat from someplace (he was guessing the van), and crept up behind Kendra before whacking her in the head.

In the time it took for Rhys to spin around, Kendra was hitting the pavement, her face a bloody, pulpy mess. Any movement she was making was due to gravity. After her initial scream, she'd not made a sound, and she'd made no attempt to brace her fall. She went down like a stringless marionette.

Rhys and Sandy locked eyes briefly. That was when he raised his arm and pointed the gun directly at her chest.

While all this was happening, Travis was also reacting.

He'd had his hands in the air, pleading for his life, tears running down his cheeks, wondering how something as minor as trespassing could result in a death sentence. A couple of cops catch you making out on private property, you figure the worst that could happen is you get a ticket. In most cases, they'd give you a stern lecture and order you to get lost.

But the guy had pulled a gun! What the hell was that about? What kind of cops would react that way? Travis hadn't threatened them. He wasn't armed.

So when Travis heard the commotion happening behind him, he turned around.

He could not believe what he was seeing.

Sandy standing there with his Louisville Slugger, now smeared with a dark red blotch, in her hands. The woman cop was on the ground, not moving, blood all over the place. The male cop had his back to Travis and was aiming his gun at Sandy.

Travis didn't think. He just acted.

He wasn't even six feet from Rhys, but in that short distance he worked up some speed and leapt onto his shoulders, wrapping his arms around his neck and holding on to him as though he were about to go on a piggyback ride.

As Rhys was thrown off balance, the gun in his hand went off. But the bullet went wild, whizzing past Sandy and pinging off the upper shipping container.

Rhys shouted, 'Get the fuck off—'

But that was as far as he got because Travis had moved his hands up from Rhys's neck and was now grabbing him around the eyes and nose. A finger slipped into his mouth and Rhys bit down, hard. Travis cried out in pain, but he held on.

And Rhys released his grip on Travis's finger when Sandy took the bat to his left knee.

It folded on him like an old, rusted lawn chair. He hit the pavement, Travis still clinging to him. Rhys didn't release his grip on the gun, at least not until Sandy swung the bat down hard onto the back of his hand.

The gun slipped from his fingers and skittered across the pavement. As he struggled to get Travis off his back, Sandy ran for the gun and scooped it off the ground, holding it as though it were radioactive. She looked about frantically, wondering what to do with it.

She pitched it skyward, hoping to land it atop the shipping containers, but her throw came up short and the gun bounced off the side of the upper container and clattered back to the ground. She stood, torn about whether to go after it or take another swing at Rhys as he lay on the ground.

Sandy chose the latter.

She took a couple of wild swings, the first more or less aimed at his thigh, because if she went for his upper body, she was just as likely to hit Travis. The bat caught him a few inches above the knee that she'd already hit.

Travis scrambled off him, scurrying a couple of yards along the pavement like a crab before he got to his feet.

He pointed to the van and screamed:

'GOGOGOGOGOGO!!!'

Kendra still wasn't moving, and Rhys was struggling to get up. As Travis and Sandy ran for the van, Rhys tried to get to his knees, but could put no weight on the left one. That bought Travis and Sandy enough time to open the driver and passenger doors and get in. The retractable side doors remained open.

362

The key had never been removed from the ignition. Travis put his foot on the brake, turned the key, and the engine came to life.

Rhys was on his feet, limping in their direction.

'He's coming!' Sandy screamed.

Travis, looking ahead through the glass, could see that. By the time he had moved the shifter into Reverse, Rhys had gotten to the open side door and was reaching for the handle to haul himself in.

But Travis hit the gas and the van shot backward, tires squealing. He abandoned the idea of making a three-point turn to get the van pointed forward. He was afraid that would give Rhys an opportunity to jump in.

So he shifted around in his seat to see where he was going, one hand over the back of the seat and one on the wheel, and he backed up all the way along the side of the disused warehouse, the transmission whining like a banshee as the car went far faster in reverse than it was ever designed to do, and when Travis got to the gate he just kept on going, knowing it was not locked and would swing out of his way.

The gate, however, was installed to swing in the other direction, so while it did give way when the van hit it, it snapped violently off its hinges and bounced off the side of the vehicle with a huge metallic crashing sound.

Travis didn't slow down. Since he'd kept his eyes

on where he was going, he didn't know whether they were still being pursued.

'Is he coming?' he shouted.

'No!' Sandy said.

He kept reversing the van until he had reached the street, cranking the wheel to line up with the road. The front end of the van swerved hard before he brought it to a stop and threw it into Drive. Fast-food debris and the pink blanket slid off the back seat and went flying out the door.

Travis floored it.

'What the fuck was that?' he shouted.

Sandy, stammering, her voice shaky and high-pitched, said, 'I decided – I came back – I saw them – he had a gun – he was pointing it – I grabbed the bat – oh my God – fuck I think I killed her – oh fuck oh fuck oh fuck did I kill a cop?'

'Why would they want to kill me?' he asked, his hands gripping so tightly on the wheel they felt welded to it. 'The police don't kill people for trespassing!'

'He was pointing the gun right at your head!' she said. 'He was going to do it! I swear he was!'

He glanced over at her quickly. 'You fucking saved my life!'

Sandy, too stunned to acknowledge the comment, had her hand braced against the dash, as though expecting them to crash at any moment.

'It was them,' she said suddenly.

'Them?'

'The two people in the bowling alley. The ones I thought were watching us.'

'Are you sure?' Travis asked.

'You didn't get as good a look at them as I did. It was *them*.' She shot him a wary look. 'Why would they have been watching you?'

'Me?' he said. 'No reason. Maybe they were watching *you*.'

Travis swerved to avoid a dog that had darted out into the street. He cranked the wheel hard left, then right, the van feeling like it was going to roll over for a second.

'You gotta slow down,' she said.

Before easing his foot off the gas. Travis made a few random turns, figuring that if they were being followed, this would shake any possible tail.

Once he'd slowed the van to something close to the speed limit, he said, 'What do we do now?'

'Maybe close the doors before one of us gets thrown out?'

He pulled over to the curb, slipped between the two front buckets, slid the doors shut, then got back behind the wheel. He put the van back in Drive and kept moving.

'Okay, now what *else* do we do? Go to the police? Tell them what happened?'

Sandy's face paled. 'Are you kidding?'

'What?'

'They *were* the police!'

'I don't think so,' Travis said. 'I mean, maybe, but they never let us get a close look at their ID,

365

they never identified themselves, and like I said, cops don't go around killing you for being on private property.'

'No,' Sandy said. 'No no no no no. Not a good idea.'

'But what you did, it was justified,' Travis said. 'He was going to shoot me! In the head!'

'I have to think about this,' she said, suddenly going very quiet. Then, 'Pull over! Pull over!'

'What?'

'Pull over!'

He hit the brakes and veered over to the side of the road. Sandy barely had her feet on the ground before she bent over, put her hands on her knees, and threw up.

Travis jumped out, ran around to the other side of the van, and rested a comforting hand on her back. He could feel her heart pounding.

When she believed she was done vomiting, she spat a few times, dug a tissue out of her pocket and dabbed her lips, then stood up straight and looked at him.

'No police,' she said. 'Promise me.' When Travis didn't respond right away, she added, 'It's how you can thank me for saving your life.'

She put a hand atop his shoulder and squeezed.

'Okay,' he said.

'Motherfucker,' Rhys said as he gave up trying to run after the van.

His knee, while still barely workable, was

throbbing. He leaned over, touched it delicately. His upper thigh hurt, too, and he'd no doubt have a hell of a bruise there, but it was the knee he was more worried about. He wasn't sure, at this point, whether it was broken, but he sure wanted to get some ice on it as soon as he could.

'That bitch,' he muttered under his breath.

How the hell didn't they hear her come back? Why weren't they watching for her?

Stupid stupid stupid.

He hobbled over to retrieve the gun that Sandy had tried to throw on top of the shipping container. He picked it up and gave it a cursory inspection. He'd have to fire it to be sure, but it appeared to be in working order. It was a wonder it didn't go off when it was thrown.

Then he looked over at Kendra.

He limped to where she lay on the pavement and, with considerable difficulty, knelt down beside her. Had the girl killed her with a single blow to the head? She sure as hell had made a mess of her face. The woman's nose appeared to have been turned inside out.

'God damn it,' he said.

And then she moaned.

'Kendra?' he said.

Her eyelids fluttered.

Rhys took her hand. 'I'm here. It's Rhys. You've been hurt bad. Fucking bitch came at you with a bat.'

Her lips moved but no words came out.

'They got away. We fucked up.'

Rhys noticed the rectangular bulge in the front pocket of her jeans and fished out her cell phone. He took her hand and pressed her thumb to the home button to unlock it. Then he went into the settings and deactivated the touch password so he could use it himself.

The app they'd used to track the Roben kid's van was open. He and the girl were already miles away, but Rhys could find them if he wanted to.

But did he?

His gut told him it was time to abort. At least temporarily. If Roben went to the cops, told them what had happened, they could be here very soon. Then again, he and the girl might be too scared to go to the authorities. If they still believed he and Kendra were police, they might lie low.

But Rhys couldn't be sure. He had to move.

Except he had a wounded associate to deal with. He couldn't take her to a hospital. And he certainly didn't know how to treat her himself. Sure, Rhys had some basic first-aid skills, but Christ on a cracker, Kendra here needed emergency surgery. It was remotely possible there were under-the-radar local resources, someone outside of a hospital with medical training who could look at her. Retired doctors, or ones who'd lost their licenses to practice.

Fucking veterinarians, if it came to that.

Kendra moaned again. This time, she managed

to open her eyes all the way and she trained them on Rhys.

'Hey,' he said.

'Blerm,' she said, blood seeping out from between her lips.

If he was going to have even a chance of saving her, he would have to run back for their rental, bring it here, load her into the back seat, get as far away from here as possible, as *fast* as possible, and get on the phone to see if there was someone who could tend to her wounds. Rebuild her fucking face, basically.

Rhys thought about all that.

And then said, aloud, 'No time.'

He bent down and whispered into her ear, 'Sorry, Kendra. Only one way this can go.'

Putting as much weight as he could on his good knee, he stood, aimed the gun at Kendra's forehead, and pulled the trigger.

CHAPTER 42

New York, NY

Roberta was in her first-floor office in Jeremy's brownstone, sitting at the computer, trying to reply to several dozen emails but finding it very difficult to concentrate. This whole business with Nicky was dragging on too long. She understood Jeremy had specific people in mind for an assignment of this nature. This was a very delicate task, not the sort of thing to be left to an amateur, and Jeremy was willing to wait for a person with the requisite skills. Such a person was supposed to be coming soon.

There were only a few people in the building who knew about Nicky. Herself and Jeremy, of course. The housekeeper, who was undocumented and definitely not going to call the authorities. And Boris, the security guard. Not even Antoine, who made the meals that Roberta took up to Nicky's room, knew who that extra plate was for, and no doubt assumed it was for some random staff member.

370

She was thinking about all of this when Boris came into her office and said, 'Problem.'

Roberta looked at him wearily. 'What now?'

'Front door.'

Roberta pushed back her chair and followed him through to the front of the house. Along the way, Boris explained that a friend of Nicky's was on the step, asking for her.

Roberta opened the door and gave the girl standing there a businesslike smile. She was fifteen or sixteen, short black hair, and about the skinniest thing Roberta had ever seen aside from a garden rake.

'May I help you?' Roberta said.

'I'm looking for Nicky?'

'Nicky?'

'Nicky Bondurant? She's a friend of mine?'

'And who are you?'

'Stacey.'

'Do you have a last name, Stacey?'

'Booker. Stacey Booker. Is Nicky here?'

'There's no Nicky here,' Roberta said. 'Do you have the right house?'

Stacey took two steps back and looked up at the number over the door. 'Yup,' she said.

'Trust me, no one named Nicky lives here.'

'I didn't say she *lived* here,' Stacey said. 'I've been to her apartment. But I've walked with her to this address before. I've been trying to find her. She hasn't been at school. They said she had mono but she's not at her place.'

'I'm sorry,' Roberta said. 'We hire a number of people for functions, but we're not hosting one at the moment, so even if we had ever hired someone named Nicky, she would not be here now.'

'Well, would you know—'

'I'm sorry, I can't help you,' Roberta said, and closed the door in the girl's face.

She saw Boris standing at the base of the broad stairwell and said, 'If she comes back, toss her ass onto the sidewalk.'

Rather than go back to her office, she ascended the stairs, continuing past the second floor and on to the third, through the doors with the security keypad, down the wide hallway lined with erotic, black-and-white photography.

She found Jeremy not at his desk but in the Winnebago. The door was open, and she saw him sitting inside at the tiny dining table, working on a laptop.

Roberta poked her head in and said, 'Permission to come aboard.'

Jeremy looked away from the screen and smiled. 'Permission granted.'

She stepped in and squeezed onto the cushion bench on the other side of the table. Jeremy's attention had gone back to the screen.

'I love working in here,' he said. 'A mini-office within the larger one. It feels like I'm somewhere else, on the road someplace. I'm doing a piece for the *Times*. Promised to get it to them by this evening. It's for tomorrow's edition, although they're going to post it online soon as it's ready.'

Roberta, who didn't give a rat's ass about what her boss was pontificating about for the *Times*, did not ask. Although she had to give him credit: the man could multitask. He could keep a young girl prisoner in his home and still bang out a think piece for the country's biggest newspaper. Nothing was going to stop him from sharing his brilliance with as wide an audience as possible.

She said, 'This issue has to be resolved.'

A brief look of puzzlement crossed his face, as if wondering what she was referencing. Roberta glared at him, figuring he'd piece it together eventually.

'Oh, yes,' he said.

'We just had one of Nicky's friends at the door, asking if she was here. One of the first rules of the house is, you don't tell strangers you work here. That stupid Nicky. If she told that girl, who else might she have told? What if, at some point, someone in an official capacity comes knocking?'

'I'd make a call. Get the chief on the line, tell him we were being harassed.'

'That might not work. They come with a warrant, there's really nothing we can do.'

Jeremy strummed his fingers on the tabletop. 'If somebody comes, gag her, sedate her, stuff her somewhere until they're gone. Move her off the property if you have to.'

'And take her where?'

'Roberta, why do I employ you?' Before she could offer a response, he said, 'I pay you to solve problems. I pay you to put out fires.'

'With all respect, Jeremy, this place is going to burn to the ground if you don't sort this out soon.'

Jeremy tented his fingers. 'Sit tight. Help is on the way.'

CHAPTER 43

New Haven, CT

They'd gotten off to a late start.

Shortly after Miles had told Chloe to get ready to go, Dorian received two unrelated messages about ongoing issues at Cookson Tech – one was a frivolous lawsuit by another software developer who'd alleged one of Cookson's travel apps infringed on its copyright, and the other was an update on a medical app that would help people self-diagnose – and Dorian felt strongly that Miles needed to make some decisions with regard to them.

That ended up taking nearly two hours, and by then it was time for lunch, so they didn't leave for wherever it was Miles wanted to go until nearly one in the afternoon. Chloe made two calls. One was to the diner to tell them she had a family emergency, which she chose not to elaborate on, and would be gone indefinitely. The other call was to reply to a voice mail from her mother, wanting to know where she was and when she would be coming home.

'I'm gonna have to tell her,' she said to Miles.

'Your call,' he said.

So she retreated to the guest room for privacy and phoned her mother. When she answered, Chloe said, 'I found him. I found my real father.'

Her mother was stunned into speechlessness to the point that Chloe thought the call had dropped out.

'Are you there?'

Finally, her mother said, 'Found out . . . who he is? Found out where he lives?'

'Yes, and yes, and I'm with him right now.' She told her mother his name and where she was.

Another moment of silence. 'How did you – was it that WhatsMyStory thing again?'

'Not this time. It's a long story. I'll tell you all about it when I get home. And I'm okay. Trust me.'

Chloe's mother asked, 'Is he . . . nice?'

'Yes.' She paused to make sure she had control over her voice. 'And he's sick. He's not so bad right now, at least most of the time, but he's going to get worse.'

Her mother's voice softened. 'Then it's a good thing you found him when you did.'

When Chloe ended the call, she sat on the edge of the bed and started to cry. She'd been caught off guard by her mother's reaction. She'd expected her to be angry. But what really released the tears was telling another person Miles was dying. Verbalizing it made it all the more real.

She'd known this man for such a short time, but she felt a connection.

Chloe *liked* him.

She realized that she genuinely cared about him, and hoped that they'd be able to get to know each other before his illness got much worse. She wanted to spend time with him, catch up on a lifetime of separation.

She grabbed a tissue and dabbed her eyes. She didn't want to head back out there having anyone think she'd lost it.

Miles had explained to her earlier where they were headed: the ReproGold Clinic in New Rochelle. And he'd also explained why he wanted her to tag along.

'You're smart,' he'd said. 'You've got a good head on your shoulders. If I lose focus, you can put me back on the right path. And with all that's been going on, I feel better knowing where you are. At least you're not going to disappear on me.' After a pause, he'd added, 'And you're good company.'

So, after lunch, Miles and Chloe were in the back of the limo, Charise behind the wheel.

'Mr Cookson, Ms Swanson,' she had said, opening the door for them. Charise had quietly asked Miles what Chloe's last name was so that she could address her appropriately.

'I think she'd be okay with Chloe,' he said. 'And you can call me Miles.'

'I'll keep that in mind, Mr Cookson.'

Once they were on their way, Miles shifted in his seat so he could look at Chloe more directly. He reached into his pocket for his phone. 'When we get to the clinic, I'm going to have a few questions for Dr Gold. I'm going to asking him specifically about these people.'

He opened a document on the phone's screen and handed it to her. She looked at it and said, 'Who are these people? I see my name and Todd's and . . .' She looked at him. 'Holy shit. This is them.'

'Yeah.'

'These are my half brothers and sisters.'

'It's time for you to know everything.'

'Who are the missing ones?'

'Katie Gleave, Jason Hamlin, Dixon Hawley. You recognize any of those names?'

Chloe read through the list twice. 'No.'

'None of them have been in touch?'

She shook her head. 'Maybe Todd and me are the only ones who used WhatsMyStory. But this is for real? These are, like, these are your kids?'

'Sounds funny putting it that way, but yes.'

'So this clinic we're going to, that's the one you went to, way back when?'

Miles nodded. 'I went to see him once before, since I got my diagnosis. He wasn't very helpful. I'm hoping he'll be more so, this time.'

Chloe grinned. 'We're going to rattle his cage.'

'Something like that.'

When they reached the clinic, Miles wondered

if it had gone out of business. The waiting room was empty.

But the receptionist Miles had seen here on his previous visit, the one who'd provided the list of names, was at her desk behind an open sliding-glass panel. Julie Harkin did a double take when she looked up and saw Miles standing there, Chloe just behind him.

'I'm here to see Dr Gold,' he said.

'He's not in today,' she said quietly. 'He's canceled all his appointments for the rest of the week.' Her eyes narrowed. 'You were here before. You're Mr Cookson.'

'Yes.'

She glanced about, as though checking to make sure there really were no other people in the room, and when she looked back at Miles she spoke in a voice that was barely above a whisper. 'You sent that woman.'

Miles nodded. 'I did. Thank you for helping.'

Julie did not look like she was going to say, *You're welcome*. She asked, 'What did you get me into?'

'Nothing,' Miles said. 'I haven't said anything about where we got the information.'

'But things have started happening,' she whispered accusingly. 'Bad things. And the doctor's freaking out about something. And it's all happened since you were here. What have you done?'

Then Julie looked past him, as if noticing Chloe for the first time. 'Who are you?'

'Chloe Swanson,' she said, offering up a small

wave. Then she looked about the room and glanced down the hallway at the doors to various visitation rooms. 'So it all began for me here, huh?' She nudged Miles with her elbow, trying to lighten the mood. 'Which room did you do it in?'

'Stop,' he said.

Chloe stopped.

Miles said to Julie, 'Where is he?'

'I don't know,' she said. 'Maybe at home, maybe out drinking somewhere. I have no idea.'

'I really need to talk to Dr Gold. Please.'

Julie bowed her head briefly, as though reluctant to look him in the eye. 'You know, I looked you up. I know who you are. I wondered who'd have that kind of money, to pay for confidential information. Your name was on all those files. You're trying to find your biological children.'

Miles nodded. 'I had different . . . motivations in the beginning. But now they've changed. You said bad things are happening, and you're right. Those children I fathered, they're in danger. I don't know exactly why. That's why I want to speak to Dr Gold again.'

Julie studied him for a moment before she made a decision to pick up the phone and enter a number. After about ten seconds, she said, 'Dr Gold? It's Julie. I know, I know you didn't – something has come up and I need to know – I can't really say what it is, but if you—'

Julie looked at Miles and Chloe. 'He hung up.'

'Shit,' Miles said.

380

'But there was an echo,' she said. 'Like the walls were metal. I'm betting he's at his storage unit.'

Julie wrote down the address on a piece of paper, then two other numbers. One was three digits, the other four. 'That first one is the unit number,' she said, 'and the second is for the keypad at the gate.' She looked defeated. 'I was going to ask you not to tell him where you got the names, but it doesn't matter anymore. I'm finished here.'

The storage facility was not far, and Charise had them there in less than ten minutes. She drove the limo right up to the gate, powered down the window, entered the four-digit code into the keypad, and waited while the gate retracted.

Once in the compound, she drove up to a drab, windowless, two-story structure. There were access doors at each end, both equipped with keypads.

'If you need me, sir, I'm available,' Charise said as she held the back door open for Miles. She stood there, taking a stance. 'One thing in my work history I didn't mention was bouncer.'

Miles couldn't help but grin. 'Good to know, but I think we'll be okay.'

Once they were inside the building, Chloe asked Miles to read off the unit number from the slip of paper Julie had given him.

'It's two-oh-four.'

'Upstairs,' she said, checking the signs.

They found a stairwell around the corner from a freight elevator, reached the second floor, and started looking for numbers.

'This way,' Chloe said, grabbing Miles's sleeve and taking him down a corridor in the opposite direction he'd been headed.

About thirty feet ahead, a storage unit door was raised to the open position. Someone could be heard moving things around. There was a buzzing sound that lasted several seconds, then a pause, then the sound of more buzzing.

They closed the distance and saw Martin Gold, in a blue suit and tie, feeding papers into a shredder that had been set up on the edge of a box, the spaghetti-like strips of paper being fed into a green plastic garbage can.

'Dr Gold,' Miles said loud enough to be heard over the buzzing of the shredder.

Gold looked up, startled. He stopped feeding paper into the machine and the buzzing stopped.

'How did you get in here?' he said.

'We—'

But before Miles could say another word, the cell phone tucked away inside his jacket started to ring. He dug it out and saw DORIAN.

'Hang on.' He tapped the screen and put the phone to his ear. 'Look, Dorian, let me call you back in—'

'We got the results already,' she said.

'What? Are you serious?'

'Yeah.'

Miles turned away from Chloe and the doctor and took a few steps away from them. 'Is she okay? Does Chloe show any signs?'

'Chloe doesn't have Huntington's.'

Miles sighed and smiled. He felt the weight of a dozen cinder blocks lifting from his shoulder. 'That's wonderful.'

'There's something else, though.'

Miles felt the blocks drop back into place. He recalled Chloe's fear that she might test negative for his disease but be found positive for a totally different condition. 'She has something else? Christ, what is it?'

'She's perfectly healthy,' Dorian said. 'But they compared your profiles. Yours and Chloe's.'

'Okay,' he said slowly.

'There's no DNA match between the two of you.'

Miles couldn't find any words.

Dorian added, 'You're no more related to her than I am to the Queen of England.'

CHAPTER 44

Somewhere over Pennsylvania

Rhys Mills normally liked an aisle seat, and as close to the exit as possible. It was a control thing. Whenever possible, he liked to be first off the plane. And he hated the window seat, being hemmed in by someone, having to maneuver around them if you wanted to use the bathroom.

But today, booking at the last minute, Rhys had few options. He had asked the middle-aged woman on the aisle if she would like the window, trying to make it sound as though he was doing her a favor, but she wasn't interested. Had a very active bladder and might need to get to the bathroom lickety-split, she told him, like he was dying to hear every possible detail about her urinary situation. So here he was, leaning into the fuselage, looking down through the clouds at the state of Pennsylvania.

Heading home.

It was usually a good feeling. But Rhys was filled with dread, as well as heavy-duty painkillers for

384

his knee. The assignment he and Kendra had been sent on was unfinished. Worse, Kendra was dead. If he was to finish this job, he'd need a new partner. This had not been the kind of gig, to use Kendra's word, one could do alone.

Every time he closed his eyes, he saw her lying there, her face a mess of raw hamburger. Saw his hand pointing the gun downward, squeezing the trigger.

He told himself it was the right thing to do, not just for himself but for Kendra. It was highly likely she would have died without his intervention. He'd spared her considerable suffering. And if she could have been saved, what sort of future awaited her? Years of reconstructive surgery. Plus, if Roben and the girl went to the police, and the cops put it all together, Kendra'd be spending her time in prison instead of the plastic surgeon's waiting room.

Rhys, too.

No, it was better all around that Rhys put that bullet in her brain. Better for the client, too. Had she lived, she might have talked. Once the police had you in a box, you had to do what you could to save your own neck.

Would have been better if he'd gotten rid of her body, though.

At least he'd stripped her of any ID – not that any of it was legit – but even fake ID, once police had run some checks, would raise questions.

Would Roben and the girl report this? Hard to say. The girl would have to admit what she did. A confession would pose considerable risk if the cops didn't buy her story. By the time Rhys boarded his plane out of Fort Wayne later that day, there hadn't been a word online about her body being discovered.

He closed his eyes again, and this time, instead of remembering her as he'd last seen her, he pictured her coming to his motel room in the middle of the night, pushing him onto the bed, having *her* way with *him*. Her entire body was hungry, and when it was satisfied, she left. Kendra was no sentimentalist. If he'd been the one caught in the face with that bat, she would have handled things the same way.

'Well, here we go,' said the woman sitting next to him, unbuckling her seat belt. 'The Pepsi's found its way through me already!'

Rhys offered a thin smile and looked back out his window.

When he landed, he'd head home first, have a couple of scotches, take a shower, maybe find a woman – there were a couple he could call on short notice – all before breaking the news to the client and deciding where to go from here.

There'd been some suggestion, in a cryptic text, that another job, tangentially related to the one he'd been on, awaited him. But he wouldn't need the bleach this time.

This one would be on the house. When you fucked up, when you were in the client's bad books, you didn't nickel-and-dime him.

CHAPTER 45

New Rochelle, NY

When his call with Dorian was finished, Miles stood there in the storage facility corridor, unable to move. It wasn't a symptom of his disease. It wasn't his muscles refusing to respond. It was the shock of the news just delivered to him that had frozen him to this spot.

Chloe was not his daughter.

The hallway seemed to be spinning, and he threw out a hand to steady himself against the wall.

Chloe said, 'Miles?'

When he said nothing, she ran to him, ducked under his outstretched arm, and put her arm around him. The phone was still in his hand.

'Who was it?' she asked. 'Who called?'

Miles tried to say something but nothing was coming out.

'Is something happening to you? Do you need a doctor, because, like this guy *is* one. I don't know if he's the best guy but he might know *something.*'

'It's . . . okay,' Miles whispered. 'Just . . . something kind of came over me.'

'Who called?'

Miles moved his dry tongue around in his mouth, trying to create some moisture. 'Dorian,' he said. 'They did the test.'

'Oh,' she said.

'I know you said you didn't want to know the results, but I might as well tell you.' Miles needed a second to form the words. 'You're fine. You don't have it. Or anything else.'

Chloe's face crumpled. 'Okay,' she said, her lip quivering. 'That's good, right? Isn't it?' She gave him a squeeze.

'It is,' he said, and squeezed her back. 'It's good.' He put his arms around her. 'So happy.'

She hugged him back, and when she pulled back, tears in her eyes, she said, 'So that's why you went all funny? *That's* how you handle good news? What would you have done if it was *bad* news?'

He offered something approximating a smile. 'I felt a little overwhelmed.'

'Okay, well, this is all great, but remember you asked me to come to help you focus? The doc looks like he's ready to wet his pants, so maybe we better go talk to him before he has to change his diaper.'

Miles nodded. 'Okay, okay, let's do that.'

Together, they made their way back to the open storage unit, where Gold had stopped shredding and was eyeing them like a cornered rat.

388

'How'd you find me?' he asked again. Rather than wait for an answer, he looked at Chloe and said, 'Who are you?'

'Chloe Swanson.' She smiled and pointed a hitchhiking thumb at Miles. 'This dude's daughter.'

Miles felt those invisible blocks on his shoulder grow heavier.

On the way here, in the back of the limo, Miles had gone over with Chloe the questions he'd intended to ask Gold, but now he could hardly remember what any of them were. She was looking at him, as if wondering when the grilling would begin.

But Miles said nothing. Chloe looked at him expectantly, waiting. After a few seconds, she prompted him. 'You up for this?'

Miles said, 'Chloe, wait in the car.'

Her eyes popped. 'Excuse me?'

'I want to talk to Dr Gold privately.'

'Why?' she asked. 'We're a team. What's the deal?'

'I've reconsidered.'

'You don't have to protect me, you know. Whatever's going on, I can handle—'

'*Chloe!*'

Her body trembled as though he'd zapped her with a taser.

'*Please* go to the car,' Miles said.

A silence hung between them for several seconds. Finally, Chloe let out a theatrical huff and walked off. Miles waited until he could hear her steps on the stairs before focusing in on Gold.

'You've got some explaining to do,' Miles said.

'Me? Who the hell do you think you are?'

Miles almost laughed. 'You know, right now, I have no fucking idea. I thought I knew. But now, not so much.' He waved a finger at the pile of shredded paper. 'If I could magically tape all that back together, would I find my name? And Chloe's? And the others'?'

Gold said nothing.

'Your assistant says you're falling apart. Does that have anything to do with Todd Cox? Or Katie Gleave? Or Dixon Hawley? Or Jason Hamlin? Or Chloe?'

'I don't know those people.'

'No? You helped bring them into the world. Their mothers were all patients of yours. Want me to run through them?'

Gold stared at him. 'No.'

Miles looked down and kneaded his forehead for a moment. 'I thought I knew what I'd ask you, but that call . . . Those names I mentioned, according to the files, I'm their biological father.'

'How could you know—'

'Except I'm not, am I?'

Gold eyed him coldly.

'I don't know what you're talking about.'

'Apparently . . . I'm not Chloe's father. So maybe I'm not Todd's. Or Katie's. Or Dixon's or Jason's or Nina's or Colin's or Barbara's or Travis's. Maybe I'm no one's fucking father.' He laughed. 'How about that! All this worrying I've been doing,

390

about these kids, whether they might develop what I've got, the plans I had to make their lives better, it's all a farce.'

Gold was looking past Miles, as if planning an escape.

'So, what's up, Doc?' Miles laughed sardonically at his own joke. 'They're dying, or disappearing. At first I thought, a wild coincidence, you know? No more. Not since the guy under the bed, the lady in the van.'

'What?'

Miles waved the question away. 'There's only so many people who'd know the connection between them. You're at the top of that list. Why are they disappearing? What's going on?'

Miles took two steps into the storage unit, prompting Gold to move back without looking where he was going. When he did, he stumbled over one of the boxes of files and landed on his butt. He got back on his feet.

'I've nothing to say. My patients are entitled to their confidentiality.'

Miles said, 'We're way past that.'

'You don't know what you're getting into,' Gold said. 'Walk away from this. You've got no connection to these people, these grown children. They're not your responsibility.'

Miles let that sink in. 'So it's true. None of them are mine.'

'Walk. Away.'

'How is that possible? Why's my name on the

files?' Miles felt his anger rising along with his voice. 'Who *is* the biological father of these people? What the fuck is going on?'

Gold raised a trembling hand and pointed at Miles. 'Go away. Just go.'

Miles suddenly had a realization. 'Christ, it's *you*. I've heard about sick bastards like you. Every single woman who's been to your clinic, every couple who's come to you looking for help, the whole thing is a sham. Stupid idiots like me come in, provide a sperm donation, it's pointless. *You're* the one impregnating all those women.'

Gold said, 'You have no idea what you're talking about. If you care anything about yourself – about that girl you came in here with – then forget all about this.'

'Is that a threat?'

'It's good advice.'

Miles pointed a finger. 'Yeah, well, listen up. If you're not going to answer my questions I'll find someone who will. Or go to the authorities, who can bring pressure to bear in ways that I can't. Maybe I'll bring them back with me.'

Miles waited another moment, realized there was nothing more to be gained here, and headed back down the corridor for the stairs.

Gold, breathing heavily, heart racing, found a pile of boxes steady enough to hold him, and sat. He took out his phone, entered a number, and put the phone to his ear. When someone finally answered, he said, 'It's Dr Gold. It's urgent.'

And then he waited more than two minutes to be connected to the person he needed to talk to.

'Cookson was here . . . He's got half of it figured out . . . Of course I didn't tell them, but he's not going to drop this . . . He's got one of them with him. The Swanson girl . . . Whatever he knows, she seems to know . . . Shredding, that's what. I'm shredding everything, just like you told me—'

The other party had ended the call.

Gold slowly lowered the phone to his lap and started to cry.

CHAPTER 46

New Rochelle, NY

When Miles got back to the car, Chloe was in the back seat, arms crossed, looking straight ahead, refusing to acknowledge him when he got in.

'Hey,' he said.

Chloe stayed silent.

Charise, tucked in behind the wheel, said, 'Where to now, Mr Cookson?'

He had no idea. Where to, indeed? What should he do next? Was there anything left *for* him to do? What was his responsibility now? What did he owe the young men and women on the list? He certainly didn't have to worry about their medical future, at least not where his genes were concerned.

'Mr Cookson?'

The fact he wasn't their father didn't mean they were no longer in danger. He still had to warn them. And there was the matter of his name being in those files, recording him as the donor when he wasn't.

Was it time to turn this over to the police? Would the FBI be the appropriate body?

'She's *asking* where you *want* to go,' Chloe said, annoyed.

'Oh,' Miles said, drawn out of his thoughts. 'Um, home, I guess.'

'Yes, sir,' Charise said, and turned on the engine.

'That's not where I'm going,' Chloe said. 'Nearest bus or train station will do fine. I've got to get to Springfield and get my car.'

'Chloe,' Miles said. 'You don't have to do that. I mean, if you want to go home, that's fine. But Charise can drive you there. She can drop me off on the way.'

'We were supposed to go at that guy together,' she said.

'Chloe, I'm sorry I sent you away. I needed to talk to the doctor alone.'

'I don't get it,' she said. 'You get the test result, tell me I'm okay, which should be, like, good news for both of us, but instead of being happy about it, you suddenly freeze me out.'

'It's complicated,' Miles said.

'What's complicated about my being okay?'

'Nothing. That's good.'

'So what is it? Did something else happen on that phone call?'

Charise put the car through a three-point turn and powered down the window to enter the code again on the keypad by the gate.

'So am I heading to the closest train station?' she asked.

'No,' Miles said at the same moment Chloe said, 'Yes.'

Charise sighed. 'I'll head for New Haven while you two come to a decision. Plenty of train stations along the way.'

'Are we a team or not?' Chloe asked.

'We are,' Miles said, but the words almost caught in his throat. Were they? Really? Their bond was now based on a fiction, a fraud.

An overwhelming sense of emptiness washed over him. All these years, even when he hadn't known the identity of the children he'd believed he'd fathered, their existence had been something of a comfort. He was leaving something behind. He had a legacy. An anonymous one, but still, it was out there.

But no more.

No legacy.

And he was going to have to break it to Chloe that she hadn't been reunited with her father after all. He was still out there. And he was very likely a despicable fertility doctor who had violated every ethical standard in the book.

What the hell was he supposed to tell her?

As Charise headed for I-95, Miles and Chloe entered into a period of silence. About ten minutes went by before Chloe broke it.

'So what's next, Pops?'

It was a peace offering. He turned his head,

looked at her, and smiled sadly. Her hand was resting on the leather upholstery, and he placed his on top of it and gave it a squeeze.

Chloe, so annoyed with him earlier, appeared concerned. 'You okay?'

'Yeah,' he said.

'You're holding something back.'

'No, I told you what Dorian said.'

Half of it.

She gave him a brief, skeptical glare, but then said, 'I guess we should carry on, find the others.' To Charise, she said, 'Forget the train station.'

Miles said, 'Maybe it's too much for me. For us. Maybe it's time to go to the police.'

Chloe rolled her eyes. 'Yeah, like they'd be any help. You know where I'd suggest we go first?'

'Where?' he said wearily.

'I was thinking Fort Wayne.'

'Travis Roben.'

'Right,' she said. 'I've already started doing some research.' She waved her phone. 'When I got back to the car, I entered in the names, one at a time, to see what I could find on them. Roben's kind of a weird, geeky guy. I don't mean that in a bad way. He's on Instagram. He's a graphic novel nut.'

'You mean he's into them, or he writes them?'

'Both. Well, he's trying to do one. He posted a few pics. He's not that great an artist, but his story lines are kind of interesting. The good news is, he's not dead or missing or anything like that.'

'That's a plus.'

Miles didn't have the heart to tell her Dorian and Heather had compiled profiles. Besides, Chloe might have found some new, interesting tidbits.

As if they mattered.

'Okay,' Chloe said, 'so this Nina Allman, she lives in Seattle and works at something called Pike's?'

'Pike Place Market. Top tourist attraction in the city. You can get fresh fish, vegetables, anything. Great restaurants.'

'And Barbara Redmond?'

'Yes?'

'She's an actress. Did you know that?'

'I did.'

'So I've got a half sister who's done *NCIS* and *The Good Place*? Looking at IMDb, they haven't been big parts. Yogurt seller? Dead body?' She paused. 'That's not a good omen.'

'I hadn't looked up her acting credits.'

'And this Neaseman guy, he's not that far from Nina. He's in Portland. The Oregon one. So what I'm thinking is, you start in Fort Wayne, since that's closest, and blow this Roben guy's mind by telling him you're his dad and that maybe someone wants to kill him, then—'

'Just another day.'

Chloe shrugged, and continued. 'And then you head to the coast, since everyone else is along there. Seattle, Portland, L.A. Start in the north and work south. You know I've never been west

398

of Albany? Too bad I don't have a half sibling in San Francisco. I'd love to see San Fran.'

Miles's heart was pounding. He bit his lip, almost hard enough to draw blood.

'You're right,' he said.

'About what?'

'Dorian did tell me something else.'

Chloe blinked. 'What?'

'When they did the test, they were comparing your profile to mine.' He paused. His mouth was getting very dry. 'Charise, do you have any water?'

'Yes, sir,' she said.

Keeping one hand on the wheel, Charise unzipped a small bag on the seat next to her. She pulled out a bottle of Aquafina and extended it, backhand, over the seat. Miles took it, but when he tried to unscrew the cap, he couldn't make his fingers close around it.

'Here,' Chloe said, taking the bottle, cracking the seal, and returning it. Miles took a long sip and set the bottle into a cup holder between the seats.

'You were saying,' she said.

'They looked at my profile, and . . .'

Chloe's face fell. 'You're sicker than you thought. This thing you've got, it's moving faster?'

'No, not that. Something . . . worse. I think. Depending on how you look at things.'

'Jesus, just tell me,' Chloe said.

'I'm not your father.'

Her face did not move. She was dumbstruck.

For several seconds, she had no words. Slowly, she retreated to her side of the car, leaning up against her door.

'I was as stunned as you are,' Miles said. 'There's no DNA match between us. I don't know exactly what happened. It's something Dr Gold did. He falsified the records. I don't know how, and I don't know why, but he—'

Chloe erupted. 'If you're not my father then who the fuck is?'

'I don't know.'

'Oh, oh, that's great.' She put a hand to her forehead and turned away, as if trying to escape him. 'This is just absolutely fucking terrific. So he could be anybody. Anybody in the whole goddamn country.' She pointed to a man on the sidewalk, walking back and forth in front of an electronics store, wearing a sandwich board. 'Maybe it's him.'

Miles was betting it was Gold himself, but without proof he did not want to speculate. He said, 'Chloe, I feel terrible about this.'

'Oh, *you* feel terrible? I thought one of the great mysteries of my life had been solved but it turns out it was all bullshit, but *you* feel terrible?'

Miles had no words.

Chloe shook her head and bit her lip. Her chin trembled. 'I can't believe this . . . I just can't . . .'

She sniffed, and as her eyes began to mist she turned away so Miles couldn't see her. 'All of this was for nothing. I don't really mean anything to you. You're not anything to me.'

The words went into Miles like a knife.

'I can't deal with this.' She leaned forward and said to Charise, 'Stop the car.'

'Ms Swanson, I'm about to get onto the interstate.'

'Stop the car.'

'Chloe, please,' Miles said. 'It's not like that. All I wanted to do was—'

'Stop the fucking car!' she screamed.

Charise hit the blinker and steered the limo over to the side of the road.

'You don't even know where we are,' Miles said.

Chloe waved her phone. 'You of all people should know there's an app for that.' She pulled on the door handle, undid her seat belt, swung the door wide open, and got out.

'Please, Chloe!' Miles shouted.

But she had slammed the door before he could get her name out. Chloe slammed her hand on the car's trunk as she walked off in the direction they'd come from.

Charise asked, 'Do you want me to go after her?'

Miles had no doubt Charise could catch up with her, pick her up, and bring her back, but he couldn't see the point.

'Let her go,' he said.

CHAPTER 47

New Haven, CT

Caroline had received a text from him, that he was back after attending to some out-of-town business, so she found herself once again at the Omni Hotel – as always, in one of the nicer suites on an upper floor that afforded a view of Yale and much of the city – standing by the window, wearing the lingerie he'd laid out for her, silk blindfold in place, waiting for Broderick to arrive.

Sometimes she thought that this part, the anticipation, was what she enjoyed most. It was better than the actual sex itself, which was nothing to complain about. Waiting for the sound of the door opening, his barely perceptible steps across the carpet, his soft breathing, directly behind her. She was not allowed to turn around until after he had touched her. There were times when he would stand there for several minutes, so close she could feel the heat coming off his body, saying nothing.

Building the suspense.

Other times, things would move much more

quickly. He'd walk right over and grab her. *Yeehaw!* That was fun, too, but she much preferred it when things moved slowly.

When she arrived, as always, the tub had been run. The champagne was open and chilling. She had filled one flute and sipped on it while she luxuriated in the tub.

She wondered what he did during this time. He would have had to come to the room first, prepare things, then leave. Caroline guessed he went down to the bar and had a drink. Was the anticipation as much fun for him as for her?

This time, it wasn't just the sex that filled her with anticipation. She wanted to hear how things were going. She wanted an update.

When she'd first told him about her situation, about the terrible thing her brother-in-law had done, essentially cutting Gilbert – and by extension, her – out of his will, Broderick had seemed skeptical that there was anything to be done about it.

But it was so unfair, Caroline pleaded. Leaving his estate to a bunch of total strangers. Okay, sure, maybe they were the product of his seed, but that was a very clinical connection. Gilbert was his *brother*. Was there a stronger bond than that? The two had grown up together, shared a room when they were younger. How do you cut out someone like that and give the money to people you've never spent one moment with in their entire lives?

It was a gross injustice.

I'm no lawyer, Broderick had told her. Maybe she should talk to one. But it really should be Gilbert who initiated any legal action. Or maybe, he said, Caroline should talk to Miles and explain how devastating his decision had been to her husband.

He'd see right through that, Caroline thought. 'And we have a bit of a history,' she admitted, without getting into details.

But she did have an idea for a new scheme. Certainly more ambitious than her attempt to get Google to invest in her idea, which actually had been pretty clever. All she lacked was the technical expertise to make it work. Was lying about Miles being a backer really that big a deal? If Google had gone for it, she would then have gone to Miles, shared her idea with him, told him Google was a backer – which would have been true – and he'd probably have invested in it.

Or so she liked to tell herself.

But this new idea, it was different. And she thought someone with Broderick's background might be able to not only advise her, but roll up his sleeves and help her out.

'Wow,' Broderick had said when she'd shared the plan with him. 'That seems pretty . . . out there.'

He'd given her a look, like he thought she was crazy. Yeah, *right*. What did they say? Crazy like a fox? That was her.

'And what would my role be?' he'd asked her.

She'd told him. In the beginning, he'd be more

of an adviser, a go-between. And then, later, if the first part of the plan went okay . . . maybe he could play a more direct role? Doing what he did best?

He had reservations. 'This sounds like something that could go off the rails very easily,' he said. 'A lot of variables, a hard situation to control. Emotional unknowns. An extra personality playing a major role. Are you really sure you want to go that route?'

'Are you saying it couldn't be done?'

'No, I'm not saying that.'

'If the first part went okay, then—'

'I get it.' In the end, he'd said, 'Let me think about it.'

'I'd make sure you were properly compensated,' she'd said.

And he had shot her a look suggesting that was a given. In fact—

Hang on. She could hear the hotel room door opening.

He was here.

He never let it slam. He closed the door gently.

Her breathing became shallow and rapid.

I don't want to wait. Not this time. Let's get to it.

She sensed his approach. He couldn't be any more than a foot or two behind her. She couldn't take it anymore. She was going to break the rules. She was going to speak.

'Do me,' she whispered.

And he said, 'What the fuck is going on here, Caroline?'

Her heart stopped.

She whirled around, whipping off the blindfold at the same time. There he was, standing right there before her.

Gilbert.

Broderick was, in fact, killing time in the bar. He'd taken a seat that afforded him a view of the hotel lobby.

He usually enjoyed this time. The anticipation. Going up to the room, getting things ready, then slipping away before she arrived. He even took the stairs back to the lobby level so he wouldn't accidentally run into her coming off the elevator.

He would order his drink and think of the pleasures to come, no pun intended.

Also, if need be, he'd get a few things done. Check his phone, answer emails, respond to texts.

One had come in while he was on his second drink. Short and sweet:

ITS ALL GONE TO SHIT. CANT DO THIS.

Hmm, he thought. There was trouble in Fort Wayne.

He looked up from his phone, glanced in the direction of the lobby, and that was when he saw Gilbert Cookson.

Broderick knew what the man looked like. When he'd gotten mixed up with this woman, he'd made a point of finding out what he could about her husband. Learned his routine, his cell phone number, places he hung out.

But Broderick had not seen this turn of events coming. Caroline's husband was crossing the lobby tentatively, as though unsure about whether he should be there or not. He was turning his head from side to side. Was he looking for her? Had he followed her in? When his eyes landed on the entrance to the bar, he came that way, took two steps in, glanced about, then retreated.

Yeah, he's followed her here, Broderick thought. He suspected his wife was up to something and he'd tailed her. She must have screwed up somewhere. Maybe he'd found a hotel napkin in her purse. Maybe he had that phone-tracking app.

Could have been any number of things. One thing was for sure. The message he'd received from Fort Wayne could just as easily apply to his situation here. It was all going to shit. Once the husband was involved, well, nothing good could come from that.

He'd been thinking of bailing for a while now, anyway. Cutting things off with Caroline, walking away from the mess she'd started. He didn't want to be a part of it anymore. A great fuck was not worth this much hassle. The woman was nuts, didn't think rationally.

I'm out.

He downed the last of his scotch and left enough cash on the table to cover it. He took the key card

407

from his wallet and held it firmly in his hand as he exited the bar.

Headed straight for Gilbert, who stood in the middle of the lobby looking bewildered and apprehensive.

Fucking loser, Broderick thought. No wonder Caroline was looking elsewhere for what she needed. In more areas than one.

Broderick pretended to be distracted by something else, and deliberately bumped into Gilbert.

'Oh, sorry,' he said. 'Wasn't watching where I was going.'

'No problem,' Gilbert said.

Broderick kept on walking until he was out on the sidewalk. He stopped, took out his latest burner phone, and entered a number.

Three rings later, Gilbert said, 'Hello?'

'There's a key card in your pocket,' Broderick said. 'Eleventh floor. Third room on the right after you get off the elevator.'

He ended the call, tossed the phone in a garbage can at the corner of Temple and Chapel Streets.

Chuckled.

CHAPTER 48

New Haven, CT

'So, Dorian has explained some of this to me, but why don't you start from the beginning.'

Her name was Lana Murkowski, and she was not only a friend of Dorian's, but an agent with the Federal Bureau of Investigation, and she had met Miles a few years before, when the Bureau was conducting a wider investigation into cyber-hacking by the Russians. She also happened to live in nearby Darien, was on her day off, and was here in an unofficial capacity as a favor to Dorian. She had put a call in to Lana while Miles was in the limo on his way back from New Rochelle, without, as it turned out, Chloe.

Miles didn't want to talk about it.

A few hours later, Lana showed up at the Cookson Tech offices, and they'd taken one of the conference rooms for a private chat.

Dorian had brought in coffee and snacks and had asked to sit in, provided Miles had no objection.

'No,' he said. 'You need to be up to speed on this, too.'

409

When Lana asked Miles to outline the situation for her, he took a breath and did his best. He started with his first visit to Dr Gold and his acquiring the list of women who had been impregnated with what he had thought at the time was his sperm.

'How'd you get that list?' the agent asked.

Miles glanced at Dorian and back to Lana. 'Is that important?'

'Yes.'

'We bribed someone at the clinic to get it for us.'

'Who did that?'

'Heather,' he said. 'The company investigator.'

'Wouldn't it be helpful to have her here today?'

'It would,' Dorian interjected. 'But her mother went into the hospital last night. Possibly a heart attack. Heather's off the map for the next few days.'

Lana said, 'Go on with your story.'

Miles said that once he had the list, Dorian and Heather ascertained the names of the children those women had given birth to, tracked down their whereabouts, and compiled as much information on them as possible.

And soon after that, they began to disappear.

'Let's go through them one by one,' Lana said.

Miles did. Most of the information he and Dorian had on Katie Gleave, Jason Hamlin, and Dixon Hawley came from media reports. Miles had learned firsthand that Todd Cox was missing. So far, the remaining individuals had not met with misadventure.

'But I'm worried,' he said.

'Okay,' Lana said. 'Let's see what we have here, starting with this Todd Cox. For all you know, that hand under the bed belonged to him.'

'No,' Miles said quickly. 'Because of the finger.' He explained.

Lana nodded. 'Okay. But the woman in the van? There's no proof she had anything to do with this.'

'What about the two cups of coffee?' Miles asked. 'That deer?'

Lana flashed him a patronizing smile. 'Deer run pretty fast and it would have been easy for your driver to miss it. And she could have had an old cup of coffee that had gone cold and bought a new one that was hot.'

Miles was undeterred. 'What about how clean Todd's place was?'

Lana shrugged. 'Some people are tidy. And if they're moving on, they want to leave the place in good shape. Look, I'm not saying this doesn't all seem a bit strange, but if you want to get the authorities involved, you need something a little harder. You don't have any bodies. No concrete evidence of foul play. It could all be coincidence.'

'No,' Miles said. 'What about the doctor?'

'He's worth talking to, sure,' Lana said. 'Sounds like he's covering up something.'

'Miles has a theory,' Dorian said, 'that the doctor is impregnating all these women himself.'

'Wouldn't be the first time something like that

has happened,' Lana said. 'Say that's the case. How does it explain the disappearances? How do those things connect?'

'I don't know,' Miles said. 'But Dr Gold as much as threatened me if I didn't drop this.'

'You bribed his employee for private information,' Lana said. 'If I were him I might have threatened you, too.'

'I don't think he knows how I got the names.'

'He knows you got it from somewhere.'

Dorian looked at Lana. 'Isn't there anything you can do? At least the Bureau could find the remaining kids – okay, they're not really kids anymore – and warn them?'

'What would you have the FBI tell them?'

'That they're in danger,' Miles said.

'From whom?'

'Granted, that's not clear yet.'

'And *why* are they in danger?'

'Chloe had a theory. If you reduce the number of people I was intending to give the money to, whoever's left gets a larger share.'

'That suggests that one or more of these people who you had believed were your biological children could be behind this. Doesn't that seem a little out there? How would they even know? You'd not yet communicated your intentions to them, and there's nothing to suggest any of them, except for Todd Cox and Chloe, availed themselves of the services of WhatsMyStory.'

Miles sighed.

Lana wasn't done. 'Let's suppose the FBI were to impart this sketchy information to these people. How are they supposed to act on it? What would you have them do?'

'Be on guard,' Miles said.

'Be on guard,' Lana said. 'Suppose someone came to you, out of the blue, and said you might be about to disappear but they didn't know why and they didn't know who might make it happen. How would you handle that?'

Miles was searching for the words but could not come up with any.

'I haven't got enough to go back to the Bureau and open a file on this. Certainly not officially.'

Miles said, 'Couldn't you at least go to the various local law enforcement agencies involved, including the police in Paris, and ask them to provide whatever information they had? Then you could look for commonalities? I'll bet none of the departments working these cases are even aware of the possible connections with other departments.'

'If there are any,' Lana said.

'I give up,' Miles said.

Lana gave him a sympathetic look. 'Mr Cookson, I want to ask you something and I mean no disrespect at all. But I need to pose the question.'

'Go ahead.'

'Is paranoia one of the symptoms of your disease?'

Miles eyed her icily. 'No.'

'Okay,' she said. She gave Miles and Dorian a

concluding nod and rose from her chair. 'If something develops, get in touch. Dorian, Mr Cookson.'

And with that, Agent Murkowski departed.

Miles looked dejected and defeated.

'Miles,' Dorian said, 'maybe she's right. Maybe it's time to step back, let this go. You've done what you could. But everything has changed.'

'What if it happens again?' he asked. 'What if the others start to disappear? What if there was something we could have done? How will we feel then?'

'But maybe nothing will,' Dorian said.

Miles closed his eyes, as though suffering a migraine. He lowered his head for several seconds, then suddenly raised it and opened his eyes.

'I didn't know about Heather's mother.'

'It just happened.'

'You'll send flowers to her hospital room?'

'Of course.'

'We can't impose on her for the next few days. And our friendly, neighborhood FBI agent doesn't give a shit. So the next step is up to me.'

'Next step?' Dorian asked.

'Did you charter a plane? Because I'm going to Fort Wayne to find Travis Roben. And then I'm heading to the west coast.'

'Alone?'

'If you're asking whether Chloe'll come along for the ride, I'd say fat chance.' He paused. 'But I'll give her a try.'

Dorian nodded and got up. 'I'm on it.'

Miles, too weary to get up and follow her out, sat there for a moment, gathering his thoughts.

His cell started to ring. He took it out of his pocket and saw that Heather was calling.

'Heather,' he said. 'I heard about your mother. How is she?'

'We thought it was a heart attack but now it's looking like it may be some kind of severe muscle spasm. They're going to release her later today. Thanks for asking.'

'Take all the time you need,' Miles said.

'I appreciate that, but listen, that's not what I was calling about.'

Miles felt his body tense. He didn't know how many more surprises he could handle. 'Go ahead.'

'Gilbert came to me,' she said.

'What?' The idea that Gilbert would approach the firm's investigator was right out of left field.

'He said he'd been to see Dorian about this, but then came to me with it, too.'

'What?' Miles asked.

'He told me about what Caroline had done before, the game she ran on the Google exec. I got the idea that this was something you'd brought to his attention, so now he was on guard, watching for that kind of thing. He was worried she was at it again. That she might have set up some fake corporation, Excel Point, and was billing Cookson for thousands.'

Miles thought back to something his brother had

said, before they went for the ride in the Porsche, before he'd handed over the keys.

'He'd mentioned the name,' Miles said.

'So I did a little digging.'

Miles held his breath, waiting. The last thing he needed was more dissension between himself and his brother over things Caroline might have done.

'Gilbert was right. There was a dummy corporation, and you've been paying it some substantial sums.'

'God,' Miles said wearily. 'Caroline is something else. She gets caught, and she tries something else.'

'But it wasn't Caroline,' Heather said.

'So someone's been sending us bogus invoices and we're just paying them? How could we be that stupid?'

'The thing is, Miles, no one was raising questions because it was being done internally.'

Miles held his breath for a second. 'Someone on the inside.'

'That's right. I followed the money, Miles.'

He didn't want to ask, but he had no choice. 'Where did it lead?'

'Dorian.'

Miles was sure he'd misheard. 'That can't be.'

'I wish I were wrong,' Heather said.

Me too, thought Miles.

416

CHAPTER 49

Providence, RI

'So he conned you?' said Chloe's mother, Gillian, early the next morning.

'It's not like that,' Chloe said, 'and I wouldn't say no to a little more support and a little less judgment.' She rummaged through the top drawer of her bedroom dresser, dressed only in underwear and a long T. The bed covers were a mess, and she had only been up for a few minutes. 'I should've done a load last night. I've got nothing for work.'

'I did it. The basket's right out in the hall,' Gillian said. 'You're lucky they'll take you back, the shifts you've missed without giving them any kind of notice.'

'Yeah, what a break. The shittiest diner in Rhode Island isn't going to fire me.'

'This guy, this Miles, he walks into the diner and tells you some wild story that he's your father and you just leave with him?'

'I'm telling you, *he* believed it! He thought I was his daughter.'

417

'Sure,' Gillian said. 'With no proof. At least with this Todd Cox there was proof from that testing company. But Miles, he tells you he's seen the file. Did *you* see the file?'

'No.'

Gillian nodded knowingly. 'Exactly.'

'And he never said *he'd* seen the file. He had this detective lady get the names from the clinic.'

'So he says.'

'Jesus, Mom, you really think some guy from New Haven hatches this elaborate scam to come all the way to Providence to tell some piss-poor waitress that he's her dad and he's got a fatal disease and he wants to give her a shitload of money? Why would someone do that? What sense does it make?'

'The world is full of strange people,' her mother said. 'I told you it was a bad idea. I told you not to send in your DNA sample.'

'This had nothing to *do* with that,' Chloe said, turning to look at her mother and banging her fist on the dresser in exasperation. 'Jesus! You seemed so understanding about this when I phoned you. I never should have told you about any of this.'

'You should have told me everything at the beginning, when he first approached you. But instead you head off all over the place and then spend the night at his home?'

'What, Mom? Are you worried someone who thought he was my dad came on to me?'

'There are plenty of cases of real dads who've

418

come on to their daughters. They have a word for that.'

'I can't take this anymore.' Chloe's eyes began to mist. 'I think he was pretty devastated.'

'About what?'

'When he got the results of my test. To see if I had the disease he's got. When we were talking to that doctor, and Miles got the call. I didn't know what it was about at the time, but that was when he found out there was nothing between us. He looked . . . crushed.'

Chloe sat down on the end of the bed. 'He's not my dad but he's the closest thing I've ever had to one. That day with him, even when the creepy shit was happening at Todd's place, was one of the best days ever. Those hours, while I was really believing it, they were pretty amazing.'

Gillian sat next to her and pulled Chloe's head into her shoulder. 'I'm sorry, honey. I am. All I've ever wanted is for you not to be hurt. In any way. That's all.'

Chloe got her arms around her mother, hugged her, and let the tears come.

'I was hateful to him,' she whimpered.

'Oh, sweetheart, he's the one who owes you an apology.'

'No, no, he was trying to do the right thing. He's *dying*. And I just fucking lost it and abandoned him.'

'You have to look after yourself. This is his problem. Not yours.'

419

'But maybe it still is my problem. What about the others? Even if Miles isn't their father, they might still be my half brothers and sisters. What about the ones that are missing? What about the ones that are still around?'

'Have you seen anyone suspicious hanging around?' Gillian said. 'I sure haven't. No strangers coming to the door or watching the house. No one's looking for you.'

Chloe's cell phone, sitting atop her dresser, lit up and began to ring. She untangled herself from her mother, reached for the phone without having to get off the bed, and looked at the screen.

'It's him,' she said. 'It's Miles.'

'Don't answer it,' Gillian said. 'You were smart to walk away when you did.'

Chloe had her thumb poised over the screen. 'I think I should—'

'No,' her mother said, and snatched the phone from her daughter's hand and pressed the button to decline the call.

'Mom!'

'It's the right thing!' her mother said forcefully. 'Put this behind you. I'm serious.'

Chloe held out her hand, waiting for the phone to be returned to her.

'Are you going to call him back?' Gillian asked. When Chloe did not answer, Gillian asked again.

Finally, Chloe said, 'No, I won't.'

'Promise me.'

Chloe waited a beat before saying, 'I promise.'

Gillian gave her back the phone. Chloe noted the time on the screen: 7:30 A.M.

'I'm gonna be late. I'm supposed to be there by eight.'

'Get dressed. I'll drive you. Tomorrow, we'll drive up to Springfield and get your car back.'

After her mom left her bedroom, Chloe noticed that she had a voice mail. Miles had left a message.

'Chloe, I'm sorry about how things have turned out. But I feel like we're still a team. I'm heading out to Fort Wayne, then the west coast. I'm not letting this go. I could use your help. I can send Charise to pick you up. But it's up to you. I'll understand if you want to be done with all of this. And with me. Let me know.'

She deleted the message.

Chloe made it to the diner by ten after eight – her mother blew through all the stop signs and one traffic light – just as the place was starting to fill up. She exchanged only a few words with the other staff, getting straight to work, and she was so consumed with thoughts of what had happened over the last couple of days that she got something wrong on nearly every order. One guy who asked for his eggs over easy got them scrambled. A woman who wanted decaf coffee got tea. She mixed up all the orders for one table with all the orders for another table.

Vivian, who worked the cash register and waited

421

tables when they were short-handed, said to her when the shift ended at two, 'You okay, honey?'

Chloe shook her head. 'No.'

Vivian gave her a hug. 'You messed up big-time today, but hey, nobody died. You'll be back on top of your game soon. I don't know what happened, and it's none of my business, but if you ever want to talk, I'll listen.'

'Thank you.'

'How you getting home, sugar? Saw your mom drop you off this morning.'

'I told her I'd walk. I need to clear my head.'

'We'll see you tomorrow, then.'

Chloe nodded, dropped off her apron in the back room, and left out the side door. She heard the limo before she saw it as the tires crunched on the gravel parking lot. When it was up alongside her, the front passenger's-side window powered down.

The driver, a man, called out to her: 'Chloe?'

She looked. It wasn't Charise, but maybe she'd taken the day off.

'Yeah?' she said.

'Someone would like to talk to you,' he said, pointing his thumb toward the back seat.

But did she want to talk to Miles? She'd promised her mom not to *call* him, but she hadn't promised not to *talk* to him if he came all the way up here to see her. The message he'd left her made it clear he was trying to make things right.

And the truth was, she wanted to apologize for

422

how she'd left things. Getting out of the car, leaving him at his lowest point – the more she thought about it, the more she regretted it.

'Okay,' she said.

The driver hit a button and she could hear the car doors unlock. She opened the back one on the passenger side and got in.

Once she had the door closed, she turned to look at the other person in the back seat.

It wasn't Miles.

It was a woman.

'Who the hell are you?' Chloe asked.

That was when the woman gave her a shot of pepper spray and the driver floored it.

CHAPTER 50

Fort Wayne, IN

Travis Roben had not left the house for a day and a half.

Except to go to the bathroom and have meals, he had barely left his bedroom. It was on the second floor of the house with a view of the street, and he spent most of his time perched by the window, watching for the police to show up.

So far, nothing.

There hadn't even been anything on the news about the woman Sandy hit with the bat. The back side of that warehouse was clearly not a well-traveled spot. Travis thought the occasional security guard might have wandered that way.

Unless . . .

She didn't have to be dead. Sandy had given her a good whack in the face, but it didn't have to be a fatal blow. Could be the woman's partner took her to the hospital, got her fixed up. Maybe it wasn't as bad as it looked, but holy fuck, it sure had looked bad. That would explain why a body hadn't been discovered. And if those two were *fake*

424

cops, it also explained why there hadn't been a story about the woman being attacked. If they weren't real cops, they wouldn't be going to the authorities to report what had happened.

Or . . .

They *were* real cops, but the whole thing was being kept secret until he and Sandy were found and arrested.

Regardless, Travis still couldn't figure out why they would want to kill Sandy and him. For trespassing? Seriously?

Nothing about it made any sense, which made it even scarier.

Sandy was as freaked out as Travis. So far as he knew, she was hiding out at her place just as he was hiding out at his, afraid to go out in public in case anyone was looking for them.

Travis's mother repeatedly asked what was wrong, and he'd done his best to persuade her he had some sort of stomach disorder, although the fact that he was still able to consume the meals she made for him had left her unconvinced. He wasn't ready to tell his parents what had happened. First, he'd have to tell them he had an actual girlfriend, which was going to make the story sound pretty fantastical before he'd even got started. (His mother had noticed his slightly less nerdy appearance of late, and when asked about it Travis had said he'd simply looked in the mirror one day and decided a change was in order.)

He and Sandy had texted back and forth several

times, each asking the other whether they had seen or heard anything.

Nothing.

Until this morning, when that car with an Uber symbol in the windshield stopped in front of the house.

Travis had left his bedroom lookout point for only two minutes to take a leak, and when he returned, a black Prius was at the curb. There was a man in the back seat. Fortyish, moving kind of slow, dressed casually in a sports jacket, jeans, and a pair of high-end runners. He opened the door, got out, stood in front of the house and took it in.

'Fuck,' Travis said. This was not good.

But this man couldn't be a cop. Nothing about him said law enforcement. First of all, what cop showed up in an Uber? And he didn't look cop-like. He didn't have the bearing or the swagger, and it didn't look like he had a badge clipped to his belt or a holstered weapon under the flap of his jacket.

So who was he and what was he doing here?

The man approached the house, mounted the steps to the porch.

Travis heard the doorbell ring.

Not going down. Not going down.

He heard faint footsteps on the floor below. His mother heading for the door. He considered shouting down to her to ignore it, but if he did, the man at the door would surely hear him.

Maybe the man was not here to see him. It was

possible he had some business with his parents. Maybe this guy was a lawyer or a real estate agent, and his parents were making a will or putting the house up for sale.

This guy did not look like a lawyer or a real estate agent.

But still, it was possible that – 'Travis!'

He debated whether to respond. Trick his mother into thinking he'd left the house. The trouble with that was, the only escape route would have been right by the kitchen, where his mother had been for the last hour.

If he didn't answer her, she'd come upstairs looking for him.

So he called back, 'Yes?'

'Someone here to see you!'

He swallowed. 'Kind of busy right now.'

What a stupid answer. What could he be so busy with that he couldn't come downstairs? *Could the man come back when I'm done jerking off?* No, that wasn't going to fly.

'Travis!' his mother said sharply.

'Who is it?' he called back.

There was a pause, a murmur of conversation. 'A Mr Cookson!'

Cookson? Who the fuck was Cookson?

'What's he want?'

This time, his mother did not reply. What he heard, instead, was her stomping up the stairs. Seconds later, she was standing in his doorway, hands on hips.

427

'What is wrong with you?' she asked. 'How can you be so rude? A man is here to see you. Get your ass down there and find out what this is about. And then you can tell *me*.'

Travis slunk down the stairs behind his mother, who flashed the man an awkward smile and said, 'Look who I found!' She slipped into the kitchen while Travis held a position on the bottom step.

'You're looking for me?'

The man nodded. 'Travis, my name is Miles Cookson. I wonder if I might speak to you about something.'

'What?'

Miles hesitated. 'An opportunity.'

'What kind of opportunity?'

From the kitchen, his mother snapped, 'Just talk to the man!'

'Who are you, exactly?' Travis whispered. 'Are you with the police?'

'The police?' he replied, keeping his own voice low. 'No. I run a tech company that designs apps. I'm from New Haven. I flew here last night, to see you.'

'To see me?'

'That's right.'

Travis had his phone in hand and asked, 'What'd you say your name was again?'

Miles told him and Travis typed it into his phone, waited for search results to come up. He tapped on Images and compared the headshots that came up to the man standing before him.

428

'Satisfied?' Miles asked. 'What do you say we take a walk?'

'I don't think so.'

'Maybe just sit on your porch? My legs are a little wobbly today. But I have a story to tell you. It's going to sound kind of fantastical, but I'm going to ask you to keep an open mind and listen to what I have to say.'

'What do you mean, "fantastical"?'

Miles paused. 'I don't want to alarm you unnecessarily, but it's possible you could be in some danger, and I want to warn you about it.'

Travis said, 'You're a little late.'

Miles raised his eyebrows. He extended his arm toward the door.

'Okay,' Travis said, and the two of them went out to the porch. Travis closed the door so his mother wouldn't listen in, and they each settled into a wicker chair.

Before telling his story, Miles was hoping for a sense of whether Travis knew he was the product of an artificial insemination. As he'd discussed with Chloe, it was a real double whammy to find out that (a) your dad's not your real dad, and (b) someone might be out to get you.

Miles had reviewed the materials Dorian and Heather had compiled, and seen from Facebook postings that Travis did not look much like his father.

Looking at Dorian's notes, Miles could not stop thinking about what Heather had learned. His assistant had been ripping off the company. He was so consumed with tracking down the remaining men and women on his list that he'd forced himself to push the Dorian issue out of his head. It was an issue he would have to deal with later. The strange thing was, he felt no anger. Just overwhelming disappointment.

But right now, in this moment, he had to focus on Travis Roben.

'What do you know about your history?' Miles asked.

'History?'

'Your background. Your . . . family background.'

'I don't know. The usual stuff, I guess.'

'What I'm wondering is, have you ever, for example, used one of those services you see advertised on TV that can shed light on your ancestry? Like WhatsMyStory, which tests—'

'I know what it is. And no.' He squinted at Miles, as if that would help him see the man's true motives. 'I would never do that.'

'Why not?'

'I wouldn't want to hurt my dad's feel—'

He cut himself off.

'Why would an ancestry search hurt your dad's feelings, Travis?' Miles felt a need to go slowly. 'Because it would make him think you didn't view him as your real father?'

Travis glanced back at the door, double-checking it was closed. 'My parents, they had some . . . issues when they wanted to have kids.'

Miles nodded slowly. 'Okay.'

'I guess they tried a long time, and didn't, you know, get anywhere.'

'So your parents decided to explore other ways.' Travis nodded.

'Your mother, she went to a fertility clinic?'

'You know, this is pretty personal stuff to talk about with someone I don't know.'

'I get that. But am I right?'

'I guess . . . she would have had to,' Travis said.

'And this clinic, so far as you know, where was it?'

'Around New York. Where my parents used to live.'

Miles looked satisfied. 'I won't pry anymore. I'm going to tell you my story. Interrupt at any time.'

And Miles laid it out, just as he had with the FBI agent, but without revealing the names of the people who were most likely half siblings to Travis. To Travis's credit, he let Miles tell all of it and asked only a minimum of questions.

'So you're not my biological father,' Travis said, when Miles finished.

'No. I mean, I don't think so. A test would confirm it. But I'm not related to the first person I contacted, and my name was on that file. I'm guessing it'll be that way with all of them.'

'Did that bum you out?' he asked.

'Yes. So, the first thing you said to me was that I'd gotten here late. What'd you mean by that?'

431

'These two people, they tried to kill us.'

'"Us"?'

'Me and my girlfriend, Sandy.'

'They tried to kill you?' Miles was wide-eyed.

Travis told his story, including the part where Sandy whacked that woman in the face with the bat.

Miles said, 'You didn't go to the police?'

'Too scared,' Travis said. 'What if they *were* cops? Like, I don't know, a couple of sicko cops who are like, thrill killers or something?'

Miles thought about that. 'The fact there's been nothing on the news suggests that whatever they were up to, they didn't want the authorities finding out about it. What about Sandy?'

'She's scared shitless, too.'

'Look, Travis, you and Sandy need to come forward. Yesterday I was talking to a woman from the FBI, an agent, and she didn't feel there was enough here to launch any kind of investigation. But what happened to you two, that's a whole new ball game. You've got a story to tell, suspects you can describe. This could change everything.'

'I don't know what to do.' He paused. 'I'm scared.'

'You'd be nuts not to be.'

Travis managed, for the first time, something approaching a grin. 'I guess it's too bad you're *not* my father. I'd have come into a shitload of money.'

Miles smiled wryly. 'Let's go find Sandy.'

432

Travis was still holding the phone, but was hesitating.

'You need to trust me,' Miles said. 'They failed the first time they came after you. There's nothing to say it won't happen again. You need to get ahead of this. You need to let me help you.'

Travis waited another moment, nodded, and started to compose a short, simple text:

A DEVELOPMENT. NEED TO SEE YOU.

He hit Send and waited.

'She usually gets back to me right away,' he said. He stared at the phone, waiting for the telltale dots that would tell him she was replying.

He waited. And waited.

'Maybe she's in the bathroom or something,' Travis said, but there was a nervous edge to his voice.

'Forget texting,' Miles said. 'Phone her.'

Travis tapped, then put the phone to his ear. 'It's ringing.'

He let it ring ten times. Then he checked to see whether she was now replying to his text. She was not.

Miles had a flashback to when Chloe had tried to get in touch with Todd. A chill ran the length of his spine.

'We need to find her right now,' he said.

CHAPTER 51

Somewhere . . .

Chloe could feel herself slowly coming out of a deep sleep.

She'd had a dream about some woman spraying her with something awful, how she had this burning sensation in her eyes and throat and on her skin. How she'd more or less gone blind, what with her eyes stinging so badly. She'd put her hands over her face, screaming with pain, and that was when she felt something jab into her arm.

No, not a dream, she thought as she slowly regained consciousness. It had happened. When she came out of the diner, after the limo pulled up alongside her.

Thinking it was Miles.

Not Miles.

She'd had only a second to get a look at the person in the back seat of the limo. A woman, some woman Chloe had never seen before in her life. Dark hair, kind of nice looking, late forties, she thought. Maybe older. Not that she'd had

434

much time to take her in. A second, maybe? Two, tops? Chloe had barely enough time to ask who she was before she raised her hand. She'd been holding some tiny canister.

Pepper spray, Chloe figured.

Before she opened her eyes, she became aware that she was on a soft, pretty comfortable surface. She ran her fingers along what felt like a quilt, and her head was resting on a very cushy pillow.

And she could sense light coming through her eyelids. She had no idea how long she'd been out, whether it was night or day, but wherever she was, the lights were on.

Chloe fluttered her eyelids, getting adjusted to the brightness. She went to sit up, but found she lacked the strength. Whatever that bitch had jabbed into her arm was still working its magic. She'd been on her side, and slowly rolled until she was on her back. She had barely enough energy to move her head from side to side.

There were nightstands on either side of the bed, decorated with large lamps with oversized shades. There was a dresser, some landscape paintings on the wall like you'd see in a hotel.

There were two doors. One was on the wall beyond the foot of the bed, and there was a second one off to the left. Both closed.

Chloe heard some stirring, then the flushing of a toilet. It sounded as though it was coming from behind the door to the left.

She watched it.

The handle turned, and then the door opened wide. Chloe's vision was slightly blurry, but there was someone standing there.

'Oh, good, you're awake,' the person said. 'I was wondering if you were going to sleep forever.'

A woman's voice. No, younger than that. A teenage girl's voice.

The girl walked closer, grabbed a chair from a small, round dining table, dragged it over to the edge of the bed, and sat down.

'How you feeling?' she asked.

'Like shit,' Chloe said.

'Yeah. They drugged you.'

'You're in a lot of trouble,' Chloe said, her words slightly slurred. 'When they find out what you've done, you're in deep shit. This is kidnapping. You'll go to jail for a long, long time. Fuck, my head's killing me.'

'I can probably get you an aspirin,' the girl said. 'And don't blame me. I didn't kidnap you. I don't even know who you are.'

Chloe moved her tongue around, trying to get things working. 'I'm Chloe.'

The girl extended a hand, and when Chloe didn't have the strength to raise her own, the girl gave her arm a squeeze.

'Pleased to meet you, Chloe,' she said. 'My name's Nicky. Welcome to hell.'

CHAPTER 52

Fort Wayne, IN

Travis backed his van onto the street and Miles got in on the passenger side, having to haul himself up to get in. Travis tromped his foot down on the accelerator before Miles was fully settled into his seat, or had even reached for the seat belt. He blew through a stop sign and swerved to avoid a squirrel that had dared to dart into the street.

'It's not far,' Travis said, eyes straight ahead.

Miles decided against the seat belt and opted instead to brace himself against the dash. God forbid they should hit anything. A deploying airbag would snap his arms like twigs. The van made a right, then a left, then sped down a stretch lined with fast-food outlets, carpet discounters, and muffler repair shops. Travis made another right, heading away from the commercial district and into a residential area that was a mix of modest houses and low-rise apartment buildings.

He brought the van to an abrupt stop in front of an old, three-story house that might have looked majestic back when it was built sixty or seventy years before, but had not aged gracefully. The paint on the trim was peeling, the steps up to the porch sagged noticeably in the middle, many of the shingles were curled, and the front yard needed a good weeding.

'She's got a room here,' Travis said, and was out of the van and running up to the porch before Miles even had his door all the way open.

Travis tried the front door and, finding it locked, started banging on it. A few seconds later, a sixtyish, balding man Miles presumed was the landlord appeared and opened the door. By now, Miles was on the sidewalk and close enough to hear the conversation.

'I'm looking for Sandy!' Travis said. 'It's an emergency!'

'What?' the landlord said.

'She lives here! Upstairs!'

Before the man could say another word, Travis squeezed past him and entered the building.

'Hey!' the landlord cried.

Miles reached the door and caught a glimpse of Travis heading up a flight of stairs, two steps at a time.

'You with him?' the man asked Miles.

He nodded. 'It's important we find her. Something may have happened.' Miles was solemn enough that the man appeared persuaded.

Upstairs, they could hear Travis banging on a door. 'Sandy! Sandy! It's me!'

By the time Miles and the landlord reached the second floor, Travis was standing at the door, his face breaking. 'If she's here, she's not answering.'

Miles, making his voice as calm as possible, asked the landlord, 'Can you open it?'

'I don't know about that,' he said. 'Unless, it's not a drug overdose or something, is it?'

'Yes,' Miles said.

The man dug into his pocket for what Miles guessed was a master key, moved Travis out of the way, slid it into the lock, turned, and opened the door. He went in first, followed by Travis, and at the tail end, Miles.

It was one simple room, filled with mismatched furniture. A double bed, a dresser and one night-stand, a small desk, and two chairs. One was for the desk, the other an easy chair. There was nothing to suggest anyone was living here. No personal items, no clothes, no book next to the bed. Not even a phone charger plugged into the wall. The bed was made, a couple of throw pillows propped up against the headboard.

'Where's the bathroom?' Miles asked.

'Down the hall,' the landlord said.

'Is this the right room?' Travis asked. 'Isn't this Sandy's room?'

'There was a girl here, that's for sure,' he said. 'Looks like she up and left.'

Or was taken, Miles thought.

'I heard someone leave only a few minutes ago,

439

just before you got here, but I was in the back of the house at the time.'

Travis shot out of the room and ran down the stairs. 'Thanks,' Miles said to the landlord, and went after Travis.

Once they were both in the van, Travis put it in Drive and took off down the street.

'Where are we going?' Miles asked.

'I don't know,' he said.

'Stop. There's no sense driving around wildly. We need a plan.'

'I don't have a plan!' he said, on the verge of tears.

The street ended in a T, and when Travis brought the van to a stop, he had to decide whether to go left or right. He sat there, foot on the brake, the engine idling roughly.

'Tell me what to do,' Travis said.

'I don't know.'

Travis looked right, debating whether to head in that direction, then left.

'Holy shit,' he said.

'What?'

His voice was no louder than a whisper. 'I think I see her.'

Miles leaned forward in his seat to be able to see around Travis. About a hundred yards away, on the sidewalk, walking away from them, was a young woman pulling a wheeled carry-on-sized bag behind her.

'You sure?' Miles asked.

440

Travis wasn't going to wait until he was certain. He hit the gas again, cranked the wheel hard left, and sped up the street, steering over into the oncoming lane and coming up alongside the woman.

'It's her!' he said as he powered down the window. 'Sandy!' he shouted.

She'd already heard the van and was looking his way. She appeared alarmed at first, then relieved to see who it was, but then almost as quickly, her expression became one of discomfort. Miles, on the passenger side, and probably not immediately visible to Sandy, blinked several times as he tried to get a good look at her.

'I've been calling!' Travis said. 'What's going on?'

Sandy held her position on the sidewalk. 'I'm leaving,' she said.

'Sandy, why—'

'I'm freaked out. I have to get away from here.'

'Please, get in. There's an explanation!'

'A what?'

'I think I know what's going on. Get in!'

Sandy appeared to give the offer some thought. She held her ground another moment, prompting Travis to hit a button that retracted the side door behind him, inviting her in. Finally, dragging the bag behind her, she reached the open door and set her luggage in first. She must have been thinking she'd then go around and get in up front, but caught a glimpse of Miles in the passenger seat. He'd been looking at her, but turned away when she spotted him.

441

'Who's that?' she asked, her voice suddenly filled with panic.

'He's okay!' Travis said. 'He knows what's going on! He can help us! Just get in!'

Sandy hesitated one last time, decided to throw the dice, and hopped in, settling into the middle seat as Travis hit the button to close the door. He pulled away from the curb.

Miles shifted in his seat so he could address Sandy full-on.

Sandy, getting her first good look at him, said, 'Oh, shit.'

'Hi, Samantha,' Miles said.

'No, her name's Sandy,' Travis said.

'No, it's Samantha,' Miles said. 'She's my niece. My brother Gilbert's daughter.'

CHAPTER 53

New York, NY

'Jeremy who?' Chloe asked, once she was fully awake and had the strength to sit on the side of the bed.

'Pritkin,' Nicky said.

Chloe rubbed her forehead briefly, as though she recognized the name but couldn't place it. 'And where am I?'

'Manhattan. It's a big house, but I guess they want us to be roomies.'

'I'm getting out of here,' Chloe said, standing.

'You can't. The door's locked. We're prisoners. It's a nice enough cell, and I won't lie, the food's pretty good, but we're not going anywhere.'

'What do they want? Why are they keeping us here?'

'It's not a *we*. It's a *him*.'

'Who?'

Nicky brought Chloe up to speed about Pritkin. Who he was, the people he knew, and the kinds of things that went on in this house.

'He's like this megalomaniac or something. Has

443

more money than God and houses all over the world but spends most of his time here. Thinks he's some kind of superman who doesn't have to worry about what's legal and what isn't, and considering that some of his best friends are judges and cops and lawyers and mayors and shit, I guess he's right. Oh, and he likes young girls. Like me.'

Chloe was dumbstruck. 'Is *that* why I'm here? I got kidnapped by some sex slave ring?'

Nicky shook her head slowly. 'No offense, but you're a little too old for Jeremy.'

'Why are you locked up?'

'I heard something I shouldn't have,' Nicky said. 'I've told them I'd never tell, but I guess they don't believe me.'

'Why?'

'I was already thinking about telling what goes on here.'

'So, what are they going to do? Keep you here for the rest of your life?'

Nicky shook her head slowly. 'No.'

'Then what?'

Nicky said nothing, but the silence spoke volumes.

'No way,' Chloe said.

'I heard them talking. They're waiting for someone to do it. And the fact they put you in here with me, well, I guess it's going to be a twofer.'

Chloe swallowed. Her mouth was dry. She walked into the bathroom, cupped her hand under the tap, ran some water into it, and lapped it up.

'There's glasses,' Nicky said.

444

Chloe saw two clean glass tumblers on a shallow shelf above the sink. She picked one up and stared at it for several seconds before putting it back, the sides now wet from her fingers.

Chloe returned, sat back down on the edge of the bed, and asked: 'What did you hear that you weren't supposed to hear? You might as well tell me if we're both in the same boat.'

Nicky leaned in close and whispered, first giving Chloe the background of how she'd been in a position to hear Jeremy's phone conversation, and finishing with the three words she had heard that chilled her to the bone.

Kill them all.

About an hour later, they heard the door being unlocked. When it opened, a woman entered, carrying a loaded tray. There were two plates on it, shrouded with metal warming covers.

Out in the hall, just a few steps away, stood the security guard.

The woman set the tray on the top of the dresser and left without saying a word. The door closed, and locked.

'Dinner is served,' Nicky said. She took off one lid and said, 'Ooh, Italian.'

Chloe approached and lifted the lid off the second plate, slowly, as though there were a rat underneath it.

'Linguine with chicken in a garlic and wine sauce, I think,' Nicky said. 'The food's so good

445

here, I keep thinking every meal must be my last one, you know? They serve you something nice before they strap you into the chair.' She rolled her eyes. 'Actually, I don't think that's how they'll do it.'

Chloe tucked into the food. She hadn't realized, until the meal had arrived, how hungry she was. She ate standing by the dresser, and inhaled the pasta in less than three minutes.

'You in a rush to get somewhere?' Nicky asked.

Moments after finishing, the door was unlocked and opened. Standing there was the woman Chloe saw, very briefly, in the back of the limo.

'This is Roberta,' Nicky said. And then, to Roberta, she said, 'I'd introduce you but I figure you already know who she is.'

Roberta ignored Nicky's snide comment. She turned to Chloe and said, 'Your host would like a word. Come with me.'

Chloe looked worriedly at Nicky. Was this it? *Had* she just had her last meal?

'Don't be afraid,' Roberta said. 'He's really looking forward to meeting you.'

Roberta stepped into the hall and motioned for Chloe to follow. They walked a short way to the broad landing, then up to the third floor, through a set of open doors and down a hallway that was lined with windows on the street side, and black-and-white erotic photography on the other. Chloe paused in front of a four-foot-square photo of female genitalia.

Chloe asked, 'Is this you? Because you seem like a really big cunt to me.'

At the end of the hall was a set of double doors. Roberta opened them outward and motioned for Chloe to walk in first.

Holy shit, Chloe thought.

She figured this was supposed to be an office, or a library, judging by all the shelved books and the big desk in the center of the room, but there was more square footage here than in her entire home. On top of that, a goddamn RV was parked on the far wall. How the hell did *that* get up here?

But her focus quickly turned to the man sitting behind the desk. Midfifties, sixty maybe, with a full head of gray hair, neatly trimmed. Slim, tanned, handsome. Long face, chiseled jaw. Sitting behind the desk, all she could see was his shirt. Powder blue, button-down collar.

But then he stood and came around the desk. Jeans, faded, but shit, were they pressed?

'Let me look at you,' he said.

Oh no, Chloe thought. Maybe she really had been brought here to be part of some sex thing.

'Please, sit,' the man said, motioning to the leather chairs on this side of the desk.

Chloe sat.

Roberta said, 'Would you like me to stay, Jeremy?'

'If you wouldn't mind waiting in the hall,' he said.

With that, Roberta slipped away, closing the double doors behind her.

'I'm Jeremy Pritkin,' he said, sitting in the chair next to hers.

'Figured,' Chloe said.

'How are you enjoying your stay, Chloe?'

'I thought the pasta had a titch too much garlic in it.'

He nodded. 'If there's something else you'd like, we could fix it up for you.'

'I'd like a ticket out of here.'

Jeremy smiled. 'Tell me something about yourself.'

'Like what?'

'What do you do?'

'I'm a waitress. At a diner in Providence.'

'I see. You've been at that for a while, haven't you?'

Chloe's eyes narrowed. 'Why do I get the feeling you already know the answers to the questions you're asking?'

'It's true, most of them I do,' Jeremy Pritkin said. 'I know your history. About your mom, and her partner. That she passed a few years ago. I would get occasional reports.'

What the fuck? Chloe thought.

'They were . . . disappointing,' he said. 'You weren't exactly a straight-A student, were you?'

'I don't understand,' Chloe said.

'Have you never aspired to anything more? You're content to be a waitress for the rest of your life?'

'No,' she said.

'What then? Please, indulge me.'

'Film,' she said. 'Documentaries, stuff like that. I would like to make them.'

Jeremy brightened. 'That I did not know. You have a talent in that regard?'

'I have no idea,' she said. 'But I'd like to do that.'

Jeremy nodded thoughtfully. 'Well, that's something, I suppose.'

'I still don't . . . what is the point of this?'

Jeremy looked down into his lap. A sadness seemed to have come over him. 'This is very difficult for me, Chloe. I don't expect you to understand, but believe me when I say that it is. Very difficult. To see you, sitting here.'

Jeremy sighed. And then, before her eyes, he appeared to transform. His forlorn expression turned into something harder, like warm water suddenly turning to ice.

'There are some things I need to know,' he said.

'Right back atya,' she snapped.

'I need you to tell me everything that you and Miles Cookson have learned.'

'Why do you care? What's it to you?'

'Don't make this any more difficult than necessary,' Jeremy said. 'For your own sake.'

'Fuck that,' Chloe said. 'You want to know something, then you go first. Tell me what this is all about.'

Jeremy sighed. He raised his head and called out, 'Roberta!'

The woman reappeared. This time, she had something in her hand. It was hanging at her side.

A belt.

Jeremy stood and then, with great solemnity, placed his hand gently on Chloe's head, felt the texture of her hair on his palm.

He closed his eyes.

Chloe froze, so taken aback by the gesture that she did not know what to do.

After several seconds, Jeremy opened his eyes and took his hand away. Chloe watched him walk to the door, nod to Roberta, and leave.

Once in the hallway, he closed the doors behind him. The first time he heard Roberta lash Chloe with the belt, and the young woman's simultaneous scream, he flinched, ever so slightly.

But when the second strike came, and then the third, and the fourth, it was like he wasn't hearing anything at all.

CHAPTER 54

Somewhere over Pennsylvania

Miles and Samantha had left poor Travis pretty much in a state of bewilderment. Miles hardly knew what to tell him. He was as shocked to find Samantha was his 'girl-friend' as Travis was to learn that Sandy was not really Sandy.

But Miles did take time to offer the young man some advice.

'Get out of town. Go away for a few days and don't tell anyone where you're going. Don't take this van. They know what it looks like. Take a bus or a train and pay cash. Ditch your phone and get a burner or something.'

Travis had been shell-shocked.

'Do you understand me?' Miles had asked.

Finally, he'd nodded. 'What'll I tell my parents?'

Miles had paused. 'You might want to consider taking them with you.'

Miles had given him a number to call in a week's time. By then, Miles hoped he'd be able to tell him whether it was safe to come in from the cold.

Then Miles took Samantha to the airport. On the way back to Connecticut, in the private jet he'd chartered, Miles got the full story from Samantha.

Her mother made her do it.

Miles listened to the tale with nothing short of absolute amazement. It was the kind of story that, if he'd read it in a newspaper, he'd have thought someone had to be making it up. It reminded him of that story from more than twenty years ago. That woman in Texas who wanted her daughter to get picked for the cheerleading team and was arrested for trying to hire a hit man to kill the mother of her daughter's rival. A family tragedy, the woman figured, would leave the other girl too distraught to try out for the team.

Couldn't have happened. Yet it did. What Caroline had put her daughter up to rivaled what that Texas mom had tried to do.

No, it was worse.

'She said we'd be doing it for Dad,' Samantha confessed, teary-eyed. 'Mom said you had done a terrible thing to him, cutting him out of your will. Which, I won't lie, sounded kind of shitty, considering everything. You were going to give all your money to these biological kids, strangers, Mom said. Wasn't right, she said. She had a plan to make everything okay but needed my help.'

Samantha said her mother had a list of the heirs and researched them online to determine the best one to target. The women were excluded – Caroline

452

had found nothing in their online profiles to suggest any of them were lesbians – so that left the five young men. Jason Hamlin's profile suggested he was in a relationship. Dixon Hawley retweeted a lot of stories about gay rights. There wasn't a lot of information on Colin Neaseman or Todd Cox. But Travis Roben ticked all the boxes. He wasn't much to look at, showed no evidence of being in a relationship, and had nerdy interests. Caroline was betting there wasn't a girl out there who'd ever given him a second look.

He'd fall for Samantha in an instant.

'How did she know?' Miles asked. 'How did she have the names?'

'There was a picture,' Samantha said. 'Of the list.'

Miles thought back to when he was in the Porsche with his brother, getting out briefly when he did not feel well. A printout of the list had been in the car. Gilbert would have had enough time to take a picture.

'So your dad was in on this, too?'

Samantha shook her head. 'No. Mom came up with a story about me going to London. To see a whole bunch of plays in the West End, because I've been majoring in theater.'

Caroline, Miles figured, must have known about the picture, sent it to herself off Gilbert's phone. She wasn't exactly the type to respect her husband's privacy.

'Instead, you went to Fort Wayne to give the

performance of your life. I don't understand. What was the plan? So you find a way to meet Travis. What then?'

This part was hard for Samantha to talk about. She was ashamed of what she had done, what she had been talked into, how outrageous the scheme sounded when she said it out loud.

'I'd meet him. Become his girlfriend.'

'Go on.'

'We'd get . . .'

'Jesus. Not marry him.'

'Mom said it wouldn't have had to be for long.'

'What did she mean by that?'

'She was never very specific,' Samantha said. 'Anyway, we'd become a thing. Live together. And when Travis got all the money—'

'—you'd find a way to con it out of him,' Miles said.

'Mom said that's when we would make everything right for Dad. Get the money to him. At least a share of it.'

'But really, it was for your mother. How were you going to trick him into giving you his money?'

'She hadn't talked about that,' Samantha said quietly. 'I'm not sure that was the plan.'

Miles waited.

'If . . . if something happened to Travis, the money would go to me. That's w-why,' she stammered, 'when those two came to, you know, kill us, I thought somehow the wires had got crossed. That someone had been told to do it. But too

454

soon. And thought it was supposed to be both of us.'

Miles studied Samantha for several seconds, wondering if he'd really heard her say those words.

'I need to stretch,' he said.

He unbuckled his seat belt, stood, and took what was a short walk to the back of the plane, dropped into one of the other empty seats and looked out the window.

Was it possible? Miles wondered. Could Caroline be behind everything? Was she trying to whittle down the list so that a greater share would go to Travis, and ultimately to her and Samantha? Even for Caroline, that seemed too diabolical. Mounting something of that magnitude – tracking down people across the globe and disappearing them – would require the help of other people, people who were *professionals* at that kind of thing. It would also require a lot of money.

She might have it.

Maybe Caroline's approach to the Google executive hadn't been the only one. It was the only one Miles *knew* about. If she'd pulled off a successful scam with someone else – maybe an individual instead of a company – she'd have the money to hire some help. She did work in the criminal justice system. Had she crossed paths, at some point, with someone who could help her with this?

And it didn't have to be someone charged with a crime. He thought back to that story out of New York from fifteen or more years ago. The two cops who were doing hits for the Mafia. Hadn't Travis said the two who tried to kill them had identified themselves as police?

He was willing to believe anything at this point.

Miles had decided getting Samantha home took priority over heading to the west coast to find the others on the list. From the plane, he had made an awkward call to Dorian and asked her to get back to that FBI agent. There was more than enough evidence now, Miles believed, for the authorities to step in.

'Okay,' Dorian said. 'On it. Anything else?'

He wanted Charise waiting for him when he got back. He wanted to take one last run at Dr Gold, press him even harder this time. Maybe it was time to take Charise – former bouncer and wrestler – up on her offer of assistance. He had a feeling she could be very intimidating if the circumstances called for it.

'Is everything okay, Miles?' Dorian asked.

'Is that a serious question, Dorian? Considering everything I've been through?'

'I know, but you sound . . . funny. Is there something you're not telling me?'

Miles wanted to fire the same question back at her, but not yet. The truth was, he still needed her help.

'No,' he said, and ended the call.

And then Miles called Chloe.

The call went immediately to voice mail. 'It's Miles. Please call me back,' he said. Then he added,

'There's been some big . . . developments. You're still important to me, Chloe.'

For good measure, he sent her a text message saying basically the same thing. He watched to see whether the text was delivered.

It was not.

Miles decided to try again later.

He went back to his seat, across from Samantha, and asked, 'What did you do after those two tried to kill you? Did you tell your mother? Did you call your dad?'

'There was this other person I was supposed to contact, a kind of middleman?'

'Do you know who that was?'

She shook her head. 'I sent texts but there was no response. The last one I sent said everything had gone wrong. I couldn't call Dad because he didn't know anything about it. And Mom had told me not to contact her directly. And I knew she'd be mad, that the whole thing had fallen apart.'

Miles had been wondering when to break it to her. That the entire scheme was pointless. Now seemed as good a time as any.

'There's new evidence, a new DNA test, that suggests I'm not Travis's biological father,' he said. 'He's not in line for any windfall.'

Samantha, what with the roar of the jet engines, thought maybe she'd misheard. 'What?'

'It's got something to do with the doctor at the fertility clinic. So far as I know, I'm no one's father, biologically speaking.'

She was stunned. 'It never would have worked.'
'No.'

Samantha looked out at the clouds. 'I couldn't have gone through with it. Travis and I . . . we were in the back of his van, and . . . I couldn't do it. I don't think I could ever have done it. Not for all the money in the world. I mean, he's actually a nice guy, you know? I was actually getting to like him, and that was why I *couldn't* do it. I didn't want to go through with it. If those two hadn't come along, I think I would have found a way to end it, to walk away. Even if Mom went nuts on me.'

'I still don't get why you agreed to do it. How your mom talked you into it.'

Samantha looked at her uncle as if he were a dumb two-year-old. 'Because she's my *mom.*'

Before they landed in New Haven, Miles persuaded Samantha to call her father and tell him what had happened. When they landed outside New Haven, Gilbert was waiting. Samantha ran into his arms. After they'd had a private moment together, Gilbert approached his brother.

'I had no idea,' Gilbert said. 'I can't believe she did this to our daughter. It's unforgivable.'

'Samantha's going to need a lot of support,' Miles said. 'Maybe even therapy. It's like she needs to be deprogrammed from what Caroline did to her.'

Gilbert looked like he'd consider stepping in

front of a bus if one had happened to go by at that moment.

'There's more,' he said. 'And maybe it's connected.'

He told Miles he'd seen Caroline heading into the Omni, that someone had slipped a key card into his pocket and told him where to find her. Caroline had been waiting for another man.

'She hasn't come home since.' He hung his head, then looked up. 'And when I got the call from the plane, I phoned her, confronted her with that. She didn't even try to deny it. Normally, that'd be her default position, but I knew too much for her to say none of it was true. She started crying, said it was all for me. I've called a lawyer. I'm getting the locks changed.'

Miles said something his brother already knew. 'There's no telling what she might do. Maybe to herself.'

Gilbert nodded.

'Go be with Samantha. She barely scratched the surface when she talked to you from the plane.'

When Gilbert left, Miles tried to reach Chloe again. She didn't answer, and another text went undelivered.

He tried to remember the name of the diner where she worked. Finally, it came to him. He opened a browser on his phone, found it, tapped the number.

'Paradise Diner,' a woman said. 'You got Vivian.'

'Yeah, hi. I wonder if it would be possible to speak to Chloe.'

'I'm wondering the same thing. She's not here.'

'When's her shift?'

'Right now,' Vivian said. 'She hasn't shown up, isn't answering her phone, and I'm shorthanded. If it's not one thing with that girl it's another. You wanna leave a message?'

CHAPTER 55

New York, NY

Nicky had run a washcloth under very cold water in the bathroom sink, wrung it out and folded it into a compress. When Chloe was brought back from her meeting upstairs with Jeremy, she was crying. When she collapsed facedown onto the bed, Nicky could see streaks of blood seeping through the back of her blouse.

Nicky had rolled up her top to reveal the belt marks on her back. Chloe winced as Nicky applied the cool cloth, moving it from one wound to another. Chloe's bravado, her flip attitude, were gone. She seemed to Nicky somehow smaller, as though her encounter upstairs had diminished her, made her less of a person.

'I told them,' she whimpered. 'I told them everything they wanted to know.'

Nicky dabbed her cheek. 'Sorry I don't have ice.'

Chloe said, 'I think he knew most of it already. Someone had told him. He was confirming things.'

461

'Take it easy,' Nicky said. She took the cloth off Chloe's back. 'This is warm already. Let me make it cold again.' She went back into the bathroom and ran more water into the sink, holding her finger under it to test the temperature.

'He was kind of weird with me,' Chloe whispered when Nicky returned. Nicky had told her she thought their conversations were monitored, so they were talking as quietly as possible.

'Weird how?'

'He put his hand on my head for a long time. Just holding it there. He ever do that with you?'

'You mean like if he's holding your head down on his—'

'No, not that. Putting his hand on my head, like – this will sound totally nuts – like he was feeling my life force or something.'

'I can honestly say he's never done that with me,' Nicky said.

Chloe struggled to sit up on the side of the bed, letting her toes brush the carpet. 'He really is going to kill us, isn't he?'

Nicky sighed. 'I keep thinking, because it hasn't happened yet, maybe it won't.'

Chloe said, 'Suppose he opened the door tomorrow and told you to leave. What are you going to do? You're going to go to the police, right?'

'I guess.'

'You *guess*?'

'I don't know. I'd be so grateful to get out, maybe I wouldn't talk.'

462

'He can't take that kind of chance,' Chloe said. 'We need to get a message out to someone, anyone.'

Miles, she thought.

'Closest I got was when I picked up a Wi-Fi signal by the window,' Nicky said. 'But they found out before I could send a message.'

'If we could set off an alarm or something.'

'Thought of that,' Nicky said. 'Was going to try to start a fire one day but couldn't figure out a way to do it.'

'There must be something.'

Nicky went quiet for several seconds, and when she did talk, her whisper was almost inaudible. 'I had this one idea, but I don't know how to do it. But you're older than me, so maybe you've got, like, skills I don't.'

Chloe leaned in closer. 'Try me.'

Roberta rapped lightly on the door to Jeremy's office before entering.

'He's here,' she said.

Jeremy, sitting at the computer, looked her way. 'Send him up in five.'

Exactly five and a half minutes later, there was another soft knock on the door. Jeremy, not taking his eyes off the screen, said, 'Come in.'

A man walked into the room and stood on the other side of the desk. Jeremy didn't stand or extend a welcoming hand.

'Sit,' he said.

The man sat, settled into the chair, and crossed his legs. Jeremy entered a few more keystrokes, did one last, dramatic tap on the Enter key with his index finger, then turned and looked squarely at his guest.

'So,' Jeremy said. 'You ran into some problems.'

The man nodded. 'I can finish the job, but I'll need a new partner. There's someone I've worked with in the past. I'll give him a call.'

'What happened to her?' Jeremy asked.

'You really want to know?'

'I wouldn't have asked otherwise.'

'She was caught off guard by the subject's girlfriend,' Rhys said. 'We fucked up.'

'You see any way that we're exposed?'

'No.'

'Her prints are nowhere on file?'

'No.'

'She had no record?'

'None.'

'No identifying marks? No tattoos?'

Rhys thought back to that night.

'No. When her body's finally found, and they try to dig into her past, they'll get nowhere. She has no past.'

Jeremy sighed. 'As it turns out, we have one of them under our roof.'

Rhys, usually good with a poker face, could not conceal his surprise.

'Who?'

'Chloe Swanson.'

Rhys wondered if it was the Chloe from Todd's trailer. When he heard her voice, he'd know.

'Plus, the one we were waiting for you to deal with when you returned,' Jeremy said. 'Roberta's been quite anxious for you to get this done. I didn't want to bring in anyone else.'

'Sure.'

Jeremy placed his palms flat on the table. 'I don't want it done on the premises. Take them elsewhere.'

'Understood.'

Jeremy smiled. 'Maybe tell them you've organized an outing. A reward for good behavior. An excursion to the Central Park Zoo. Feed them to the snow leopards.'

Rhys stood. 'I'll drop by, introduce myself as part of your legal team. Tell them we're drafting some nondisclosure agreements for them to sign, after which their release will be expedited.'

Jeremy nodded. 'It has the ring of credibility. Throw in some financial compensation.'

He turned back to his computer, signaling that they were done. Once in the hall, his back to a large black-and-white photo of one man mounting another from behind, Rhys took out his phone, entered a number, and waited. After twelve rings, a pickup, followed by silence.

'It's me. We need to talk,' Rhys said, and ended the call.

He took his time heading down the hallway, checking out the pictures as though he were in a museum.

The world may think Jeremy Pritkin is normal, but he is one crazy motherfucker, Rhys thought.

His phone, still in his hand, rang.

'Hey,' he said. 'How's things?'

'Okay.'

'What's your availability?'

'Depends. What've you got?'

'Two projects. In Manhattan.'

'I'm in town.'

'What are you doing in an hour?' Rhys said.

'Usual place?'

'Yeah.'

'I'll be there.'

Rhys put his phone away and smiled. It was good to have Broderick aboard. The guy was a pro, and he owed him one.

Chloe and Nicky were sitting on the bed, backs to the headboard, legs crossed, watching TV. Nicky had the remote and was going through the channels, spending little more than three seconds on each. There was nothing else they could do right now, but given how hard it was for them to actually focus on anything, they weren't settling on any one show.

The door opened.

That gave Nicky more of a start than it did Chloe, because Nicky was used to the routine around here, and this was not a normal visiting time. Dinner wouldn't be until later. Breakfast arrived at eight, lunch at half past twelve, dinner at seven. Every Monday, around nine, housekeeping arrived with fresh sheets and towels.

Rhys stepped into the room.

They both sat up a little straighter, but neither of them got off the bed.

'Relax,' he said, raising his right hand in a nonthreatening gesture. 'My name's Rhys. I represent Mr Pritkin, and we've come to a conclusion about how to resolve our current situation with you two young ladies that I think you'll find very satisfactory.'

He smiled reassuringly. 'You'll be coming to our offices to sign some papers. Nondisclosure agreements. I'm sure you're familiar with those. Very common practice these days. You'll sign, promising never to disclose to anyone what has happened here. There will be significant financial compensation for the inconvenience we've caused you.'

Nicky asked, 'How much?'

Chloe shot her a look that said, *Seriously?*

'To be determined,' Rhys said. 'But you'll be pleased by the amount. Anyway, pardon the intrusion. We'll see you shortly.'

He backed up a step, tapped the door, waited for someone in the hall to open it. When he was gone. Nicky turned to Chloe and said, 'That's good, isn't it? I'll sign anything they want if it means this is over.'

Chloe did not look encouraged.

'Did you see his hand?' she asked.

'His hand?'

'His pinkie finger. Most of it was missing.'

'So?'

Chloe sighed. 'Big-time lawyers don't hide under beds.'

468

CHAPTER 56

Mount Vernon, NY

Martin Gold loved bridges.

His fascination – he supposed it was fair to call it an obsession – with them went back to his earliest childhood years. Using the most basic wooden blocks, little Martin would construct bridges to drive his cars and trucks over. His favorite toy, without question, was a Kenner Bridge and Turnpike Building Set. Inside that box were hundreds of tiny red plastic beams and girders and road pieces that could be used to build the most elaborate structures. There was even a motor for operating a drawbridge. By combining several sets, Martin made bridges with massive spans, long enough to go from one side of his bedroom to the other.

His father, a dental surgeon who shared his son's love of bridges and probably would have felt more fulfilled had he become a structural engineer instead of someone who poked around inside people's mouths, enjoyed indulging Martin. Whenever possible, when out in the car, they

469

would take a route that included a bridge. One day, his father planned an all-day trip to New York that was built around bridges. They drove over the Queensboro, the Manhattan, the Williamsburg, the George Washington, but when it came to the Brooklyn Bridge, Martin's dad had a special treat. They parked the car and walked it, starting on the Manhattan side, had lunch in Brooklyn, then walked back, enjoying the view of the Manhattan skyline as it grew closer with every step.

Martin Gold remembered it as the best day of his life.

Throughout the years, wherever he and his wife vacationed, Gold would search out the most interesting bridges. When they went to San Francisco, he walked the Golden Gate. When they went to Australia, not only did he check out the Sydney Harbour Bridge, he did the climb, hooked up safety cables so he could traverse the top span. It was as close as Gold had come to a religious experience.

Gold remembered thinking, at the time, *I could die right now.*

But he didn't, of course. He came back to New Rochelle and continued to run his fertility clinic. (His love of bridges had never turned into a career. Bridges were fine as a hobby, his parents said, but his destiny was to become a doctor.) He had managed, at least while in Australia, to forget that there was a metaphorical bridge always

470

hanging over him, a bridge always on the verge of collapse.

It was a terrible thing he'd done, more than twenty years ago. He knew it was wrong. How could he not? But when someone had a hold over you, possessed incredibly damning information, you found yourself capable of unimaginable things. He'd made a god-awful mistake. He'd tried to rationalize his behavior. He'd taken these actions to protect not just himself, but his wife and their young son. If he were to be disgraced, they would be, too. Their lives would be ruined.

So he did what he believed he had to do.

He knew there had to be pictures, maybe even videotapes. If they were sent to his wife, that would be bad enough. Maybe, when she saw him getting it off with a girl who was barely old enough to vote, she'd seek a divorce. And he wouldn't blame her. A divorce, as horrible as it would be, was something he could ride out. But what if the tapes were made public? Sent anonymously to the state medical board? He'd be ruined professionally. The clinic would be shut down. God, he might even face criminal charges. He'd be lucky to have a job as a Walmart greeter by the time the dust settled.

And as more time passed, it became harder to do the right thing. The noose around his neck tightened.

It had all started from a chance encounter. A grateful couple he'd helped to conceive twin boys

471

had rewarded Gold with dinner at Windows on the World atop the North Tower of the World Trade Center, more than two years before that day that changed the world. They were well connected, these people, and during the meal they spotted one of their idols, whom they knew personally, several tables over.

'Oh,' they'd said to Gold, 'you must meet our friend Jeremy.'

And when Jeremy Pritkin learned what Gold did for a living, he took an immediate interest.

Gold had to admit that he'd allowed himself to be dazzled by the man. Jeremy was rich, charismatic, possessed of an overpowering personality. To be taken under his wing, to be considered his friend, to be admitted to the inner sanctum that was that massive brownstone on East Seventieth Street, left Gold spellbound.

When he was behind those doors, it was like being admitted to one's own private Playboy Club. Dear God, the people Gold met there. Mayors and governors and movie stars. Even the odd royal! About twentieth in line to the throne, but so what?

And of course, there were the girls.

As it turned out, Martin Gold and Jeremy Pritkin had similar tastes. They liked girls on the young side. Oh, they weren't pedophiles, for God's sake. Nothing like that. These were not *children*. These were girls coming into womanhood. Lots of respected, famous men fancied women much

472

younger than themselves. Even a president, for crying out loud. And from everything Gold could tell, these girls – no, let's be clear about this, these young *women* – were treated well by his host. From what he'd heard, they were well paid as hostesses, and pretty much guaranteed some sort of future role in the Pritkin organization.

Jeremy had made that very clear to him.

Jeremy was, let's face it, a big talker. He had a pretty grand impression of himself, and not without reason. He'd already made billions in the business world – this was before he'd sold his company – and as a result of his generous donations to museums and theaters and the like, he was a darling of the arts world. He backed politicians. He was a go-to guest for political talk shows.

Was it little wonder he thought highly of himself? In fact, he confided to Gold one day that he was of superior genetic stock. A kind of superman.

'How do you mean?' asked Gold. He thought, initially, that Jeremy was just kidding around.

'I really need to explain?' Jeremy replied.

At Gold's encouragement, he listed the reasons. He was, first of all, an above-average physical specimen. He was fit, he had never been sick a day in his life, and he was, by societal standards, exceedingly handsome. But then you added in his astounding intellect, his ability to comprehend complicated issues that left most people perplexed.

473

His IQ was reportedly 179, and as everyone knew, anything over 160 was considered genius. So Jeremy was 'genius plus.' He'd put his significant skills to work in the business world.

You put it all together, and he was as close as someone could be to a superman without donning tights and a cape, flying out the window, and letting bullets bounce off his chest.

Jeremy had gone on to say ('Just between us, you understand') that his voracious sexual appetite and his interest in women – especially younger ones who were, as he described them, 'prime breeders' – was nature's way of urging him to procreate.

'It is, in effect, a force beyond my control,' he had said. 'Mother Nature *wants* me to spread my seed. I am among a select few who have been chosen to better the human race. It's imperative that I propagate.'

It was, in short, his destiny.

By this point, Gold realized his host was serious. He believed the shit he was saying.

'You're a good-looking guy, there's no doubt about it, a regular Marlboro Man,' Gold said, adding a small, nervous laugh.

'I have this idea I've been thinking about for a long time, and you're just the man who could help me with it,' Jeremy said, putting his arm around Gold's neck and pulling him in close.

Martin Gold was stunned by what Jeremy would propose.

Jeremy wanted Gold, as an expert in fertility medicine and the director of a clinic, to impregnate several women with Pritkin's sperm. The files, of course, would have to be doctored to show it was someone else's donation. It would be a long-term experiment. Jeremy's people would keep tabs on these offspring as they matured to see whether they inherited any of his greatness. Much would depend, of course, on the recipients of his donation. Jeremy stressed that any woman who received his sperm would have to be above average, too. Healthy, attractive, intelligent. While he understood it would be difficult to find female recipients as remarkable as he was, Gold would have to do his best. Pritkin wanted to be clear that there were plenty of women happy to sleep with him, but not necessarily on board with having a child with him. Besides, Pritkin didn't want the responsibility. What he wanted needed to be done in a scientific, clinical way.

And really, Jeremy argued, what difference did it make if his sperm was substituted for someone else's? The women didn't know, really, what they were getting anyway. They chose from a profile without actually knowing who the person was. And Jeremy's profile would undoubtedly be superior to any other they might receive.

The man was crazy.

'No,' Gold said.

'I'm sorry?'

'No. No. No. No. I can't make it any clearer.

That violates more ethical standards than I can count. No, I'm sorry, Jeremy, it's out of the question. I'm sorry. Look, I like you. You're a wonderful guy, and maybe, maybe you're right. You're as perfect a human being as there could be. You're Paul Newman and Albert Einstein and Warren Buffett all rolled into one. But what you're asking, that's simply not possible.'

Jeremy was unable to hide his disappointment. He took his arm from around the doctor's neck. 'Oh, Martin, I had such faith in you. I was sure you'd be able to do this for me.'

'Jeremy, if there was anything else, believe me, I would do it. But not this.'

Jeremy shook his head sadly. 'This is not what I wanted to hear from you.'

Gold had not known what to say. He definitely wasn't going to suggest he try some other doctor. *No* doctor should be involved in anything like this. Jeremy did not believe basic societal rules applied to him. What could you say to a person like that? Gold hated to disappoint him, because knowing this man, having access to this exclusive world, was the best thing that had happened to Gold since he walked the Brooklyn Bridge.

'What's your wife's name again?' Jeremy asked.

'I'm sorry?'

'Your wife. Her name?'

'Elspeth. You met her at that function last year. The museum fundraiser.'

'Lovely woman.'

Gold's insides started to turn to jelly. 'Why do you ask?'

'No reason.'

'Jeremy, please.'

'I'm just imagining her reaction when she sees a clip of you with your head between Whitney's legs.'

And Jeremy smiled.

So there it was.

How many others were similarly compromised? The police chief? The governor? Judges and prosecutors?

Gold wrestled with the request for only a few days before bending to Jeremy's will. He disposed of a sample provided by one Miles Cookson, but attached his name to the files of nine women implanted with Jeremy's sperm.

Who could have guessed, back then, that in less than two decades there'd be thriving businesses devoted to testing your DNA and linking you to relatives you never knew you had? And that Jeremy's sister would send in her DNA sample and be startled to learn there was at least one person out there who was very likely her niece? And that it didn't make any sense at all.

That was when Jeremy realized the seriousness of his situation.

Those nine grown children out there. Living, breathing evidence of his arrogance and grandiosity. One day, more of them might send samples to WhatsMyStory or some other DNA service, and be linked back to Jeremy's sister and, in turn, to him.

Jeremy was apoplectic.

His grand 'nature vs. nurture' experiment had to be brought to an end prematurely. All evidence had to be destroyed.

Evidence being, of course, the people themselves.

It wasn't enough that they be killed. They had to be vanished. DNA could be recovered from a corpse, even years into the future. A body could be exhumed, tested.

Not only that, DNA traces could be left behind. In hair-brushes, on phones, towels, sheets. Two of the best ways to eliminate DNA were bleach and fire. If the residences of these people couldn't be burned to the ground, then they had to be thoroughly cleaned.

This string of murders would never have happened if Gold had not caved to Jeremy's outrageous demands two decades earlier.

Gold knew that Jeremy had employed people to monitor his nine biological children over the years. Followed their academic progress, their interests. And, as the years progressed, which colleges, if any, they chose.

Before learning that his sister had sent her DNA to WhatsMyStory, what had distressed Jeremy Pritkin most was how *normal* these children were.

Oh, sure, some had shown some minimal talent in certain areas. One wanted to be an actress, another a graphic novelist. The one out in Portland was interested in medical research. But where were the child prodigies? The kid who could play Mozart on a piano at the age of four? The youngster who could solve a scrambled Rubik's Cube in fifteen seconds? The computer geek who could figure out how to hack the Pentagon from his bedroom before puberty?

Normal. Or, to put it another way: *disappointing*.

It took a little of the sting out of it for Jeremy. In some ways, erasing these children from the face of the Earth was a way to hide his failures.

Or so Jeremy had told Gold.

There was one bridge, in neighboring Mount Vernon, that Gold viewed with special affection. It was by no means the longest bridge in the world, or the highest, and it certainly was not the most beautiful. It was no Golden Gate, and it sure as hell was no Sydney Harbour Bridge.

But he liked it because it reminded him of the bridges he built as a child.

It was the South Fulton Avenue bridge in Mount Vernon that spanned the Metro North Railroad line.

A simple Pratt through-truss bridge, two-lane, slightly more than 150 feet. Long enough to span the four tracks below. Partway across, a set of covered stairs that headed down to the tracks, and signs that read: MOUNT VERNON EAST STATION. TO STAMFORD AND NEW HAVEN, TRACK 4.

Once you crossed the bridge, the road became North Fulton Avenue. It was a dividing line between north and south, an equator of bridges.

Gold knew the history here and was happy to explain it to anyone who wanted to listen. The design for the Pratt bridges, and examples of them were scattered all over the country, came from Caleb and Thomas Pratt, who developed, in 1844, a bridge constructed of wood and diagonal iron rods. It was made up of sections called trusses.

As a boy, Martin lived only a few blocks from here, and he had walked or ridden his bike across this bridge probably a thousand times.

It seemed fitting this would be the one he jumped from.

There was a fence running along the walkways on both sides, but it was not so high as to be insurmountable. Just to be sure, Gold brought along with him a small plastic step stool that he kept in his storage unit for when he needed to bring a box down from the top of a stack.

The 1349 train would be coming into the station at 11:12, from the east, passing under the bridge before it came to a full stop at the platform. Gold figured if he arrived at 11:10, parked his Lexus right on the bridge, grabbed the step stool, and hurriedly bailed from the car, that would give him enough time to leap over the fence and land on the tracks seconds before the train got there. The fall would almost certainly kill him, but in the unlikely event it did not, the train would finish him off.

Gold, always a considerate sort, would leave the key to the Lexus on top of the dash. No sense making the police have to call for a tow, or worse, dig through his pockets once the fall and the train had made a mess of him. He wondered if he should have written a note for Elspeth, explaining why he was ending his life.

No, he thought. Better that she never know.

He held back one block from the bridge, and when his dashboard clock read 11:08, he put the car in Drive and hit the accelerator. There were no vehicles in his path, nothing to stop him from meeting his train on time.

The car rolled onto the bridge. Halfway across, he stopped the car, put it in Park, and killed the engine. He tossed his keys onto the dash, then grabbed the small step stool that was in the foot-well of the front passenger seat.

He stepped out onto the bridge, walked around the back of the car to reach the pedestrian walkway on the east side. He peered over the top of the railing.

There it was. The headlight of the approaching train.

His heart hammered as he set the step stool down, got onto it, and gripped the top of the railing. All he had to do to get over was hoist himself up at the same time as he gave a good push with his legs.

The train was almost to the bridge.

It was time.

Grip. Push.

'Hey, whoa, stop it!'

He felt someone grab him around the legs. He glanced over his shoulder, saw a large woman clinging to him. She was dressed somewhat formally, in a pale blue shirt, black pants, and a black suit-like jacket.

'Don't do it, Dr Gold!' the woman cried. 'Don't do it!'

How did she know who he was? He'd never seen this woman before in his life.

'Let go!' he said. 'Let me go!'

'I gotcha! I gotcha!'

Martin Gold couldn't get over the railing. The woman had a good fifty pounds on him, he was betting. He'd lost his leverage.

The train rumbled underneath them as it slowed coming into the station stop. It was now immediately west of the bridge.

The moment was gone.

He stumbled off the plastic step, lost his balance, and hit the walkway. The woman knelt over him, straddling him. She was doing more than just trying to help him. She was keeping him from getting away.

'It's going to be okay,' she said. 'Charise is going to take good care of you.'

And that was when Gold noticed someone else on the bridge. Running this way. This person he recognized.

Miles Cookson.

Shit, Gold thought. *It's over.*

CHAPTER 57

New Haven, CT

Gilbert and Samantha stood at her second-floor bedroom window, peering down from behind the curtain, wondering what Caroline might do next. She stood in the middle of the yard, looking up, aware that they were watching her.

'I'm sorry!' she shouted. 'I'm sorry about everything!'

Earlier, she had only been crying. Now she was sobbing.

'Please let me in! I did it all for you!'

The locksmith had left only moments before Caroline dared return home with a story that would satisfactorily explain her actions. The code for the security system, mounted on the exterior door handle – and which, if entered correctly, not only unlocked the door but turned off the alarm – had also been changed.

'Maybe we should let her in,' Samantha said.

'No,' said her father.

'We can't let her stand in the yard all night.'

484

'Yes,' Gilbert said. 'We can.'

Gilbert had also canceled all their credit cards, except for his Cookson Tech card, to which Caroline did not have access.

Caroline, at one point, had gone around to the back of the house and attempted to gain entry through the sliding-glass doors that led into the kitchen, but Gilbert had made sure those were locked, too. She'd picked up one of the metal deck chairs and thrown it at the glass, but without enough force to crack it.

So she had gone back to the front yard, hoping that expressions of contrition would do the trick.

'I'm sorry!' she shouted again, figuring her family would hear her even if she couldn't see them. 'I was trying to do the right thing! I was trying to *help* us! Gil, please go to the front door! You don't have to open it. I just want to talk to you.'

So he went downstairs and positioned himself by the door. Caroline, on the other side, was whimpering.

'I was trying to get justice for you,' she said.

'No, you weren't,' Gilbert said.

'It's true. It is. I told Samantha it was all for you.'

'Go away, Caroline. Don't come back.'

'I'll talk to Miles. I'll make it all better.'

'I don't think that would be a good idea.'

Now, no words. Only crying.

Gilbert, exhausted, put his forehead to the door. 'You need help,' he said.

More crying, sniffling.

'You need to talk to somebody,' Gilbert said. 'Maybe . . . that would help. You need to figure out why you do the things you do. If you really want to do the right thing for this family, that would be a place to start.'

Still nothing from the other side of the door. The whimpering had ceased. Gilbert wondered whether she was still there. And then he heard some kind of crash. Glass shattering. Then the whooping of an alarm.

He ran to the living room window.

The windshield of the Porsche Miles had given him had been shattered, caved in. The hood was covered with what looked like topsoil and leaves. The car's lights were flashing as the alarm continued to wail. Gilbert noticed that one of the planters by the walk up to the front door was missing.

Caroline stood next to the Porsche, brushing her hands together, admiring her handiwork. She turned, slowly, to look back at the house.

Gilbert thought she suddenly looked very calm. Maybe her act of automotive vandalism had served as a kind of release.

Samantha had come downstairs. 'Did you see what she did?'

'Yes.'

He saw, at that moment, how pathetic his wife looked. Standing there, tear lines streaking her cheeks, her makeup smeared, hands covered in dirt, her hair in disarray.

Gilbert knew he should be angry, and he certainly had been, but now all he could do was pity her.

Caroline took one last look at the house, turned and walked to the curb, where she had parked her Volvo SUV across the end of the driveway. She got in behind the wheel and drove away. Calmly. No spinning of wheels. She even used her turn signal when she got to the end of the street.

Samantha asked, 'Where do you think she's going?'

Gilbert shook his head. 'As long as she doesn't come back, I don't care.'

CHAPTER 58

New Haven, CT

'This is kidnapping. You can't hold me here against my will. I'll call the police.'

Miles tossed a cell phone to Dr Martin Gold. It was the one Charise had taken off him earlier. 'Go ahead. Call them right now. Let's tell them everything.'

Gold seemed to sink into the leather couch in the living room of Miles's home. He looked from Miles to Charise, who was standing nearby, arms crossed, ready to throw him back onto the couch if he considered making a run for it.

Once Miles had returned from Fort Wayne, he'd had Charise drive him back to the ReproGold Clinic. When the doctor turned out not to be there, they went to his home, but a block before they reached it they spotted the doctor behind the wheel of his Lexus, headed in the other direction.

They followed.

They trailed him to the Mount Vernon bridge, and were puzzled, at first, when he stopped his car in the middle of it. But his intentions soon became clear.

'Oh, my God,' Miles had said. 'He's going to jump.'

Charise had not waited for instructions. She'd bolted from the limo and run onto the bridge, then grabbed Gold, hauled him off the railing, and sat on him so he could not get away.

She had then whispered in his ear that if he did not come back to the limo with her, she would do something so horrible to him that he'd beg her to let him try jumping off the bridge again to make the pain go away.

After she had him in the car next to Miles and was back behind the wheel, Miles had said, 'That was amazing.'

Charise had said, 'Compared to what I used to do, sir, this was like subduing a five-year-old girl.'

Miles had wondered, briefly, whether they should be taking a suicidal man to the hospital, but believed getting some answers from Gold took priority. They could get him the help he needed later. So Miles had directed Charise to take them to his home.

Dorian was waiting at the house when they got there, and reported that a call had been made to the FBI's Lana Murkowski. So far, she had not called back.

When Gold did not call Miles's bluff and call the police, Miles took the phone back. He handed

489

his own cell to Charise and asked, 'Can you keep trying Chloe?'

Dorian said, 'I can do that.'

'No, it's okay,' Miles said. He had not looked Dorian in the eye since they'd returned. To Charise, he said, 'Chloe has to turn her phone back on at some point.'

'Chloe,' Gold said. 'The girl who was with you before.'

'Yeah,' Miles said. 'So, you were going to jump. Why?'

Gold took a moment to answer. 'I've had enough.'

Miles perched himself on the coffee table, in front of Gold, and said, 'Why does someone consider taking their own life? Depressed, surely. Or maybe to avoid something worse than death. What have you done, Dr Gold? Tell me what you've done.'

Gold couldn't look at him.

'Tell me about Caroline Cookson,' he said.

Gold's head jerked. 'Who?'

It was a shot in the dark. Miles didn't know if Caroline had a connection with Gold, or whether the stunt she'd pulled was in any way related to everything else that was going on, but he wanted to see the man's reaction when asked. Miles repeated the name.

'Who's that?' Gold said. 'Cookson? A relative?'

'Sister-in-law,' Miles said.

'Did she come to my clinic? I don't know the name.'

Miles believed him and went in another direction. He told Gold what had gone down in Fort Wayne, the attempt to kill someone whose mother had been to Gold's clinic years ago, before moving to Indiana. As Gold listened, he grew increasingly agitated.

'Why would someone want Travis Roben dead?' Miles asked. 'Or the girl in Paris? The student in Maine? All children of women who came to your clinic.'

Charise waved the phone in the air and said, 'Still no answer, Mr Cookson.'

Miles leaned in close to Gold, close enough for the doctor to feel his breath on his face. 'You told me I had no idea what I was getting into, who I was dealing with. It's time you explained what you meant by that.'

When Gold said nothing, Miles turned to Charise. 'Back in your wrestling days, was there a favorite move you used?'

Charise thought for a moment. 'We had something we called the tombstone piledriver. It was actually so dangerous we weren't supposed to use it. You turn someone upside down, then drive his head into—'

'I think we get the idea,' Miles said. He turned his attention to Gold again and waited. Gold raised his head and looked into Miles's eyes. There was the sense of a dam about to burst.

'Pritkin,' he said.

'Pritkin?' Miles said.

'Jeremy Pritkin.'

'*The* Jeremy Pritkin?'

Gold nodded. 'It's him.'

'What do you mean, "it's him"? What's "him"?' Miles was aghast. 'Pritkin? You're not serious.'

Gold's head went up and down.

It all came out, in a rush. A man who hours earlier was ready to end his life evidently no longer felt a need to keep secrets.

Gold related how Jeremy believed he was a superhuman being with an extraordinary genetic profile, and he wanted his sperm implanted in women who were, essentially, unwitting test subjects. He wanted to try it with ten women, but one miscarried. Miles's donations were discarded, but his name went on the files.

Then commercial DNA testing came along.

'It wasn't enough that they die,' Gold said. 'They had to be erased.'

'I set out to find children I thought were mine to help them, while their true biological father set out to destroy them.'

Miles had to get up and walk. He paced the room, went to the window, and looked out into a nearby wooded area.

'It's unthinkable,' he said. 'How could one person be that—'

Gold said, 'He's not who he appears to be. When you get a look behind the curtain, you see what he really is. He makes the devil look like Mr Rogers.' He paused. 'And that's why I was on that bridge.'

Gold said to Charise, who was still holding Miles's phone, 'You still haven't reached her, have you?'

Charise shook her head.

The doctor looked at Miles. 'After you came to the storage locker I . . . I called him.'

'What did you say?' Miles asked.

'That you and Chloe were putting it together.'

'What are you saying?' Miles said. 'You think he's got her? You think he's *killed* her?' He became unsteady on his feet, placing a hand on the back of a chair to steady himself.

Gold said, 'I don't know. I think he'd try to find out what she knows first. To find out if he's vulnerable. Exposed.'

Dorian rushed to Miles's side in case he lost his balance or collapsed, but he pushed her away. Dorian looked as though she'd been struck.

Miles said, 'Where would she be? If he has Chloe where would it be?'

Gold said, 'Probably at his place, in Manhattan. It's massive. Two or three brownstones joined together. He could easily keep her under wraps there. He's protected. He knows everyone. Cops, judges, politicians. No one's going to go busting in on him unless they're really sure he's done something wrong. And even then, who knows? He's had me in his pocket for two decades. God knows what he has on everyone else.'

'Are you saying if we call the police, he'll be tipped off?'

493

The doctor shrugged. 'Maybe. And you have to know, once he's done with Chloe, he'll be coming after you.'

Miles handed Gold's phone back to him. 'Call him,' he said.

'And say what?' he asked, his voice on the verge of squeaking.

Miles considered the question. 'Tell him . . . no, first, find out if he has her. If he does . . . shit, let me think.' He walked away, started pacing again. 'We have to find a way to stall. To buy some time.' He turned to Dorian and spoke to her for the first time since they'd all been in the room together. 'Still nothing from Murkowski?'

'No,' said Dorian. 'And if he's to be believed, even she could be compromised. Or if not her, whoever she brings in on it.'

Miles put his hand to his forehead. 'Jesus.'

Gold said, 'I have an idea.'

Miles waited.

'I tell him, if he has her, I need . . . I need to get a DNA sample from her.'

'Why?' Miles asked.

'Because, because . . .' Gold struggled for a reason. 'Because I need to compare her against some other adult children. That I may have made a mistake with the filing, there might have been more than nine women impregnated with his sperm. That he might have more children out there he needs to track down.'

Miles was skeptical. 'Does that even make any

494

sense? Why would you need her DNA? Wouldn't a sample of his suffice? What about—'

'Shut up!' Gold said. 'Just . . . shut up. It's the best thing I can think of right now. I know the science better than he does. I might be able to bluff my way through.'

Miles looked like a man who had run out of options.

'Do it,' he said.

Gold entered a number on the phone and waited. Finally, he said, 'It's Martin. I need to speak to Jeremy.' He was put on hold. 'Waiting,' he said, looking at Miles.

'Put it on speaker,' Miles said.

Gold tapped the screen, held the phone a few inches in front of his mouth. The wait went on for the better part of a minute before there was the sound of someone at the other end.

'Jeremy?'

'No,' a woman said. 'Dr Gold?'

'Yes. Who is this?'

'Roberta.'

'Roberta, I need to speak to Jeremy.'

'He's busy,' Roberta said.

'It's urgent.'

'What's it concerning?'

'The Swanson girl.' He paused, and lowered his voice conspiratorially. 'Is she there?'

'Why would you think that?'

Gold's eyes danced while he tried to think of something, and Miles shuddered inwardly. Why

495

would Gold think that? How would he have been tipped off?

Gold decided to go with a version of the truth, since it would sound the most credible. 'Cookson called me. The girl's disappeared. I'm just connecting the dots.'

'Suppose she were here,' Roberta said. 'What's that to you?'

'I wanted to discuss an issue with Jeremy.'

'Discuss it with me.'

Gold took a breath and said, 'I need a DNA sample from her. I need to run a comparison between her profile and some others. It's rather complicated.'

'You think I wouldn't be able to understand it?' Roberta asked.

'No, no, not at all. But it makes more sense for me to explain it to Jeremy directly.'

There was silence at the other end. Charise and Miles exchanged glances, wondering if maybe the signal had been lost.

But then Roberta spoke.

'You'd have to come here to do this, of course?'

'Yes,' Gold said.

'When?'

'Tomorrow?'

Another moment of dead air. When Roberta came back on, she said, 'That would be too late. I'm sorry, Dr Gold, but we're not going to be able to accommodate you on this.'

'But you see—'

'Goodbye,' Roberta said.
'Hello? Don't hang up. Are you there?'
She was not.
'He's got her,' Miles said.
Charise said, 'I'll bring the car around.'

CHAPTER 59

New York, NY

Rhys and Broderick had each ordered a beer. They'd taken a booth in a bar on Third a couple of blocks north of Bloomingdale's.

'Been a while,' Rhys said.

Broderick nodded. 'We haven't talked since my legal problems.'

Rhys smiled. 'All seems to have worked out okay.'

Then Broderick smiled. 'Could have gone another way if it hadn't been for you. I owe you one.'

'Kinda why I got in touch,' Rhys said. 'I've had a little trouble recently. You heard of Jeremy Pritkin?'

'That's like asking if I've ever heard of money.'

'Been doing some work for him,' Rhys said. 'Big job, not finished. Things went sideways.'

'Like?'

'Lost a partner.'

Broderick smiled. 'So what's the job?'

'Pritkin has two girls at his place. They're a liability. He can't release them into the wild,

498

but they think they're getting their freedom, that they've got an appointment with a lawyer to sign some NDAs, walk away with a substantial cash settlement to keep quiet. That way, they leave the building without trying to make a break for it, and it gets them out of there so we can do what we have to do off-site.'

Broderick nodded. 'What's it all about?'

'Do you *want* to know what this is all about?'

Broderick shrugged. 'Curious.'

'Even I don't know the scope of it. Pritkin's needed some people to disappear. Completely. No DNA traces left behind. They're all over. We ran into a problem in Fort Wayne.'

'Fort Wayne?'

'Yeah.'

Broderick moved his tongue around, poking it into his cheek. 'Hadn't thought of Fort Wayne in a million years and now it pops up twice in a very short period of time.'

Rhys waited.

'Met this woman. Had a scheme to get a fortune that should go to her husband, but he got fucked over by his brother. Got her daughter to make nice with this nerd who was going to come into a lot of money, eventually.'

Rhys's eyes narrowed. 'You got a name for this nerd?'

'Travis Roben.'

Rhys leaned back in the booth and shook his head. 'You're shittin' me.'

499

'No.'

Rhys said, 'That's the thing that went sideways.' He gave Broderick the bullet-point version. 'Small fucking world.'

'Not really,' Broderick said. 'Not a lot of people in our line of work. Sometimes our interests overlap.'

'You know what?' Rhys said. 'Bringing you in, it was meant to be.' He raised his bottle and clinked it against Broderick's. 'I got a good feeling about this.'

CHAPTER 60

New York, NY

Chloe and Nicky decided to they would do it after dinner, which, as it turned out, was pretty damn good. Veal lasagna and chocolate mousse for dessert.

'This is even *better* than usual,' Nicky whispered to Chloe. 'They probably *are* getting ready to kill us.'

Their occasional attempts at gallows humor did not mask how scared they were.

Nicky, whispering to Chloe with the television volume turned up, had gone over, several times, how things worked around here. Whenever anyone came to the room, like the maid or Roberta, they couldn't leave until someone responded to their rap on the door. The man who stood guard at the top of the stairs, a short distance down the hall, would come open it, then return to his station. Like in a prison movie, when the lawyer lets the guard know he's done talking to his client.

The door was always open for a few seconds. Now that there were two of them, there was a better chance that between them they could keep that door open long enough to escape.

What about the guard? Chloe had asked.

He was big, Nicky said, but that also meant he was slower than them. And the thing was, he wouldn't be standing where they intended to go.

'You ever play basketball?' Chloe had asked.

'Sure.'

'We fake him out. Look like we're going one way, he moves to block, we go the other way.'

'He'll think we're heading for the front door.'

Chloe said, in a voice loud enough to be picked up by their captors, 'Gotta pee.'

She went into the bathroom and closed the door. She grabbed a hand towel, wrapped it around the drinking glass sitting on the shelf above the sink and lightly rapped it on the edge of the porcelain sink until she heard it shatter.

Then she set the towel down in the bottom of the sink and carefully unwrapped the glass, now in several pieces. Chloe examined the shards and picked two larger pieces she believed would suit their purposes. They needed to be large enough to be effective, but small enough to be concealed in their hands. About the size of a book of matches.

She set the two curved pieces next to the taps, then gathered up the rest of the shards in the towel and put them in the garbage receptacle. She wadded up some tissues and tossed them over the glass to hide it. She flushed the toilet, for the benefit of any bedroom listening devices, and rejoined Nicky on the bed.

They were sitting atop the covers, their backs propped against the headboard. Chloe tucked one of the two pieces of glass just under Nicky's jeaned leg. They were both fully dressed, shoes on.

'It's sharp,' she whispered.

'Duh,' Nicky said.

The glass briefly caught on the bedspread as Nicky reached down and palmed it. Then, in a normal voice, she said, 'I gotta move around.'

She hopped off the bed and began to pace the room, her path taking her close to the door with every lap. The plan was simple. When the maid came back for their tray, Nicky would keep the door from closing while Chloe kept the maid in check by threatening to cut her.

Simple.

Nicky might have tried something like this long before now, but the rest of the escape plan needed Chloe's skills to be executed.

Nicky, still speaking so that she could be heard, 'Tell me again what a DNA agreement is?'

'Not DNA,' Chloe said. 'NDA. Nondisclosure agreement. We sign it, they pay us, and we agree never to be tattletales.'

'But what if we told anyway?'

'They could sue us and we'd have to give the money back and maybe even more. And we'd have to hire lawyers to fight it for us and we'd be in debt up to our assholes.'

'Even if holding us here is against the law?'

Chloe shrugged. 'You really want to challenge this? If it gets us out of here? You don't want enough money to have you set for life? Because believe me, they're going to have to pay up to keep us quiet.'

They believed their performance was Oscar-worthy.

'Fine,' Nicky said. 'If all I got to do is sign something, I'll do it. How much money you think they'll give us?'

Chloe shrugged. 'Thousands, I bet. This Pritkin guy's loaded, right?'

'Uh, look around,' Nicky said. 'He's got more money than—'

Knock knock.

Chloe got off the bed. Nicky stopped her pacing two feet from the door.

Chloe felt the glass shard digging into her palm as she delicately closed her hand around it. The slightest squeeze and she'd start to draw blood.

Nicky was doing the same. They exchanged a quick glance.

Here we go.

The door began to open.

CHAPTER 61

New York, NY

On the first part of their trip into Manhattan, as the sun was setting, Dorian had asked to sit in the back with Miles. Gold was put up front next to Charise.

Dorian, her voice low, said to Miles, 'What's going on with you? You've been acting funny. Freezing me out.'

'We can talk about it when this is over,' Miles said. 'This isn't the time.'

'No,' she said. 'Now.'

Miles wouldn't look at her. He faced his window. Dorian went to place her hand on his arm, but held back. The realization had set in.

'I'll pay it back,' she said.

Miles, still avoiding eye contact, said, 'It's not about the money. Keep the money. I don't care about that.'

'How long have you known?'

'Heather called me, after the FBI meeting.'

Dorian struggled to hold back tears.

'Maybe you could just tell me why,' he said.

'I thought . . . I deserved it,' Dorian said.

Miles slowly turned and looked at her. 'That's probably true. You did deserve it. I know you probably feel I've taken you for granted, but that's not true. I've always been grateful for your help. I couldn't have had a better assistant.'

Dorian did not miss the *had*. 'You should have come to me, made your case. I'd like to think I'd have listened. But the trust is gone.'

She wiped away a tear on her cheek. 'I could get out right now. Uber back.'

Miles shook his head. 'No. Let's see this through.'

Dorian asked Charise to pull over next chance she had so that she could switch seats with Gold.

Charise drove them into Manhattan by way of the Triborough Bridge. As they crossed, Gold, in a rare moment of detachment from the crisis at hand, said, 'The formal name for this bridge is the Robert F. Kennedy. It's actually three bridges, and it was built in 1936.' He turned to look at Miles, who was sitting next to him in the back seat, and asked, 'Did you know that?'

'No,' Miles said flatly. 'I did not.'

'Did you know that every three and a half days, someone tries to jump off the George Washington Bridge?'

This time, Miles turned and looked at him. 'I didn't know that, either.'

'Maybe,' Gold said quietly, and in total

seriousness, 'Charise could give me a lift there when this is over.'

'One thing at a time,' Miles said.

Shortly after they'd gotten off the bridge and headed south on the FDR, the traffic had slowed, and by the time they were passing 118th Street, it was down to a crawl.

'If it's still bad at 106th I'll get off there and work my way down,' Charise said.

She'd been glancing repeatedly in her rearview mirror, and Dorian had noticed a worried expression on her face.

'Everything okay?' Dorian asked quietly.

'I think it's nothing,' Charise said. 'Feel like I've had the same car behind me for a long time. But I don't know. It's dark. I could be wrong.'

Dorian turned, tried to see out the back window. 'How could you even tell?'

'Different kind of headlights. Used to be they were all round. Nowadays, every manufacturer has its own style.' She glanced again. 'Okay, I don't see them. Maybe I'm just paranoid.'

The car moved, inch by agonizing inch, until Charise was able to edge the car over to the right and get to the 106th Street exit. But she was not the only one who'd chosen that route as a way to escape the FDR.

'Shit,' Dorian said.

Charise started laying on the horn. It didn't get anyone to move out of her way, but it made her feel better.

'Call them again,' Miles said to Gold. 'Tell them you're in the neighborhood. That you *have* to see Chloe.'

Gold protested. 'I already tried once. Roberta—'

Miles exploded. 'Try again.' He handed Gold the phone. Gold entered the number and waited.

'It just keeps ringing,' he said. 'Hang on.' Someone was picking up. 'Hello, it's Dr Gold. Roberta, is that—'

Gold lowered the phone. 'She hung up.'

'Christ.'

'How about this?' Dorian said, turning around in the seat to face them. Miles looked at her but said nothing. 'Call the fire department.'

'Say again?' said Charise.

'We say we just drove by the address and saw flames coming out the window. That should buy us some time. They're not going to try anything with the fire department on their front step.'

Charise said, 'I like it.'

Miles, with some reluctance, said, 'Me too.' He took Gold's phone back from him.

'Hey, not from *my* phone,' he protested. 'They'll have a record. I'll be charged with making a false report.'

Miles gave him an incredulous look. '*That's* what you're worried about?' He made the call.

CHAPTER 62

New York, NY

The door opened an inch, but no farther. Before Nicky could think about grabbing the knob from the inside and yanking the door wide open, she saw, in the sliver of an opening, a man standing there. The one who'd visited earlier with the NDA proposal. The one with part of his finger missing.

'Stand back,' he told her. When Nicky moved away no more than a foot, Rhys said, 'More.'

Nicky gave Chloe a surrendering, hopeless look. She did as she was told and took several steps back. The door opened wide and Rhys stepped in, followed by a second man. They closed the door behind them.

Click.

Nicky and Chloe thought, *Shit.*

Chloe had not counted on there being two people. Two *men.* The guy with the tiny pinkie was formidable enough on his own, but this second dude was just as big and as menacing looking,

509

even if he was in a suit and tie, trying to look all lawyerly.

'You girls ready?' Rhys asked. 'Sooner we get this done, sooner you'll have your money and you can get back to your regular lives.'

'Who are you?' Nicky asked the other man.

Rhys provided an introduction. 'This is my associate, Broderick. He's drafted the paperwork you'll be signing.'

Chloe asked, 'Why couldn't you bring the papers here? Then we could just walk out the front door and be done with this dump.'

Rhys nodded understandingly. 'Of course, I can see how you might feel that way, but there's quite a lot to sign, and the checks are at the office. That's the way it's done.'

'Oh,' said Chloe. 'Okay, then.'

The glass shards were getting damp with sweat in her and Nicky's hands. If either of the men had noticed they were keeping their right hands closed, they'd given no indication.

'Is there anything we have to bring?' Chloe asked.

Rhys grinned. 'I'm guessing you didn't have a chance to pack before you got here.'

'No shit,' Chloe said.

'Can I come back and get my stuff later?' Nicky asked the men.

'Sure,' said Broderick.

Chloe said, 'Do you hear that?'

'Hear what?' Rhys said.

'Sirens.'

Rhys shrugged. 'You must not spend much time in New York.'

But the sirens were getting more intense. They were getting closer. The two men traded concerned glances. Someone rapped on the door. Rhys walked over and opened it an inch.

The man from the stairs could be heard saying, 'Sit tight. Something's going on.'

The door closed. Rhys turned and smiled.

'We're going to wait for an all clear.'

'What's going on?' Chloe asked.

Rhys said, 'Shut up.'

Roberta had the brownstone door open before the first firefighter had mounted the steps. The street, totally choked off with FDNY emergency vehicles, was ablaze with pulsing red lights from two pumpers and a ladder truck. For good measure, there were two cars from the NYPD.

'What's going on?' she asked, descending the front steps and meeting a helmeted fireman decked out in full regalia.

'We have a report of a fire at this address,' he said.

'That's ridiculous,' she said. 'There's no fire here. Not so much as a slice of burnt toast.'

The fireman tipped his head back, scanned the brownstone from top to bottom. 'Someone called it in, said there were flames visible from the street.'

'Do you see any flames?' Roberta asked.

'We need to come in and check,' he said.

'That's not necessary,' Roberta insisted.

'I'm sorry,' he said, stepping around her and heading for the door.

'Honestly!' Roberta said, chasing after him. 'Everything's fine!'

She'd left the front door ajar, so all he had to do was give it a push. She caught up to him in the lobby.

The fireman was greeted by Jeremy Pritkin descending the stairs. He smiled broadly and extended a hand.

'Well!' he said. 'Isn't this a surprise!'

The fireman stopped, did a double take. It was clear he recognized Pritkin. There wasn't a person in New York who wouldn't have.

'We had a call,' he said.

'I've no doubt,' Jeremy said. 'Seems we're the target of some harassment. Been getting calls all day. Had twenty pizzas delivered to the house an hour ago that we did not order. Had a bomb threat on my cell, which I know you probably think should worry me, but I get these sorts of things all the time. I'm guessing it has something to do with what I said on *Anderson Cooper* the other night. Got a few of the crazies fired up. And now, you're here. I am *so* sorry you had to be dragged into whatever nuisance campaign is being directed against me. I've already got a call into the chief of police to see if he can assign someone to get to the bottom of it.'

The fireman nodded. 'That's a shame, Mr Pritkin. Okay then. Well, ordinarily we'd do a walk-through, but it sounds like everything's okay here. You have a good evening.'

As he turned, Pritkin walked with him, putting a friendly hand on his shoulder. 'It's an outrage, you guys wasting your time here when there could be a real fire going on somewhere else. It's unconscionable.'

'Happens all the time,' he said. As he stepped outside, he gave Pritkin and Roberta a wave. 'Take care now.'

'Thank you!' they said in unison.

And as they went back into the brownstone, Pritkin whispered to Roberta, 'Something's wrong.'

Upstairs, Rhys had one arm wrapped tightly around Chloe, his other hand clamped tightly over her mouth. Broderick had a similar hold on Nicky.

Their arms were pinioned in their grips. The pieces of glass were still in their hands, but there was nothing they could do with them. Chloe tried to tamp down the panic she was feeling. If these men took this to the next step, if they gagged them and tied their hands, not only would the glass shards prove useless, the rest of their plan would go out the window.

'Just be very, very quiet now,' Rhys whispered into Chloe's ear. 'Soon as we get the all clear, we can carry on with our business.'

If Chloe had had any doubt before, lawyers did

not manhandle you and put their hands over your mouth.

Killers did.

There was another knock at the door. From the other side, a voice that was clearly Roberta's said, 'We're good. You ready?'

'A minute!' Rhys shouted. He relaxed his grip on Chloe, took his hand from her mouth. 'Sorry,' he said. 'We don't need anything interfering with you getting out of here. No sense having to answer a lot of unnecessary questions.'

Act like you believe them, Chloe told herself. *Play along*.

'Okay,' she said. 'But that wasn't nice.'

'Yeah,' Nicky chimed in once Broderick released her.

Chloe looked at her fellow prisoner and something caught her eye.

Blood.

There was blood dripping from Nicky's right hand.

514

CHAPTER 63

New York, NY

Charise figured the quickest route to the Pritkin address was to head south on Park, then take a left onto Seventieth, a one-way street running east. The brownstone was in the block between Park and Lexington. She was betting by the time they got there, the street would be clogged with fire trucks and other emergency vehicles, assuming the bogus call to 911 from Gold's phone worked as they'd hoped it would.

'Whatever they're up to, they're not going to be able to do it with the FDNY and the NYPD on their doorstep,' Miles said hopefully.

Charise said, 'And when we get there?'

Miles said, 'We tell whoever's there – the police, the fire department – we have reason to believe someone's being held against their will inside. They'll *have* to listen to us.' He looked at Gold. 'What do you think?'

Gold, the picture of defeat, said, 'I don't know anymore.'

'Okay, only a few more blocks,' Charise said encouragingly. 'Passing Seventy-Second. We got a green light ahead.'

Miles looked out his window, mesmerized by the dizzying display of lights. He'd always loved New York, had never failed to enjoy the excitement of driving into the city. Never, until now. All he felt now was anxiety.

We're coming, Chloe. We're almost there.

'One block to go,' Charise said. 'I'm not . . . seeing any fire trucks or anything.'

They had reached Seventieth Street. Charise steered the limo hard left, waiting for a break in traffic.

'It didn't work,' Gold said, peering down the street. 'There's no fire trucks.'

Miles said, 'Shit. What now?'

Charise said, 'What if we—'

And that was when the Volvo SUV rammed full speed into the driver's side of the limo.

CHAPTER 64

New York, NY

Caroline Cookson was delusional enough when she drove away from her house that she still believed she could make this right. Sure, the odds were against her. Her husband had caught her in an affair. And he'd found out about how she had used their daughter, Samantha, in a fantastical scheme to get her brother-in-law's money. And no question, these decisions were hard to defend.

But it wasn't as though she'd broken any actual laws, was it? Affairs weren't illegal. Okay, maybe conspiring to get money from Travis Roben was on the wrong side of the law, but the plan had not been carried out. Broderick had pretty much vanished – she'd tried to reach him but her ALLCAPS texts had gone undelivered and she had no idea where he really lived – so he wasn't going to tell the police what she'd done. And Samantha certainly wasn't going to testify.

After all, Caroline was her *mother*.

517

And when you got right down to it, the real victim here was Caroline herself.

Maybe if Gilbert had been a better husband, a more *attentive* husband, a more *imaginative* husband, a husband more *sensitive* to her needs, then she wouldn't have found herself looking for excitement elsewhere. And maybe if he had been a more persuasive *brother*, he wouldn't have found himself shut out of Miles's good fortune, except for that stupid Porsche.

Miles, she believed, was the key to making things right.

She would talk to him. She could confess her sins. She would throw herself at his mercy. Talk to Gilbert, she would say. Make him understand that what I did was as much for him as it was for myself.

Butter him up, if need be. Tell Miles he was a brilliant man, but she also knew he was a compassionate man, that he was capable of forgiveness.

Yes, yes, that might work.

So when she drove away from her home – she would get back there, she *would* – she found herself driving to Miles's place.

She was almost there when she saw the limo pull out of his property and onto the road. She saw him in the back seat, up against the driver's-side window.

If she were to have a chance to talk to Miles, she would have to follow him. And she kept on that limo's tail, all the way into Manhattan. Along the way she kept asking herself, *Where the hell is he going? When will he ever get there?*

At one point, going into the city, the limo made a short, unexpected stop. Long enough for a front-seat passenger to trade seats with one in the back. Before Caroline could decide whether to act on the opportunity, the limo was on the move.

More than once, she considered whether to abort. Take the next exit and head back to New Haven. She was starting to feel the way she did when she'd call an airline and be placed on hold.

Your call is important to us.

The longer you waited, the less you were convinced of that. But you were afraid to disconnect, fearing that any second they'd get to your call. You might be next in line. She kept thinking Miles had to be close to his destination. But then the limo would keep on going, and going.

And then the red warning light had appeared in her gauge cluster, telling her she would soon be out of gas.

She was driving down Park when reality began to kick in.

Miles would never listen to her.

Miles would never see her side of things.

Miles would laugh in her face.

This entire drive into the city had been a colossal waste of time.

She hated it to have been for nothing.

The rage began to simmer. The world seemed

to be turning red, as though her eyes were misting over with blood.

All of this was Miles's fault. His greed, his ungrateful attitude, his disrespect for his brother.

No, no, his disrespect for *her*.

When the limo made that turn at Seventieth, when the headlights of Caroline's SUV caught Miles's profile in that back window, she floored it.

She didn't make a conscious decision to do it. Something just snapped.

And a second later, there was a bone-jarring jolt, the explosion of an airbag, the thundering sound of metal hitting metal, and the shattering of glass.

Screams.

From inside her car and beyond.

And then everything went black.

CHAPTER 65

New York, NY

Chloe forced herself to look away from the bloodied carpet and the red drops coming from Nicky's closed hand. She didn't want Rhys and Broderick following her gaze. She wasn't sure Nicky was aware the glass shard in her palm had broken the skin.

'Can we just go and sign the papers and be done with this?' Chloe asked. 'I really want to go home.' And, continuing with the act, she asked, 'Can you give us a hint how much money we're going to get?'

Rhys smiled. 'I'll tell you this. You'll probably never be able to spend it all. We got the car parked around back so let's—'

'What the hell?' said Broderick.

'What?' Rhys asked.

'I got blood or something on my foot.'

They all looked down at the splotches atop his right shoe. His shoes were black, so the redness of the splotches didn't stand out. But

521

the drops on the pale gray rug right next to his shoe certainly did.

Nicky's eyes went wide. She looked at her own hand and saw the blood.

'Oh, shit,' she said.

'How'd that happen?' Broderick asked.

Everything from that moment on happened very quickly.

'Probably like this,' Chloe said. Taking half a step back, holding her piece of glass firmly in her hand, she raised her arm and swung it sideways across Rhys's face.

The edge of the glass sliced diagonally across his cheek half an inch below his left eye. The cut was a good inch and a half long, and blood started spurting from it immediately. He screamed, 'Fuck!'

His left hand went instinctively to his cheek. Blood was already streaming down the side of his face and seeped through his fingers as he tried to stanch the flow.

When Broderick turned to see what had happened to his partner, Nicky took her own piece of glass, already bloodied from the small cut in her palm, and drove it into the side of the man's neck.

'Bitch!' he screamed, turning, raising an arm defensively.

Nicky kept a tight grip on the shard and managed to cut him again, on the side of his throat, just below the jawline. Broderick slapped his hand over the wound and started to make gagging noises.

Even with one hand on his cheek, Rhys tried to grab Chloe with his free hand. He gripped her left arm, but he would have done better getting hold of her right, since it was the one wielding the glass.

Chloe struck him again, aiming high.

She didn't slash this time. She used a pointed end, much as Nicky had with her first strike against Broderick. But Chloe did not get Rhys in the neck.

Chloe got him in the left eye.

The man's scream was primal. He released his grip on Chloe and now had both hands on his face, one over his cheek and the other over his left eye.

Broderick continued to make choking noises as blood flooded his windpipe.

Chloe and Nicky, glancing briefly at each other, understood that this was it.

Do or die.

This was their only chance. But they still had to get out of the room. The men's anguished screams were sure to bring someone to that door. Chloe, forcing herself to keep a clear head in the face of epic chaos, positioned herself by it and waited.

She did not have to wait long.

The door began to open. A woman yelled, 'What's going—'

Roberta.

When she was halfway into the room, Chloe rushed the door, arms out straight, palms flat and up. She hit the door with everything she had, catching Roberta's left leg in midstride. Roberta screamed as the door crushed her upper thigh. She went down.

Once Chloe had disabled Roberta – she dropped to the floor like the sack of shit she was, Chloe thought – she pulled the door open again, turned to Nicky, and shouted, 'Come on!'

Chloe held the door until Nicky reached it. They stepped over Roberta, who'd been clutching her wounded leg but made one futile attempt to grab Nicky's ankle as she ran past.

They sprinted down the hallway as far as the stairway landing, where it was just one flight down to the front door. As expected, Boris, the security guard, was stationed at the top of the stairs that led down. He'd heard all the commotion, especially Roberta's cries of pain, and when he saw Chloe and Nicky running in his direction, he broadened his stance, getting ready to block their path.

He even grinned. The very idea that these two girls thought they could get past him.

But they had no intention of trying to get past him.

When they reached the landing, they quickly pivoted away from the guard and headed for the ascending staircase.

They were going up.

CHAPTER 66

New York, NY

After the explosive crash, the silence was deafening.

The left side of the limo was seriously mangled. Several side airbags had deployed, but no one in the car had escaped unscathed.

Some were worse off than others.

The car itself had been knocked several feet to one side, and the SUV that had hit them had bounced back from the impact, its front end a crumpled mess, the hood buckled, the windshield spiderwebbed. A bloodied, deflated airbag was visible beyond the glass.

There hadn't been time for anyone in the car to scream. No one had seen it coming. They were talking, waiting to turn onto Seventieth, and then there was the incredible crash, the disorientation.

And then, briefly, the quiet.

It was Charise who spoke first. 'Is everybody okay?'

Clearly, she was not. Blood was streaming down the left side of her face. Her door had caved in about six inches, and when she looked down at her leg, covered in crystallized glass, she saw blood.

Gold said nothing.

Miles had heard Charise call out, but her voice had sounded like it was coming from underwater.

Dorian said, 'Miles, Miles, talk to me.'

Miles looked down at himself and was surprised not to see blood. But his left shoulder was aching, his head hurt, and he wondered whether he'd suffered a concussion. He turned to check on the doctor, whose head was sitting close to sideways on his shoulder.

'Gold,' Miles said, his voice echoing in his own head. 'He's not moving. I think he broke his neck.'

Charise said, 'My leg.'

Dorian opened the front passenger door – easily done since the car had not been hit on that side – and staggered out to the street. She needed a moment to get her balance. She opened the rear door. Gold rolled out with it, his body half in the vehicle, half out. Dorian reached around him to undo his seat belt.

'Shit,' Dorian said. 'I think he's dead, Miles.'

Dorian, summoning a strength she did not know she had, gently dragged Gold from the car and placed him carefully onto the pavement.

There was a smell of gas.

Miles's door was too damaged to open, but as he went to slide across the seat toward the other side he found he couldn't move.

'Miles,' Dorian said, 'come on.'

He felt paralyzed. He didn't think he'd been injured, but his body wasn't getting the message he was sending it, which was: *Get out!*

Dorian went headfirst into the car, got her arms under Miles's shoulders, and started to drag him out.

'Anybody else smelling that?' said Charise, trying without success to open her door.

Dorian had Miles halfway out when he said, 'I'm okay, I can move.'

The messages were getting through. The moment he was on the street he looked down and saw gas flowing across the ground.

'Charise, get out,' he said.

'Door won't open.'

'Scooch over!' Dorian said.

'My leg,' she said again. She tried to shift across the seat but was moving slowly.

Dorian reached in and grabbed Charise's right arm with both hands, pulling hard enough to almost take it out of the socket. When Charise reached the door, she had to put an arm around Dorian's shoulder so that she could stand. Her left pant leg, below the knee, was torn and bloody.

A crowd had formed. People were rushing about. Someone was on a cell phone, calling for help. Another was taking video, something they could sell to the local newscasts.

Sirens.

Miles, wobbling some because of some soreness in his left knee, got around the other side of Charise to help Dorian get her away from the car. He yelled at the rubberneckers, 'Get back!'

Charise said, 'I never saw . . . came out of nowhere . . .'

When they were about twenty feet away from the limo, Miles asked Dorian, 'You got this?'

'Yeah.'

Miles let go of Charise and went to check on the car that had hit them.

'I know that car,' he said under his breath.

He limped along until he was at the driver's door. The window had shattered, and he could see the woman behind the wheel.

The airbag, having exploded and collapsed, looked like an enormous, melted marshmallow dribbled with strawberry syrup.

'Caroline,' he said.

She did not hear him. Her head sat at an odd angle on her neck. Her eyes were closed. Miles reached out tentatively, touched her below the jaw.

'Caroline,' he said again.

It wasn't up to him to make the call, but he had little doubt she was dead. He stood and looked at her for another moment, believing it and not believing it, and then limped his way back to the limo.

An ambulance was already pulling up to the scene. Seconds later, another one. There were more sirens in the distance.

A paramedic ran over to Miles. She said, 'Sir, are you hurt?'

Miles looked down Seventieth Street. They'd almost made it.

He said. 'Look after the others.'

As the limo started to erupt in flames, Miles hobbled his way to Jeremy Pritkin's brownstone.

CHAPTER 67

New York, NY

Chloe and Nicky successfully faked out the security guard. He was ready to block their way down the stairs, but as they hightailed it up the steps to the third floor, they were leaving him in their dust.

They hoped a few seconds' head start would be all they needed.

They sprinted, side by side, to the closed doors that led down the wide hallway to Jeremy's office. Nicky quickly entered the four-digit password into the keypad and pushed the door open. They flew past the erotic art on one wall and the windows on the other one. When they opened the second set of doors at the end of the hall, Nicky was relieved not to find the man of the house there. That would have been a complication.

Nicky ran straight to Jeremy's desk and slid open the drawer she had seen him take the gun from the night she'd been discovered in the Winnebago. 'It was here,' she said breathlessly.

She found the gun immediately, but set it aside on the desk.

'Don't we want that?' Chloe asked.

'He doesn't keep it loaded,' Nicky said.

They could hear someone running down the hall.

'Where *is* it?' Nicky said. She was tossing everything from the drawer onto the desk. Pens, small Moleskine notebooks, computer sticks, reading glasses—

'Yes!' she said, taking out a key ring with a two-inch silver *W* attached to it. There was only one key on the ring.

She came running around the desk and headed for the Winnebago's side door. She swung it open for Chloe, who jumped in first. Nicky followed, and slammed the door shut behind her at the same moment the security guard came storming into the study.

'Lock it!' Chloe screamed.

Nicky reached for the deadbolt above the knob and turned it. The guard ran across the room and tried the outside handle. Finding it locked, he banged on the door with his fist.

'Open up!' he demanded.

'Fuck you!' Nicky said.

Jeremy could be seen beyond the study doors, running down the corridor.

'He's coming,' Nicky said.

Chloe got behind the wheel of the Winnebago and placed her palm on the center of the steering wheel and applied pressure.

531

The vehicle's horn began to blare.

This had been the plan. It was simple enough. Grab the keys to the RV, get in and lock the door, then lay on that horn until help arrived. And as simple as the idea was, Nicky wasn't sure she could pull it off alone. She might need Chloe to stall while she looked for the key. Plus, she'd had to admit to Chloe that she didn't actually know where the horn would be. On the steering wheel, sure, but would it be a little button on the spokes? Would it be in the center?

Chloe had thought the idea was worth trying.

Someone would hear it. Someone *had* to hear it. If they couldn't start a fire and set off the smoke alarms, this was the next best thing. As thick as the window glass was, the noise would carry down to the street. Even in a place like New York, where the strangest things could happen and people didn't bat an eye, the sound of a horn blaring from within a brownstone had to turn some heads, didn't it?

Jeremy was at the door. He tried to open it and slapped it twice with the flat of his hand.

'Nicky,' he said, raising his voice to be heard above the noise of the horn, 'stop this nonsense. Unlock the door.'

'No,' she shouted.

Jeremy looked at the security guard and pointed to his desk. 'Key,' he snapped. 'Top drawer.'

But that was when Jeremy noticed several items from that drawer, including the gun, were on the desk. The guard peered into the drawer, then looked at Jeremy and shook his head.

'This is not funny,' Jeremy shouted. 'Nicky, Chloe, get out.'

Chloe had been holding the horn down for a full minute now. She was starting to wonder whether this plan was so brilliant after all. If Jeremy could get that door open before any help arrived, well, there was no doubt about it. They'd be fucked.

Jeremy was shouting something else to the guard. He picked up the gun, walked it across the room, and gave it to Jeremy. Then he ran back to the desk, opened a lower drawer, and started dropping into his hand what appeared to be bullets.

'Oh, shit,' Nicky said.

Jeremy shouted, 'Nicky, I'll shoot this door open if I have to!'

'Fuck you!' she yelled.

'You don't leave me much choice!' There was a brief pause, and then: 'Chloe! Chloe! It's you I want to talk to!'

Chloe let up pressure on the horn. 'What?'

'You know, don't you? You know what you are to me.'

Chloe said nothing, but she felt her insides turning, as though a virus had entered her system.

She'd been thinking this from the moment she'd left Jeremy's office. That it had to be him. But she hadn't wanted to verbalize the question. Didn't want to ask him, didn't want to ask Roberta.

Didn't want to know.

'You knew when I put my hand on your head,' Jeremy said. 'I think . . . I think that you're the one. Of all of them, you're the one with potential. You're the only *worthy* one.'

'Nicky,' Chloe whispered. 'Give me the key.'

'Why?' Nicky whispered back. 'You don't need it for the horn.'

'Chloe,' Jeremy said, 'if you're willing to put this behind us, we can have a future together. We can. You're my daugh—'

'Don't say it!' Chloe screamed.

'But's it's the truth. Now that we've met, that I've touched you, it's different.'

'The key,' Chloe whispered to Nicky.

Nicky tossed the key to Chloe, who snatched it out of the air. She inserted it into the ignition. Nicky had told her the RV had only been installed recently.

Maybe, just maybe, there was still a trace of gas in it. Maybe in the fuel line, if not the tank. If she could start it, she could run it straight into the window. Send a shitload of glass raining down onto the sidewalk.

That would get some attention.

The guard dropped the bullets into Jeremy's hand and he began to load them.

'Chloe, one day, everything I have would be yours. I'd see to it.'

All these rich dudes, wanting to give me their money.

Chloe, through gritted teeth, whispered, 'Burn in fuckin' hell.'

She turned the key.

The engine rumbled to life.

Jeremy screamed: 'NO!'

He ran around to the front of the Winnebago, standing between them and the floor-to-ceiling window. He pointed the gun at the windshield.

Chloe put her foot on the brake, and shifted the Winnebago into Drive.

She thought back to that trip she'd done with her mom. She'd driven a rig like this before. How hard could it be, once you ignored the part about there being no road, and that they were on the third floor of a *building*.

She took her foot off the brake and hit the gas. Chloe figured Jeremy would leap out of the way, but he held his position for a second longer than she thought he would.

Could she really run someone down?

Could she run her *father* down?

Instinctively, she cranked the wheel, the tires squeaking on the floor as they did a dry turn. Jeremy vanished from her field of vision, having jumped at the last second. The vehicle was now pointed at the doors, and the broad hallway beyond.

Chloe held her foot over the gas.

Nicky said, 'What are you doing?'

'You might want to buckle up,' said Chloe, who had seconds earlier fastened her own seat belt.

535

Nicky jumped into the passenger seat, grabbed the seat belt, and clicked it into place. Jeremy was running alongside the Winnebago now, banging on the sheet metal below Chloe's side window.

'*Stop!*'

Chloe punched it.

The RV shot across the office. It burst through the double doors, ripping them off their hinges. Behind them, a shot rang out. The Winnebago's rear window shattered.

The vehicle had minimal clearance as it went down the hall. Barely two inches on each side, and that did not take into account the oversized mirrors mounted left and right. They were immediately buckled back toward the vehicle, scraping the street-side window, and on the other side, stripping the framed photos from their hooks. The pictures hit the floor, glass shattering everywhere.

But the RV kept on plowing through.

Heading for the stairs. Almost on them now.

Nicky was too terrified to scream.

'Are the stairs wide enough?' Chloe shouted above the clatter. Nicky did not respond. Chloe thought, *I guess we're going to find out.*

The front wheels dropped over the top step. From the two seats up front, it felt like going over the edge of a cliff.

Nicky's eyes were wide, her mouth open. She spoke:

'*No no no no no!*'

Chloe took her foot off the gas and feathered the brake. Gravity would be doing most of the work here.

KATHUMP KATHUMP KATHUMP.

The rear tires were now on the steps, the rig fully committed to its downward, forty-five-degree plunge. Chloe believed she'd heard another shot – Jeremy was evidently in pursuit – but it was hard to tell, what with the noise of the engine, people screaming, the RV crashing into walls and banisters.

The RV was half a dozen steps from the landing. Chloe was going to have to execute a left, followed by another left to get her on the second descending flight.

She turned the wheel, putting her shoulders into it.

The front left fender of the Winnebago ripped out the railing, the tire an inch from going over the edge of the stairs and dropping into the open atrium. If that happened, if the wheels lost purchase, their ride would be over.

The vehicle made the turn, the right side scraping the wall of the landing area. Chloe kept turning left, fighting the obstacles in her path, holding the wheel firm.

She made it to the flight of stairs that led to the first floor.

KATHUMP KATHUMP KATHUMP.

The security guard had somehow gotten ahead of the vehicle. He must have fled the third floor before Chloe turned down the hallway, and was now trying to avoid being run over. Ahead of the security guard was a frazzled-looking Roberta, limping as she descended the stairs on her towering heels.

When the guard reached the bottom step, he spun around. He was armed, as well, and was going to try to fire off a round before the Winnebago reached him.

The windshield shattered. Tiny shards of glass rained down on them inside the cab.

Chloe had ducked at the first sight of the gun, and now was driving blind. But she hadn't slowed, and the next thing she heard was a loud *THWOMP*, and when she glanced up, she caught a half-second glimpse of the guard's head appearing briefly above the lower edge of the windshield opening.

He slipped quickly from sight.

The Winnebago came to a crashing halt as it reached the bottom of the stairs. The front bumper of the RV hit the floor, but momentum carried the vehicle a couple of feet farther. The wheels no long had purchase. The front two were suspended above the floor, and at the back end, the rear bumper rested on a step, the back tires hanging in the air.

The brownstone's front door was only ten yards away.

'Out, out, out!' Chloe said.

She and Nicky unbuckled their belts and nearly

fell out of their seats, since the RV was pitched forward. It might have been faster to go out the open front window, but the sill was a row of jagged glass teeth. So they climbed three feet to reach the RV's side door, and once they unlocked it and pushed it open, it swung back on its hinges. One at a time, they jumped out.

The two of them came around the front of the monstrously damaged Winnebago, its engine still running, the smell of exhaust and fuel in the air.

They started for the door.

But standing there, between them and freedom, was Jeremy, haggard and wild-eyed, both arms raised, his hands wrapped around the gun.

He had it pointed straight at Chloe.

Jeremy was so focused on her, he barely noticed Roberta running past him. In her rush to flee the building, to get away before the police arrived, she tripped over the corner of a rug, her left stiletto flying off her foot. She hit the floor, but wasted no time getting up, and didn't bother to retrieve her shoe. She kicked off the other one, opened the front door, and ran off into the night.

On the front step, arm raised as if ready to knock, stood Miles.

He took about five seconds to take it all in. The Winnebago at the bottom of the stairs. Debris everywhere. A dead man under the vehicle.

A man standing with his back to him, only a few feet away, pointing a gun at someone.

Chloe.

The man glanced over his shoulder momentarily, long enough for Miles to recognize him. He'd watched the news. He'd read countless online stories. He recognized the man as Jeremy Pritkin.

A man who was determined to kill the very people Miles had set out to save. A man who was willing to destroy his own flesh and blood to save his own skin.

And now he was going to kill Chloe.

Instinctively, Miles started to run toward Jeremy, to jump him, tackle him, anything to keep him from shooting Chloe. But he'd only taken a step when he spotted one of Roberta's discarded shoes.

Saw that sharply pointed, four-inch heel.

He bent down, grabbed the shoe by the toe, grasped it firmly, and charged Jeremy.

The man heard him coming and made half a turn, just in time, from the corner of his eye, to see Miles swinging the shoe at him, overhand, cutting through the air like it was an ice pick.

If Jeremy had been able to raise his hand in time, or fire off a shot, he might have been able to stop Miles from driving that spiked heel right into his skull.

ONE WEEK LATER

EPILOGUE

New Haven, CT

Miles could hear the car approaching the house before he saw it. He slid off the stool at the kitchen island, where he'd been sipping on one of his fancy coffees, went to the front door and opened it.

Chloe's Pacer was coming down the driveway. The car had sounded ragged enough when Chloe had driven Miles to Springfield in it, but it was sounding even worse now. A hole in the muffler, most likely.

The car came to a stop near the front door, and when Chloe killed the engine, it continued to cough and sputter a few times before finally giving up. Miles walked over to the car as Chloe opened the door.

'Hey,' he said.

'Hey yourself,' Chloe said, lifting the door slightly as she closed it to make sure it latched. 'How's it going?'

'It's been a long week,' he said. 'But I don't have to tell you.'

543

He glanced into the back of the Pacer. The rear seat was folded down, and there were several soft-sided travel bags there.

'Going somewhere?' Miles asked.

'Kinda,' she said. 'I was going to talk to you about that.'

'Come on in,' he said. 'Pick a pod.'

When she got to the kitchen, she did exactly that. 'I want something with mocha,' she said. She found one she liked, inserted it into the machine, and while it percolated, she turned and noticed a stack of what looked like contracts and other documents on the island.

'Sup?'

'Legal shit.'

'What kind?'

'My will, succession plans. Lots of things to sort out before I retire from the company. I want to do some other things before my health forces me to step down. Get it all organized now. An orderly transition.'

'You got someone picked to take over?'

Miles smiled. 'Gilbert.'

Chloe nodded. 'Makes sense. How's he doing?'

'Caroline's funeral was yesterday. He and Samantha will be okay. Better, actually. I think he'll make a good leader. He's stronger than I thought. I made a big mistake with him. I'm going to try and make it right.' He waved his hand over the paperwork. 'Dorian and I are going through a list of good causes. I want to set up a fund for Huntington's research. That's where a lot of the money will go.'

'Dorian?' she asked. 'I thought she was gone.'

Miles nodded slowly. 'I've been rethinking that.'

'Up to you,' she said. 'What about me and the other four? Guess we all gotta fend for ourselves, huh?'

'No one's health is at risk. None of you have my genes. But I was thinking, if you need anything . . .'

'Look, I don't need your money. Give it to research. And anyway, me and the others are looking at getting a shitload from Pritkin's organization. That lawyer you suggested, he's forming a class action. We're heirs, right? And we can prove it. The dude may be in a coma but we can still get his DNA.'

Miles's face fell. 'I had to stop him.'

'And thanks for that,' she said. 'Listen, by the time this is all over, I'll be able to buy myself a second Pacer.'

That made Miles laugh. But he quickly turned serious. 'How you dealing with that?'

'What? That the biggest scumbag in the world is my biological poppa?'

'Yeah, that.'

She shrugged, but it was a fragile shrug, lacking her usual flippancy. 'I'm blocking it out. I'm going to imagine it's someone else.'

The words hung there for a moment before Miles said, 'How's Nicky?'

'Good. Her mom's a ditz, but she's got other

545

family up near Albany, so she's gone to stay with them for the time being. For a while there, they were talking like she'd get charged with killing that Broderick guy, but then everyone came to their senses about that. And my lawyer says I got nothing to worry about with the guy we ran over, or the one whose eye I sliced open.'

'No one should have to go through what you've gone through,' Miles said.

This time, her shrug appeared more carefree.

'And that Roberta bitch, she's ready to tell all if she can cut some kind of deal that'll keep her from spending the rest of her life in jail.'

Even with Martin Gold dead, everything he and Jeremy had done was coming out into the open. Between what he'd told Miles, the information his assistant, Julie, could provide, and with Roberta eager to talk, the authorities were putting the story together.

'The others on the list, the ones you didn't get to,' Chloe said. 'They're going to find out who their daddy is?'

'I think so, but it's out of my hands. Everyone from the FBI to CNN will be talking to them.' He brightened, remembering something. 'I heard from Charise yesterday. She's on crutches, but a couple more weeks, she should be off them.'

Chloe smiled.

'So tell me,' Miles said. 'Looks like you've got everything you own in the car. Where you headed?'

'I'm there,' Chloe said.

Miles blinked. 'Say again?'

'I'm staying here. I'm moving in. I know you've got space.' She came around the island and plopped onto the stool next to him. 'But I might jazz up my room some. It's pretty minimalist. Needs some pillows and shit. Some movie posters.'

'Chloe.'

'Did you know there's a film school in New Haven? I'm looking into that. There'd be time in between other stuff.'

'I don't understand.'

'Are you saying I'm not welcome?'

'No, but Chloe, I'm not too bad right now, but I'm going to get worse. I'm going to reach a point where I need constant care, constant attention.'

'Why do you think I'm moving in, dumbass?' she said.

'Chloe—'

'I've thought about this a lot. There's no point trying to talk me out of it. I'm staying.' She paused. 'As long as I can be of help.'

She had to look away for a second, compose herself.

'Chloe, really, it's going to be rough. You're young. You've got a life. Don't let me drag you down.'

'Drag me down? What the fuck.'

'I didn't mean it like that. I hate to see you make that kind of sacrifice.' He took a deep breath. 'Here's the thing, Chloe. I'm not your father. You're not my daughter.'

'I'm thinking,' she said, 'that this whole father-hood bullshit is more than a genetic thing.'

He thought back to what she had said when she'd bailed from the car. 'But I'm nothing to you,' he said.

Chloe slipped her arm into his and rolled her eyes. 'You dumb shit,' she said. 'You're everything to me.'